HISTORIETAS

A series of short stories told in the vernacular by Vincent Livelli
Compiled and edited by Lewis Lazar

First Edition.
First printed in 2016 by Lewis Lazar.

Designed by Emily Gasda.
Set in Williams Caslon.

ISBN
978-0-990-66439-0

LCCN
2016936108

CONTENTS

A NOTE ON THE FIRST EDITION:

This "Birthday Edition" of *Historietas* has been assembled to print the core narrative of Vincent's visual and literary patchwork in time for his 96th birthday. It is in no way a finished or final edition of this work but rather a presentation of what, with a little more work, could be a definitive volume.

There is a whole host of untyped material, specifically a portion of work centered around the subject of Santería, that is not included.

This edition owes its existence to the patient help and labour of:

ALEX TRAUB
JUDEE
EMILY GASDA
MICHAEL LEVITON
CORNELIA LIVINGSTON
LEWIS LAZAR
HEATHER BOO
KELIN DILLON
BOB GALLAGHER
And last but not least… VINCENT LIVELLI

A LETTER FROM THE EDITOR

        VINCENT LIVELLI WELCOMED ME IN TO HIS LIFE LIKE A
        LONG LOST FRIEND WHOM HE HADN'T SEEN FOR 70 YEARS.
          WE ARE BORN BUT ONE DAY APART AND SHARE MANY THINGS
IN COMMON THOUGH OUR AGE DIFFERENCE SPANS A LONG LIFE
        TIME (HE WAS BORN IN 1920 and I in 1990)

  I MET VINCENT IN A CAFE IN THE WEST VILLAGE WHEN I OVER
      HEARD HIM TALKING ABOUT HAVANA IN THE 40s.   *invited*
        AFTER INTRODUCING MYSELF HE BRUSQUELY LED ME TO HIS
   APARTMENT TO TALK MORE, AND IF I HAD TIME, TO HEAR SOME
   OF HIS STORIES. I REALISED THAT TELLING STORIES IS ONE
OF VINCENT'S GREAT JOYS. NOT ONLY BECAUSE HE IS A NATURAL *BORN*
   RACONTEUR AND HAS BEEN ENTERTAINING PEOPLE HIS WHOLE
      LIFE, BUT ALSO BECAUSE HE REVELS IN THE WONDER OF
      HIS OWN STOREHOUSE OF MEMORIES AND AT TIMES FINDS
        IT HARD TO BELIEVE WHAT HE ACCOMPLISHED AND
EXPERIENCED, BEING BUT A HUMBLE ITALIAN FROM BROOKLYN
   BORN IN TO THE GREAT DEPPRESSION.   *boy*
          VINCENT HANDED ME LARGE VOLUMES OF SCRAP BOOKS
   WITH PICTURES OF THE SHIPS HE SAILED AROUND THE WORLD *in*,
     AFRO CUBAN MUSICIANS HE DANCED TO, LOVERS HE HAD KNOWN
   WRITERS, ARTISTS, STORIES ABOUT CRIMINALS, THE
     WAR..A LIFE STRANGER THAN FICTION.
     HIS APARTMENT IS A SHRINE OF CREATIVITY AND CULTURE, WI
WITH TAPESTRIES AND FABRICS BROUGHT BACK FROM MORROCCO
AND IRAN AND INDIA COVERING EVERY INCH OF WALL SPACE.
     THERE WAS NOTHING UNDER WHELMING OR SHORT OF AWE INS
INSPIRING ABOUT VINCENT. HE SEEMED TO HAVE LIVED LIFE
     FULL OF EXPECTATION, HOPE AND AN INFINITE APPETITE
     FOR ADVENTURE, *which was faithfully rewarded to him,*
HE*NEVER*HAD*TIME
     ALTHOUGH HE HAD CREDENTIALS: FORMER PUBLICATIONS, TIES
     WITH THE SMITHSONIAN, CORRESPONDANCES WITH SCHOLARS HE *who*
       SOUGHT HIM OUT FROM FOR FIRST HAND INFORMATION
     ABOUT THE VILLAGE, MUMBA MAMBO AND AFRO CUBAN MUSIC *(Robert Farris Thompson)*
       HE RARELY TOOK THE TIME TO COMPOUND ALL HIS WEALTH
OF EXPERIENCE AND OBSERVATIONS. HE WROTE PROFUSELY
     BUT HIS SHORT STORIES, OR 'HISTORIETAS', LAY PILED
       UP AND OR UNORGANISED AMONGST SCRAP BOOKS, COLLAGES
AND OUR MANY CONVERSATIONS LATE IN TO THE NIGHT.
     SLOWLY OUR FRIENSHIP EVOLVED IN TO MY ASSISTING HIM
ORGANISE ALL THINGS TOLD, AND ALL THINGS WRITTEN THAT
     FLOWED FROM HIS MEMORY. IT HAS BEEN MY PLEASURE THUS
     FAR TO PARTICIPATE IN THE ASSEMBLING OF A WORLD
     OF EXPERIENCE AND OF VALUES THAT NO LONGER EXISTS.
     IT IS THE WORLD OF THE XXTH CENTURY. A CENTURY OF TUMULTU
     OUS UPHEAVELS THAT VINCENT RELISHED, LOVED AND SAILED
     THROUGH LIKE THE DANCER HE IS, WILDLY, COMICALLY
     AND GRACEFULLY. THE QUALITIES HE ADMIRES IN DANCE, HE
     POSSESSES AS AN OBSERVER AND IN TURN AS A WRITER.
     HERE IS AN EXCERPT OF HIS HISTORIETAS: A WELL TRAVELLED
     VIEW OF THE WORLD OF THE LAST CENTURY: ALL THINGS TOLD

   LEWIS LAZAR

Introduction

Vincent Livelli at 90 is a fascinating gentleman. Storyteller, raconteur, teacher, ladies man, adventurer, dancer, lover of music: he has made his life his art, his story is at once a piece of the New York bohemian saga and a global chronicle of wanderlust and the insatiable search for knowledge of other cultures and places. Livelli is full of humor but has strong opinions that can make him seem outspoken, but he always backs up his points of argument with thoughful thoroughness based on a wealth of experience and deeply held convictions.

Though his seemingly endless treasure trove of stories is as varied and multi-leveled as the most incredible of libraries, he does have a lion's share of stories about music, dane and his love affair with all things Afro-Cuban. This is where I first encountered him, in the part of his overstuffed brain that knew the 'rhumba', in the time before mambo, salsa, hip-hop. I was fascinated hearing about Vince's experiences in the Village with intellectuals like Anatole Broyard, and curious to hear of New York Latin dance culture before it hit the Palladium, before *I Love Lucy* was on in everyone's living room. Livelli had been there, dancing int he 30's and 40's at clubs like The Park Plaza uptown in Spanish Harlem or La Conga in Midtown. He tells of seeing Tito Puente when he was just a teenager playing bongos with a young Noro Morales at the piano, and testifies to the fact that back in the early 40's, the sultry *chanteuse* Graciela Peréz's double entendre lyrics were truly revolutionary. Through Vince I learned the little known fact that there was an important connection between New York Chinese restaurants and the support of Latin music, and to hear him tell of setting up a Latin dance club in warn-torn Tokyo is nothing short of thrilling.

What makes Livelli doubly valuable to historians is the fact that he is a living link with a bygone era, experiencing firsthand the sublime yet little-known dance moves of Afro-Cubans like René and Estela, Electric and Midnight, and making the acquaintance of a young Miguelito Valdés, the great talent who brought African language into the popular consciousness through popular Cuban song. In 1937, Livelli befriended the seminal Afro-Puerto Rican *bongocero* José "Buyú" Mangual, but perhaps most importantly, he made the friendship of Mangual's compatriot, bassist Julio Andino, best known for his work with Frank "Machete" Grillo's orchestra, the Afro-Cubans. Before anyone else, Andino had wanted to form a big brass band to take his beautiful Afro-Cuban music from the Latino ghettos of NYC and make the move to Broadway, transferring the segregated Ango world downtown, where he felt sure whites would love it. A few years later, he and Machete, along with Graciela, Marlo Bauzá, and others, would change Latin music forever with their super-charged orchestral New York style mambo, making it popular all over the world, but especially in midtown Manhattan among Blacks, Italians and the Jewish population. Andino and his contemporaries had brought Afro-Latin culture to Broadway and the social changes this move incurred would reverberate down the decades. Mambo was in effect introducing Afro-Cuban culture through the back door, infiltrating popular music with subliminal Africanisms that helped convert and entire mambo-mad populace with their really being cognizant of the significant of what was taking place.

In Cuba in 1941, Livelli received a prophecy from a *bablawo*, Juan Bessón, a priest of divination in the Yoruba-Cuban religion known as La Regla de Ocha. Bessón directed him to make it his mission to spread the music, and hence an appreciation of the culture, to all the corners of the globe. In his way, Vince was doing the same as Machete, Pérez Prado, Tito Puente, and so many others – taking Afro-Cuban music around the world – but through the medium of dance, as he became entertainment director for several international cruise ship lines for many years, teaching passengers to rumba across the waves; and bless him, Vince has been spreading the gospel of Afro Cuban music ever since.

Robert Farris Thompson

CHILDHOOD

PHILIP J. MASSARO, P.L.S.
518 County Route 10
Germantown, NY 12526

THE JOY OF GROWING UP ITALIAN

I was well into adulthood before I realized that I was an American. Of course, I had been born in America and had lived here all my life, but, somehow it never occurred to me that just being a citizen of the United States meant I was an American. Americans were people who ate peanut butter and jelly on mushy white bread that came out of plastic packages. Me? I was Italian.

For me...as I am sure that most second generation Italian American children who grew up in the 40s or 50s, there was a definite distinction drawn between US and THEM. We were Italian. Everybody else - the Irish, German, Polish, Jewish They were the "MED-E-GONES". There was no animosity involved in that distinction, no prejudice, no hard feelings, just -well we were sure ours was the better way. For instance, we had a bread man, a coal and ice man, a fruit and vegetable man, a watermelon man, and a fish man; we even had a man who sharpened knives ad scissors who came right to our homes or at least right outside our homes. They were the many peddlers who plied the Italian neighborhoods. We would wait for their call, their yell, their individual distinctive sound. We Knew them all and they knew us. Americans went to the stores for most of their foods - What a waste.

Truly I pitied their loss. They never knew the pleasure of waking up every morning to find a hot, crisp loaf of Italian bread waiting behind the screen door. And instead of being able to climb up on back of the peddler's truck a couple of times a week just to hitch a ride, most of the "MED-E-GONE" friends had to be satisfied going to the A&P. When it came to food, it always amazed me that my American friends or classmates only ate turkey on Thanksgiving or Christmas. Or rather, that they ONLY ate turkey, stuffing, mashed potatoes and cranberry sauce. Now we Italians - we also had turkey, stuffing, mashed potatoes and cranberry sauce but - only after we had finished the antipasta, soup, lasagna, meatballs, salad and whatever else mama thought might be appropriate for that particular holiday. This turkey was usually accompanied by a roast of some kind (just in case somebody walked in who didn't like turkey) and was followed by an assortment of fruits, nuts, pastries, cakes and of course, homemade cookies. No holiday was complete where you learned to eat a seven course meal between noon and 4 p.m., how to handle hot chestnuts and put tangerine wedges in red wine. I truly believe Italians live a romance with food.

Speaking of food - Sunday was truly the big day of the week! That was the day you'd wake up to the smell of garlic and onions frying in olive oil. As you laid in bed, you could hear the hiss as tomatoes were dropped into a pan. Sunday we always had gravy (the "MED-E-GONES" called it SAUCE) and macaroni (they called it PASTA). Sunday would not be Sunday without going to mass. Of course, you couldn't eat before mass because you had to fast before receiving communion. But, the good part was we knew when we got home we'd find hot meatballs frying, and nothing tastes better than newly fried meatballs and crisp bread dipped into a pot of gravy.

There was another difference between US and THEM. We had gardens, not just flower gardens, but huge gardens where we grew tomatoes, tomatoes and more tomatoes. We ate them, cooked them , jarred them. Of course, we also grew peppers, basal, lettuce and squash. Everybody had a grapevine and a fig tree and in the fall everybody made homemade wine, lots of it. Of course, those gardens thrived so because we also had something else it seemed our American friends didn't have. We had a Grandfather!! It's not that they didn't have Grandfathers, it's just that they didn't live in the same house, or on the same block. They visited their grandfathers. We ate with ours and God forbid we didn't see him at least once a day. I can still remember my grandfather telling me about how he came to America a young man, "on the boat". How the family lived in a rented tenement and took in boarders in order to help make ends meet, how he decided he didn't want his children, five sons and to daughters, to grow up in that environment. All of this, of course, in his own version of Italian/English which I soon learned to understand quite well.

So, when he saved enough, and I could never figure out how, he bought a house. That house served as the family headquarters for the next 40 years. I remember how he hated to leave, would rather sit on the back porch and watch his garden grow and when he did leave for some special occasion, had to return as quickly as possible. After all, "nobody's watching the house". I also remember the holidays when all the relatives would gather at my grandfather's house and there'd be tables full of food and homemade wine and people everywhere. I must have a half million cousins, first and second and some who aren't even related, but, what did it matter. And my grandfather, his pipe in his mouth and his fine mustache trimmed, would sit in the middle of it all grinning his mischievous smile, his dark eyes twinkling, surveying his domain, proud of his family and how well his children had done. One was a cop, one a fireman, one had his trade of course there was always the rogue. And the girls, they had all married well and had fine husbands and healthy children and everyone knew respect.

UNQUALIFIED FOR LIFE

(A.A.D.D.)

WE ARE MARRIED TO OURSELVES. TO DISCOVER VERY LATE IN LIFE THAT BEGINNING IN INFANCY, YOU HAVE BEEN LIVING WITH A VERY IMPERFECT PARTNER ALL THESE YEARS CAN BE A SHOCK. IT INVOLVES THE HISTORY OF YOUR ENTIRE EXISTENCE. NOW YOU RETROSPECTIVELY UNDERSTAND REASONS, MOTIVATIONS AND MYSTERIES THAT HAVE FASHIONED YOU AS WHAT YOU ARE. SOMETHJNG WAS AMISS, CAUSING YOU TO MISHANDLE YOUR LIFE.

ONE DAY, YOU MAY LEARN AS I DID RECENTLY, THAT THIRTY MILLION OF US HAVE A.A.D.D.,ADULT ATTENTION DEFICIT DISORDER. IT HELPS CLARIFY THE REASONS FOR OUR EDUCATIONAL FAILURES, LAZINESS, DISMISSED OPPORTUNITIES AND STUPIDITY. IT CAUSES DAY DREAMING WHILE PROVOKING IMAGINATION. IT IS THE CAUSE OF A BASKETFULL OF SILLINESS, ODD ERRORS, NEEDLESS SACRIFICE, IDIOSINCRACIES AND WORST OF ALL REVERSALS OF FORTUNE. IT IS TRULY AN INTERNAL DEVIL AT HOME IN YOUR BRAIN LIKE A PATIENT ASSASSIN. IT IS AN AFFLICTION THAT SABOTAGES WITH GREAT GLEE YOUR MOST PRECIOUS ACCOMPLISHMENTS. SOME SAY THAT LEAD IS THE CULPRIT AND THAT PLUMBING MAY HAVE BEEN ONE OF THE FACTORS IN THE FALL OF ROME. BETTER TO HAVE DISCOVERED THIS SELF-BETRAYAL LATE IN LIFE(SINCE THERE IS LITTLE IN THE WAY OF TOTAL CURE)INSTEAD OF GOING THROUGH LIFE EMBITTERED AGAINST YOUR SELF. WHERE YOU THOUGHT YOU WERE DOING WELL, YOU NOW SEE WHERE YOU COULD HAVE DONE BETTER AT EVERY TURN. IF YOU ATTEMPT TO PIN YOUR LIFE DOWN, TO CHARACTERIZE IT, YOU FEEL ITS IMPROPER CONDUCT. ON THE OTHER HAND YOU FEEL YOU MADE THE MOST OF WHAT YOU HAD TO WORK WITH.

ONE OF THE INSIDUOUS ASPECTS OF THIS CONDITION IS THE AURAL IMPLICATION. . UNAWARE, COMPLETELY OF MY HEARING DEFICIT UNTIL MID-LIFE, I WAS FORTUNATELY ABLE TO PARTIALLY CORRECT IT THROUGH TECHNOLOGY. HOPEFULLY, MEDICATION IS BEGINNING TO APPEAR ON THE SCENE. UNTIL THE SOLUTION IS FOUND, I SPUTTER ALONG LIFE'S HIGHWAY, OUT OF SYNC SINCE INFANCY WHEN I FIRST INGESTED LEAD CHIPS. IT PERHAPS MADE ME MORE ATTUNED TO SOME INNER GUIDANCE SINCE I COULD HEAR THE HIGHER REGISTERS OF LAUGHTER WHILE THE LOWER REGISTERS OF

SADNESS WERE MUFFLED. AT NIGHT, I LAID MY CAREFREE HEAD ON CLOUDS OF PUFFED PILLOWS. WHAT IF I HAD KNOWN THAT I WAS UNQUALIFIED FOR LIFE...WOULD MY SLEEP HAVE BEEN SO UNDISTURBED? TO HAVE BEEN SO FRETLESS WAS AN IRONIC JOKE OR WHAT ROMANS CALLED 'MANUS E NUBIBUS', A HAND FROM THE CLOUDS. WAS IT A DESIGN WITHIN A DESIGN WITH AN ALTERIOR PURPOSE TO REFASHION HUMAN INTELLIGENCE? NO WONDER THE GREEKS, UNAWARE OF AADD AND THE BEHAVIOR OF CHEMICALS THAT BEFUDDLED HUMANS BLAMED SUCH ODD BEHAVIOR ON THE GODS. LEAD PREVENTS DECAY, E.G. LEAD COFFINS, BUT ALSO PRODUCES HEARING DISTORTIONS. IT CAN MAKE THEM MORE INTRICATE, MORE RECEPTIVE TO THE VERY MYSTERY OF SOUND ITSELF, CARRYING COMPREHENSION TO ANOTHER LEVEL. BEFORE TOTAL EXTINCTION, IT CAN FLARE UP TO FLASH WITH BEETHOVIAN OUTBURSTS LIKE DYING STARS. THOSE NAGGING VOICES THAT DON QUIXOTE ENDURED, LEADING HIM ON IDEALISTIC ADVENTURES WAS PROBABLY A LIKELY SUFFERER.SOME POISONS STIMULATE AURAL NERVES, INCREASING THE ABILITY TO HEAR, BUT THE AFFLICTED HIDALGO, BEDEVILED BY INNER VOICES,BECAME COMPULSIVELY INFATUATED WITH A CHIMERA AND DIED SOBBING. BUT IF ONE IS FORTUNATE, THE LYRICAL SOUNDS OF MUSIC LEAVE A TRAIL OF LINGERING EMISSIONS..TRACES RESOUNDING AS MELODIOUS MEMORIES IN THE BRAIN THAT CAN MAKE BOTH NORMAL AND ABNORMAL HUMANS DANCE. SWEET MUSIC AND CHORAL VOICES CAN INSPIRE, ANAESTHESIZING THE STING OF MISFORTUNE.

WHATEVER ONE MISSES OUT ON IN LIFE DUE TO AADD, FAMILY LIFE MOST OF ALL,CAN BE COMPENSATED BY GOOD FRIENDSHIPS, GOOD EMPLOYMENT, A WARM BED WHEN MOST NEEDED OR AN INGROWN INDIFFERENCE TO PRO LONGED CONCERNS. IT CAN BRING A COMBIN. ATION OF NAÏVE BLISS, A FOGGY MIST OF ALMOST PLEASURABLE CONFUSION LIKE A PERPETUAL INEBRIANT. CONTRADICTIONS IN LIFE ARE NECESSARY, LIKE NIGHT AND DAY. THERE MAY OCCUR A MORE EUPHONIC EXISTENCE GIVEN TO CELEBRATION ; IT CAN , LIKE A BAR TENDER INHALING THE VAPORS OF HIS ALCOHOLIC ENVIRONMENT OR THE PAINTER WITH HIS PAINTS,PRODUCE GOOD CHEER. IT MADE ME FOLLOW THE UNREAL WORLD OF ENTERTAINMENT, SAILING THROUGH LIFE AS A CRUISE DIRECT OR WITH THE EVANGELICAL ATTITUDE TO, AS THE HYMN SAYS, 'LIGHTEN THE CORNER WHERE YOU ARE...'' THERE WERE "NO SAD SONGS FOR ME" OR CALLOUSED PALMS. I ONCE THOUGHT MY VALUE SYSTEM ACCOUNTED FOR MY NOT BECOMING WEALTHY..A CONVENIENTLY SIMPLIFIED SELF-APPROVAL , BUT ERRONEOUS. IT WAS MORE THAN SUCH AN ELECTIVE CHOICE THAT GAVE ME MORE OUT OF LIFE THAN WHAT I HAD PUT INTO IT. IT MAY HAVE BEEN AADD THAT WATERS DOWN AMBITION, THUS AVOIDING EXCESSIVE FAILURES. OR IT MAY HAVE BEEN THE LESSONS LEARNED FROM THESE FAILURES THAT HELPED UNDERSTAND THEM.

A DOCTOR ONCE SAVED MY LIFE BUT COULD HAVE ENDED UP KILLING ME. HE HAD READ THE X-RAYS BACKWARDS. WHEN AN IMPERFECT WORLD COMBINES WITH INNER IMPERFECTION, SUCH AS AADD, THE ODDS ARE PRECARIOUS. THE SUPER-SURVIVORS ARE NOT PLAYTHINGS OF LUCK BUT OF LOGICAL STATISTICAL PROGRESSIONS THAT HAVE NOTHING TO DO WITH AADD. TRUE SURVIVORS ARE THOSE WHO NEVER ARE EXPOSED TO DANGER IN LIFE. AS FOR THE DEATH·BED SCENARIO,.THAT WELL- ESTABLISHED BLUEPRINT FOR HUMAN PROGRESSION, IT MAY BE EASED IN THE SAME WAY ONES ATTENTION IS DISTRACTED..LACKING CLARITY BECAUSE OF AADD, IT SERVES TO DISTRACT, LIKE MORPHINE'S MIRACLE, TO MAKE ONE LESS FOCUSED ON DEATH AS ONE WAS LESS FOCUSED DURING THEIR LIFETIME.

ADDENDA

DYSLEXIA AFFECTS SENTENCES, BUT AADD AFFECTS JUDGMENT. AADD REVERSES DECISIONS. IT IS A LIFE SENTENCE THAT HAS YOU SLEEPING WITH YOUR ENEMY, IT IS PARASITIC, IF 3 GOOD FRIENDS GIVE YOU THE SAME ADVICE; TAKE IT BEFORE YOUR HUNCHES, IF YOU THINK YOU HAVE AADD.

DON QUIXOTE AND THE DOCTOR ARE EXAMPLES OF AADDISTAS. WHEN THE SERGEANT YELLS, "ATTENTION", "RIGHT FACE", LAUREL TURNS LEFT IN THIS LAUREL + HARDY WORLD. DON QUIXOTE'S MADNESS IS BLAMED ON TOO MANY ADVENTURE BOOKS, LIKE COMIC BOOKS TODAY.

WE NEED "ENTRANCE EXAMS" FOR WORLD LEADERS. WHO MAY HAVE AADD. WE ALSO NEED AADD ANONYMOUS MUCH MODERN ART IS THE HANDWRITING ON THE WALL. ASTROLAGERS SHOULD STUDY EFFECT OF METALS FOUND IN PLANETS AND IN OUR BRAINS. PERIODIC INFLUENCE? WE COME FROM THEM.

<u>VIOLENCE ON THE HOME FRONT</u>

    TO ESCAPE CONSCRIPTION INTO THE AUSTRIAN ARMY OCCUPYING GENOA, MY GRANDFATHER CAME TO GREENWICH VILLAGE ONLY TO FACE CONSCRIPTION INTO THE UNION ARMY. ALTHOUGH HE WAS A PACIFIST, HE WAS ALSO A PATRIOTIC FOLLOWER OF GENERAL GIUSEPPE GARIBALDI(THEN LIVING ON STATEN ISLAND IN 1861). THIRTY TWO OF HIS "RED SHIRT" VOLUNTEERS DIED AT GETTYSBURG, MEMBERS OF THE "GARIBALDI BRIGADE".

    WHEN PRESIDENT LINCOLN CALLED UP THOUSANDS OF YOUNG MEN IN 1863, DRAFT RIOTS ENGULFED THE CITY. SOMEHOW MY GRANDFATHER SCRAPED UP THE THREE HUNDRED DOLLARS NEEDED TO BE EXEMPTED. UNFORTUNATELY, ALTHOUGH IT MAY HAVE SAVED HIM HIS LIFE, IT CAUSED THE DESTRUCTION OF HIS FAMILY AND THE LOSS OF THE PROPERTY HE OWNED AT 117 SULLIVAN STREET. THOSE WHO HAD ESCAPED THE DRAFT WERE TARGETED BY FAMILIES THAT HAD LOST LOVED ONES. FURTHERMORE, WE WERE HATED CAPITALIST LAND- LORDS. WE WERE ALSO GENOESE AND THE TENENTS SICILIANS WHO VANDALIZED OUR BUILDING. WHEN THE WAR ENDED MY GRANDFATHER DIED AND BROTHER FOUGHT BROTHER IN THE FAMILY OVER THE ESTATE. MY COUSINS, WHO WERE MY PLAYMATES, LEFT THE VILLAGE TO LIVE IN HOBOKEN NEVER TO BE SEEN AGAIN. TENANTS WOULD WAIT AT THEIR WINDOWS TO SPIT ON MY MOTHER AS SHE WALKED ME HOME FROM SCHOOL (TODAY CALLED CHELSEA VOCATIONAL). MY CHILDHOOD MEMORIES BEAR THE SCARS OF BEING BITTEN,TOUGH KIDS WHO STILL CALLED OUT TO EACH OTHER, "HEY, WHYO" (A TERM USED IN 1866 AMONG ITALIAN STREET GANGS, SIMILAR TO BLACKS CALLING OUT "NIGGA" TO EACH OTHER TODAY), AND RUNNING INTO ST. ANTHONY'S CHURCH FOR PROTECTION FROM ATTACK. I REMEBER MY DAD BEING PULLED BACK FROM THE WINDOW LEDGE..THE CITY MARSHALS WHO PUT OUR FURNITURE OUT ON THE SIDEWALK, WHERE I HAD TO STAND GUARD OVER IT, AS WE WERE CONSTANTLY BEING EVICTED. WE CALLED IT "MOVING DAY", PUTTING FURNI- TURE OUT OF THE WINDOW AT NIGHT..LANDLORDS WAITING TO CONFISCATE OUR BELONGINGS AS COMPENSATION FOR NON-PAYMENT OF RENT..PROCESS SERVERS, NOTICES IN THE MAIL. BUT ASIDE FROM WHAT TERRIFIED MY CHILDHOOD THE MOST WAS NOT THE THROWING OF PLATES, AND YES, KNIVES, THE SCREAMING..IT WAS THE WORD "DIVORCE" THAT I BARELY UNDERSTOOD.

    THE THREE HUNDRED DOLLARS HAD BOUGHT RESPITE BUT NOT EXEMPTION FROM THE VIOLENCE THAT FOLLOWED IT.

He achieved his goal in coming to America and to New
Jersey and now his children and their children were achieving
the same goals that were available to them in this great
country because they were Americans. When my grandfather
died years ago at the age of 76, things began to change.
Slowly at first, but then uncles and aunts eventually began
to cut down on their visits. Family gatherings were fewer
and something seemed to be missing, although when we did get
together, usually at my mothers house now, I always had the
feeling that he was there somehow. It was understandable of
course. Everyone now had families of their own and
grandchildren of their own. Today they visit once or twice a
year. Today we meet at weddings and wakes.

Lots of other things have changed too. The old house my
grandfather bought is now covered with aluminum siding,
although my uncle still lives there and of course my
grandfather's garden is gone. The last of the homemade wine
has long since been drunk and nobody covers the fig tree in
the fall anymore. For a while we would make the rounds on
the holidays, visiting family. Now, we occasionally visit
the cemetery. A lot of them are there, grandparents, uncles,
aunts, even my own father.

The holidays have changed too. The great quantity of
food we once consumed without any ill effects is no good for
us anymore. Too much starch, too much cholesterol, too many
calories. And nobody bothers to bake any more - too busy -
an it's easier to buy it now and too much is no good for you.
We meet at my house now, at least my family does, but it's
not the same.

The differences between US and THEM aren't so easily
defined anymore, and I guess that's good. My grandparents
were Italian Italians, my parents were Italian Americans.
I'm an American Italian and my children are American
Americans. Oh I'm an American alright and proud of it, just
as my grandfather would want me to be. We are all Americans
now - The Irish, Germans, Poles and Jews. U.S. citizens all
- but somehow I still feel a little bit Italian . Call it
culture, call it tradition, call it roots, I'm really not
sure what it is. All I do know is that my children have been
cheated out of a wonderful piece of the heritage. They never
knew my grandfather.

Loosies

(In memory of Eric Garner)

Loosies (loose cigarettes sold one cigarette at a time):

Working as a delivery boy after school in 1936, I earned $10 a week, part of which was from tips and part in cigarettes. A pack of Lucky Strikes or Old Gold cost $.15 and contained ten cigarettes. In the college cafeteria, I sold each individual cigarette for $.02, making a daily profit of $.20, or an extra dollar a week.

Every penny I earned was given to my parents, to be put in the bank and to give me a small weekly allowance. I thought of expanding my income with chewing gum, but there was little demand. Gum was not addictive.

My first sally into business was pitiful, but the power it gave me among the student body propelled me into college politics. I was selected to run as candidate for student council. My chances of election were good until the fraternity I pledged for rejected me on the basis of my pro-Mussolini position, that joined many Americans, such as Henry Ford, Charles Lindburgh, who supported the corporate state solution for the economy and its opposition to communist ideology. This was before Hitler entered the picture.

I was labeled a deprecating term, *fascist*, by the liberal student body and lost the election, as well as admission to the fraternity I had pledged for. I withdrew from Brooklyn College

THE DUMBEST KID IN THE CLASS

By

Vincent Livelli

If you had attended six universities your mother could boast,
"..my son, the intellectual".

My education was not an average one, nor were my grades average.
It was the kind of learning that orphans receive shuttling
back and forth between foster facilities.

As a child I had been eating lead paint, drinking from lead
pipes, eating from lead-lined cans, chewing my lead pencils
and playing with lead soldiers. My teeth were filled with lead.
Cars fed lead into the air. I played in construction sites,
scavenging lead scraps left by the pipe fitters. Junkmen came
to the house to buy my lead. By the time I was ready for college,
my brain was loaded with lead. I was a lead junkie.

The first university was one of the ten most difficult in the
country. I was thrown in with cut throat high achievers on
their way to becoming lawyers and doctors. Pledging for a
fraternity, I was rejected. They wouldn't accept me, me the
dumbest kid in the class, perhaps in the whole school, perhaps
"unteachable".

Determined to get an education, I dropped out. Perhaps another
college, other than Brooklyn College would be wiser. In 1940,
I enrolled at the University of Miami, unaware that it was an
anti-academic "country club". Suddenly my grades were A's and
B's. Teaching Conga at Miami Beach hotels paid for my tuition.
I then applied and received an Exchange Grant to studyat the
University of Havana. International Law sounded interesting.
I enrolled in it under Professor Bustamonte, known to his
students as "El Sordo", the Deaf One. My own hearing had been
damaged by lead. Sitting in the back of the class because of
my height and with limited command of the language, I nevertheless was happy in Havana, enjoying academic freedom and rumba.

But wait, what about CCNY? The Army had sent me there in '43, "awaiting assignment". (Evidently the authorities were puzzled by my record that even listed "Institute for Advanced Studies, Princeton, New Jersey-- Portuguese Monitor".) In a half empty classroom, I sat like a ward of the State, institutionalized.

Undoubtedly, this was all a continuation of a childhood pattern. During the Great Depression, families were constantly evicted. Attending a variety of High Schools and Sunday Schools seemed normal and fun. At home, we spoke English. Relatives spoke Genoese, Sicilian, Neapolitan and neighbors spoke Portuguese and Yiddish, etc. At age seventeen I was enrolled in a night secretarial course at Bay Ridge High School--an all-girl school. Later, I would crash The New School to hear Meyer Shapiro talk about Mondrian's "endless contingencies".

One day a mental breakthrough occurred. I wasn't a dumbhead after all! The smartest kid in our Spanish Class was failing the easiest language. By tutoring him I discovered my way out of the blackboard jungle. Qui docet discit.

SUMMARY. This all-expense paid, generalistic experience was a full school bag of international travel/adventure, warfare manuals, an unsuspected handicap and bibliotherapy.

NON SCOLAE SED VITAE DISCIMUS.

"XXth Century multiplicity"— Henry James

SALSALIVELLI . BLOGSPOT . COM

Google

I PAY CASH FOR OLD CLOTHES

by

Vincent Livelli

During the days of the Great Depression you would hear under your window someone singing, "O Sole Mio", "I Sharpen Knives", or "I Buy Old Clothes." Today, because of some bad luck, I'm living like a peddler out of a suitcase.

Because so much of my life has been lived on the go, this is not an entirely unaccustomed situation for me. For many years I lived on ships, sleeping in small cabins with tiny closets. Travel became my way of life, frequenting thousands of eateries that were my kitchens so to speak, and living in hotel rooms that served as my homes while working on the road and seas as a tour director.

As an itinerant, I've been lucky traveler. This is why, now that I find myself living in a tiny room furnished not to my admittedly odd tastes, I can easily make my way through life's pathways and lesser alleyways. This set up, though not of my choosing is good enough when compared, to say, Daniel Boone who lived in and off a forest all his life.

Sobering moments enter the picture of my life. When in a thrift shop I catch myself paying cash for old clothes. Just like back in the day of the Great Depression.

VINCENT LIVELLI

212 255 0576

44 Perry Street   New York, New York   10014

Dear Henry! Your interest in Greenwich Village shows me that
you are an artist at heart. With me, it was an accident of
birth that placed me here, fortunately. I say fortunately, because this is where I feel I most belong. If I could have had
a choice it would have been here or Paris, so much so, that when
I meet a Parisian, I feel I have much in common with him.

This is where I awoke from infancy when my mother took me to
the window to show me snow in the back yard. *MY FIRST VIEW
OF THE "WORLD" WAS A BEAUTIFUL ONE.* Because the 9th
Ward (as Greenwich Village was once called in the early part of
the 20th century) was so overrun with violence from street
gangs it was unsafe for me to play in the street. Furthermore,
since we were landlords, there was much envy and hostility
toward my family. I was only allowed out inthe company of my
grandmother or my uncle on their daily visit to St. Anthony's
Church (Shrine)..that my grandfather was instrumental in establishing on Thompson Street. He hoped to help the community
and at the same time increase property values in the ~~neigh~~ *NEIGH-*
bor,hood. Today, his dream is realized, I'm happy to say.
He admired and spoke often of the Germans, a more settled
element in the city. "A walk in G.V." refered to "Row houses"
north of Washington Square Park. These stately mansions were
called,in my grandfather's time and even today,"The Rhineland-
ers Estates" (now owned by NYU). He traveled all over Germany
as his old passport shows and was in the "piano string busieass"
at 5 Bedford Street with a German family. He may very well have
built the hurdy-gurdy organ that he carried around Europe as a
"musiker". He owned a stable and opened a bar to sell German
beer. In those days, the Genoese families in the Village drank
beer more than wine since it was more readily available. Wehn
I was 9 or 10, I would go for Beer for the men working on West
Broadway, bailing paper. They called such young children "go-
fors" in English even though the men working the hugh compacting
machines were all Italian-Amercans. My father was a journalist
having been born in NY and having graduated High School. He began his newspaper career as Arthur Brisbane's office boy an
worked his way up to Investigative Reporter with the NY WORLD
and the NY American (Hearst newspapers.)He may also have worked
on the Old NY POST,(Editor,a certain Mr. SWOPE.) The Village at
this time was very crowded with poor immigrant families. Walking
to P.S. 1o2, on Varick St. I would be bullied and sometimes spit
on. from tenants up at windows who identified me with my landlord
family. Soon I was not allowed the natural pursuits of young kids
and was kept tied to the fireescape. A cousin older than I would
walk me up to Central Pk and back, especially in the winter to
ice skate on the lake. He would have to carry me home on his shoulders since it was quite far for me to walk. He would skate with me
on his shoulders as well. His mother, my aunt Tessie and my unmarried Uncle John,my grandparents and my mom & dad were all obliged to live in the building. For safety, my Dad moved me and
mom to Brooklyn when I was 10 or 11. I had originally been born
in Brooklyn at the time when all the apartments in my grandfathers'
building at 117 Sullivan Street were taken.

(Now SoHo)

BACK

18

As soon as a vacancy opcured, my Dad [HAD] moved into my Grandfathers
building when I was 6 months' old so I consider myself a villager.
I remember the Jefferson Market Courthouse Library when it had a
Womans' Prison attached to its property. It was torn down around
1960 espially since the ladies would be yelling down from the
barred windows at friends and passersby in the street (6th ave.).
I played, jumping in the mountains of sand being excavated while
they were building the 6th Avenue subway, coming home all sandy.
My real playground was Washington Square Park where I was taken
daily,(after visiting Pompei Church and St. Anthony's) to ride
my tricycle..the envy of the neighborhood kids whose families
could not buy them one. We sat by Garibaldi's statue since my
grandfather was a "Garibalino", instrumental in raising money
for the statue. He came to America in 1861 to join Garibaldi
who was living on Staten Island at that time prior to leaving [STATEN ISLAND]
to fight in Peru against the Spaniards. He bought acres of
empty land in Rego Park and Forest Hills but sold it in order to
finance his son,Dominick (my uncle) who was running for Mayor of
Hoboken where there was a very large community of Sicilians
(who were being oppressed by the Irish political machine and made
to work of a dollar a day paving streets) He lost the election
and we became much poorer over time. Today the rent for an apt/
in my grandfathers' building on Sullivan St. is averaging $2000.00
a month. Next to this builing I remember "out houses" before there
was central plumbing. The people called them "back houses" as
Barry Lewis mentioned. In Italian, "Bacahows" or "Cesso".(the
word comes from cesspool in English.) Today you enter a tight alley
to go into the back yard of the two bulldings where there is now
a small cottage. This occured in many instances where the space was
used to build small cottages where formerly there where crude "toilets".
Even as late as the sixtied thre was a public toilet (men and women)
around #17 Perry St.Most of the kids were poisoned eating lead paint
chips as they still are today in poor neighborhoods in the Bronx and
elsewhere in the city. My mother loved dancing and spoke of the
cabaret named "The Black Cat" (I think it was on West third st.)
in the twenties. "Mori's"was the popular restaurant on W.4th St [IN 45]
and had a fountain in the interior yard. MacDougal St. was lined
until just after the WW2 with privat mansions with ironwork balconies
and railings. And at the Provincetown Playhouse was in 1946-48, a nice
club called "Salle de Cahmpagne" hwere guests sat on cushioned seats
and drank champagne. A Jazz spot named George's was at the corner (NE)
ofBleeker and 7th Ave. and then after WW2 was "Louie's" on W. 4th &
Barrow (where "One if by land" restaurant is located down the street),
In the hot summers, horses would die in the streets, cops would shooT
them, flies entered windows before screening, stable smell to this day
keeps me from liking horses..I lit the gas lamps in the hallways of my
grandpas' bulding while carried on the Dad's shoulders. The communal
[WC] toilets on each floor served three families and where the coolest places
to escape the hot apts. My dad bought me clothes on Orchard St and I was
[8YRS—] always wearing a hat (that I took off to greet people as I bowed in front
of them). My best friend was the son of the Jewish candy store owner on
Prince St. when I was 9.My childhood in the Village was proper and not
difficult compared to other kids, many of whom went to jail. Today, my
Village is my house of memories that will be with me forever.

THE ADULTURATED SCRIPTURES

by

Vincent Livelli

I was 13, walking with two Jewish friends on my way home from school. We all saw clearly in the sky, three beautifully clothed figures in flowing robes, and the central figure being unmistakably the Virgin Mary. This upsetting vision so startled us that we separated, speechless. So mystified were we that each went off in different directions, scattering from shock. Thousands of faithful adherents as well as determined skeptics have been involved in this matter of faith in the shadow of doubt.

While I was in Ephesus, on a tour called, "In the Footsteps of St. Paul" it was the effect of my entering the abode of Mary that highlighted my trip. John the Baptist is said to have escorted the Mother of Jesus from Jerusalem to Ephesus where he had a small stone house built for her.

A house is "second removed" from its occupant whose spirit it inhabits. Perhaps that is why, while the guide and my tourist group waited below, I chose to climb a rocky hill in order to go inside this sanctified dwelling. Completely devoid of furnishings, the air remained one of mystery. I found the same "presence" evident in the church of Saint Cyprian in Carthage which was completely emptied by Muslims, as in the now shell-stripped, bare, and enormous shrine to St. Nicholas in Smyrna, and in the Moscovian Orthodox church with its pews removed to discourage religious worship. The massive "presence" in these cases means "less is more."

Following the crucifixion, Mary Magdalene, and her Mother-in-Law the Blessed Virgin were obliged to flee from Roman authorities. Mary Magdalene fled to the south of France, protecting the unborn child. The two parted with the tearful knowledge that the Grandmother would never see the boy or girl grandchild.

There are two reasons as to why the marriage that resulted with the pregnant Mary Magdalene was kept secret. It was prudent, because of the Roman hostility, and of course the tremendous embarrassment to church dogma, especially since it forbade abortion. The two Marys would never have separated at such a crucial time had the welfare of an unborn child not entered the picture.

When I passed out the back door of Mary's house, as if following a rite of passage, and I rejoined my party, I was never closer to the Holy Mother. My departure from the tour group, and entering such sanctity had brought to mind my first encounter with her.

If the catholic hierarchy is feeling threatened, let them fear not, for the Bible says, "The truth shall set you free…" The unadulterated truth, that is.

Thou shall not commit adultery.

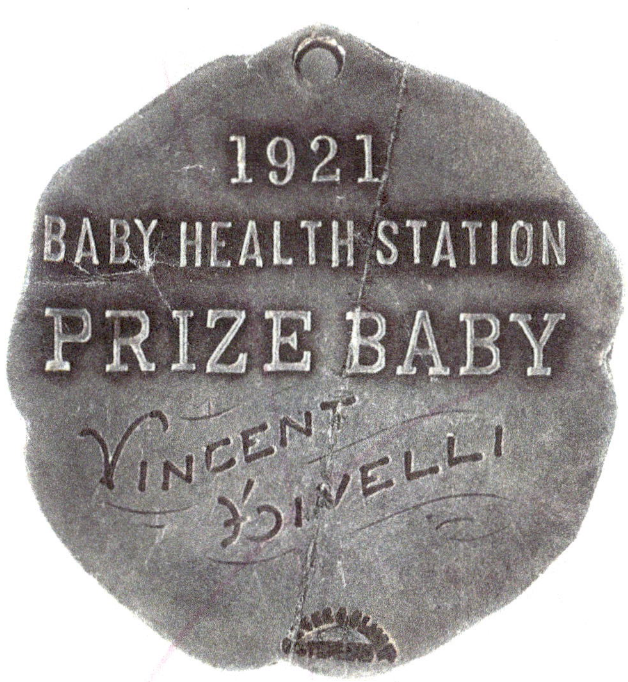

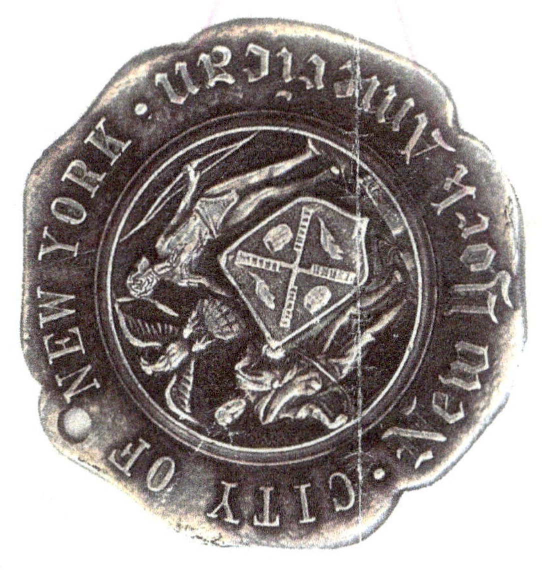

1921
BABY HEALTH STATION
PRIZE BABY
VINCENT LIVELLI

CITY OF NEW YORK
New York American

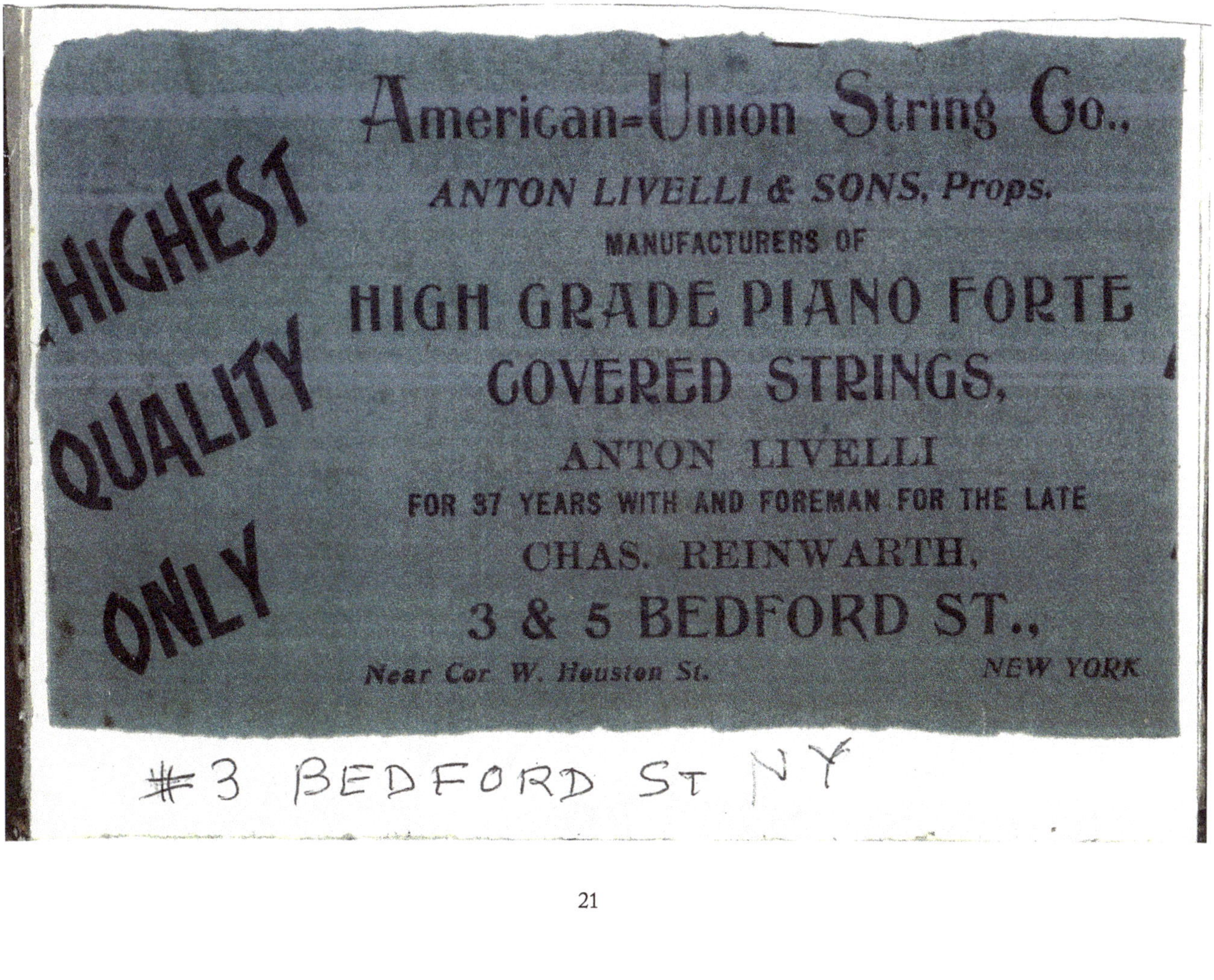
HIGHEST QUALITY ONLY
American-Union String Co.,
ANTON LIVELLI & SONS, Props.
MANUFACTURERS OF
HIGH GRADE PIANO FORTE
COVERED STRINGS,
ANTON LIVELLI
FOR 37 YEARS WITH AND FOREMAN FOR THE LATE
CHAS. REINWARTH,
3 & 5 BEDFORD ST.,
Near Cor. W. Houston St.
NEW YORK
#3 BEDFORD ST NY

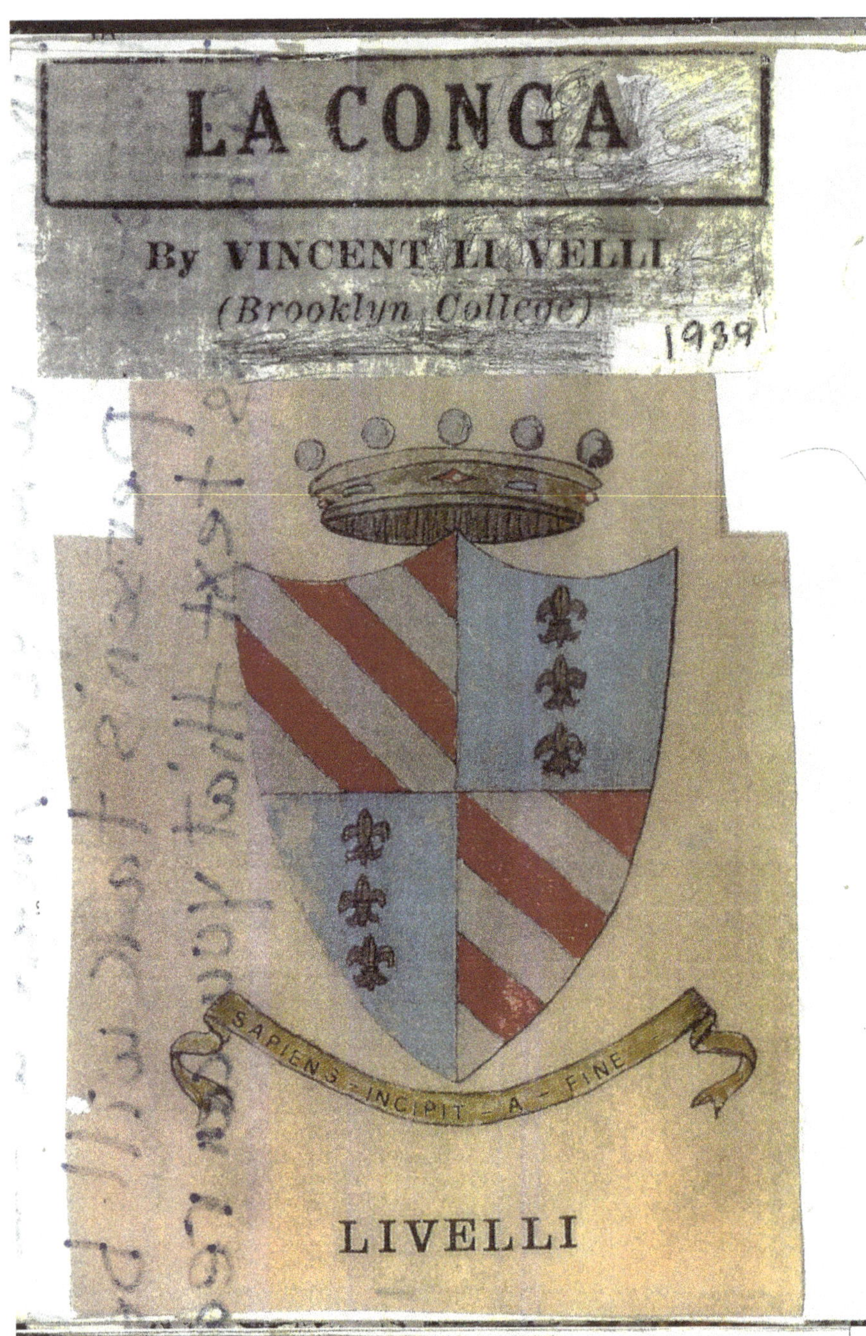

LA CONGA

By VINCENT LI VELLI
(Brooklyn College)

1939

...in Rythms
...VINCENT LI VELLI
(Brooklyn College)

...opularity of music of the Latin
...is increasing. The reason for
...immediately when
...is evid... the rythm, the melody
...listens teauty of any Tango,
...nd the b Conga.
Rhumba or primitive, exotic and
...It is the ppeal of this music that
suggestive ...ed the peoples of the
...attrac...e Rhumba is danced in
...Japan and Scandinavia
...a no hay fronterra" as the
...say.

...ew York, the Rhumba has its
...support in Society. At Miss
...enda Frazier's debut. Emil Cole-
...an, who specializes in Latin music,
and a Gypsy Ensemble provided the
entertainment.

Meanwhile, the Waltz is coming
back and Swing is dying from over
work. Cuban style night clubs and
orchestras are multiplying.

Tango, Rhumba and Conga dancing classes are crowded. The steps
are simple and the rythm is accented and easy to follow the "Bongos"
"Claves" and "Maracas" will a...
you in this.

There is, however, a distinction...
to how it's done at the La Rain
Casino in Harlem and at the...
bow Room in Rockefeller Center.

The success of The Peanut Ven-
der, The Isle of Capri, Serenade in
the Night, and Tip! Tin shows the
trend to be toward that type music.

The World's Fair has invited the
best orchestra in Cuba—the Ca...
De La Playa—to New York.

As for the future, I pred...
"Jitterbugs" will be trample...
"Rumberos".

GREENWICH VILLAGE

II

GREENWICH
VILLAGE

" U VilAGIO "
and
U VILAJ
(SICILIAN)

DEAR BLISS: HEATED DISCUSSIONS CONCERNING LITERATURE AT THE
"REMO" OFTEN REQUIRED DEFINITION OF TERMINOLOGY AND MODERATION.
YOUR DAD REFEREED A CERTAIN DECORUM AND RESPECTFUL APPROACH TO
THE IMMORTAL AUTHORS UNDER SCRUTINY. THIS WAS SLIGHTLY INCONGRUOUS
IN A BAR ATMOSPHERE. WHEN RETURNING HOME DRUNK, THOMAS WOLFE WAS
KNOWN TO ENTER DICTATING PASSAGES, WHILE HIS SECRETARY SCRAMMBLED
FOR A PENCIL. AT TIMES, TALK TURNED CONTENTIOUS REGARDING THIS
OR THAT WORK OR AUTHOR. YOUR DAD ORCHESTRATED THE PEPPERY CON-
FRONTATIONS, BEING A MASTER OF QUOTATIONS, PARABLES, REFERENCES
AND CHAPTER AND VERSE. NIMBLE WITH WORDS, HIS SENTENCES SKIPPED
ALONG, CHURNING THE AIR WITH WORDS NEVER HEARD BEFORE. HIS WAS
THE SOURCE OF THE BRILLIANCE. WHILE TEASING MILTON KLONSKY, WHO
WAS STEEPED IN BLAKE, DANTE, DICKENS AND D'ANNUNZIO AMONG OTHERS,
YOUR DAD WOULD CALL ON AUDEN, TRILLIN OR CLEMENT GREENBERG IN
RETORT. THERE WERE TIMES OF HARMONY AND AGREEMENT BUT ALSO DAYS
WHEN THEY WOULD CROSS THE STREET TO AVOID EACH OTHER BECAUSE OF
PROUST. WE ALL LEFT THE TABLE SATISFIED WITH OUR SELVES AND OUR
MEAL WHICH WAS USUALLY MANICOTTI, CHEAP AND FILLING, LIKE A POT
BOILER.

LATE IN THE FORTIES, THE VILLAGE BEGAN TO ACQUIRE THE APPEAL OF
A CIRCUS AND AN ATMOSPHERE OF A FREAK SIDE SHOW. MANY CAME TO
WATCH THE SICKOS AND SICKIES THAT BEGAN TO MULTIPLY AROUND US.
IN A TOLERANT COMMUNITY, WITH MANY HANG-OUTS AND BARS, WE SAW
THE BEGINNING OF UGLY ATTITUDES CONSIDERED FASHIONABLE. SOME
CAME FOR ARTSY-CRAFTSY REASONS. THERE WAS A CULTURAL VACUUM TO
BE FILLED POST-WAR AND THE VILLAGE WAS THE BEST PLACE OUTSIDE OF
PARIS FOR EXPRESSION. THE PLACE ASSUMED THE MYSTIQUE OF AN EGYPT
WITH LITERARY MONUMENTS. OVERFLOWS FROM THE BOWERY, WHO FORMER-
LY FEARED THE LOCALS, WERE MORE IN EVIDENCE, ALLOWING ARTISTS
TO DISCOVER SOMEONE TO PITY OTHER THAN THEMSELVES. DELINQUENTS
AND ADMIRERS OF BAD GUYS WERE FOUND AMONG US. LOSERS BECAME THE
WINNERS, LIKE LENNY BRUCE. BUSES PARKED AROUND THE ARCH AND THE
CIRCLE BECAME PRE-WOODSTOCK WITH A PSUEDO-"GAIETE PARISIENNE".
NYU BEGAN EXPANDING ALL OVER THE PLACE, CHANGING STREETS AROUND.
BACKYARD GARDENS DISAPPEARED OVERNIGHT. ORNAMENTAL IRON GRILL-
WORK WAS SCRAPPED, DALI PERFORMED FANTASY-INSPIRING ANTICS.
ANAIS NIN OPENED HER DIARIES, SARTRE'S "HUIT CLOS" OPENED ON
BROADWAY. 9 AND 5 WERE UNLUCKY NUMBERS, LOCALS BEGAN TO REBEL

William Gaddis   1991 2

I MUST HAVE CAUGHT HIM OFF GUARD SINCE I NEVER REMEMBER HIM
SMILING. HE INTRODUCED ME TO HIS WIFE WHOSE NAME I CAN'T RE-
MEMBER. WE DRANK SOME WATER WHILE HE SHOWED US WHERE HE DID
HIS WRITING. (AUTHORS I'VE KNOWN ALWAYS SHOW ME THEIR WRITING
SPACE..THE SCENE OF THE CRIME). HIS WAS IN A SMALL GARAGE WITH
AN OVERHEAD SOLITARY BULB, FREEZING IN THE WINTER, I'M SURE
UNCOMFORTABLE AS HELL, LIKE A MONKS CELL. ANATOLE SHOWED ME
HIS AS SOON AS I ARRIVED AT GREENS FARM WHERE HE HAD MOVED
TO, IN CONNECTICUT WITH SANDY. BEING ON THE TOP FLOOR OF A TWO
STORY HOUSE, IT WAS LIKE UP IN AN ATTIC AWAY FROM THE REST OF
THE PLACE. HE MADE ME SIT IN HIS FAVORITE CHAIR..WHICH HAS
A SPECIAL NAME AND IS A COLLECTORS' ITEM TODAY. IT WAS THE LAZY-BOY
CHAIR, ONLY PADDED, BLACK LEATHER WITH EXTENDED FOOT REST AND
LAY-BAK FOR COMFORT AND CONTEMPLATION. THE ROOM ITSELF WAS
LARGE AND ALMOST BARREN. WILLIE'S WAS AN UNLIKELY CHOICE AND ODDLY
UNCLUTTERED BEING AS IT WAS A GARAGE WITH NO CAR OR TOOLS.
I COULDN'T PICTURE WILLIE USING HIS HANDS SINCE HE RESEMBLED
AN ENGLISH COUNTRY GENTLEMAN. WE DIDN'T STAY LONG AND WHEN I
MADE A MOVE TO LEAVE EARLY, HE DIDN'T PRESS ME TO STAY WHICH
I REGRET, HE WASN'T LATIN IN THE LEAST IN THAT WAY OR PERHAPS
HE WAS POLITE NOT TO HOLD ME BACK. I HAD PHONED IN ADVANCE.

NEXT TIME, AT THE MAIN BRANCH, NY PUBLIC LIBRARY, WITH 500 +BLISS
PRESENT, HE APPROACHED THE LECTERN TO SPEAK ABOUT HIS 2nd.   BROYAR
NATIONAL BOOK AWARD. HE WAS WALKING TO THE PLATFORM WHEN I
COULD HAVE GREETED HIM, BUT SOMETHING HELD ME BACK. HE WAS
ON HIS WAY TO ADDRESS A CROWD AND I THOUGHT BETTER THAN IN-
TERUPTING HIS THOUGHTS AND COMPOSURE. HE SPOKE FOR A FEW MINutes.
NATURALLY, HE WAS SURROUNDED AT THE CONCLUSION AND I LEFT. IT
WAS NOT A GOOD MOMENT TO CHOOSE TO TALK, LIKE SEEING AN OLD
LOVER WITH A NEW GIRLFRIEND.

I DECIDED THAT HIS FRIENDSHIP COULD BE RE-STARTED BY WRITING
TO HIS LAST MANHATTAN ADDRESS, SENDING HIM THREE FRONTPIECES,
XEROXED FOR HIM TO SIGN, (SINCE I DIDN'T WANT TO SEND HIM THE
RARE COPIES OF HARDCOVER "THE RECOGNITIONS", j r and carpenters
     --THIS TYPEWRITER ONLY WORKS ON UPPER CASE---
HE MAY HAVE RESENTED THIS APPEAL OR GOD KNOWS WHY HE DIDN'T
RESPOND. IT WAS A STRANGE REQUEST BUT I WAS TAKING ADVANTAGE
OF THE FACT THAT HE PUT ME IN "THE RECOGNITIONS". VALENTINE
WAS WHAT THEY CALLED ME IN THE SAN REMO.."valentino" HE MEN-
TIONS ME WEARING BLACK AND WHITE SHOES WHICH WAS MY TRADEMARK
AS A RUMBA DANCER IN THE OLD MIAMI BEACH / GROSSINGER HOTEL DAYS.
WHEN HE MET ME IN SOUTH MIAMI, HIS CONVERSATION WAS CRYPTIC
CONCERNING HIS FORD FOUNDATION ASSIGNMENT. HE, AND MANY FREINDS
OF MINE THOUGHT I WAS DOING SOME SECRET WORK FOR THE GOVERNMENT
AND RE-ACTED IN A CONSPIRATORIAL MANNER DURING OUR CONVERSATIONS.
IN SOME WAY, AMERICANS ARE SUSPICIOUS OF CITIZENS THAT TRAVEL
AROUND OUT OF THE COUNTRY TO FOREIGN CULTURES GATHERING GOD
KNOWS WHAT.

                              SHUE
HE AND ANATOLE DIDN'T SEE THAT SHERI WAS ON DRUGS (SUPPLIED BY   THE
HER LOVER EDDIE SHOE, (SAXIPHONIST EXTRAORDINAIRE). I DID, SINCE QUEEN
SHE USED ME AS A FATHER CONFIANT. HE GAVE UP SHERI, SHOCKED LIKE
THE YOUNG ENGLISH POET WHO FAINTED WHEN HE LEARNED THAT HER MAJESTY
URINATED AS WELL AS EVERYONE ELSE. SHERI SPOKE WITH A HOLLOW VOICE
AS THOUGH AT THE END OF A LONG TUNNEL, CURLING HER HAIR WITH HER FORK
GETTING IT CAUGHT IN THE MUSIC BOX SHE WOUND UP & CARRIED WITH HER.

JAY, DEAR JAY: I WILL ALWAYS ANSWER YOUR LETTERS. THEY ARE KISSES.
THAT I RESPOND TO. I'M WORKING ON TWO PIECES, "TWICE IN A LIFETIME"
ABOUT THE "QUEEN MARY" and "DO NOT TOUCH", ABOUT EXPERIENCES IN
MUSEUMS. I'M OVERFLOWING LIKE A BATHTUB WITH WORDS AND IDEAS ABOUT THE
PAST...SELF-MEMORIALIZATION. YOU HAVE GIVEN ME PERMISSION TO DO SO.
YOU GENEROUSLY GAVE ME BOOKS THAT I WILL NEVER PART WITH. TRY TO
GET YOURSELF "IN RECOGNITION OF WILLIAM GADDIS", SYRACUSE UNIVERSITY
PRESS, STEVEN MOORE, JACK KUEHL. THEY WERE BOTH AT MY PLACE TAKING
NOTES AND GAVE ME A PLUG IN THE INTRODUCTION. MISTRUSTFUL GENIUS
THAT HE WAS, HE NEVERTHELESS COULDN'T BE HIS RECLUSIVE SELF WITH
ME SINCE I MET HIM DURING HIS FORMATIVE (OUR FORMATIVE YEARS). IF
HE, WILLIE, LIKE KLONSKY, THOUGHT THAT "SILENCE IN THE NIGHT" WAS
WHEN IDEAS CAME, TO USE KANT'S CONCEPT, HE IS EXCUSED SINCE IT DID
WORK FOR HIM. HE SHUT HIMSELF UP ON A MONASTERY IN ESTREMADURA. I'VE
BEEN TO THAT BARREN PLACE, PERFECT FOR ISOLATION AND HIDING FROM
SOCIETY. ITS LIKE NEBRASKA, ONLY DRY AND HILLY..SO BORING TO ITS
FOLK THAT THEY LEFT IT FOR PERU AND MEXICO IN THE 16th CENTURY TO
DIE ABROAD. YOUR BROTHER KEPT NOTES WHICH IS LIKE CHEATING ON YOUR-
SELF. MILTON WAS A HUMOUROUS JEWISH CONVERSATIONALIST LIKE A RABBI,
BUT WILL' WAS A CLOSE-MOUTHED ENGLISHMAN, MINUS THE PIPE. HE (W.) MUST
HAVE REALIZED EARLY ON THAT HE WAS A WRITER WITH TALENT IN THE RIGHT
DIRECTION, ORIGINALITY. HE SAVED CONFUSION FOR HIS PLOT PURPOSELY
AND CARRIED IT INTO HIS INTERPERSONAL RELATIONS. HIS SILENCE WAS
PERPLEXING TO PEOPLE AND HE ENJOYED THEIR SPECULATION LIKE A CHILD
PLAYING HIDE & SEEK WITH WORD GAMES. HIS REBELLION TOOK THE FORM
OF MAKING THE READER SUFFER (DID HE HATE HIS PARENTS?) AND THE ENTIRE
LITERARY ESTABLISHMENT AS WELL. I FELT SORRY FOR THE REVIEWERS WHO
WERE ASKED TO TACKLE HIS WORK. IT TOOK ME MONTHS TO FINISH "THE
RECOGNICTIONS" EVEN THOUGH EACH PAGE WAS SO RICH IN SPECULATION AND
THE HISTORY OF OUR VILLAGE DAYS..OR TO SAVOR EACH WORD SELECTIVELY.

WE WERE BOTH 28 WHEN WE MET, OUR FORMATIVE YEARS, PREPARING US FOR
ADULTHOODS' CHALLENGES. HE COULDN'T FOOL ME SINCE HIS WEAKNESSES
STOOD OUT. BASICALLY, I WOULD CLASSIFY HIS ATTITUDE   TOWARD
LIFE AS MISCHEVIOUS AND TIMID IN A CLEVER MANNER. WHEN HE PHONED
ME OUT OF THE BLUE ONE NIGHT IN SOUTH MIAMI, WE HAD SOME AMONTILLADO
AND WHEN ASKED WHAT HE WAS UP TO..THE WAY YOU AND I EXCHANGE GOOD &
BAD NEWS.."I'VE BEEN DOING SOME WORK FOR THE FORD FOUNDATION, GOOD
MONEY, BUT I DONT GIVE A HOOT FOR THEM", HE TOLD ME. THIS KIND OF
REPLY BEGS FOR FURTHER COMMENT OR EVEN A LONG DISCOURSE AND EXCHANGE
OF INTIMATE DETAILS, ETC. BUT I WOULDN'T PLAY HIS GAME, LETTING IT
DROP. HE WANTED TO BE RECOGNIZED I THINK, WHICH IS VERY WELL WHEN
ONE HAS LOTS OF TIME. THE REASON I'VE GOTTEN SO MUCH UNDER MY BELT
IN LIFE IS BECAUSE I HURRIED WHILE OTHERS TARRIED. ANSWERS WILL CROP UP.

THREE INCIDENCES BEAR RELATION. MY GIRFRIEND AND I DROVE UP THE
HUDSON RIVER VALLEY TO "GROTON-ON-HUDSON" (AN ADDRESS HE HAD GIVEN ME).
IT SOUNDED LIKE HIM. WHEN WE ARRIVED THERE WAS AN OVERTURNED TRYCYCLE
AND A RED CART AND A SWING, EVIDENCE OF A CHILD, BUT THE PLACE WAS
EMPTY. PERHAPS SINCE WE ARRIVED UNNANOUNCED, HE DIDN'T ANSWER THE DOOR.
DROPPED A NOTE AND LEFT UNEASY. THE PLACE WAS SPOOKY, LIKE A HASTY
DEPARTURE OF SOME SORT. THE NEXT TIME I VISITED HIM WAS IN PIEMONT,
WHERE WOODY ALLEN FILMED "RED ROSE OF CAIRO". WHEN HE OPENED THE DOOR,
I THRUST A BOX OF CANNOLI IN HIS HAND AND SNAPPED A PICTURE OF HIM SMILING

(RIGHT) WILLIAM GADDIS
SOUTH MIAMI 1958

TWO-TIME NATIONAL BOOK
AWARD VILLAGE ORIGINAL
FROM THE MID 19 HUNDREDS

WROTE "THE RECOGNITIONS"

JAY LANDESMAN   2002
ISLINGTON LONDON

ROCCO LANDESMAN'S UNCLE

V.L. WILLIAM GADDIS
SOUTH MIAMI
1958

IT HAPPENED OVERNIGHT

by

Vincent Livelli

Sandy Broyard believed that by removing Anatole from his *hanky panky* playground he would be reformed into a normal husband. If she could change his wayward ways she would find peace in herself, since she also had a temptation similar to his. Hers came from both her alcoholic parental family history among Norwegian drinkers and from the justifiable desire to totally own Anatole for herself. But Anatole was "tied to the skirts" of the very desirous and young Smith College beauties that were flooding into the Village in the late 1940's.

These prime targets came seeking "Anatoles", the writers and artists who provided delights of romance and erudition. Since there was only one true "Anatole" to be found among the denizens of Washington Square Park, they were obliged to line up to meet him. He of course was readily obliging, even if not always available. He once told me, while teaching at Cambridge, another young active playground, and without detail, "I can't handle them."

2   Once the girls returned to the North, and to the Boston suburbs, they found more reasons to explain their Village behavior and forgive their indiscrete activities. Bostonian men were seen to be more strictly conservative by comparison. They knew what they needed, and what they had been deprived of by law and by unwritten law. This was conveyed in girl talk that spread around the various campuses, including the bastion of feminine high morality at Sarah Lawrence.

When Sandy succeeded in kidnapping Anatole from his Village buddies, she actually jumped from a hot plate into the fire. Cambridge was ripe and waiting for an Anatole. He was brought to where his many conquests were still smoldering from his expertise, which was the epitome of rampant masculinity. Boston males were more interested in rowing on the Charles River than in rolling in bed.

<u>CELEBRITY PHOBIA</u>

        I CAN'T SAY THAT I'M NOT IMPRESSED BY CELEBRITIES, BUT BACK IN
1938 SOMETHING HAPPENED THAT LEFT A SHOCKING FEAR OF THEM. STRANGELY,
THEY SEEMED TO BE ATTRACTED TO ME, POPPING IN AND OUT OF MY LIFE.
WHEN I WAS 17, I THOUGHT I WOULD COLLECT AUTOGRAPHS OF THE FAMOUS,
AS MANY YOUNGSTERS WERE BEGINNING TO DO AT THAT TIME. AT IDLEWILD
AIRPORT, I SAW MARTHA RAYE APPROACHING AND, LIKE DIVING FOR THE
FIRST TIME, I EXTENDED BY PAD AND PENCIL. SHE WAS A STRONG WOMAN,
USED TO ENTERTAING G.I.'s OVERSEAS. "OUT OF MY WAY, YOU ---!" I
was pushed emotionally and physically. NEVER HAD I HEARD A WOMAN
CURSE LIKE A MAN, NOR DID I KNOW SHE WAS FAMOUS FOR HER BIG MOUTH
AND SALTY LANGUAGE. AFTER RUNNING INTO ABOUT A HUNDRED CELEBS,
THERE IS ONLY ONE THAT I HAVE, CARMEN MIRANDA. IT WASN'T HER AUTO-
GRAPH THAT I WANTED, IT WAS HER LIP PRINT ON A PIECE OF KLEENEX.
I WAS NOT BEING BRAZEN WHEN I ASKED HER FOR IT SINCE SHE HAD JUST
KISSED ME AND ACTUALLY I WAS WIPING ROUGE OFF MY FACE. SHE KISSED
ME BECAUSE I SPOKE SOME PORTUGUESE WHILE WE WERE FILMING HER IN
HER DRESSING ROOM. SHE HANDED ME THE TISSUE, SIGNED IT WITH A HUGE
LIP PRINT ADDED TO IT. SHE WAS AN EXCEPTION.

        AN ENCOUNTER WITH WORLD CLASS CELEBRITIES OCCURED IN PORTOFINO.
THE FISHERMEN AND THEIR FAMILIES RETIRE VERY EARLY AND THE PLACE
WAS SILENT AND VERY DARK. ON OUR WAY TO THE "PIRASCOPO" RESTAURANT,
A COUPLE APPEARED OUT OF THE DARK..THE DUKE AND DUCHESS OF WINDSOR
WITH THEIR TWO SMALL DOGS. SUDDENLY DOGS BARKING WOKE UP THE PLACE.
LIGHTS WENT ON HERE AND THERE. THE DOGS HAD RUN INTO MY MALTESE,
A VERY VOCAL YAPPER. OTHER DOGS JOINED IN. WHEN I SAW WHO I WAS
IN THE COMPANY OF, I NOTICED THAT THE DUKE'S COLORFUL BAHAMIAN SHIRT
WAS IDENTICAL TO MINE. THERE WAS ONLY ONE TAILOR IN NASSAU THAT
MADE THEM IN 1952. FELLOW DOG LOVERS AND COINCIDENTAL FASHION CON-
CIOUS CHARACTERS OPENED A CHANCE TO CHAT,HOWEVER, HINDERED BY THE
HISTERICAL BARKING AND A GROWLING STOMACH, WE PARTED COMPANY.

        ANOTHER ODD COINCIDENCE HAPPENED AT THE CARLTON IN CANNES.
IN THE TINY ELEVATOR. ED SULLIVAN WAS WEARING A RED JACKET AND
PASTEL PINK PANTS. I WAS WEARING A PASTEL PINK JACKET AND RED PANTS.
THE LADIES LAUGHED BUT AS WE EXITED WE DIDN'T WALK TOGETHER IN THE LOB
AT THE TEATRO PAYET IN HAVANA IN 1941, I WAS EMBARASSED BY MAESTRO
ERNESTO LECUONA .HE WAS FOR ME A MUSICAL HERO AS HE WAS TO EVERYONE
WHO FOLLOWED HIM. HIS FIRST VIOLINIST HANDED ME A NOTE.INVITING ME
TO THE DRESSING ROOM AFTER THE PERFORMANCE. WITH THE NOTE IN HAND AND
HIS MUSIC IN MY EARS, I COULDN'T BE HAPPIER, SITTING THERE IN THE DARK
IN THE DRESSING ROOM, THE MAESTRO AROSE FROM HIS SMALL PIANO AND AFTER
A WELCOME TO CUBA, HE SAT DOWN SAYING, "YOU ARE THE FIRST TO HEAR THIS
SONG I HAVE JUST FINISHED COMPOSING". WHAT LUCK IT WAS A "PRECIOSO
BOLERO","YOU ARE ALWAYS IN MY HEART". "WE'RE HAVING A PICNIC AT THE
FARM ON SUNDAY.." IT WAS TIME TO LEAVE WHEN HE GAVE ME A KNOWING LOOK.
ANOTHER HASTY EXIT OCCURED AT THE BEACHCOMBER. SHE WAS SITTING RINGSIDI
WITH HER BACK TO HER TWO COMPANIONS WHO WERE IGNORING HER. APPROACHING
HER FOR A RUMBA, SHE JOINED ME ON THE FLOOR. WHEN I ASKED HER NAME,
"VIRGINIA HILL", SHE REPLIED IN MY EAR. "BUGSY AND MEYER LANSKY", I
SHUDDERED PULLING APART FROM HER, THANKING HER FOR THE DANCE.

        LEO DUROCHER WAS RINGSIDE AT THE HOTEL NATIONAL, HAVANA. IT WAS
RUMBA MATINEE AND HE CALLED OUT, "WHERE YOU FROM?"CURIOUS ABOUT THE E
STEPS PERHAPS. "BROOKLYN", I SAID. "COMING TO THE GAME TOMORROW?", HE
ASKED. "WHAT GAME?",WAS ALL I COULD THINK OF. THAT ENDED THE ENCOUNTER

See glossary of travel encounters in chapter "Lists and Miscalleny'.

Hoping for ever closer contact with celebrities, I applied
for a position with a large banking and travel company without
mentioning stuntman on my resume. Wearing a uniform and a smart
hat inscribed in gold braid "Uniformed Representative", I would
be meeting and greeting celebrities daily, who arrived at docks,
terminalsand airports. Soon, I graduated to a category called
"Special Services", a blanket title that involved confidential
assignments. Since the work was secret, I had to give up my flashy
prized uniform as well as my contact with celebrities.

One of my riskiest assignments involved smuggling drugs
through customs.The child of one of the company's foreign managers was dying, requiring a special medication. There existed a
political stand-off between the manager and the local dictator,
On a mission of mercy, I was to take the drug into the country
in question, illegally. In a sense the child was held hostage
if the drugs were discovered and confiscated if sent by mail.
When my bags were inspected by the foreign Customs officials,
I produced a signed prescription in my name. The child was saved.

Entering a wild animal into the States proved to be tough,
even though the Endanged Species Act was not as yet in effect.
A senior company official had promised his son a surprize birthday present. They asked me to pick up an Amazonian wild cat in
Manaus and bring it to Miami. However, the captain of the ship
we were aboard refused to carry animals. When we docked in Belem,
I rushed off since we were in port for only four hours. This
meant finding someone with a wild cat for sale, The first stop
was at the local zoo where I bought the animal, had it innoculated,
filled out the documents required, arranged a "despachante" to
handle the bureaucratic formalities, the crating and shipping to
a veterinarian in Miami..all this in a Latin country where things
of this sort normally took weeks, bribes and luck, plus phone calls.

<u>FORSAKING ALL OTHERS</u>

DEAR BLISS: WHY DID YOUR DAD FAVOR ME OVER SUCH BRAINY GIANTS
AS WILLIAM GADDIS, KLONSKY, DELMORE AND ALL THE OTHERS? HOW COULD I
EXPLAIN THIS DEMONSTRATION OF LOYALTY THAT ENDURED TO THE END?
IT REMINDED ME OF THE TIME MY SWEETHEART BROKE A DATE WITH FRANK
SINATRA TO BE WITH ME.

YOUR DAD HAD A FRISKY CHALLENGING, ALBEIT GOOD-NATURED STYLE.
"WHAT HAVE YOU BEEN READING?", HE WOULD SUDDENLY ASK. WITH WHAT
WAS UNCANNY LUCK, EVEN THOUGH I HADN'T READ A BOOK IN AGES UN-
TIL THE DAY BEFORE, I ANSWERED TRUTHFULLY, "CERVANTES". I EVEN
QUOTED "EN UN LUGAR DE LA MANCHA..". THERE WERE MANY SUCH CLOSE
CALLS. NO USE TRYING TO HIDE BEING CONFOUNDED BY POETRY'S BEAUTY
IN THE PRESENCE OF POETS OR A SLOPPY GRAMMER. SILENCE ONLY LEAVES
ONE EMBARASSED LIKE AN UNPREPARED STUDENT CAUGHT BY SURPRIZE.

LEAVING BROOKLYN COLLEGE BEHIND, WE MOVED INTO THE "SAN REMO",
WHERE AN ALTERNATE INTELLECTUAL ENVIRONMENT WAS SET UP..THE
BEGINNING OF NEW LIFE STYLES, ITBECAME "ELAINES'" OF THE 1940'S
FOR LITERARY CELEBRITIES. UPTOWN, IT WAS THE PERIOD OF "CAFE
SOCIETY" WITH BRENDA FRAZIER, TOMMY MANVILLE AND PATRICIA WARD.
AT A BOOTH TABLE THAT GREW IN IMPORTANCE, CHAIRS WERE PULLED UP
TO IT BLOCKING THE AISLES. THERE WOULD SIT YOUR DAD, PLAYING VERBAL
CHESS AGAINST FOUR WRITERS AT A TIME. OCCASIONALLY, A BASEBALL
BAT WOULD APPEAR FROM BEHIND THE BAR AND BANGED ON THE BAR-TOP
MORE FOR EFFECT THAN TO RESTORE ORDER. ON THE WAY TO EARLY DINNER,
YOUR DAD REHEARSED HIS LINES WITH ME, PERFECTING QUOTATIONS HE
WOULD LATER EMPLOY WITH EASE, NEEDING NO PROMPTING FROM ME. HE
WAS A LITERARY CARD SHARK WITH THE MEMORY NECESSARY FOR THE TASK.
SANTOS, THE WAITER/BOUNCER,KEPT THE MACDOUGAL STREET ENTRANCE
TABLE FOR US. IMAGINE BEING SQUEEZED BETWEEN GADDIS AND MILTON
AND SHERI MARTINELLI. LIKE SITTING BETWEEN MOZART AND OFFENBACH.
YOUR DAD WORKED ON ESTABLISHING HIS REPUTATION. HE BECAME COM-
PETITIVE,"TRES SPORTIF". HE WAS A GOOD RUNNER WHO BROKE THROUGH
THE RACIAL "WALL". WITH HIS MENTAL WARM-UPS AND CEREBRAL WORK-OUTS,
HE MADE HIMSELF A CHAMPION.

TODAY, WRITING TO YOU, BLISS, I PUT TOGETHER PIECE-MEAL A CASSAROLE
OF LEFT-OVERS, LIKE A WIDOW LOOKING BACK ON HER LONG MARRIAGE.
WITHOUT GLORIFYING THE PAST AND DISREGARDING THE NATURAL TENDENCY
TO MELLOW WITH AGE, I TRY TO ANSWER, "WHAT DID HE SEE IN ME?".
COULD IT HAVE BEEN AN ASTROLOGICAL ALIGNMENT BLESSING TWO INDI-
VIDUALS,BONDED IN A LIFE-LONG FIDELITY? HOW ELSE TO EXPLAIN THE
HUNDREDS OF READY ANSWERS TO EPISODES LIKE THE "DON QUIXOTE" ONE
MENTIONED ABOVE. WAS THIS FRIENDSHIP SUCH, THAT LIKE TWINS, WE
COULD READ EACH OTHERS MIND? WHEN I BROKE A DATE WITH MY GIRLFRIEND
TO BE WITH HIM.,THAT WAS THE MOMENT WHEN WE BOTH KNEW THAT WHAT WE
SHARED WAS TO BE TREASURED. FOREVER.

CROSSROADS OF THE WORLD
(AN OPEN LETTER TO BLISS)

    FORGIVE ME BLISS, IF WRITING TO YOU ABOUT YOUR DAD IS A PRETEXT
FOR WRITING ABOUT MYSELF. IN GREENWICH VILLAGE, YOU DAD FOUND A
WORLD HE COULD CALL "HOME". IT GAVE HIM AN INTELLECTUAL ENVIRONMENT
ROOTED IN LITERATURE AMONG FRIENDS HE FELT COMFORTABLE WITH. IT GAVE
HIM HIS BELOVED BOOKSHOP ON CORNELIA STREET AND EVENTUALLY A RESPECT-
ABLE POSITION AT THE NEW SCHOOL,SURROUNDED BY FASCINATED STUDENTS.
I, ON THE OTHER HAND, MY VILLAGE HAD BEEN MY CHILDHOOD PLAYGROUND;
WASHINGTON SQUARE PARK WITH MY BYCYCLE, P.S.201, ST. ANTHONY'S AND
A GIGANTIC SAND BOX TO ROMP IN WHEN THEY WERE BUILDING THE 6TH AVE.
SUBWAY. FURTHEMORE, MY PARENTS TAUGHT ME TO AVOID BOHEMIANS.

    IN 1946-47, CONVERSATIONS AT THE SAN REMO, THAT GATHERING PLACE
OF EXISTENTIALIST THINKERS, WERE BECOMING MORE AND MORE RARIFIED.
TALKING OF HENRI MICHAUX OR MRS. BLOOM WENT EVEN FARTHER AND I FOUND
MYSELF FALLING BEHIND, AS THOUGH UNPREPARED FOR AN EXAM. I SQUIRMED
TO ESCAPE A GROWING EMBARASSMENT, AS I TOOK A BACK SEAT AT TABLES.
AS A WAY OF PRESERVING A CERTAIN DISTINCTIVENESS I HAD ACQUIRED IN
THE SHADOW OF YOUR DAD, I SOUGHT TO EXCUSE MYSELF WITH MY REPUTATION
STILL INTACT, TO EXIT WITH DIGNITY.

    SAN FRANCISCO WAS STILL VERY FAR AWAY AND THETHOUGHT OF LEAVING
THE WOMB OF THE VILLAGE WAS QUITE FRIGHTENING. VILLAGERS GRAVITATED
TOWARD THE "NAVEL OF THE UNIVERSE", THE CIRCLE IN THE SQUARE IN THE
PARK. THEY IGNORED THE HUDSON RIVER, WHICH WAS TO BECOME MY ESCAPE
ROUTE. TO UPHOLD MY STANDARD IN THIS BRAINY COMMUNITY AND EVEN ADD
TO MY PRESTIGE, I CONCOCTED A MYSTERIOUS DISAPPEARANCE. WHEN THEY
ASKED ABOUT MY WHEREABOUTS, ONE WOULD ANSWER, "HE'S ON A SHIP SOME-
WHERE". I ASSUMED THE AURA OF A LOST EXPLORER. I NOW RANKED WITH
MILTON KLONSKY WHO HAD GONE TO TEACH AT THE UNIVERSITY OF IOWA, OF
ALL PLACES! SOON MASON HOFFENBERG RAN OFF TO PARIS, FOLLOWED BY
BEAUFORD DELANEY AND AL LETTIERE. PEGGY GUGGENHEIM LEFT ABBINGDON
SQUARE FOR VENICE.

    NOW, AS I BEGAN TO SPECULATE SERIOUSLY ABOUT A LEAVE OF ABSENCE
FROM THE VILLAGE, EVERYTHING MATERIALIZED INTO A MIRACULOUS ESCAPE.
I SHIPPED OUT ON A VOYAGE TO THE FIRST OF 80 OR MORE COUNTRIES. WITH
A FEW "SAD" GOOD-BYES, MOSTLY TO BARTENDERS WHO WOULD RE-COUNT MY
DEPARTURE, I FOLLOWED THE TRADITION OF MEN WHO WENT TO SEA BY
ABANDONING MY LOVE. FOR CONSOLATION, I MUSED, "CLOSER APART, THAN
MANY WHO ARE TOGETHER". I WAS NOT TO FOLLOW THE FOOTSTEPS OF "ON
THE ROAD", BUT RATHER ADVENTURES MADE IN HEAVEN. INTRIGUING ESCA-
PADES ADD SPICE TO ONE'S TRAVELS, JUST AS AN ESSENTIAL MISCHEVIOUS-
NESS ADDS DISCOVERY TO SEX.

2

When Anatole became identifiable as what I call Village nobility, he became just a bit more sophisticated by dressing nattily or with smart sweaters and khakis that predated sport clothes. He wore his popularity well, underpinned by l'air sportif. He was not calculating, but spontaneous, with comments that were very much alive. More than something he'd mention was the nerve, the response he provoked in you as a verbal fencing master. He was one of the first to visit a psychoanalyst at that time. His "one drop" predicament encased him on four sides, he said, until he "climbed out of the box from the roof." He used Baudelaire's tragic example to caution us against Dr. Leary's "drop out," "if it feels good, do it" slogans. He was removed by his proper marriage from the poetry of the uncommon Village streets to a comfortable country family setting, where he felt boxed in once again.

This time it was by his own doing and not by a circumstance of Nature's coloration. He was apologetic, ashamed of his cubicle office on Madison Avenue and even Castro-phobic working in the Battery Park Whitehall Building, with its view of the Statue of Liberty, and among the tightly-knit desks at the New York *Times*. In his longing to be free, he established a new "freedom of expression" desire among Villagers. He was motivating attention to the Village at a time when it was still a "nice, quiet neighborhood," an orderly, though tough-working class in a majority Italian-American community. He brought Afro-Cuban and mambo music down from the Park Plaza Dance Hall in El Barrio, and was seen playing bongo while they were still unknown or called tom-toms. He jived in Spanish, using *hombre* before "hey, man." In his neat appearance he detained the appearance of ugliness in clothing that was to follow. Anatole, while helping out needy friends, including addicts, he cautioned against drugs by saying, "I want a clear head." much attraction to and from the opposite sex, no woman gave him what I may have, namely, the freedom to feel himself as well as freedom from his literary world.

We melded in silent interaction. It was fellowship without the trappings of bonding or the horsing around of brotherly love. Astrologers call it the placement of our "nodes." He made free love more acceptable,

Although we lived apart from each other for ninety percent of our lives, we were forever bound by a secret we shared. We alone, by chance, witnessed the moment and place when the Village changed goals, ideals and vision. The world as well, we can say, lost its self-respect, due to the wrong friends (the Beats), but worst of all, the wrong reading material.

ANATOLE'S UMBRELLA
(ANIMATISM)

To wait out a rain shower, I entered a thrift shop where, for three dollars I bought myself another umbrella. I had seen one like it in an old English movie. With it gnarled handle and sturdy frame, when tested, it popped open like a cork from a bottle of fine champagne, proud of its aristocratic essence.

When I left, the sun was shining making me an oddity, carrying two umbrellas on a sunny day.

With weather still uncertain, Anatole came to meet me for dinner. Waiting on the stoop, I was surprised to hear him say, as he approached me, "Ah, Brooks Brothers."

For reasons of embarrassment as well as snobbishness, I refrained from mentioning the source or the price of my umbrella but I felt that I was hiding a secret from a friend; it was like harboring an unspoken lie, concealing the truth.

As we headed to the San Remo, the rain began. The umbrella opened like a soldier snapping to attention. As we pressed on, huddled against the angry gods of a storm·tossed sky, he was allowing me the greater protection. I responded equally, in a reverse tug-of-war, With the mutual concern found in honest friendship, I revealed the origin of the umbrella. It became a symbol between us so that when, due to a fire it was destroyed, I felt it had been baptized in water, consecrated in fire, and lost like a deceased member of the family. CONTRARY TO THE OBSTANCY OF INANIMATE OBJECTS IS THE COOPERATION OF INANIMATE OBJECTS IN JOINING US. Today, in the rain, I feel every drop that falls on me is a visit from Anatole. How many umbrellas are seen laying like dead birds with their skeletal framework exposed in the gutters of New York? We all forget umbrellas, but none with such long term memory of loss as Anatole's umbrella.

1

<u>The Birth of the Bookstore: A Story of Life and Death</u>

"If we can get her off Courvoisier and onto rum, we may be able to save her. If not, I give her six months," her doctor told me. This is the story of the strange demise of the bookstore's angel, Janet. It is a tale as dramatic as any on the bookshelves. Without this benefactress there would not have been the Cornelia Street Bookstore in 1945. "With luck," the doctor continued, "we can perhaps interest her in something to occupy her and take her mind off drink."

Who was I to disagree, even knowing it would never happen. The last stages of the situation were evident: the time it took Janet to answer the door, the shakes and rages, the blackouts and loss of memory, the spurts of clarity, the cross-eyes, the march toward death. That's what finally happened, but not from drink, a fall, or some accidental development. It was to be a gentle departure with dignity, painless, one that one would wish for oneself. A death process well ahead of its time, an unavoidable event, *deus ex machina*.

"We can open a flower shop," I suggested to Janet as we discussed her salvation, since she was frightened about her survival. "Or a bookstore," I added as a sudden thought that occurred to me. Anatole Broyard had often spoken of opening one. Janet had taken a small studio apartment at 32 Cornelia Street, and a store was available to rent at 18 Cornelia. Perhaps she could help out at the store as part of her recovery or occupational therapy.

A lawyer's meeting was set up, a large sum — a thousand dollars — was arranged as a loan to Anatole. The bookstore was born, only to be short-lived. Anatole had hoped it to be a well of knowledge for the young Village writers, offering rare names such as Henri Michaux, Frans Kafka, Celine, Cummings, Gide — authors favored by Anatole but comparatively unknown by the young unsophisticated customers. Worse, still, for stock customers these authors were difficult to find anywhere around town in 1945. Often there would be a request, a possible sale, but no book to sell. Orders were taken but not filled. It was like running a business backwards, with demand, but no supply. We can today look back at what was the classic pioneer's frustration, facing what is ahead of their time.

I had met Janet at the Club Bali in Miami in 1941. The beach season had ended and dance teams and entertainers either returned north or found work in the city. After each show, as per the club's policy, we were obliged to mingle. At ringside, a pleasant-looking young woman wearing a starched white outfit smiled up at me. I asked politely for a dance and was refused politely, with the suggestion that I might dance with her friend seated with her. Too late to decline, I discovered that Janet's nurse had lured me into an offer I couldn't now refuse. Janet couldn't stand very well off-balance, much less rumba. I accepted a drink, as the club encouraged us to do, and eventually, the crafty young nurse had us manipulated to where I ended up in Janet's bed somehow or other.

Janet was generous, wealthy, and grateful, as I began to become a male nurse for her, as well as her "dance teacher." Making frequent bar scenes with her in Miami and New York was injuring a weak kidney that I was unaware of. Over time I developed hydronephrosis, pylonephritis, and hypertension. One kidney began to atrophy after I received by accident a Mickey Finn destined for her at the 5 o'clock Club, where Janet had heckled the singer loudly. After one spinal tap and three cystoscopies (scheduled for a fourth) at St. Clare's midtown hospital and at Dr. Oswald Lowsley's Park Avenue office and overnight at the Leroy Pavilion on the Upper East Side, I left Janet since she was returning to Peoria for a visit home.

Working as a trainee now for the Sterling Drug Company, a subsidiary of I.G. Farben (Bayer), I was to be a future "detail-man." I was in daily contact with calmatives, spasmotics, aphrodisiacs, and remedies with names like thalidomide.

When I received a sudden call from Janet, I was surprised to hear that she had checked herself into a Central Park West sanitarium. When I visited her, I could not refuse her the favor she asked of me. "Next time, can you bring some Lucky Strikes and something to help me sleep?" she asked.

In 1945 we didn't know much about uppers and downers washed down with Courvoisier. When I honored her request, as I was leaving she handed me a gift, her wedding ring. On my next visit, I was told that Janet had checked out. It was just about six months. We had closed the bookshop. It was as if Janet had taken it with her *in extremo libro* (at the end of the book).

He had dropped out saying "it doesn't coincide with my frame of mind." For me, it was "Life, not school is the teacher" (Non scuolie sed vitae discimus). Had I never known him would I have left the Village to enjoy Latin inscriptions in Rome or the WILD writings of James Joyce? How can we classify him? Less agitating than Vidal, more wholesome than Kerouac, less egomaniacal than Mailer, soberer than Capote, less elusive than Gaddis, more ribald than Campbell, more secure than Styron and handsomer than Adonis. The enormous collection of books that he bequeathed to the Connecticut Library system was overwhelming. I recall him fondly wrapping a book do be mailed to a customer in the Cornelia Street bookshop. It was obviously troubling him to part with it, as though he were burying the family pet.

Walking in the Park with Gala, his 4 year old daughter, he would stop and ask her if she was happy. She would say, "Yes". He would then have her say"happiness".and as we walked along she would say "ha-pee-ness" to people we passed. Anatole was enrolling her in higher education as he did all of us. His Socratic attraction established a spirit, a sense of importance for book-lovers. He legitimized them. There was as much diversion in a library as in a disco.

Attention NY Landmark Commission: A plaque , nay, a statue in Washington Square Park is properly needed. Let it read: ANATOLE BROYARD July 16, 1920 – October 11, 1990. Villager, Litterateur, Culturist to a Generation.

7   At the end, Anatole had asked Sandy to have me stand beside her at his internment, along with his son Todd and daughter Bliss in Martha's Vineyard, so that she might, as a widow, chose me as a replacement when he was gone. She would never have considered me, since I was the original influence that involved him in "U Vilaj" in the first place. That night in 1938, when I introduced him to the San Remo on Bleecker and Mac Dougal, had it been instead, let's say, the Village club Vanguard, where he would have more likely joined the jazz Black crowd, having originally come from New Orleans but where he would have not, "fit in" as well as he did with the crowd of his own making, namely, the crowd that made writers like Kafka and Henry Michaux the rage, until Ginsburg, Kerouac, and Burroughs won over the minds they brainwashed with drugs and a counter-productive culture.

8   Anatole would have perhaps preferred to have lived a life more like mine with abundant voyages around the world that left little opportunity for academia. Whereas, I definitely would have preferred a life more like his, surrounded by good reading, and writing, and intellectuals in a world of ideas. What we both were happy to have had in common were the many women who happily shared our lives with us, even though briefly.

9A   My career, as well as Anatole's, owed much to women. One set me sailing around the world for most of my life, the other had me prepare to function in the competitive environment of show business, having given me Afro-Cuban dance moves that few men had ever been exposed to.

These two women seemed to have done you good, why not mention their names?

Anatole never, in all his hundreds of liaisons from Susan Santary to Sheri Martinelli, would have liked very much to boast. He was never boastful regarding his affairs, to me at any rate. I could boast, but I never did to him of my international roster of lovers (not the correct word, since they were mostly of a one night or, of a one hour quickie, duration) from Anais Nin, a Catalonian, to assorted mobility. To know a foreign country and its female components is to have the cake with a cherry, and to have it and eat it. To leave Thailand, for example, without feeling her in your arms, is missing the flavor the place, the desert that make the meal sweeter. In addition, to know the women of Cuba or Brazil can satisfy to only a certain degree, since it leaves more to be desired, like ice cream.

11   Anatole and I were similar as quasi-misfits all our lives, while still being envied by many. At the height in our careers, we could not have been more blessed with enjoyment. Life has its own purposes, since we erroneously accepted good fortune as normal, once accustomed to it. Popularity was a spotlight that blinded us from actuality. After his saying no to drugs, "I want a clear mind," he would ask, as a buddy, (his family called him Bud) and as a well-meaning friend, if I would care to enjoy the effects of something unknown as such, that today would be called Viagra, but much more harmful, something liken to offering me a stimulating glass of champagne to enliven my next liaison. Had he, or had we all known that Speed could be addictive, many of us would have said no thank you. I happened by chance to decline more out of the moment's inconvenient timing than out of the fear of this unknown pill. Ironically, he didn't need any additional stimulant in his sixties, nor did I.

That pill was what caused stress on his body, innocently overused caused the damage it did. It also interrupted his memories of the Village that were to continue benefiting those of readers interested in Greenwich Village as a nucleus of the 20th century's creative process. So, we lost both Anatole and the wisdom he would have granted us.

In my case, what I had to grant any readers was to be an insight into, not the world of travel, which they can discover for themselves, but admittance into the world of Afro Cuban music and Santeria. To run out of time, to tie a ribbon on one's life is the saddest part when family, friends, or projects of all sorts are involved. No one seems to be spared such conclusions. Time leaves us behind inexorably, hopefully with a graceful exit, while foregoing dignity. Vanity must remain outside the door in the hall. To enjoy privacy after a life on the stage is like saying, no flowers, please.

In addition to having brought Anatole into the turf of the Italian San Remo Social Club and restaurant, I also opened his eyes and ears to Afro-Cuban music. Through both of these means, plus supplying him with the financial essentials that produced the bookstore on Cornelia Street in 1946, Anatole was able to climb out of the box of a Bed-Sty background with success, guaranteeing his overall brilliance, charisma, and ambition, all qualities I lacked. My spotty flashes of creativity were based on duplicity, uncovering the counterfeit quality of life. As for charisma, my linguistic prowess in five languages made a noticeable impression on others, but with the combination of my low self-esteem, ADD, dyslexia, hearing impairment, and no one yet such as Anatole to emulate, I retreated, while all my peers progressed. As a left behind, slow to learn specimen, my teachers called "un-educate-able," I was condemned, seemingly to be a sad failure, that is until Anatole took me into his life.

We both withdrew from Brooklyn College (although I returned to finally secure a B.A.) We both moved to different locations at the same time, and both, unprepared for family obligations, married in haste for the same reason, a love child's arrival.

To explain our mutuality, we turned to the fact that we had been born the same year and two months apart, "under the influence of the moon" as astrology indicated in our overall charts. We lived for seventy-five to eighty per cent of our lives apart, he at home, and I abroad and aboard ships, which leads me to claim that many apart are closer than many together. Life, like water finding its level, does change with time, whereas, our lives were linear to the end. In order to succeed one must change friends, but in our case this maxim did not apply, even when life's major events like marriage, or distance, intervened. Ours was an unceremonious allegiance that could be said to have been made in heaven. At least that is what seems to have been the case.

anyone who has been fortunate enough to have been locked in the jaws of an exclusive neighborhood, knowing the local Sicilians as "U Vilaj" even today , 2015, it is only San Francisco that claims to be the crown of America's primary location. If San Francisco has Hollywood, the Village has Cambridge, both centers of creative avant-gardism.

SAN REMO NIGHTS

One evening in 1939 I invited Anatole Broyard to dinner at the San Remo and by 1940
we had dropped out of Brooklyn College and moved in together in the Village. By 1945
the booth by the MacDougal street "Ladies Entrance" had become reserved more or less
for him. The Bleeker street entrance served the local bar customers and the card players
while the MacDougal entrance led to a modest dining room that had an air of refinement.
A brightly polished brass rail curved around the edge of a long wooden-topped bar,
sawdust was spread across a black and white tiled floor and tablecloths were the typical
red and white checkered designs that were intended to lend a homey atmosphere. Prior to
going to the Remo, we would meet at Pete's Bookstore on W.4th street, where we could
browse while awaiting each other. While walking over to the Remo we wouldreview
what we had browsed thus preparing ourselves to meet the hungry literary lions waiting
there for us. Milton Klonsky, Dick Gilman, Chandler Brossard, Mason Hoffenberg were
seated, talking books and authors. Every one had been talking about Hemingway and for
the last few days it had been Nathaniel West. Anatole had wisely armed himself with
quotations from Hemingway that he had memorized while on route to the Remo
If Klonsky switched to Blake, Anatole was ready with Blake's influence on Picasso's
minotaur. To counter Klonsky's Blake, Anatole would inject Henri Michaux, a
watercolorist and poet like Blake knowing Klonsky's weakness when it came to Michaux.
Comments such as these were thrown on the table like poker chips. For revenge, Klonsky
gave signed copies of his published work "Blake's Dante" to everyone except Anatole.As
Santos cleared off the dishes, Anatole would pause in the middle of analyzing the three
versions of "Lady Chatterly's Lover" for clever suspense. And so it went, night after
night.

Never having had a full time job, Milton devoted hislife to the classics. He
represented the camp of the Old School i.e., Dickens (his favorite author), Chaucer,
Dante, O'Henry, etc., and as a liberal, Steinbeck, Dos Passos,George Sand, etc. But
Anatole was excited by the modern writers and poets. He looked toward Europe for fresh
air., Kafka, Sartre, Michaux, Rimbaud, Verlaine. He championed Henry Miller, the Deep
Southerner, Faulkner and more conservative writers. In order to overcome Anatole's
Michaux advantage, Klonsky tried a leap-frog tactic coming up with Tolkein. For a while
they were pushing these two authors until discovering that their Village followers were
not quite ready to tackle either Michaux or Tolkein. It seemed that Klonsky and Anatole
were with their desperate head butting, trying to advance their own personal
importance—using literature as a tool, getting us caught up in their quarrels. While it may
be that Tolkein went on to take the day, perhaps Michaux will one day emerge victorious.

In order to arouse the sleeping interest in good books in general which was prevalent at
the time, Anatole concentrated on Eros. Henry Miller or the Marquis de Sade's 'Venus in
Furs" were very much in fashion. Employing Ovid's poetry as an erotic device seduced
numerous bed-mates, while adding to his charm. At the MOMA, where he was an early
member, he would steer Smith College coeds to "Les Demoiselles D'Avignon",
Picasso's favorite prostitutes, leading them by the elbow on a path to the bedroom. He
used Gorky in place of Georgi (vodka). Mentioning Gabriele D'Annunzio, the great
poet/hedonist he found favor with the local Italian card players in the Remo. He set up
shop, as it were at his booth, turning it into a miniature "Salon" in addition to his
bookshop Cornelia Street . It no longer was necessary to gather on the hard benches in
the Park or the windy corner by Pete's. While few of us had the money to buy books, it
seems as though everyone was suddenly seen carrying them, trafficking in books. We had
become a crazy literary hootenanny. Our only competitors were Hot Jazz and Country
singers. It was The Village Vanguard or The Village Barn vs. the Remo. To improve
musical appreciation, we tried to introduce Hindemith, Mahler and the great Latin
pianist,Noro Morales. Hungry writers, hungry for quality, crowded at his feet. He
dispensed a free education of pre-digested knowledge and tutored us with his NY
Times Book Reviews. His fragil bookshop was an overnight failure with its empty
bookshelves but its mere concept inspired us to write. He was obliged to buy books from
Pete in order to fill orders he received for out-of-print or rare books . At times he was
seen canvassing the shops over in the East Village on 4th Avenue. In this way, he became
known in the downtown literary community. It was he who " put out the word". Should
someone overhear him mentioning Camus or Celine, there would be a rush to the library.
If he spoke of Brancusi, they'd visit theMOMA. Fire Island, the Park Plaza in Harlem
were popularized by him. From the halls of academia to the dance halls of Harlem, his
irresistibility was gossip with girls everywhere. Among his confreres in the writing
community however, his uniqueness was over-looked. Years later, Alfred Kazin
wondered how it had taken him so long to meet Anatole. There may have been two
reasons for the protracted indifference among members of the literary fraternity. One, his
multifold liaisons were such that personal secrecy and respectful discretion favored a low
key exposure. Secondly, writers are a jealous bunch like actors. There were forces intent
on minimizing his growing influence over a generation of young writers. Politically, he
chose Kafka's Das Schloss over Das Kapital. Sequestered in the Village of the forties we
may have been offending conventions but let us imagine after a span of sixty yers, the
Village could have progressed to become a present day counter-part of say, the court of
Francis the First. "The King" is not Nashvillian nor the Master a writer of mystery
stories. Imagine a world free of industrialized rock and roll..free of a clownish culture!
When he emerged from the virgin forest of enchanting evenings at the Remo, he was
promptly labeled a hipster and later denigrated, maliciously ignored, denounced unjustly,
belittled, besmirched and willfully neglected by his peers.

Sheri didn't cook and took her lunch at Joe's Luncheonette
(where Junior, Joe's handsome son kept after Sheri like a
wolfhound and she was flattered in front of your Dad). ...
Dinner was at "remo" every night. Some nights on occasion
I would step across Bleeker to bring back some cannoli for
desert cheaper than ordering them in the "Remo", like
bringing your own wine,it was frowned upon by the Santini
brothers but I got away with it). There were lots of
arguments about Sartre's philosophy, about Neitsche and
our voices rose as though drunk on literature..we were high
on literature, as your Dad said many times.
The day I first met Sheri on Cornelia Street,I was drunk.
Never given to drinking, the affect was so much more enhanced. It seems the Italian owner of the building invited
your Dad and I to the basement under the bookstore to sample
some Grappa, pure alcohol remaining from his wine press.
As we were climbing back . to street level, I saw this young
girl (we were all mid-20's) coming down the middle of the
street. There are . hardly ever any cars on Cornelia Street .
The sidewalks being so narrow,they were not fit for dancing
gaily along as she was doing out in the street. When she
saw your Dad, she did apirouette as she reached us and bowed.
She was nicely dressed in a flaired dirdle skirt (but not
New Yorkish- a bit peasantly, I thought. Later, I realized that
she favored hoop skirts to hide her pear-shaped.. bottom, that
was contrary to your Dad's rigid preference for shapely ballet
dancer types. I thought she was a ballet dancer at first since
that was what usually found favor with your Dad (One of the
more famous dancers, D.L. was on the Cover of LIFE, photo by
Marcus Blechman). Sheri was glowing with no make-up- just having
fallen in love with your Dad. I would say, that it was the most
ideal manner to meet a person, when one is happily high on grappa
and the person you meet is happily in a new found love on a   -
warm afternoon on Cornelia Street, a block unlike any other,
in a Village unlike any other,and,I add,at a time unlike any other.

Sheri found her lost daughter in your Dad and she was not
about to let him stray or be taken from her. She avoided
Anais, knowing that Anais was a man-eater. When in a playful
mood, Sheri was as unpredictable as a firecracker that could go
off in your hand. One evening, in Pete Martin's bookstore,
I waited outside while Sheri and your Dad squeezed between
the bookshelves reading titles. The shelving was such that
you had to turn sideways to look down at the bottom books.
The shop was smaller than a candy store. Mom & Pop, Pete and
his wife were small people in this closet full of books with
some outside on a wooden bench. Business was always very bad.
Pete had a perpetual worried look and his wife was impolite
to customers and to your Dad in particular since she considered
him a discount bookdealer and a bad moral influence on Pete.
This particular evening, in walked W.H.Auden of all people.
Your Dad I'm sure wanted a word with him if possible but
Sheri, in one of her diabolical moods, somehow or other caused
Auden to trip and fall at the narrow doorway as he was trying to
back out of the store, seeing it was so jammed and trying to
avoid rubbing against Sheri. It was a contrived collision.
Remember it was considered fun to tease homosexuals in order to
enjoy their emotional reactions. Remember also, how your Dad
and I picked heavy Dante Pavone up bodily and threw him out
into the street hurting only his gay pride. To further compound
the spectacle, Sheri managed to land on top of Auden in a kind o
sexual embrace. Your Dad was, as was everyone present, horrified
At the 'Remo", with its oversized large booths that have since
disappeared from restaurants, we sat six, plus two on the aisle.
When dishes were cleared and coffee served the number at the boo
would increase as friends joined . While there were no books
around the walls, there was present the spirits of the authors
that were being discussed. The place smelled of beer, tomato
sauce, wine, Di Napoli cigars and sawdust. The cardplayers
would suddenly yell out "Scopa", as one would scoop up his winni
This was the closest one could come to Europe's popular culture
in a pub-like enviroment. It was like a masculine club with won
allowed and welcomed although few were ever present. One was
a gal named Stella Brooks who later went out with Jack Kerouac
and another big gal named Georgia who went out with everyone.

*SAMPAS
ANOTHER WAS HELEN PARKER, A YOUNG MOTHER, BUT SHERI WAS SHE

Both Sheri and Anais dressed distinctively. Anais,with flowing
soft, solid colors with a touch of conservatism to match her
status as a"serious"writer coming up in the world. She dressed
the part, the way Milton Klonsky didwith his tweed jacket and
wool solid brown tie that he habitually wore. All he lacked was
the pipe. Sheri made most of her own clothes out of hardship
or creative impulse,to cover her precarious financial position.
The result was unflattering in that she was obliged to be seen
in the street with her painters frock or in a long dark brown
nun-like robe which in the Village could be acceptable, even
imitated. She kept an open ironing board in her crowded kitchen
that she used as a catch all table (including uncashed checks
that she received while working briefly as a "Vogue" model for
flowing lingerei (full page!)). I feared they would be lost
or at least misplaced among all the papers, like unopened mail,
that didn't seem to bother her. Then again, she may have wanted
those checks to be seen for some reason that gave her pleasure.
When she was working on your Dad's portrait, she went on to explain her work to me but I was not able to follow her interpretation of various touches. Henri Michaux's work (portraits or
his commentaries of the human condition) were easier to grasp
visually than her barely recognizable features. In her painting of
your Dad, Sheri was showing her deep struggle to capture his
soul, trying to make him hers on a piece of canvass that showed
him agonizing for her in the confusion of colors. He told me it
was not 'him'. When Stanley Philipps showed me a picture he had
purchased from her, a self-portrait she had done on a small canvass,
it showed a young girl with a blank expression in happy colors
that did not go together very well. It seemed that she tried to
regress to a happier time in her life but could not conceal the
truth. Anais was gluttonous sexually and Sheri was starving for
one man- your Dad and affixed to him. FOR LIFE.

Yolandi: I love your closing lines —
"Wait 'til the phone rings, before
you pick it up" — classic!! SHOW BIZ!

FALLING IN STEP

by

Vincent Livelli

All Harlem went wild that night. Joe Louis had k.o'd Schmeling in 2 minutes and 4 seconds of the 1st round.[1]

Considering I was a totally rabid fight fan how was it that I was in Harlem, but not interested in the biggest fight of century? During the Great Depression, few Harlem families had radios, but could watch the fights that were broadcast at Fire Stations. That night practically everyone crowded around a radio, but I hadn't.

It was June, 1938. I was dancing at the Park Plaza on 110 Street. Heading home that night, about to enter the subway on Lenox, I found myself running in step down Lenox Avenue in a crowd of hysterically, cheering, victorious black families. I was the only white face.

In 1940 I arrived in Havana unaware it was Carnival. Exhausted from a turbulent flight, I checked into a hotel and fell asleep, fully clothed. Hours later I was awakened by the sounds of pounding conga drums and marching feet below my window. I ran down to the street and fell in step with the Negritos, parading along the Prado. Once again I was the only white face in a crowd of hysterically happy people. Cubans customarily distance from this spectacle with slavery connotations. They stood watching from balconies, and probably wondered who the white guy was.

Unless there is a *love* waiting sailors calling the same ports, sailors repeatedly become bored and seek relief and excitement in the many unsafe waterfront bars around the world. For me, taking in a movie was a more wholesome choice. So it was that I left the sun scorched streets of Bridgetown, Barbados and entered a cool and dark local theater showing a picture with an unfamiliar title. I had stumbled into pitch blackness, and watched a particularly blood-soaked move titled <u>Zulu</u>. I sat up front, due to my hearing deficit. When the lights came up, I was the only white face in the audience.

In Honolulu, an Italian film showed Japanese dialogue vertically along the left margin and English subtitles. And in 1958, in a dark, dismal, and dull Moscow with workers who retired early I chose to see a Charlie Chaplin movie. Again, in both places, I was an oddity.

Vincent Livelli is a world traveler, cruise director, tour director, social director, and performer. He has been featured in documentaries, novels, and journal publications.

Missed Encounters

by

Vincent Livelli

When it happed was probably the moment I began to back calculate the difference between my life's history as against the biographies and memoirs of others. What did I have in common with almost 100 celebrities that I had met during my lifetime? What I came up with was basically zero. Of course, meeting Ed Sullivan had little to do with comparing our lives, except for he wearing red pants and a red jacket and I wearing light red pair of pants and red jacket in an elevator at the Hotel Carlton, or that the Duke of Windsor was wearing the same Bahamian shirt that I was wearing when we met in Portofino. This is all well and good but not what my life represented compared to theirs. The Duke was not a happy man and Ed Sullivan suffered all his life with a severe backache. I never met the "Entertainer" as Charlie Chaplin was known; he fled to England to escape American justice. He left his plush life and adoring fans from Hollywood to the 4 corners of the Earth and gave up his U.S.A. citizenship to live in London's bleak and foggy climate, never to set foot on U.S. soil again.

Picasso, Sinatra, and Eva Peron could have been added to my list had I accepted the invitations to visit. Picasso cancelled for a prior engagement. Sinatra invited my girlfriend- but she cancelled Sinatra's party.

Eva cancelled due to her cancer condition.

Perhaps Lettieri could have introduced me to Liz Taylor and Richard Burton since he was living with them in their Mayfair compound.

In Havana I ignored Hemmingway who was always very drunk at the la Floridita Bar. At the upstairs bar at Maxim's in Paris, I did not approach Richard Wagner who was deep in conversation with the bartender.

I refused Peggy Guggenheim's invitation to join her to visit Jackson Pollock, who I thought of as an alcoholic mad man. In fact, I rushed away from the Duke and Duchess because I was starving not having eaten all day. I cut the encounter short, even though he seemed anxious enough to talk to me more about Nassau where I had been Social Director at the British Colonial Hotel and where he appeared to have been fond of the island and its sun shined beaches.

All this asks the question, how did they differ from me and my life's scenario? They had more money, more popularity, more talent and more assistance with press agents, script writers, wardrobe, make-up, partners, publicity agents and multiple invitations and fans. In my case I had none of these supports.

Events that don't occur naturally have an aura of mystery about them. None of my encounters has a day to day quality to them. They inhabited the realm of the night when the real world shuts down. It is then that my lack of hearing takes importance it would otherwise lack.

The day was activity and the night serenity- it was with the latter that I sensed a unique clarity and an easy, unquestioned acceptance that became status quo that was questionably abnormal but unchallenged. The inexplicable was best left alone. The best gamblers "go with the flow", since they understand where the power lies beyond their involvement. The best gamblers are cool, not effusive. It is the loser who is loud at the smallest win, only to fall silent at a loss. When I went from little over two dollars, and then on the win over one thousand in three days of winning, or better said, shooting dice, a very unlike me, ruled the day. Something outside of me had taken over the event that excluded my participation. It was a streak that defied the odds and one that had no need of me whatsoever. My presence was more the role of an obedient servant. When I became me, I had of course lost it all back, proving that lie is a gamble.

To Anatole Broyard's daughter

DEAR BLISS: WHY WAS YOUR DAD SO IMPRESSED WITH ERNEST? ERNEST WAS
DUTCH, BUT SOUNDED"AUSTRIAN"AT A TIME WHEN FREUD WAS HITTING THE
VILLAGE GOSSIP. A KNOWLEDGE OF PSYCHOANALYSIS WAS BECOMING IMPERA-
TIVE. IT WOULD ADD A NEW DIMENSION TO YOUR DADS' PERSONA AT A TIME
WHEN HE WAS BEGINNING TO REALLY FLEX HIS INTELLECT. IN 1946, YOUR
DAD WAS PROGRESSING FROM HAVING BEEN AN OUTSIDER AT BROOKLY COLLEGE
TO FINDING HIMSELF A LEADER IN THE VILLAGE. A PERIOD OF ADJUSTMENT WAS
NECESSARY FOR HIS EMERGING EGO, HIS NEW POWER. WE NOTICED A BEHAVIOR
SHIFT THAT MADE HIS FRIENDS UNCOMFORTABLE SINCE IT DIDN'T SUIT HIM.
HE CLOSETED HIMSELF WITH ERNEST, WHO WAS AN ANOMALY IN OUR MIDST.
ERNEST MONOPOLIZED YOUR DAD,LIKE A SVENGALI, LEAVING US FEELING
"DITCHED". WE AGREED THAT ERNEST WAS TO US, AN EXOTIC PRETENDER,
BUT TO YOUR DAD, HE WAS A SOURCE OF KNOWLEDGE TO BE WELCOMED.
THIS POUNCING ON KNOWLEDGE,LEONARDO'S "CURIOSITA",CHARACTERIZED
YOUR DAD. IT WAS FOR THE GOOD SINCE IT GAVE HIM A PERSPECTIVE
OF LIFE AND OF HIMSELF. ERNEST WOULD HAVE LIKED TO HAVE CHARGED
FOR HIS ADVICE, BUT ENDED UP RECOMMENDING A THREE-DAY-A-WEEK PRO-
GRAM, USING THE MONEY LEFT OVER FROM THE THOUSAND DOLLARS TO EN-
LIST THE SERVICES OF, I BELIEVE, KAREN HORNAY. UNRESOLVED VESTIGES
OF HIS CHILDHOOD WERE CLARIFIED OVER TIME AND HE SEEMED TO NOW
SETTLE INTO A MORE EVEN-KEELED POSITION AMONG US. WE COULD NOW
LOVE THE REAL ANATOLE, WITHOUT RISKING THE EMBARASSMENT OF PAN-
DERING TO HIM IN ORDER TO CONTINUE TO SPEAK FREELY.

IT WAS A TIME WHEN GENIUS WAS IN THE NEWS. EINSTEIN, KAFKA AND
OTHERS WERE CELEBRITIES. READING THEIR WORKS, YOU FELT YOURSELF
RUBBING ELBOWS WITH THE HIGHER MINDS, HOPING IT WOULD RUB OFF ON
YOU. YOUR DAD WALKED US THROUGH JOYCE, EXPLAINED THE "ORGONE BOX",
THE STRENGTH AND WEAKNESS OF PSYCHODRAMA, MONDRIAN AND HUNDREDS OF
WORKS AND WRITERS AND THINKERS. HE FED US PRE-DIGESTED SUSTENANCE.
HE TAUGHT US TO FLY. HE WAS THE ONE WHO SHOULD HAVE CHARGED A FEE!
HE DID OUR HOMEWORK FOR US, MAINTAINING A LIFELONG LOVE AFFAIR WITH
DANCERS (OF THE SPIRIT) AND PSYCHOANALYSISTS (DANCERS OF THE MIND).
HOW FLATTERED WE WERE WHEN HE ASKED US A QUESTION. (USUALY SOMETHING
LIKE, "WHAT HAVE YOU BEEN READING?" AND NOT,"HAVE YOU SEEN ANY GOOD
MOVIES LATELY?").WITH A FLAIR ADDED TO HIS TALENTS, HE WAS AT EASE
IN HIS WORLD. BEING WITH HIM WAS LIKE RECEIVING A GIFT. HIS WORDS
REVERBERATED IN YOU. THEY WOULD FOLLOW YOU DOWN THE STREET AS YOU
LEFT HIM. HE SAW LIFE AS AN INTELLECTUAL CHALLENGE. HE WAS A WINNER.

LIKE HIM, YOU POSSESS A "PRESENCE", A COMMAND QUALITY, THE EFFORTLESS
READINESS OF THE ARTISTIC PERFORMER..ONE WHO FEEDS HIS EGO WHILE
FEEDING HIS PUBLIC. ALONG WITH OTHER LESSONS THAT YOU MAY BE TAKING,
YOU SHOULD HAVE YOUR CHART PREPARED BY AN ASTROLOGER, IF YOU HAVEN'T
DONE SO.THE SOONER THE BETTER.

AT SEA, IN MY BOX-LIKE CABIN, EN ROUTE TO PENDING ADVENTURES, I WROTE.
BUT LIKE HAVING WAITED FOR THE PAINT TO DRY ON THE CANVAS OF MY LIFE,
I NOW FEEL A SURGE OF WORDS WASHING OVER ME. WHILE AT SEA, WRITING
WAS A DEVICE DESIGNED TO SEDUCE A SYMPATHETIC RESPONSE FROM A LOVE
LEFT ASHORE, WHILE BEING CONSOLED BY A GIRL IN EVERY PORT. A SAILOR
SOON FINDS A WORLD AWASH IN WOMEN. LIKE AN INCONSTANT CASANOVA, I
LED AN ILLICIT LOVE LIFE, AKIN TO ADULTERY AND THIEVERY. INDIVIDUALS,
LIKE SPECIES, DEVELOP DIFFERENTLY IN ISOLATION. I WAS FORMED BY THE SEA.
"ANATOLE" WAS FORMED BY THE LOVE HE ENGENDERED IN ALL WHO KNEW HIM..
OR OF HIM.

Vincent

Dear Earl & Yolandi

As you see, I'm still at it since Anatole's daughter has a contract to write another book about her father.

7-10-2000

When Anais Nin's book "Ladders of Fire" was published in 1946
she asked her friend, the critic Edmund Wilson, to comment.
The work was unusual and exceedingly personal like her diaries.
Parts made no sense and mimiced abstract poetry. In an English
class they would be curiousities at best and doubtful literature.
Wilson knew Anais well enough to see in them her purposefully "bizzare"
elusive flirtatious romp with the reader that exhausted one's
patience like a puzzle. Since his professional criticism was
universally admired by thousands, he was put in position where
he either endangered his friendship with Anais or betrayed
his readers. His integrety was at stake and he could very well
be facing the possibility of not recognizing the birth of a
new revolutionary style of writing which future generations
would condemn him for overlooking. In a polite, friendly letter
he mainly commented on her occasional misuse of the English
language, trying to be neutrally helpful to her, and overlooking
the fact that she may well have misued them purposefully for
effect.
As a critic, your Dad, Bliss, would have been more skillful.
He would take the work and bend it to his own ends in the
process, placing the accent on meanings within meaning that
were of his making and flattering Anais, while bringing to
the public, insights that made us forget Anais. In this way
he remained faithful to the work, playing with it. This was
your Dad's genius to where often the criticism was superior
to the work in question; one did not go on to read the work
so well examined and reviewed and digested.
Wilson had reacted like an uncertain virgin in front of Anais
who could make men uncertain of themselves if she wished,
could embarrass or win them over with coquetry and sex play.
Like Anais, Sheri was like a Spanish gypsy dancer, cleverly
ambitious but with a tragic past hidden by her gaeity.
In Sheri, your Dad met his match. It was like a retribution
for all the young souls, left-over loves, that he had withering
in his garden of delights.

* "intellectual women are neurotic" - Edmund Wilson
* "emotional algebra" - Anais Nin

Sheri and Anais were both overly ambitious in love.
Anais wrote porno poetry to support herself in order to eat.
Writing became a part of her existence that sustained her
externally and internally. She arrived in America with a
commodity that we needed after WWII, namely fresh new slants
on sex and cultures. She had "writer" written all over her
the way a dancer can be identified by his or her carriage.

Sheri was a rare,at the time, painter who exhibited successfully. She spoke poetically about her work; her ideas were
unfamiliar to us, but intriguing in their originality based
on modern art. Her vocabulary was down to earth or far out.
as the case might be, but in love both women were like
dominatrix's of men's souls.

Sheri wanted to totally have your Dad for herself.It was a
time when constancy and fidelity was falling apart among
young lovers. Now there was at last a supply of men around.
Due to a gender imbalance caused by the war, women had held on
to whatever they could get. Sheri met your Dad at the height of
his irresistability (a word that fits him so well). She had
lost her only child, her daughter, in a custody battle and
she substituted your Dad for the child. "She made love to me
for two hours", your Dad revealed to me one day. Unlike many
men, he did not boast to me, perhaps to maintain a nonchelant
attitude that was even more impressive. This exposed me to envy,
curiousity or amazement, but not to disbelief since he had no
need to exagerrate as other men did, or embelish even as a
Casanova would. This was not boy meets girl, nor was it "I
love you". It was I want you, period. They became the most
visible couple in the Village, hiding a poetic tug of war between them based on your Dad's other escapades. At a time when
Americans were becoming aware of personalities, conducts and
relationships, proper or improper ,many were embracing Picasso
and his distortions and Freud was speaking of "talk cures".

I would not claim that Sheri was inluenced by Anais..nor did
she want to fall under her influence, but both carried poetry
around in their being. An outsider would be unable to imitate
Anais, Sheri, your Dad, Klonsky, Willie or any of the "remo"
people in 1945. Even today, who do we know of that would let
us feel we were close to that time? Newcomers to that Village
had to pass an intellectual screening, had to be seen at the
right booth at the "remo" (like a chic le Cirque table)..had to
be seen carrying Kafka or Proust, had to be in the company of
your Dad especially. The atmosphere was friendly but selective
without true celbrity complications. Best of all, to have had
something published..preferably in a little magazine, or PR.

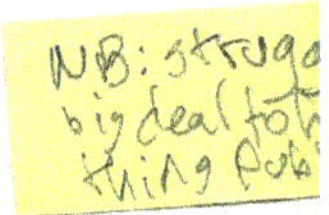

Your Dad was awash in women but he met his awakening, his
match in Sheri since he was sailing along at such a high·rate of
successful encounters. I doubt whether he even knew that women
like Sheri existed, or what hit him. She was squeezing him like
a sponge to bewitch his essence. The only happy thought here is
that I'm sure that if she ever succeeded, she would have kept
him well cared for and not cast away as might hve been the case
if the situation was reversed. Men were being spoiled by an imbalance of genders. She was able to capture and use Willie as a
pawn.   your Dad took it lightly when Sheri dropped him (something that really hit home with your Dad's ego). It probably was
your Dad's first rejection by the opposite sex. It worked for a
while but he got up and began to fight back. Sheri used your Dad's
literary knowledge as though it were originally hers to impress
Willie (who had just come to the Village from an illiterate South
American country). He had never met a girl with such brilliance,
he thought,until your Dad somehow made it clear to him that what
he was hearing from Sheri,originated, let's say the day before,
from him. She was caught and lost that round of a battle of wits.
Her style of painting impressed Willie, I suppose because he was
puzzled by it. Her small apartment was splattered with paint
drippings and Willie was rather fastidious. Villagers reflected
their personas in their apartments..Leonard Bernstein had four
walls of LP's, Milton, four walls of Dickens, Tolkein, etc. and
in Sheri's, you got high on the alcohol in the paint that surrounded
you. Sheri could flirt like a Parisian prostitute with Willie but
not with your Dad.

REMO NIGHTS   (Remembering Anatole Broyard)

In 1945, the booth at the MacDougal entrance to the San Remo was his. The Bleeker Street entrance served the local bar crowd and lively card players. A brass rail curved around the edge of the long bar, sawdust covered the tiled floor and a large mirror furnished the room. Anatole's booth was by the "Ladies Entrance" that led to the dining ROOM with white tablecloths, spotless dinnerware and an air of refinement.

We would meet for dinner at Pete Martin's bookshop on W.4th, IN THAT WAY, able to browse while waiting for each other. On the short walk to the Remo we could go over some of the stuff STILL FRESH IN OUR MINDS preparing to meet the hungry literary lions waiting at the Remo. Like a panel of experts, Milton Klonsky, Dick Gilman, CHANDLER, MASON, LA Martinelli were already seated, EATING.   What they were not aware of was the fact that we had been preparing for the battle by using a system involving memorizing choice quotations, lines of poetry and bits about the authors. It was a strategy similar to preparing for an exam, except that we knew the answers in advance.
The success of this approach was due to the fact that we ALSO knew what subjects were to be under discussion. Everyone had been talking of Hemingway for the past few days, for example. Last week it had been Nathaniel West. We threw in comments like chips at a poker table. If Klonsky mentioned William Blake, Anatole was ready with the influence of Blake's Minotaur on Picasso. To chide Milton further, he would mention Henri Michaux and Blake as painter/poets, knowing Klonsky's weakness regarding Michaux. Klonsky's revenge took the form of giving signed copies of his published "Blake's Dante" to everyone except Anatole.

With this unsportsman-like advantage, Anatole became either admired or feared. He was never revealed as a cheater, but as perhaps having a "photographic memory" together with his potent vocabulary. I recall walking with Anatole and Gala. his 4   year old daughter ,in the Park. We would stop and he'd look down at her and ask, "Are you happy?" She'd give a happy "Yes". He would then have her say the word "happiness". She would walk along saying "Ha-pee-ness" over and over. WHEN she saw someone approaching us she would look up at them and say "happiness, happiness". Anatole was enrolling her in higher education, as he did all of us.

 Back at the Remo, Anatole STOPPED talking of the three versions of "Lady Chatterley's Lover", AS Santos cleared the dishes. The treatment of women was the current hot topic as was sexual freedom among the budding writers present. To arouse interest in literature in general, Anatole concentrated on Eros. He used Henry Miller when talking about the Maquis de Sade's "Venus in Furs". He also used literature as an erotic device to secure bed-mates. At the Museum of Modern Art, where he was an early member, he would steer young coeds down from Smith College toward "Les Demoiselles D'Avignon", Picasso's favorite prostitutes, taking them by the elbow on a path that would eventually lead to the bedroom. He used Gorky in place of Georgi (vodka). He used Gabrielle D'Annunzio, the great hedonist, to find favor   the card-players
WITH

who looked up from their game at the mention of the name. As the headmaster at the Remo round table, he had set up shop in addition to the Cornelia Street Bookshop that he started. No longer was it the benches of Washington Square Park , or the corner hang-out by Pete Martin's small bookstore, next door to the candy store's newspaper stand. .Few people were buying books. Everyone seemed to be carrying them, borrowing them, writing them, exchanging them. They were talking about Sandburg and GRAVES, Gertrude Stein's lost generation or Whitman's immoralist. We'd talk until Pete turned the lights out and some of us would go to the bookstore around the corner on Cornelia to continue the conversations in the rear room.

Under Anatole's wing, we had become crazy in a literary hootenanny. Hot Jazz and Country Singers were MERE distractions, The Village Vanguard and Village Barn vs. the Remo. Fiction and non fiction rivaled Be Bops blatant message. We tried introducing Mahler and Hindemith as well as Noro Morales to maintain our standards. Anatole fitted literature the way Chaplin fitted comedy. Hungry writers, hungry for knowledge, crowded at his feet. He gave us a free education of pre-digested knowledge. Later, as the New York Times literary critic, we WERE TUTORED BY his brilliant reviews. The FRAGIL bookshop was a failure but not completely, since it produced marvels in the form of writers that were able to benefit from its stimulus. With out much stock on the shelves, that looked much like an empty cupboard, he was obliged to ask Pete for copies of books ordered by customers. He was selling out-of-print books (that he advertised but didn't always have on hand). T his obliged him to scour the book shops over on 4th A venue for help. In this way he became known in the literary community in general.

From the halls of academia to the dance halls of Harlem, his irresistibility was evident to girls everywhere. However, among people in the writing establishment his uniqueness , though evident, was over-looked. Alfred Kazin was puzzled by how long it had taken for him to encounter Anatole, for example There may have been two reasons for this protracted indifference by members of his literary fraternity. One: Anatole's multifold liaisons were such that personal secrecy and respectful discretion , favored a low key exposure. Writers are a jealous bunch. Two: There were political ramifications, forces intent on minimizing his growing influence over a generation of young writers. In the rudderless Village of 1945, Anatole's Socratic attraction established a spirit, a tone , a legitimacy for book-lovers. There was as much diversion in a library as in a disco.

STILL FREE OF GRAFFITI, THE PLACE HAD CHARM AND SUFFICIENT
NORMALCY IN CERTAIN STREETS. AT THE "REMO",THE SAW DUST FLOORS
WERE SWEPT CLEAN DAILY FOR AN UNKEMPT CLIENTLE. INSPIRATION
STILL CAME FROM SHOCK VALUE INSTEAD OF THE "STILLNESS OF THE
NIGHT" AND ODDITY PRODUCED CELEBRITY. HOWEVER, ONE COULD STILL
SLEEP ON THE GRASS, SMELL THE CAFE EXPRESSO, STILL ENJOY THE
SENSATION OF NAUGHTINESS. THERE WAS EVEN A GROWING HARD CORE
OF QUALITY ORIGINALITY AND AUTHENTIC TALENT LENDING SOME BIT
OF LEGITAMACY TO IT ALL. IMPERTURBABLE CHESS PLAYERS LENT THE
PARK STABILITY. IT WAS A POOR MAN'S TRIP TO HOLLYWOOD ON THE
HUDSON WITH AN ALL-NIGHT CAFETERIA CROWD AND CONTINENTAL DINING
AT MORI'S.

BECAUSE OF THE BENNINGTON AND SMITH LOVELIES THAT CAME TO THE
VILLAGE SEEKING TO FULFIL THE PROMISE OF THE POETS IN AN ES-
THETIC GOLD RUSH, YOUR DAD, BLISS, HUNG ON. WHO WOULD VOLUNTAR-
ILY LEAVE A BLOSSOMING GARDEN OF EDEN JUST NOW? SOON IT WAS TOO
LATE. HE WAS TRAPPED, HAPPY ALL THE TIME WITH BEAUTY AND LAUGH-
TER ON EACH ARM. HIS EDUCATION WAS A "TOOL OF POWER", ESPECIAL-
LY OVER EDUCATED WOMEN. HE SPOKE OF ALL THIS FEMININE NOURISH-
MENT WITH ASTONISHMENT ADDED TO HIS DESCRIPTIONS OF NIGHTS AND
AFTERNOONS ELEVATING THE ACT TO THE STATUS OF BALLET AND DRAMA.
HE FEASTED ON FEMALES, CONSUMING AT TIMES, TWO BANQUETS IN ONE
DAY, THE WAY HE ORDERED "TWO SCOOPS" FOR HIS MALTEDS AT BIGELOW'S
SODA FOUNTAIN

BY THE FIFTIES, WE MADE EXCUSES FOR THE VILLAGE THE WAY ONE
FORGIVES A DRUNK OR CONSIDERS OBESITY "CUTE". BUT IT WAS BE-
COMING AN UNSUPERVISED SOCIETY. TO LEAVE IT WAS TO SETTLE
FOR A WASTELAND. IT CONTINUED TO HAVE THE POWER TO INFLUENCE
THE WORLD LIKE A MOVIE INDUSTRY. WE BEGAN TO ENCOUNTER POLITI-
CALIZATION. INVITATIONS ARRIVED TO "CHINESE AGRARIAN REFORM"
PARTIES WITH FILMS OF FIELD WORKERS SINGING. THE NEW SCHOOL
SEEMED SLANTED, PSYCHOANALYSIS BECAME SUSPECT WITH FAKERS AND
ABSTRACT POETRY ADDED TO THE CONFUSION. THINGS WERE BECOMING
MISDIRECTED, MANIPULATED BY UNSEEN FORCES.

ONE DAY, WALKING WITH YOURDAD, WE PASSED THE PEACOCK CAFE.
ON THE GROUND, ALONG THE WALL, WAS STANLEY GOULD, MASON HOFFEN-
BERG, STELLA BROOKS, EARL PIGRIM, ALL OF THEM PRE-BEATS. WAS IT
A STRIKE, A PROTEST ACTION OR A BUNCH OF DRUNKS SAYING TO US,
"COME SIT DOWN", APPEALING TO OUR SPIRIT OF CAMARADERIE? NOT
AT ALL. IT WAS A RELAXED GESTURE OF CELEBRATION, A DISPLAY OF
JUST HOW WONDERFUL IT WAS TO BE "VILLAGERS". LIKE A WORRIED
PARENT, YOUR DAD AGREED WITH ME THAT IT WAS A SPECTACLE OF
PUBLIC MISBEHAVIOR, LIKE GUESTS AT A GATSBY PARTY, DONE IN JEST.
WE WALKED BY SADLY NOT BENDING TO "BOHEMIENNE" BONHOMMERIE.
THAT WAS THE DAY THE WORLD SPLIT.HISTORY WAS IN THE MAKING.
IT SAW THE BIRTH OF THE BEATS,WITH THOSE WHO COULD NOT HANDLE
WALLACE STEVENS OR AUDEN, DOOMED TO DECADENCE, TO BE FOLLOWERS
OF BURROUGHS AND OTHER DEPENDENTS. WHILE I COULD RECITE TENNYSON,
I COULD NOT DO JUSTICE TO DELMORE OR TO KLONSKY, MY GOOD FRIEND.
WHERE WAS I IN ALL THIS? WAS I TO BECOME ONE OF THEM?

ANATOLE'S COAT

IN NEW ORLEANS, WHERE THE COAT CAME FROM, IT WOULD HAVE BEEN
CONSIDERED STYLISH, BUT ON A NORTHERN COLLEGE CAMPUS IT WAS OUT-
LANDISH. IT WAS A VERY SHORT GREY OVERCOAT, UNSUITABLE FOR WINTER.
WITH IT'S HIDDEN BUTTONS, IT RESEMBLED A CAPECOAT, LIKE THOSE WORN
AT DUELS OR BY CONFEDERATES. COMING FROM DECATURE STREET IN BED-
STY TO ATTEND COLLEGE IN JEWISH FLATBUSH, THE YOUNG MAN WAS START-
ING HIS CLASSES, DRESSED IN HIS "BEST", OR SO HE THOUGHT.

IT WAS A TIME WHEN STUDENTS WORE TIES AND CONFORMED PROPERLY.
YOU EXCELLED SCHOLASTICALLY AND NOT BY YOUR MANNER OF DRESS. THE
YOUNG MAN'S FIRST DAYS ON CAMPUS DREW STARES AND SNICKERS. HE WAS
SOON IDENTIFIABLE BY ALL..A WALKING CURIOSITY. POSSESSING ETHNIC
SENSITIVITY AND SURROUNDED BY INTELLECTUALLY AGGRESIVE STUDENTS,
HE FELT MISPLACED, MISMATCHED, LIKE HIS CLOTHING. HIS CLASS MATES
CAME FROM WEALTHY, WELL-EDUCATED EUROPEAN REFUGEE FAMILIES. THE
YOUNG MAN WITH THE ODD NAME "ANATOLE" WAS SEEN IN THE CAFETERIA
ASKING IF SEATS WERE FREE, PASSING FROM TABLE TO TABLE LIKE A
BEGGER. THE COAT WAS TO BLAME.

"SIT DOWN", I BECKONED AS HE APPROACHED. AS AN OUTNUMBERED
CATHOLIC, COMING FROM FORT HAMILTON, A SCANDINAVIAN NEIGHBORHOOD,
I WAS LIKEWISE A MINORITY MEMBER. MY DEPRESSION-ERA SNEAKERS WERE
TIED WITH STRING. MY INK WAS HOME-MADE, WATER MIXED WITH BLUE DYE.
TO GET TO SCHOOL, I RODE ON THE OUTSIDE OF THE BUS OR SQUEEZED
THROUGH IRON BARS AT EXITS AND CROSSED TRACKS NIMBLY. I HOPED
HE WOULD BUY THE PENNY CIGARETTES I WAS SELLING CALLED "LOOSIES".
I WAS THE "SUPPLIER" IN THE CAFETERIA TURF. WHEN I NOTICED THAT
HIS HAIR WAS AS LONG AS MINE, AN IMMEDIATE SYMPATHY AROSE IN ME,
LIKE A BATTLEFIELD CLOSENESS. SOON OUR ATTITUDES MERGED AND, AS
MISFITS, WE WERE TWO ORPHANS WHO ADOPTED EACH OTHER.

ONE DAY, I DISCOVERED THE CAPECOAT IN A STREETCORNER BASKET.
HE HAD SHED HIS UNWANTED IDENTITY. HAVING NO COAT OF MY OWN, JUST
LAYERS OF SWEATERS, I FELT I HAD FOUND A TREASURE. BESIDES, I HAD
ALWAYS ADMIRED THE COAT IN A ROMANTIC SORT OF WAY. GIRLS EXCHANGED
CLOTHES, I ARGUED, WHY NOT US? WOULD I RISK ASSUMING HIS IDENTITY?
ANATOLE WAS RIGHTFULLY SENSITIVE, WHERE I WAS THICK-SKINNED. I HAD
BECOME DESENSITIZED, ADJUSTING MYSELF TO DIVERSE BROOKLYN NEIGHBOR-
HOODS. DAD WAS A "RENT-DODGER", ALWAYS PACKING AND UNPACKING, LIKE
TOURISTS; WE LIVED FLEEING LAWYERS AND LANDLORDS. THE FIT WAS A BIT
OFF, BUT WITH SUCH APPAREL, WHO COULD TELL? IT LOOKED BETTER ON ME
THAN IT HAD ON HIM, I WAS CONVINCED. HIS FATHER WAS AS TALL AS I WAS,
AND HE HAD WORN IT. MY FATHER WAS SUSPICIOUS. WHO THREW OUT A COAT?
I INVITED ANATOLE TO VISIT US TO PROVE THE COAT WAS NOT STOLEN.
AS HE PUT IT ON WE CIRCLED ROUND HIM. LOOKING IN THE LARGE PARLOR MIRROR,
HE WAS SURROUNDED AS FOR A PHOTO. HE HAD BECOME "FAMILY".

The coat hung in the closet like a good friend to
be called on when needed

                    VILLAGE NOBILITY

        ALTHOUGH WE LIVED FAR APART FOR 90% OF OUR LIVES
HOW COME ANATOLE BROYARD WAS A CRADLE TO THE GRAVE FRIEND?
WE WERE TOGETHER FOR A SHORT TIME AT BROOKLYN COLLEGE AND
IN THE VILLAGE. AT THE END, IN MARTHA'S VINEYARD HE HAD
ASKED THAT I STAND WITH HIS WIDOW, HIS SON AND DAUGHTER
WHILE A CROWD OF FAMOUS DIGNITARIES LOOKED ON FROM A DISTANCE.
"CLOSER APART, THAN MANY WHO ARE TOGETHER", I ONCE WROTE HIM.

        LOOKING BACK FOR ANSWERS, NOTHING JUSTIFIED SUCH LOYALTY.
I CAME UP WITH OVER A DOZEN POSSIBILITIES, TRYING TO DISCOVER
WHAT MUST HAVE IMPRESSED HIM. WHEN TAKEN AS A WHOLE. WAS IT
THE FOLLOWING THAT IMPRESSED HIM?

THE SAN REMO. IN 1940, IT WAS A HANG OUT FOR LOCAL CARD PLAYERS
AND NEIGHBORHOOD FRIENDS. IT WAS UNLIKE A CORNELIA STREET BAR
THAT HAD AN IN-HOUSE PROSTITUTE. WITH A RESTRICTIVE POLICY OF
SORTS, THE SANTINI BROTHERS GRANTED ME ENTREE SINCE MY FAMILY
OWNED 117 SULLIVAN STREET AND MY GRANDFATHER HELPED ESTABLISH
ST. ANTHONY'S CHURCH. IT BECAME ANATOLE'S LITERARY HEADQUARTERS.
BROOKLYN COLLEGE IN 1939, ANATOLE AND I MET AS I HAPPENED TO BE
RUNNING FOR STUDENT COUNCIL. I DROPPED OUT TO LEAVE TO STUDY AT
THE UNIVERSITY OF MIAMI. HE DROPPED OUT AS WELL, SAYING, "IT
DOESN'T COINCIDE WITH MY FRAME OF MIND".WAS I AN INFLUENCE?
UNIVERSITY OF MIAMI WHEN I RECEIVED AN EXCHANGE GRANT TO
STUDY AT THE UNIVERSITY OF HAVANA AND LATER AT THE UNIVERSITY
OF BRAZIL, WAS THIS IT? HE WAS TEACHING AT THE NEW SCHOOL.
THE DANCE HE LOVED TO DANCE. I HAD BEEN A PROFESSIONAL LATIN
DANCER AND DANCE TEACHER IN 1939. I TAUGHT HIM SOME STEPS AND
SOME SPANISH, BUT SO WHAT.
ROUND THE WORLD IN 1952, IT WAS A REAL ACHIEVEMENT. THIS
MUST HAVE HELPED WIN HIS ADMIRATION WHEN HE FOUND OUT I DID IT.
ANAIS NIN ANAIS CELEBRATED PUBLICATION OF "LADDERS OF FIRE".
AMONG THE LITERATI PRESENT, SHE CHOSE ME FOR A LIAISON . HE
WAS HOPING TO HAVE BEEN CHOSEN.
DELMORE SCHWARTZ ANATOLE WAS ACHING TO MEET THE RECLUSIVE
DELMORE. THANKS TO MILTON KLONSKY, I WAS INVITED TO MEET HIM
ON CHARLES STREET. DELMORE THREW US BOTH OUT AFTER I HAD SAID
SOMETHING ABOUT HIS LIBRARY, COMPARING IT TO MILTON'S.
MILTON KLONSKY MILTON AND I WON "HONORABLE MENTION" IN A
NEW YORK TIMES HIGH SCHOOL WRITING CONTEST. HE CAME TO LIVE
WITH ME FOR A WHILE IN SOUTH MIAMI WHERE I HAD TWO HORSES. I
SUPPOSE WORD GOT BACK TO ANATOLE.
WILLIAM GADDIS ANATOLE AND WILLIE WERE RIVALS OVER SHERI
MARTINELLI. AS A VERY RESERVED FELLOW REGARDING HIS PERSONAL
LIFE, WILLIE NEVERTHELESS CAME TO ME FOR SOLACE, ESPECIALLY
SINCE SHERI ENTRUSTED HER SECRETS TO ME.

VILLAGE NOBILITY

<u>TED SHAWN</u> THE EDITOR-IN-CHIEF OF THE "NEW YORKER" WROTE
ME SAYING HE LIKED MY "V-J DAY IN YOKOHAMA". IT WAS EVENTUALLY
PUBLISHED IN ANOTHER MAGAZINE. IN 1947, EVERYONE WAS WRITING.
CHANDLER BROSSARD, WILLIAM GADDIS, KLONSKY AND ANATOLE. SOME-
ONE CRIED OUT, "I WILL BE THE FIRST TO BE PUBLISHED!" WHEN I
PRODUCED A COPY OF "LANGUAGES FOR WAR AND PEACE", HAVING
COLLABORATED WITH PROFESSOR MARIO PEI OF COLUMBIA, DATED 1943,
THAT WAS THAT.
<u>PAUL BROYARD</u> ANATOLE HAD JUST GAINED STATUS WITH "WHAT THE
CYSTOSCOPE SAID". IT WAS HIS FIRST STORY AND WAS PUBLISHED IN
TED SOLOTAROFF'S "AMERICAN REVIEW". STRANGLY, HIS FATHER, PAUL
AND I WERE EACH UNDERGOING CYSTOSCOPIES THE SAME WEEK. I HAD
HAD THREE IN A ROW, SCHEDULED FOR A FOURTH. WAS IT THE PAIN
THAT ANATOLE SUFFERED UNDERGOING HIS OWN TOWARD THE END THAT
JOINED US AS ONLY PAIN CAN?
<u>HENRI MICHAUX</u> ANATOLE DISCOVERED MANY LITERARY GEMS. HE TURNED
US ON TO THEM, I.E., KAFKA. WHEN ANATOLE WAS ENRAPTURED OF
HENRI MICHAUX'S POETRY AND PAINTINGS, I MUST HAVE IMPRESSED HIM
BY BUYING TWO OILS AT THE GALLERY "RIVE GAUCHE" AND HAVING MOVIES
TAKEN WITH MICHAUX.

NONE OF THE ABOVE COULD COMPARE WITH ANATOLE'S ACHIEVEMENTS,
ADVANCEMENTS AND ACCLAIM. MY RECORD LOOKS LIKE A PLAYFUL PASS-
TIME WHILE HE, AS A CRITIC, HAD TO INTERPRETE AND REFINE OUR
THINKING OF A WORLD OF LITERATURE. I USED THE WORLD SELFISHLY.
HE WAS SCHOLARLY, YET WITTY, COMPETITIVE, YET POPULAR. HE WAS
A SPRY PERSON WITH LIFE LONG CONTRIBUTIONS TO UP GRADING ONE'S
INTELLIGENCE. HE FATHERED A MODERN PROGENY BY WORKING HARD.

<u>THE ANSWER TO"WHY ME?"</u> ANATOLE AND I SHARED A SPECIAL KNOWLEDGE.
WE WERE THE ONLY TWO WITNESSES TO A VISION THAT EVAPORATED BEFORE
OUR EYES. GREEENWICH VILLAGE WAS THE MOST BEAUTIFULLY INSPIRING
PLACE ON THE FACE OF THE GLOBE JUST AFTER WORLD WAR II. IT CAME
AND WENT LIKE A FLASH, SO FAST THAT MANY WERE UNAWARE OF WHAT
WAS BEING LOST. LOST TO MANKIND. THAT PERIOD OF WHOLESOME FLOURISH-
ING OF CULTURAL TRENDS BECAME ENDANGERED AND DIED. TOWARD THE END,
ANATOLE SAW ME AS AN OLD GATEKEEPER ON A PROPERTY IN RUINS, STILL
LIVING IN THE VILLAGE. HE MUST HAVE RECALLED THAT HE ONCE ACCUSED
ME OF "ESCAPING", WHEN I SHIPPED OUT TO SEA. BUT WHEN HE LEFT THE
VILLAGE PERMANENTLY, HE MUST HAVE FELT LIKE A GUILTY ESCAPEE.
AS A SOLE SURVIVER NOW, I WALK THE VILLAGE WITH HIS GHOST,KNOWING
THIS IS WHERE HIS HEART STILL RESIDES, AMONG THE LANDSCAPES OF
OUR HAPPY YOUTH. THUS WE ARE TOGETHER, JOINED NOT IN SADNESS,
BUT RATHER IN THE FEELING THAT WE WERE SO CLOSE TO A MIRACLE THAT
WE COULD HAVE SAVED THE WORLD.

VILLAGE NOBILITY

DEAR BLISS: THE LOVERS, DANTE PAVONE AND BEAUFORD DELANEY
NEVER APPEARED TOGETHER AROUND YOUR DAD AND   NOR WOULD YOU
SEE THEM WALKING IN THE PARK TOGETHER. DANTE WOULD VISIT US AT
THE W.4th STREET PLACE, THE HOUSE IN THE BACKYARD. WHEN BEAUFORD
WOULD WAIT FOR DANTE, HE WOULD BE FOUND SITTING ON A BENCH CLOSEST
TO W. 4th STREET. IF NOT, HE WOULD SIT CLOSER TO HIS LOFT ON GREENE
STREET, UNDER THE GARIBALDI STATUE. BEAUFORD WORE A HAT LIKE GARI-
BALDI'S. ONE DAY I BEGAN TO TRY TO UNDERSTAND HIS SUBLIME COMPOSURE.
"HOW DO YOU MANAGE TO GET ALONG WITH NO MONEY?" "I ONLY WORRY WHEN
I DON'T FEEL WELL", WAS HIS GENTLE REPLY. ALTHOUGH IT WAS A BITTER
DAY, HE EXUDED A WARMTH THAT CAME FROM HIS "PERSONALITY", OR WAS
IT SOMETHING MYSTERIOUS OR DREAMY, LIKE SLEEPING PILLS. HE HID A
SECRET KNOWLEDGE THAT I LATER DISCOVERED WAS THE INCOME HE WAS
RECEIVING FROM HIS FRIENDSHIP FOR HIS ADMIRERS, HENRY MILLER AND
MRS. ROZENWALD ASCOLI AND OTHERS. HE WAS CHEERFUL AND CLEVER LIKE
A PIXIE. CHUBBY GOD OF PLENTY. TO SHOW HIM MY FRIENDSHIP, I PRESENTED
HIM WITH A JAPANESE CEREMONIAL NAIL-STUDDED DRUM, THAT I HAD CARRIED
ACROSS THE PACIFIC, TO ADD TO HIS MODEST COLLECTION.

BEAUFORD RESEMBLED MILTON, WHO APPARANTLY HAD NO SOURCE OF INCOME,
EXCEPT FOR HIS BROTHER, A MARITIME LAWYER IN BOROUGH HALL, BROOKLYN,
AND THE GENEROSITY OF HIS FEW FRIENDS. YOUR DAD BEGAN THE EULOGY AT
MILTON'S WAKE BY SAYING "MILTON NEVER HAD A JOB". WHEN THE SHIP
CAME INTO NEW YORK, I WOULD BRING HIS FAVORITE BRAND OF CIGARETTES
TO SELL TO HIM AND FINALLY TO REFUSE THE MONEY. TAX FREE LIQUOR
WAS ALSO SOMETHING HE ASKED ABOUT, SEEING THAT AS A CREW MEMBER
IT WAS ALSO TAX-FREE TO ME. WHEN HE ASKED ABOUT PERFUME, I ASKED
FOR PAYMENT OF SORTS SINCE IT WAS THE "HANDLING" THAT BOTHERED ME,
BEING HELD UP IN CUSTOMS BECAUSE OF HIS GIFTS. YOUR DAD AND I GAVE
HIM MONEY TO BUY HIS LUXURIES IN THE NEIGHBORHOOD. MILTON READ AND
RESEMBLED KAFKA, WHILE BEAUFORD WAS MORE PROUSTIAN. THEY BOTH WORE
WOOL SCARVES AND, SPOKE PROFOUNDLY AND WERE RECLUSIVE BUT OPEN TO
CONVERSATION. PROUST WORE A NIGHT CAP IN HIS ELEGANT BEDROOM WORLD
AND BEAUFORD WORE ONE AS WELL IN HIS FRIGID FLAT, LIT WITH CANDLES
(NOT FOR EFFECT) AND HIS SMALL WOOD BURNING, COAL BURNING STOVE.
PROUST WROTE THE STORIES OF HIS ABSENT SOCIAL WORLD AND BEAUFORD
PAINTED A WORLD IN THE VILLAGE THAT WAS ALL TOO PRESENT IN HIS MIND.
PROUST STRUGGLED WITH THE PAST AND BEAUFORD WITH THE PRESENT. THE
VILLAGE PRODUCED MIRACLES AS WELL AS ARTISTS AND AUTHORS. BEAUFORD
AND MILTON WERE THE LIVING PROOF. DANTE WAS PRIEST-LIKE EXCEPT FOR
A LONG STEMMED CIGARETTE HOLDER AND CONVERSATIONS ABOUT DRUGS. BEAU-
FORD POSED IT SEEMED LIKE A ROUND-FACED BUDDHA OR WISE OWL WHO WORE
HIS HAIR LIKE NAT KING COLE. ALL WOULD HAVE BEEN FRIENDS OF WM. BLAKE.

ONE AFTERNOON, JAMES BALDWIN CAME FROM THE BAR AT THE CARLTON,
WALKING WITH BEAUFORD, BOTH LOOKING AROUND AS ONE DOES WHEN IN THE
MAIN AREA OF THE WALDORF. HE GAVE ME HIS NUMBER AND WHEN I CALLED
HE SAID HE WOULD DO A PORTRAIT OF ME. IN THE STYLE OF MATISSE OR
VAN GOGH, OR BOTH, I WONDERED? HE ONCE SANG FOR ME TO KEEP THE
COLD AT BAY AT HIS WIND-SWEPT   "I ONCE WAS LOST BUT NOW AM
FOUND, WAS BLIND BUT NOW I SEE..". BOTH HE AND MILTON CAME FROM
A BEAUTIFUL, NOBLE STOCK AND ADDED TO THE LORE OF GREENWICH VILLAGE.

        IMAGINE ESCAPING FROM THE VILLAGE WHERE EVERYONE WENT TO
ESCAPE. WAS THERE SOMETHING WRONG WITH ME AS THERE WAS WITH
MANY AROUND ME? WAS ESCAPING ITSELF A WAY OF BEING "ORIGINAL"?
YOUR DAD, BLISS, WAS AN AUTHENTIC ORIGINAL, A KIND OF LITERARY
FASHION DESIGNER WHO LIVES AND BREATHES ORIGINALITY. IN THE
FORTIES, VILLAGERS COMPLAINED THAT THEY WERE "BORN IN THE WRONG
CENTURY". WAS I BORN IN THE WRONG COUNTRY? WHERE THEY COLLECT-
ED PROUST, I COLLECTED KAFKA. THEY COLLECTED FIRST EDITIONS,
I COLLECTED FOREIGN DICTIONARIES. WITH OUR "IMPETUS JUVENILIS",
WE FELT WE WERE KEEPING THE WORLD WAITING FOR OUR MANY TALENTS.
TODAY, THEY FEEL THE WORLD MAY WELL DISAPPEAR WITH OR WITHOUT
THEM, CAUGHT AS THEY ARE, BETWEEN ESCAPING AND COMPLYING.

        MY FAMILY WAS A CASSEROLE OF NORTHERN AND SOUTHERN ITALIANS
WHO WANTED A PRIEST IN THE FAMILY, OR AT LEAST, A FOREIGN
MISSIONARY. I WAS HOPING TO BE A FOREIGN CORRESPONDENT. DURING
THE WAR, I WAS IN "FOREIGN LIAISON". WHEN I FAILED THE FOREIGN
SERVICE OFFICERS EXAM AND WAS LATER REJECTED BY THE ITALIAN
FRATERNITY AT BROOKLYN COLLEGE, I JOINED THE LUSO-AMERICAN CLUB
(PORTUGUESE), SEEKING A FOREIGN IDENTITY. SAILING UNDER A VARIETY
OF FOREIGN FLAGS, MY SHIPBOARD AND OVERSEAS ROMANCES WERE A MIXED
SALAD, SEASONED WITH FRENCH, RUSSIAN, ITALIAN, WEST INDIAN AND
SOUTH AMERICAN DRESSINGS.

        IT IS NOT ENOUGH TO READ ESCAPIST LITERATURE AND MYSTERY
STORIES OR TO ATTEND LONDON THEATERS ON A WEEK-END SPREE. THE
TRUE ESCAPE ARTIST LEAVES HOME BEHIND IN ORDER TO ENTER THE MANY
MYSTERIES OF THE WORLD; TO UNRAVEL HIMSELF BY CLIMBING ABOVE
NEPAL OR BEYOND THE ATLAS MOUNTAINS.

        THE "REMO" IS GONE, TAKING MUCH OF THE CENTURY WITH IT.
THE LOCALS LEFT WHEN THE DRINKERS CAME. DRINKERS LEFT WHEN THE
CRITICS AND POETS CAME. THESE LEFT WHEN THE HIPPIES CAME. THE
HIPPIES LEFT WHEN THE GAYS CAME AND THE GAYS LEFT WHEN THE
TOURISTS CAME. TO THE TOURISTS BELONGS THE WORLD. BY MY WORKING
WITH FOREIGN TOURISTS, I SEE AMERICA THROUGH THEIR EYES AND BY
EMPLOYING COMMENTARIES OF HUMOROUS CONTRASTS, THEY CAN SEE THEIR
COUNTRIES THROUGH MY EYES IN A WORLD MADE ONE.

        WHERE AND WHEN WILL MY PARTICULAR SAFARI END? WHERE ELSE
BUT BACK HOME AT THE END OF THE CENTURY, SURROUNDED BY STRANGERS
AND FOREIGNERS IN TIMES SQUARE. I HAVE A SPOT PICKED OUT. IN
CENTRAL PARK SOUTH THERE IS A HUGH ROCK, WHERE, OVERHEAD A FLOOD
OF FIREWORKS WILL SPLATTER THE NIGHT SKY WITH GRAND FINALES
AND STRAIGHT AHEAD, DOWN OLD BROADWAY.. THE WORLD PREMIER OF
THE TWENTY FIRST CENTURY!

At the Bar the San Remo   Dec. 1999

Leaving Greenwich Village in 1948, where my family had arrived in 1861 proved n[...] be a foolish mistake but a true blessing. My low level of intelligence restricted my entering the circle of literati such as Delmore Schwartz, Milton Klonsky or William Gaddis. The weight of my ignorance was embarrassing as I remained silent at the San Remo dinners in their company. They had been reading Kafka's nightmarish plight, Thoreau's rough natural environment, Orwell's future, Nathaniel West's well·intentioned defeats. They quoted paragraphs from Huxley's medicated future world, Coleridge, Leary and Baudelaire- all of whom were searching for Utopias of one sort or another and for one reason or another. When I witnessed my Village becoming attractive to hippies and druggies, I began to ponder leaving while also attempting to read Finnegan's Wake or about Dedalus, who left Ireland for religious reasons. Boccaccio, because of the plague, left Florence for a safe utopia called Fiesole. But it wasn't until I read Henri Michaux thanks to Anatole Broyard's recommendation that I was able to sneak away to sea to what the Greeks called, utopia, "the empty space". Michaux wrote about "L'Espace du dedans", "The Space Within" and "Ailleurs", "Elsewhere", writing, that I understood as a message to me. There was no longer a need to read about Brave New World's mysticism or Emerson's transcendentalism or about some "remote Western isle" by O'Flaherty. Perhaps Thomas Wolf, who left his town in the south for the wider world of Harvard University, like Michaux, whose work included what is known as "the marvels of journeys", convinced me to leave the Village. Since I could not catch up with the brilliant friends surrounding me and with my only sharp weapon being my dominance of foreign languages (that encountered no one to duel with), I picked up and left for where my knowledge was put to good use beyond Greenwich Village.

To begin with a clean slate. I had to find my utopia, a space where I could construct a world within an already fertile environment. Having red Mathew Arnold who, while on a voyage to Margate, wrote how better behaved people were at sea than on land. Tantamount to winning a lottery that I had NOT nto purchased a ticket for, I was dealt a good luck hand a Royal Flush that washed away what I left ashore and a Full House that became my home at sea. I landed a job as cruise director in a virgin industry in 1948 and began settling into a career that spanned 30 years. By setting up a Program of Daily Activity and an enthusiastic cruise staff, a hostess and a Travel Officer to assist, I fashioned a life-style for my-self that became my utopia. Sailing first class with an unlimited bar account, with semi celebrity status among celebrities, all-expense paid lifetime of vacations, I was cloistered in a wholesome, glorified existence with forty ways to make money, plus many "extras". I did alright,

It wasn't long before successful wealthy passengers or member of the crew asked me, "How did you get a job like this?" to which I still have no answer.

"The greatest loss is to remove oneself from the physical world," someone once said. Many who wished to change the world or their plight in it through nature, drugs, cults, communes or escapes that were legitimate experimentation, freedom of expression or plain folly, failed. Going to sea actually brought me in closer touch and familiarity with the bigger physical world. It seemed that my childhood stamp collection sprang to life with visits to eihty countries including Brunei, Borneo, Burma, Sarawak, Lapland, with duplicate visits to Israel, Egypt and others and to rarities like Papua, Andorra, San Marino, Lichtenstein, Algeria. To sail over sixty ships I had to "Jump ship" leaving one company in order to join another that called at places I had yet to visit. Holland American Line boasted the Rotterdam flagship, the Nieuw Amsterdam, the New Amsterdam, Statendam, Veedam, Volendam, Maasdam. I worked all of them except the latter. It added up to a million dollars if you include all the privileges, invitations, extra income and even better in a way, the access to hundreds of restricted, off limit or reserved venues such as for examples, the kremlin or the Shah of Iran's Treasury while on shore excursions.

Good luck followed me favored by "wind and weather". When I was discovered signing my bar tabs for fictitious "mixed drinks' with my unlimited bar account, drinks that I would normally have consumed, I had expected dismissal but the CEO of the company said, "Continue to do it. We need sober cruise directors." It seemed I could do no wrong! Obviously I rode the crest of a wave that carried me in luxury around the world and back to the Village when it was cleaner and a lot safer. I was a migratory bird sailing the wind from season to season. When I won a trip to Greece in a raffle, I said, "Give it to someone else," since I knew Greece so well. But the BIG RAFFLE that Lady Luck favored me with, continued. The world had become my oyster, to quote Zora Neale Hurston. In the Thousand and One Nights, you can read, "How long, how long in infinite pursuit of this and that endeavor and dispute? (On land) It is better to be merry with the fruitful grape (my ship), than to sadden after none or bitter fruit." (Ashore)

Unlike on land, I had the run of the ship with an office in Purser's Square, the headquarters of all ships and with a self-serving schedule that catered to both my passengers and to myself. At one time, Pursers once ran shuffleboard, bingo, kiddie parties or the ship's pool or dining service. New Year's Eve was celebrated with noise makers and clown hats, installed big Broadway-type entertainment aboard little by little, to overcome 38 days between New York and Buenos Aires round trip. Cheerful Cruise Directors took over from many doctors who had recommended a salubrious sea voyage as a remedy. Things were changing. When transportation became lavishly embellished with Las Vegas type casinos, sadly, the show was over for the cruise director's monopoly. Certain elements on land wanted, "a piece of the action." I had to refuse their offer. It was "come in or get out" and I was a poor swimmer. They made it their jack pot utopia with no thanks to me. Again I was lucky to escape at the right time, back to where I had started in my own back yard as though I had never left. I returned home as if nothing happened except that now I was listened to with rapt attention at the dinner table.

Author with Miguelito Valdez , <u>Beachcomber</u>, *Miami Beach, 1941.*
Xavier Cugat Ochestra.

TAKING AS MUCH OF "MY" VILLAGE WITH ME AND WITH A COPY OF GADDIS'S
"THE RECOGNITIONS"IN MY BAGS, I MADE FOR THE OPEN SEA, THAT ANCIENT
PALYMSIST. WHETHER THIS HAPPENED COURAGEOUSLY OR THROUGH COWARDICE,
QU'IMPORTE? I WAS LEAVING MY HOMELAND NOT JUST MY NEIGHBORHOOD. NOONE
EVER LEAVES A PLACE ENTIRELY. NOW, IN THE COMPANY OF ST. CHRISTOPHER
AND ST. BONIFACE, I FOLLOWED MY INTERNAL COMPASS AND GENETIC RADAR.
IT WAS LIKE RUNNING AWAY FROM HOME, LIKE LEAVING A SICK FRIEND ON
TIP TOES."ESCAPING" SOUNDED BETTER THAN "GOING TO WORK" ON A SHIP.
TODAY, FRIENDS CONSIDER ME BOTH A TRAVELER AND A VILLAGER, TWO DIS-
TINCTIONS, A SEEKER OF TRUTH IN TWO WORLDS, LIKE MICHAUX SEEKING
ANSWERS IN BOTH PAINTING AND WRITING. THE VILLAGE IS STILL AROUND,
BUT I MISS YOUR DAD. THE WAY ONE MISSES A LOVE THAT IS VERY MUCH
ALIVE BUT VERY FAR AWAY.

AFRO-CUBAN MUSIC

                    JOSE MANGUAL, Sr.,
                  (EL BONGOSERO BUYÚ)

     TO WATCH A GREAT BONGOSERO IN ACTION, PERFORMING HIS PRESTI-
DIGITATION IS AN AUDIO/VISUAL DEMONSTRATION OF HI-MAGIC. DANCERS STOP TO
BECOME LISTENERS AND LISTENERS BECOME DANCERS. HARRY JAMES COULD DO IT
AND SO COULD JOSE MANGUAL (BUYÚ).

     WE DO NOT FEEL SHOWMANSHIP IN HIS PERFORMANCE AS WE DO WITH TITO
PUENTE. RATHER IT IS THE CONTROLLED INTENSITY OF A LION TAMER AT WORK
WITH A SAVAGE RYTHM. WE CAN CALL IT AN AMAZING GRACE, AN INHERENT
NOBILITY OF CHARACTER..ONE WITH ROOTS IN HIS AFRICAN HERITAGE, IN HIS
ANCIENT WISDOM. IT IS THE OPPOSITE OFCELEBRITY, BEING AS IT IS, THE *CARAFE*
UNDISTRACTED ARTIST AT WORK, MARRIED TO HIS MUSE AND NOT SEPARATED FROM IT
BY THE DEMANDS OF POPULARITY OR FASHION. IT IS RESPECT FOR WHAT HAS BEEN
GIVEN AS A GIFT FROM THE GODS. HE HAS TAKEN A VOW OF SILENCE WHILE HIS
BONGOS DO THE TALKING, THE DESIRED INVOCATION IS AT HIS FINGERTIPS.

     ANOTHER RARE INDIVIDUEL WHO POSSESSED WHAT WE CALL MODESTY BUT
WHAT IS ACTUALLY AN AURA OF DIVINITY, WAS THE PAINTER, BEAUFORD DELANEY.
HIS ART CAN BE SEEN AT THE STUDIO MUSEUM ON WEST 116th STREET. LATINOS
CALL SUCH TALENT,"LLENO DE DULSURA", A TENDER MODESTY. IT IS A STRENGTH
THAT EXISTS IN THE ARTIST EVEN BEFORE HE SHOWS ANY OUTSTANDING ABILITY,
AS THOUGH "CHOSEN". BEAUFORD ONCE SANG TO ME, "I ONCE WAS LOST BUT NOW
AM FOUND, WAS BLIND BUT NOW CAN SEE..". WHEN I THINK OF BUYÚ, I HEAR,
"SIENT'UN BONGO, MAMITA ME TA'LLAMANDO.."

     MIGUELITO ONCE TOLD ME HE WAS TIRED OF SINGING "BABALU" (LIKE
CARUSO SINGING "O SOLE MIO"). BUYU WAS AT AARON DAVIS HALL THIS SPRING
AND AT THE "POINT" IN THE BRONX TO RECIEVE AN HOMAGE. IT'S BEEN SIXTY
YEARS SINCE WE FIRST MET AT THE "CAFE LATINO" ON BARROW STREET IN THE
VILLAGE. FORTUNE SMILES ON THESE GOOD PEOPLE, REWARDING THEM WITH
FRIENDSHIPS THAT CONTAIN VENERATION. SHE PROTECTS THEM FROM HARM LIKE
A MOTHER,IN AN INDUSTRY THAT KNOWS THE TRAGEDY OF DRUGS. IS THIS BECAUSE
THEY GIVE MORE THAN THEY RECEIVE WITH BIBLICAL APPROVAL? IN A BUSINESS
REQUIRING BOTH TALENT AND LUCK, BUYU HAD AN ADDED SUPPORT..LOVE, TO
WHICH HE WOULD CREDIT "MI ABUELA" WITH HIS CUSTOMARY MODESTY.. TO WHICH
SI ME PERMITE, WE MUST ADD, HIS SISTER, GLORIA.

Eulogy St Paul Church

Salsa 101: Reflections on Latin Music

Graciela, La Libertadora

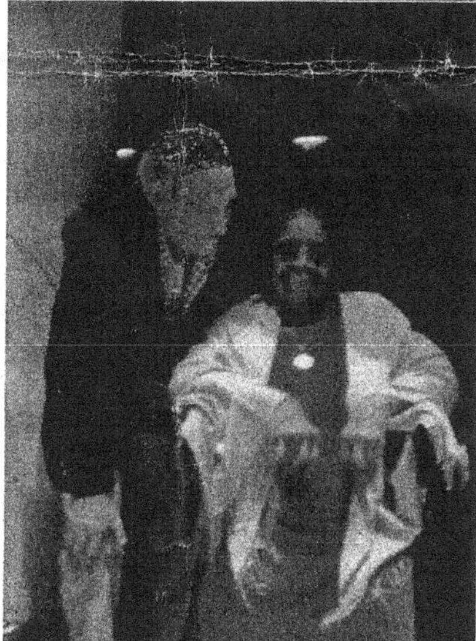

At the **La Conga** nightclub in 1945, **Graciela Perez** broke the restraints of propriety and virtuousness the night she sang "Sí Sí No No." The band fell silent, the waiters froze, the dancing stopped, and the bartender turned to witness her daring performance.

Beginning off to the side, she slowly edged center-stage under brighter lighting. She personified womankind facing an eternal seductive, copulative proposition. Her agile voice nursed a suspenseful scenario that gradually submitted to normal desire. Within this framework, Graciela reached a melodic dénouement, an artful pseudo-orgasmic celebration ending in an ecstatic climactic scream. This was music to the ears of every male present.

Her startling melodramatics had no encore. Here was a breakthrough similar to **Sally Rand's** very daring fan dance, **Josephine Baker's** nudity, and **Miguelito Valdez's** "Babalu" number at the uptight, Anglo-centric Waldorf Astoria. She hit us the way **Valentino's** tango did, then **Isadora Duncan** and **Madonna**, but without their universal celebrity. We had been presented with a revolutionary event, like a morality play vocalized. It was one that lyrically mimicked a Shakespearean dueling scene

8/28/2009 10:59 PM

between rival moral principles. Her act liberated a stale, sexually correct post–WWII America at a time when Club El Morocco denied entry to women wearing sunglasses. Graciela taunted a tight-laced society wherein any indelicate intimacy was taboo, except in crass vaudevillian skits on red-light Forty-Second Street.

The patrons at La Conga's rumba matinees were dancers and their "pupils," garment-center "cloak-and-suiters" with their models, and gigolettes. The dance floor was a smoldering tinderbox of erotic performances, with groins riveted to groins. This was reminiscent of the old **Park Plaza** where, during slow, grinding selections such as "El Negro Simón," the lyrics described a girl becoming *arrebatá,* or sexually uncontrollable. With Yoruba language working, i.e., *arrullendole caguá,* lusty interpretations were left to the inflamed imaginations of the dancers. These odd, throaty sounds seemed to imply foreplay. Since the messages in these unintelligible lyrics were decoded by each dancer according to his or her level of arousal, there was sufficient amplitude for each individual to respond physically, blaming the Afro music for their suggestive behavior on the floor. The musicians, as well as the outnumbered Latino dance couples, encouraged the Anglos to interpolate the feral sensuality surrounding them, while clownish antics of frustrated beginners were perceived with good humor by everyone.

When a Latino danced with an Anglo girl, she would perform with exaggerated responses in dances that glorified femininity and the macho man. The result was a greater abandonment with newfound freedom of movement. The male Anglo, his heretofore secure role threatened, eschewed the Afro-Cuban dance world, whereas his partner now saw it as part of her overall liberation—and would again during the 1970s, when disco dancing meant less male control. The Stonewall historical event is a good example of a revolution beginning on the dance floor.

Graciela's substantial voice that night in 1945 ignited an overheated environment. Unless you had witnessed her, you would not have realized what it all meant. Her coquettish, beguiling, pantomime with needless lyrics nevertheless left us with a climactic, playful portrayal of a female's victory over a manipulated male, despite their mutually responsive libidos. She gracefully and cleverly flaunted her newly liberalized instinct, using "Si Si No No" as a musical vehicle for freedom of greater expression without vulgarity.

Graciela came from a background where a 1930s rumba, "El Plato Roto," spoke of a broken hymen. It was one of many risqué numbers that, like spice, were welcome ingredients in Cuba's everyday life and torrid musical climate. It recalls a more restrained, delightful combination of feminine musical beauty, the eleven-piece Retunda All-Girl Orchestra, whose redolence infused Havana in the forties, as did that of **Orquesta Anacaona,** which of course, featured Graciela.

THE DANCE FLOOR, LIKE THE BAND STAND AT THE OLD LA CONGA NIGHTCLUB
WAS THE SIZE OF A POSTAGESTAMP. PERFORMING DURING THE POPULAR RUMBA
MATINEES OF THE EARLY FORTIES, NORO MORALES HAD TO SIT SIDE-SADDLE
AT HIS PIANO DUE TO HIS CORPULENCE AND THE CRAMPED ANGLE. THE PATRONS
CAME FROM THE NEARBY FUR MARKET, GARMENT CENTER AND MILLENARY DISTRICT.
THESE WERE THE JEWISH BOSSES WITH THEIR ITALIAN MODELS. FOUR HUGE
"PALM TREES" DOMINATED THE DECOR. TWENTY FOUR ROUND TABLES SEATING
FOUR WERE SET SO CLOSELY THAT CONVERSATIONS AND CASUAL COMMENTS OVER-
LAPPED ADDING TO A CLOSE CONGENIALITY EVEN AMONG BUSINESS COMPETITORS.

"RUMBAMBOLA" HAD JUST ENDED. THE PERSPIRING DANCERS WRIGGLED THEIR
WAY BACK TO THEIR TABLES LIKE BOUNCING BALLS. IN SPITE OF THE A/C ON
FULL BLAST, EVERYONE IN THE CLUB WAS WRINGING WET. WITH A CLEVER
CHANGE OF PACE, NORO WENT INTO "RUMBA RUMBERO" CAUSING THE EXHAUSTED
COUPLES TO GULP DOWN THEIR DRINKS IN ORDER TO HURRY BACK ONTO THE FLOOR.
ONE MIGHT SAY THIS WAS BAD FOR BUSINESS IN A WAY. AS SOON AS YOU SAT
DOWN, YOU WERE UP AGAIN LIKE PUPPETS ON A STRING, MANIPULATED BY THE
CORDS OF MUSICAL MAGNETISM. YOU WERE STILL JUMPING IN BED THAT NIGHT.

WHEN IT BECAME TIME TO CLEAR OUT FOR THE DINNER CROWD(WHO HAD COME TO
SEE CARMEN AMAYA, DIOSA COSTELLO, JOSE GRECO, PEDRO FLORES OR PEDRO
RAMIREZ OR TONDALEYO),THE PATRONS WERE SLOW TO LEAVE. IT WAS LIKE
EMERGING FROM A THEATER INTO SUNLIGHT. YOU WERE A PERFORMER! A STAR!
ONE FELT A RELUCTANCE, A DISBELIEF, LIKE A SHOCKING CONCLUSION. YOU
FELT THAT "I WANT MORE" FEELING UNTIL THE RHYTHYM SLOWLY EVAPORATED
AS YOU WALKED DISTRACTEDLY DOWN BROADWAY. THESE WERE THE SAME PEOPLE
WHO ARRIVED EARLY WHEN THE DOORS OPENED AND WHILE THE BAND HAD NOT AS YET
SHOWED UP, THE SAME PEOPLE WHO WOULD BRAVE THE HEAVIEST RAINSTORM TO
DANCE CARRYING UMBRELLAS INTO THE CLUB. ONCE SETTLED, THEY WOULD
WATCH THE MUSICIANS COME IN CARRYING THEIR INSTRUMENTS OVER THE HEADS
OF THOSE AT THE TABLES. THEY WOULD WATCH THE BAND ASSEMBLE. TESTING,
TUNING, GREETING ONE ANOTHER, THE MUSICIANS WERE GODS,
A CONGREGATION OF TALENT. WHEN THE BONGOSERO LIT HIS STERNO, YOU KNEW
YOU WERE IN FOR A HOT TIME. NORO, SEATED CALMLY AT THE PIANO, THE
DANCERS HUSHED AT THE TABLES, IT WAS FULL ARTISTIC APPRECIATION TO
WATCH THINGS FALL INTO PLACE. THIS PERFORMANCE REACHED ITS CLIMACTIC
MOMENT WHEN NORO WOULD RAISE HIS HAND AS IF TO SAY, AS THEY DO AT
THE LINDY 500, "GENTLEMEN, START YOUR ENGINES".

When I was a year old, Mr. William Randolph Hearst awarded me
a medal. He was running for president and the medal was a political
gimmick. To win voters, he opened "Milk Stations" with medals for
the fattest baby. In order to win, my parents fed me milk until I
was like a cow fattened for the slaughter. When my eyes became slits,
they called me "chink", a racist label attached to the Chinese in
the twenties. As I grew into manhood, the label stuck. Although
it was like living a lie, I went along with it philosophically.

In the mid-forties, the streets of Greenwich Village were empty.
"We have it in our power to begin the world over again", said patriot
Tom Paine, years earlier. Wonderful things could have happened to our
society, our world, with just a lucky shove from destiny. We already
possessed a spirit of bohemian rebellion. There was an attitude of
refined curiousity and wholesome optimism after the war. Kafka still
amused us, Orwell was still far off and "Brave New World" scared and
fascinated us. Sadly, we had not read sufficient history in America.
There was no Chopin or Verdi to compose an anthem for us, or an
Anton Dvorak to lend us militancy. Our literature was not Jeffersonian.
Like a circle of self-deluded poets, we assembled in Washington Square
Park. We were "rebels" but rebels who are today obliged to live in
an artful culture with commercial overload and a plastic philosophy.

Recently, I visited my old friend, Jose (Buyú) Mangual at
Mother Gabrini Hospital. Casually asking his nurse whether she knew
who her patient was, she replied that she didn't. "He is the world's
greatest bongo player", I said.Buyu's eyes had been closed all the
while I was in the room. He suddenly opened them and with a smile
on his face, he closed them for the last time.

"The last thing we possess is our philosophy", Anatole Broyard
once told me. But I would prefer to possess Buyu's contentment..
his rapturous response. Like the masons who built the Gothic Cathedrals, he had spent an entire life building a monument to his own
musical legacy. His was an enviable life based on truth more than on
a philosophy. His was an enviable finale.

What Music Is About

Among the ten top artistic directors and orchestral conductors is **Daniel Barenboim**, earning two million dollars a year, or should we say a season. In fact, these ten lucky individuals take in over ten million dollars in salaries! Not bad for a clique of sophisticated elitists in the symphonic and operatic establishments. Fundraising gala performances could use some housecleaning. Charity begins at home and should end in the street, where it will do the most good. To the people!

Are the complexities of Mahler's Ninth Symphony any more challenging than a salsa montuno performed by **Rene Lopez**'s twelve-piece orchestra, where a close listener can catch experimental, classical, serial, modern and postmodern influences?

Music should serve to spread the maximum good the greatest audience. It should best be out of Lincoln Center's grasp and out in the street for the people, by the people and of the people...a birthright. For every black tie fan attending the annual Mostly Mozart festival, a thousand Latinos are enjoying Marc Anthony's latest hit.

A worldwide survey found **Puerto Rico** to be No. 1, the happiest place on earth. Is it because many poor families harbor at least one musician or more? More than an evening's gala is present night and day in the Latin music that is in the air one breathes...out in the streets of P.R. It is not in the snooty confines of academic strongholds that are constantly begging for donations to stay alive while attendance dwindles. Is this not a good example of snobbism, where unknown names perform unknown opuses to a restricted, mostly tax-sheltered "select" audience?

When the average music teacher struggles to secure pupils that struggle to afford lessons themselves, this in itself restricts not only the appreciation of music but also its influence. Money should not only go into offering scholarships but also into making musical instruments available like library books to students who cannot afford to buy them, like giving them chances to learn how to fish, instead of giving a handout.

René And Estella

THE FORTIES WERE BECOMING WITTY COMPARED TO THE PRESENT SILLY CENTURY. FED BY COMMERCIAL OVERLOAD, AN ARTFUL CULTURE AND OBLIGED TO EMBRACE A PLASTIC PHILOSOPHY BASED ON SLOGANS, WE NEVERTHELESS CONSIDER OURSELVES "REBELS".

The singer's name was: DOROTEO SANTIAGO

Vince made his way to this venue for several weeks. But one of the issues he had was that by the time everything was winding down, he'd have to make the looooooooooooong trek back from the Bronx to Manhattan and into Brooklyn. In those days, there were not as many subway cars running as there are today, and standing on those platforms for long hours were pretty exhausting, not to mention dangerous. He would always arrive home at sunrise. So he discontinued his trips and began to tune into his [illegible] radio. In 1939, there was a show that was broadcast live from the Escambron club in Puerto Rico where he would be able to hear "La Musica" directly. As he recalled, many times Vincent's father would often yell "Turn off that racket! I'm trying to get some sleep here @#$%^!!" Which prompted Vincent to place his radio directly upon his ear so as not to disturb anyone else, and simultaneously get his musical fix.

Jose Mangual Sr. gave him a call and asked him:

"Hey wha' happen? Where ju be?...".

Vincent explains to "Buyu" that as much as he loved to expwerience the music, the trip to the club in the Bronx was too much of a hassle for him. He was also in the process of moving to a new apartment in his home away from home, NY's Greenwich Village.

Mangual told him: "So'kay, no pro'lem! All ju have to do is go uptown. I go to be at the Teatro Hispano and later despues I go to next door and go play with anoder conjunto. Ju go?...".

Vincent was excited as the address of the location was far more easily accessible to him than the venue in the Bronx. The address was 110th Street & 5th Avenue. The place was the Park Palace Ballroom. When he arrived, he realized he was now in the Promised Land. Afro-Cuban music in full effect. "La Musica," as he affectionately called it, was being celebrated and was in all it's glory. EVERYONE dancing. There were Jews. African-Americans. Latinos. Even his Italian compatriots were there. And right on stage was his good friend Jose "Buyu" Mangual Sr., nodding his head towards him in acknowledgement and playing tumbadora with a band known as LOS HAPPY BOYS.

"Vaya! Ju said ju was gonna come. And ju come...." said Mangual to Livelli.

The band played everything. Sones, Rumbas, Guarachas. Even a Waltz!!

Livelli wanted to show his friends -- a crew that included the novelist and critic (N.Y. TIMES)
Anatole Broyard, the poet Delmore Schwartz, and author William Gaddis -- the *2 TIME WINNER OF THE NATIONAL BOOK AWARD*

Park Palace, the dancehall he had been frequenting with his Puerto Rican

girlfriend. The Park Palace was a Jewish-owned catering hall on 110th Street

that, with the Jewish population in East Harlem in decline, was often rented out

by African-American and Latino entrepreneurs and groups from the Masons to

the Fire Department. The club had developed something of a rough reputation,

but it was the place to see the music he'd fallen for in the raw.

"We took two taxi loads up to Harlem," Livelli remembers. "At that time, 114th St.

was the most dangerous street in the city. The Depression was still in full force

up there, the people on the street were hungry. Then, just as we were going in

the door, we saw people running madly out of the place. My friends said, 'We're

not going in there!' and just turned around and went back to the Village. I acted

cool. The fights at the Park Palace came with the territory *RARE* -- my girlfriend carried

a razor in her garter."

        THEY MAY HAVE DRESSED BETTER THAN I BUT I LOOKED BETTER ON THE
DANCE FLOOR WHERE STYLE WAS IMPORTANT. THERE'S LOTS TO BE LEARNED
FROM THESE EXAGERRATED INDIVIDUALS. BUT IT MAY BE TOO LATE FOR LEARNING.
NOT ONE OF THESE CELEBRITIES IS ALIVE TODAY EXCEPT IN NAME AND FAME.
"IF YOU'RE SO FORTUNATE MEETING THESE RARE PEOPLE, THESE SUCCESSFUL
TYPES, WHY AREN'T YOU RICH?",I'M SURE FRIENDS WONDER ABOUT ME. I AM
UNABLE TO ACCOUNT FOR THIS. THERE ARE FEW MILLIONAIR DANCERS OR RICH
MUSICIANS. IS IT ALWAYS A QUESTION OF VALUES? TODAY, WE ARE ALL IN
THE SAME FIX, CELEB OR EVERYDAY GUY. UNAUTHORIZED FIREWORKS ARE PRO-
HIBITED THIS FOURTH OF JULY BECAUSE SUCH DISPLAY MIGHT INCREASE THE
DANGER IN OUR LIVES. PERMIT US A BIT OF MORBID CURIOUSITY. IF WE
ARE HIT WITH AN "ORANGE FLASH", THE RICH AND POOR ALIKE, WILL THIS
DRAMATIC THEATRICAL HAPPENING HAVE A REDEEMING ASPECT? IF WE CONSIDER
IT ALL AS HISTORICALLY INEVITABLE THEN WE ARE TRUELY LIVING IN VERY
NOVEL TIMES..AND NOVELTY IS WHAT CELEBRITY IS ALL ABOUT.

PATAKIN

PATAKIN fue formado por Louis Bauzó en 1984. El grupo presenta diferentes estilos de música afrocubana, desde la rumba hasta la música y el baile sagrados de santería. La participación de cubanos y puertorriqueños en este grupo refleja la importancia y la popularidad de dichas formas en ambas comunidades.

PATAKIN was formed by Louis Bauzó in 1984. The group performs different styles of Afro-Cuban music and dance from rumba to the sacred music and dance of Santería. The participation of Cubans and Puerto Ricans in this group reflects the importance and popularity of these forms for both communities.

INTERPRETES / *PERFORMERS*

Lázaro Galaraga	Reynaldo Rivera	Yvette Martínez	Frankie Malabé	Greg Askew
Louis Bauzó	Nydia Ocasio	Reynaldo Alcántara	Ray Romero	Edwin Rodríguez

Santería

En Nueva York, la santería es una expresión religiosa importante de los cubanos, puertorriqueños y otras nacionalidades, para las que la música cumple una función central. La santería tiene su origen en las prácticas y creencias del pueblo Yoruba de Africa Occidental. Como consecuencia de la trata de esclavos, los sistemas de creencias yoruba y de otros pueblos africanos fueron traidos al Nuevo Mundo. La santería y demás sociedades secretas tales como el Abakuá, desarrolladas durante los tiempos de la esclavitud, surgieron en Cuba después de dicha época. Las creencias de la santería se caracterizan por complejas relaciones entre la naturaleza, el concepto sobre la creación del mundo, el hombre y el panteón de deidades conocidas como orishas. Cada orisha está relacionada con mitos,

Santería

Santería is an important religious expression of Cubans, Puerto Ricans and other peoples in New York in which music functions as a central feature. *Santería* derives from beliefs and practices of the Yoruba people of West Africa. As a result of the slave trade Yoruba and other African belief systems were brought to the New World. Evolving during slavery, *Santeria* and other secret societies such as *Abakuá*, emerged in post-slavery Cuba. *Santeria* beliefs are characterized by complex relationships among nature, concepts about the creation of the world, man, and the pantheon of deities known as *orishas*. Each *orisha* is associated with myths, colors, elements of nature and musical forms. During ritual events, called *tóques* and *bembés*, an *orisha* may manifest itself in human form through possession of a

9

Carrousel Opening Heads Week's Night Club Event

Ha! Ha!, Club In Hollywood Also Bids For Pre Season Patronage; Bali Plans New Entertainment

By PETER PELL

Ben Brooks' Carrousel will reopen tomorrow nigh starting its second winter season. The huge, colorful roo has undergone several alterations, among them the additic of a new theater-stage, replacing the tiny platform of la year; a larger dance floor, and a Zombie room and bar c the balcony, the latter being a creation of Bob Feinstein.

Heading the entertainment will be Johnny Austrian's 10-piece orchestra and Sanchez' rumba band. Henry Fink will be emcee. Conga and rumba dance offerings will be handled by Pepito and Carmen, who will lead a troup of eight. The Carrousel has signed Ina Ray Hutton and the Valero Sisters for late December openings.

LA CONGA

[193

By VINCENT LI VELLI

(Brooklyn College)

Mr. Mario Tossatti has mad New York Conga—concious. The success of the second La Conga Restaurant has been due to the contagious qualities of conga music, as well as to the ability of Mr. Tossatti.

Those of us who follow the Conga and the Rhumba must applaud his efforts in championing entertainment of the Latin type. Burlesque floor shows, swing bands, tap-dancing etc. will soon all bow to the beat of a Conga drum, for what they offer reach only our outer edges— the ears and the eyes, but not the soul. Who can hear "Allegre Conga" and not feel happy?

There is an element present in music in Afro-Cuban rythmn that has the cure for the "unhappy" condition of the world.

Cuba's Cohesive Tumbao

Music is poetry in the air.... J. P. Richter

Nowhere is music more in the air than in Cuba, where the lowliest solo musician is a poet. When combined, these poets produce a *weltweisheit*...a philosophy of contentment that gives music a high priority in every Cuban's everyday life. The "Blue Danube," the waltz that swept Europe, made Vienna that gayest capital of its time. Havana may not be the gayest capital, but its music has no borders. They use their music as medicine to handle their misfortunes the way Neopolitans do..."O Sole Mio" traveled around the world but is mostly forgotten, like Argentina's tango, "Comparsita." Parma, the birthplace of Verdi's twenty-four operas, is called the City of Music, like Strauss's Salzburg, but one simple melody, "The Peanut Vendor," put Havana on the map. Paris, famous for la Gaiete Parisienne, produced the cancan, and rests on its laurels like New Orleans after Mardi Gras. The Rio Carnival is incomparable but, seemingly exhausted, retires to prepare for next year. Spanish gypsies provide excitement and merriment like the Russians and Hungarians but are basically tragically oriented with their musical bipolarity. Germany's music may start you marching but salsa stirs your toes. The Irish, like the Greeks who dance in circles, need a pint to get on the dance floor. Japan's rock and roll is imitative and in Hong Kong the sound of the cash register is music. When Um Kulsum sang in Cairo, the Muslim world came to a halt, but she is gone. Truly irresistible music is rare and most music is not. In Brazil, samba does not serve to bring sufficient joy into the life of the average Carioca the way salsa has in Cuba and Puerto Rico, where its mystique is well understood.

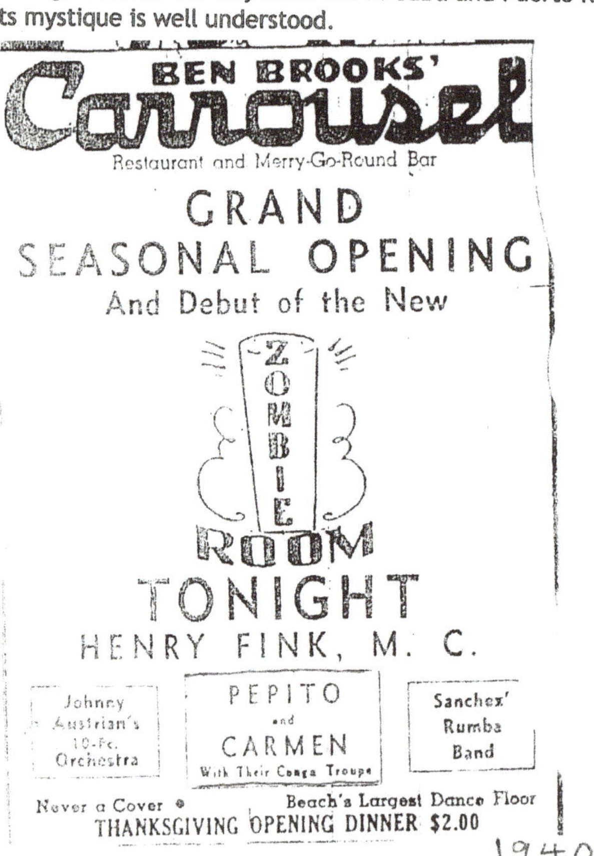

Musical Missionary

At the beginning of the last century, many Anglicans left New England bound for Hawaii, the islands of the Pacific, and China. They were **missionaries** trained in medicine who were seeking to save souls by distributing Bibles and healing the sick. Often among hostile populations, they were not always welcomed. Like the early Jesuits who spread out in Southeast Asia and Japan, they were hoping for converts. In Honolulu, someone told me, "We exchanged our land for their Bibles."

Ever since a *santero*, Juan Besson, told me that I would "carry this music around the world," I have distributed cassettes instead of Bibles to everyone who would listen to my message. I even left them in hotel rooms, like the Gideon Society leaves the New Testament. The message, or as it is called, the "good news," that I preach through Latin music is something that goes like this: "God loves music." If God is love then music is love in its most harmonious form. Where harmony is absent, love is absent. St. Paul, the fisher of men, sent Epistles all around the Mediterranean world, obeying the command of a higher power. When you hear Latin music, it is like a command to rise up and dance. For me, the music turned me into a professional dancer. But it was the command of the santero that was a religious experience that turned me into a "musical missionary."

There is a Cuban song that says, *por vivir en quinto patio / desprecias mis besos.* Basically, "You disrespect me because I am poor." Referring to the eighteen-hour documentary called *Jazz*, it is obvious to the thirty million Latinos in the USA that they are not only ignored by are used to benefit jazz. Latinos have been (ever since **Mario Bauzá** composed "Tanga," a piece rarely heard and one that jazz influenced to its detriment) "Los Amigos Invisibles" of the jazzistas. Things are changing it seems and the complacent invisible friends are emerging from the shadow that jazz cast upon them unjustifiably. The January 28 issue of *Variety* says that "The Business Now Loves the Latins." Jennifer Lopez just beat out the number one Beatles and she, like Ricky Martin, is not a true Latina. Another tune called "Cuando Llegará" can be answered now: "Ya Llegó."

To close this sermon, let me quote from Luis Pales-Matos: *"Ahi vienen los tambores! Ten Cuidado hombre blanco, que a ti llegan para clavarte su aguijón de música...te picará un tambor de danza o Guerra."*

7/19/2007 2:44 PM

We were dancing the conga on the roof of the Semiramis Hotel in Cairo when suddenly all hell broke loose. The Egyptians began shooting off fireworks, celebrating the British evacuation of the Sudan. Cheers and laughter greeted explosions, until sparks, smoke, and flames began to fall at our feet. The band kept playing and the drummer accented each burst as we began to hop and leap with every explosion like rabbits. You could say the place was really jumping that night.

More peaceful and relaxed moments on the dance floor were spent at the Rainbow Room where everyone behaved properly, unaware that they were dancing on turf owned by the Mafia management at that time.

At the Waldorf's Sert Room, Xavier Cugat presented Miguelito Valdez singing, *Babalu*. Miguel had just broken down the strict hotel policy of "no persons of color." In celebration, I got on the floor doing a <u>wild</u> rumba with my partner. The management *asked* me to leave the dance floor.

They keep the world resounding within Nature's super bowl environment. They support a mystery that sings for humanity. They seem chosen.

As an orchestral organ when silenced or expressed, the forte music of Life comes to us as grief or as gaiety from the heart. That internal metronome and ultimate timer is also a sounding board where the vibratos, crescendos, and tremolos of daily life are played by impulse, much of which is for our ears alone.

Imagine an integration of DaVinci and Vasily Kandinsky, of Franz Liszt and Hindemith, or Calder and Rodin — interesting, but one does not mess with the heart or with its music, especially since all musicians are brothers.

We are all born only once, or are some of us born "twice?" Jesus was born, died and was born again as the Christ we know today. In order to perform miracles one has to be a miracle personified and in order to become a living miracle such as Jesus, one must first die and be reborn.

When I lost my hearing and much of my ability to think and react normally, I was dead from the neck up, if not entirely so. My world was unlike others for a purpose that was to become clear to me with time. It took years to become evident to me that, like Jesus, I had a mission to perform before dying like everyone else _NORMALLY_. Because this is all virgin territory I cannot set a date but I will give the cause- "natural causes" will be on my death certificate.

What miracles can I perform knowing the power I possess, having been "born," "died," and born again? Preachers are inspired and some claim success at healing. There are cases of miraculous healing powers after the person with such power disappears after the fact, after having appeared seemingly out of nowhere. LIKE GOOD SAMARITANS,

What I can see myself doing in this world of miracles is coming to the aid of not only a needy fellow human but of all humanity. To succeed in such a challenge requires a universal phenomenon, This I call Afro Cuban TUMBAO* for once it IS UNDERSTOOD worldwide, it will be the equivalent of Nirvana, the Buddhists requirement for

* VIBRATING SOUND WAVES.

against physics and the physical world and the laws involved. The tricks that can be repeated are not miracles. To be born is miraculous, but the true miracle occurs only once. The second occurrence of one's life is ALSO A miracle. SUCH AS RECOVERING FROM "DEAD FROM THE NECK UP", TO NORMALCY, MY LIFE WAS ERASED BY DEAFNESS ONLY TO BE RESTORED FOR A PURPOSE AND THAT IS TO "CARRY LA MUSICA AROUND THE WORLD" WHICH IS WHAT I HAVE DONE OUT OF OBEDIENCE TO SANTARIA'S REMOTE CONTROL

Vincent Livelli
44 Perry Street
New York, New York 10014
212-255-0508

4-13-2015

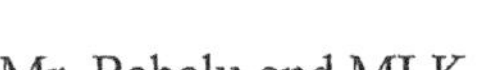

Mr. Babalu and MLK.

by
Vincent Livelli

Due to the destruction of my hearing, the world might just a well have been a frozen block of ice. A door was shut on the outside world and I was a shut-in. While the condition deteriorated I was unaware that it even existed. Loud noises further injured my aural nerve but at the same time made me aware of what I was missing. Out there were the drums that carried messages unlike more pleasant everyday normal or average reality. Drums spoke of hardships, slavery, injustice and rebellion. I heard from a more personal angle of what was in the offering approaching us. (1960's)

The civil rights movement began not in Selma but in the sugar mills of the Caribbean. In the U.S. south, women and children picked cotton where as in the islands of the West Indies, men cut down miles of sugarcane tracts under torturous conditions. In Cuba, two voices, namely, Mr. Babalu (Miguelito Valdez and Chano Pozo) sang out in agony. The music set the Afro Cuban rhythm in place to march to, while the lyrics added verbal content that solidified hopes and dreams one sang. Bruce Manigua hit everyone in the solar plexis regardless of one's racial componenet. Freedom is oxygen enshrined. It was Miguelito Valdes whose lyrics said, "Déjame morir!" (let me die!), at a time when Cuban music was romantically oriented and at a period when a slave was too valuable to allow suicide. He couldn't escape even through death.

Reading about slavery, listening to recordings like Bruce Manigua that began to take hold in 1937 on my conscience only needed to fall in step with the physical manifestation, the equivalent of the protest march, which I joined during the Carnival in Havana in 1940. This magnificent spectacle broke down centuries of injustices. You felt freedom released from its cage.

Miguel's songs sung in African foreign languages like Yoruba are like another different form of music. Sounds with meanings were now new sharps and flats in a musical sentence. The meaning ws in the climax that emphasizes the purpose desired. This may mean protest agreement, love, sympathy, or more subtle "entendres". It may be an artificial approach to understanding like sign language, but the person exposed to sound without audible words involved can hear beyond the limits of habit and academic instructions. Plug both your ears tightly and you can still hear this unused ability that has kept mankind ignorant of a means of communication without language proper. Similar to animal's behavior and more based on intuition's magic, like a grasp of life's future with unknown dimensions. Intuition is a lie-detector that reads the mind! What a blessing that could be for humanity.

What Dr. Martin Luther Kings called a dream was Miguelito's "Bruca Manigua" v

spun rapidly back up-right like a top, moving in very close to maximize velocity as a flashy finish. The music was at a very slow tempo so that the furiously spinning upright return was made all the more dramatic. He followed this with his handkerchief dance display, which also had never before been seen in New York. Picking it up off the floor with his teeth while doing a summersault in an all white suit was a high-class finale for an act full of quality and invention, elaborate as well as authentic. Meanwhile, Estela was a picture of poise, grace, and nobility—in fact, they were both Afro-Cuban royalty!

At the Park Plaza, the dance floor resembled a rush hour A train, except that the dancers were not stepping on toes. They were the very best dancers in that winter of 1938-39. The dancers named "Eléctrico," "Midnight" and "Chino" (and even an anonymous *mulata* lady who was on crutches) were competing during continuous applause from the onlookers' nonstop encouragement. Normally, though, there were no formal dance competitions back then at the Park Plaza, as there would be later at the Palladium.

The sweet scent of the tobacco of the tropics came up from the basement lounges, blending with the cologne in vogue, called Tabú. Most of the dancers were from the area around 116th Street (the main street before 125th Street became known as such), and from 114th Street. They were frenetic and exuberant under the spell of a band that brought them "home," to the islands of their enchantment, unlike the latter day Studio 54 club that set dancers adrift, lost in space. What attracted me to the Park Plaza was its unassuming simplicity, the atmosphere set by its hardcore dancers and crowded, scuffed floor. It felt authentic, there was no "glitz" at this venue, which seemed closer to the heart, soul, and sound of the music. There was a much fancier ballroom upstairs, with a separate entrance to the left, called the Park Palace, but that did not interest me as it was far too big, well lit, with deluxe décor and a shiny floor. At the Plaza, unlike the Palladium—which came later, was a giant room, and seemed such a self-conscious scene—everyone was more satisfied with themselves. The young danced with the old, in more of a neighborhood family environment. People were better behaved there. The young Latinos of El Barrio during the Depression could not afford to go in the more expensive downtown clubs (nor would they be admitted), so the scene at the Plaze was more conservative because they were dancing among their elders. The young girls were so shapely in their homemade, well-fitted dresses; the sharp guys sporting their black and white shoes, the mark of an accomplished *rumbero*. Heavily slicked-back hair managed to overcome the huge fan that was intended to cool off overheated dancers who possessed the stamina of prizefighters. There were two bouncer alarms (one in the front, the other back of the dance floor) that were heard in response to occasional trouble among the patrons.

As one of the sole sources of gaiety during thirty-percent unemployment in America, the Park Plaza's rumba world was vital. At a time when you would be asked to "please leave the dance floor" if your dancing was indiscreet

LA PLAYA DANCE TEAM
RUMBA CASINO 1939
WEST END, N. J.

universal harmony based on compassion and altruism- something that can be identified with precis, harmonic sound waves, the brain of all alpha and omega.

Why Afro-Cuban music? Because it is born from suffering- the plight of black slaves, millions of them. Their cries reached out as sound waves and "arias". Like preachers with miraculous cures that they achieve through the sound of their sermons, coupled with their personal powers that could include having been born twice, AS DISEMBODIED INFLUENCE

Some preachers may not know of it and accept their gift as itself miraculous, whereas it is actually a result of having been chosen for the task. Chosen by and how is where the creator comes into the picture. Time and place are the basic necessities for astrological phenomena. Events are created by the alignment of planets controlled by gravity and are the creator of all that occurs everywhere.

These far out fanciful speculations can get your interest going in a new direction, but without the minimal substantiations these scholarly considerations end up empty. If we need miracles badly enough like communal praying in the recovery of a selected patient, the miracle we are also at the same time seeking is not only the recovery of the patient but perhaps more startling, the appearance of a miracle itself.

When born for a second time, the person occupies a changed reality that is unlike any of his/her fellow humans. REALITY.

EACH DAY When you awake from sleep you are in a new reality, one that you had no problem doing WHILE ASLEEP without. But the "Big Sleep" separates you entirely from all that constitutes reality. This temporary absence allows whatever was, to emerge under different circumstances. This is where the miracle can become a reality prayer. It is what Einstein would call, a leap in the fabric of time. A "pause" allows the magician the time to perform his slight-of-hand. A miracle is a trick

THE DANCE FLOOR, LIKE THE BAND STAND AT THE OLD LA CONGA NIGHTCLUB
WAS THE SIZE OF A POSTAGESTAMP. PERFORMING DURING THE POPULAR RUMBA
MATINEES OF THE EARLY FORTIES, NORO MORALES HAD TO SIT SIDE-SADDLE
AT HIS PIANO DUE TO HIS CORPULENCE AND THE CRAMPED ANGLE. THE PATRONS
CAME FROM THE NEARBY FUR MARKET, GARMENT CENTER AND MILLENARY DISTRICT.
THESE WERE THE JEWISH BOSSES WITH THEIR ITALIAN MODELS. FOUR HUGE
"PALM TREES" DOMINATED THE DECOR. TWENTY FOUR ROUND TABLES SEATING
FOUR WERE SET SO CLOSELY THAT CONVERSATIONS AND CASUAL COMMENTS OVER-
LAPPED ADDING TO A CLOSE CONGENIALITY EVEN AMONG BUSINESS COMPETITORS.

"RUMBAMBOLA" HAD JUST ENDED. THE PERSPIRING DANCERS WRIGGLED THEIR
WAY BACK TO THEIR TABLES LIKE BOUNCING BALLS. IN SPITE OF THE A/C ON
FULL BLAST, EVERYONE IN THE CLUB WAS WRINGING WET. WITH A CLEVER
CHANGE OF PACE, NORO WENT INTO "RUMBA RUMBERO" CAUSING THE EXHAUSTED
COUPLES TO GULP DOWN THEIR DRINKS IN ORDER TO HURRY BACK ONTO THE FLOOR.
ONE MIGHT SAY THIS WAS BAD FOR BUSINESS IN A WAY. AS SOON AS YOU SAT
DOWN, YOU WERE UP AGAIN LIKE PUPPETS ON A STRING, MANIPULATED BY THE
CORDS OF A MUSICAL MAGNETISM. YOU WERE STILL JUMPING IN BED THAT NIGHT.

WHEN IT BECAME TIME TO CLEAR OUT FOR THE DINNER CROWD(WHO HAD COME TO
SEE CARMEN AMAYA, DIOSA COSTELLO, JOSE GRECO, PEDRO FLORES OR PEDRO
RAMIREZ OR TONDALEYO),THE PATRONS WERE SLOW TO LEAVE. IT WAS LIKE
EMERGING FROM A THEATER INTO SUNLIGHT. YOU WERE A PERFORMER! A STAR!
ONE FELT A RELUCTANCE, A DISBELIEF LIKE A SHOCKING CONCLUSION. YOU
FELT THAT "I WANT MORE" FEELING UNTIL THE RHYTHYM SLOWLY EVAPORATED
AS YOU WALKED DISTRACTEDLY DOWN BROADWAY. THESE WERE THE SAME PEOPLE
WHO ARRIVED EARLY WHEN THE DOORS OPENED AND WHILE THE BAND HAD NOT AS YET
SHOWED UP. THE SAME PEOPLE WHO WOULD BRAVE THE HEAVIEST RAINSTORM TO
DANCE CARRYING UMBRELLAS INTO THE CLUB. ONCE SETTLED, THEY WOULD
WATCH THE MUSICIANS COME IN CARRYING THEIR INSTRUMENTS OVER THE HEADS
OF THOSE AT THE TABLES. THEY WOULD WATCH THE BAND ASSEMBLE. TESTING,
TUNING,TALKING AND TURNING TO ONE ANOTHER, THE MUSICIANS WERE GOD-LIKE,
A CONGREGATION OF TALENT. WHEN THE BONGOSERO LIT HIS STERNO, YOU KNEW
YOU WERE IN FOR A HOT TIME. NORO, SEATED CALMLY AT THE PIANO, THE
DANCERS HUSHED AT THE TABLES, IT WAS FULL ARTISTIC APPRECIATION TO
WATCH THINGS FALL INTO PLACE. THIS PERFORMANCE REACHED ITS CLIMACTIC
MOMENT WHEN NORO WOULD RAISE HIS HAND AS IF TO SAY, AS THEY DO AT
THE LINDY 500, "GENTLEMEN, START YOUR ENGINES".

TITO PUENTE

ONE MATINEE, A SHORT GOOD LOOKING SEVENTEEN YEAR OLD WAS SEEN CUTTING HIS WAY THROUGH THE TABLES. HE WAS CARRYING SOMETHING HALF HIDDEN ON HIS WAY TO THE REAR OF THE BANDSTAND. HE DID THIS WITHOUT DISTURBING THE MOOD OF THE MOMENT WHICH HAPPENED TO BE A ROMANTIC "PRECIOSO BOLERO". NO DOUBT HE HAD COME, NOT TO SIT IN WITH THE BAND, BUT TO PRACTICE HIS BONGOS WITH NORO'S APPROVAL. HE SAT OFF THE BANDSTAND IN A CORNER AS THOUGH HIDDEN. IT WAS THE FIRST TIME I HEARD SOMEONE SAY, "TITO PUENTE".

THE NEXT TIME I SAW HIM WAS AT THE PAPAGALLO BAR AT THE AVILA HOTEL IN CARACAS. HE PLAYED THE CARNIVAL EVERY YEAR. WE SPOKE OF THE BILLO BOYS AND VENEZUELA'S GROWING MUSICAL INFLUENCE. THE THIRD TIME WAS AT THE ST. REGIS HOTEL BAR. HE WAS KIND ENOUGH TO GREET ME AND MY LADY FRIEND. HAVING TITO PUENTE EMBRACE YOU IN FRONT OF YOUR DATE IS INDEED A COOL OCCURANCE, A FORTICIOUS HAPPENSTANCE. THE FOURTH TIME WAS AT THE BOYS HARBOR CONSERVANCY. HE WAS ON HIS WAY TO GIVE HIS PERCUSSION LESSONS TO THE NEIGHBORHOOD KIDS, WITH HIS MANAGER, JOE CONZO. I COMPLAINED TO THEM THAT CONTRIBUTIONS TO THE TITO PUENTE SCHOLARSHIP FUND WERE NOT GOING EXCLUSIVELY TO PUERTO RICAN YOUNGSTERS AS I HAD BELIEVED. THE NEXT AND LAST TIME I SAW HIM HE WAS LYING IN STATE. HE HAD JOINED MUSIC'S HISTORIC NOBILITY. UTTERING "DESCANSE, O REY DEL TIMBAL", I TURNED AWAY CARRYING THE MEDALLION OF HIS MEMORY PINNED SECURELY TO MY HEART.

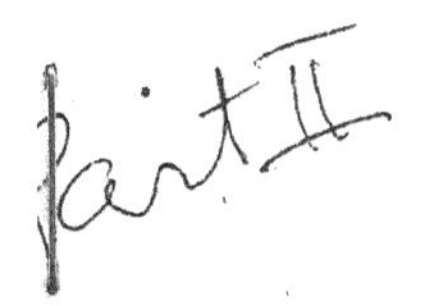

The Park Plaza

There was no mike, bandstand, spotlight, or amplifier, but two alarm bells were posted in opposite corners to alert the bouncers to where the trouble was. The printed exit sign was not lit and no fire safety equipment was to be seen. The emergency exit was surely locked to prevent illegal entry. It opened onto a narrow alley that was shared with the neighboring Teatro Hispanico, and ended out on Fifth Avenue. The entrance to the Park Plaza was through a narrow hallway, typical of Harlem buildings. On the left, a narrow stairway went up to the larger Park Palace Ballroom, which had better lighting, large windows, and twice the space, plus a bandstand with a mike. The lavatories were sanitary and brightly lit. We remember our preferring the Plaza.

Four iron columns supported the ceiling on the dance floor of the Park Plaza. The one in the darkest corners served as much to hold up the ceiling as to provide a bolster for the woman while her partner pressed his body against hers, grinding away in keeping with the music. Couples took turns. It took some skill to reach gratification before the song being played ended and the floor emptied. This unacceptable behavior was mostly conveniently ignored or politely overlooked as the exception rather than the rule. This, it must be remembered, was at a time when rooftops were obligatory venues for lovers.

"It's safer inside than outside," I told my friend Anatole Broyard, as we planned to bring some Villagers to the Park Plaza. We organized two taxi loads after briefing the party concerning proper behavior and safety measures regarding jewelry, etc. Like subway tracks in the thirties, taxi meters made loud clicking noises. We arrived in high spirits, tipping the drivers — ten cents each, the standard tip during the Great Depression, regardless of the distance traveled.

. . . making a bit of uneasiness among friends as we entered the hallway entrance to pay our admissions. Suddenly, a commotion arose inside, causing some screaming, followed by a minor stampede that plowed into our party. Half of our group ran back to the taxis and left, perhaps satisfied to do so.

With, I estimate, 200-300 Cuban and Puerto Ricans in the surrounding neighborhood, why was there never a long line waiting to enter? People desperate to dance were penniless. While some Greek and Roman stadiums and theaters charged admission, the old coliseum was free to all. Today we might consider this morale boosting as a project similar to City Meals-On-Wheels, part of a caring community that would also help unemployed musicians . . . and not a Lincoln Center scheme of some sort.

In the islands, dancing and swimming went together, as they do at Rio's Carnival when crowds swim along Copacabana to cool off, and return to continue festivities. Opposite the Park Plaza is Meer Lake. In 1939, there were three rowboats that we untied when the band took a break, allowing us to row out into the dark privacy of the middle of the lake under the stars, rowing back frantically when the sound of music came across the water to us.

In the Dominican Republic, behind the waterfront club Taino were shacks with mattresses for rent. In Montevideo dives, mattresses behind curtained areas on floor landings in the building served patrons. With no element of danger or stolen pleasure, unlike our rocking row boats, modern cruise ships are floating bedrooms with convenient cabins near your disco. Roman baths, Bangkok Brothels, Amsterdam walk in-walk out, Reno, Nevada ranches — none of these could give the romance of the open sky of Central Park's lake or the raw sex that took place against that iron column on the Park Plaza dance floor.

One of the more popular songs heard at the Plaza was "Camina Como Chencha." Chencha was a lame girl who was asked to dance every dance. This showed courage, spirit, determination, and a certain beautiful concern on the part of the males, who were determined to assure that she, in particular, enjoyed life, such as it was, in her condition. One night while saying good night to a friend living on West 114th Street, "the most dangerous street in the city," a woman ran screaming down the steps of the stoop we were on. She was being beaten by a man in front of us. Switchblades in '39 were today's box cutters. "We women carry razor blades," said my friend, showing me hers wrapped by a rubber band that she had hidden in her elastic stocking.

The enjoyment of having experienced an event like the Park Plaza compensated for having to go home by subway, or worse, for those who went to bed alone. It was when the trumpets fell silent and the bass began to pack, and the guitarists tip-toed off, that the show was over, honoring the piano that lastly tinkled good to the last note. Some New York Latin orchestras ended with "Good Night Irene." Once, while on the way out, I turned around to look at the dance floor. Nothing ever looked as vacant after that. It was a classic shock of recognition. So was the rest of the waiting world outside on West 110th Street, **where it was Ford Madox Ford's "Parade's End." [Vincent, tell me more about this!]**

The Park Plaza with the Afro-Cuban beat got a crippled country back on its feet, dancing! *Twisa Moungu, Echale Salsita,* Get Hot, Hot Shot, Hot Stuff, and that cool gal Hot Tomato, have become both hot and cool today, like those remarkable dancers at the old Park Plaza. We wonder whether our disco-club scene can do it, beginning with a cultural climate change.

Viva La Musica — Afro-Cubana!

The Park Plaza

When one steps outside the circle of the family and by doing so, encounters the true world for the first time, whatever knowledge gained in that way has a tremendous impact on the future course of one's life. Americans taking *le grand tour* of Europe returned home with a cultural concept with high values. Thus, we became a society interested in learning. Students today whose parents send them off to Cancun, Jamaica, or Nassau, for instance, expose these young minds to inferior influences. The students quickly adopt as part of their formation unrefined behavior, mediocre interests, and less sophisticated lifestyles.

Next to visiting a foreign country is the familiarization gained through the literature that country produces. Visiting the West Indian Islands, where literary achievement is scarce, it is *music* that has the power to influence and formulate the direction of one's life.

What has this to do with the Park Plaza? Like a first-time encounter with a foreign country, the Park Plaza dance hall in '37-'38 helped to fashion a more salutary individual, thanks to the musical education found there. I traveled to the Park Plaza searching for music of a certain flavor — Afro-Cuban. I couldn't dance a step, I didn't know a soul, couldn't understand a word, couldn't play a note, nor could I spare during the Great Depression the carfare and the admission. At a time when there was little joy in the world, the music gave me the reason I needed to set off from Fort Hamilton, Brooklyn up to Harlem when it was dangerous to do so.

I found what I was searching for the moment I heard the Happy Boys Orchestra as I paid my $.25 admission. The ticket window was grilled like a Bronx bodega cashier's. The bandstand was a lighted area as I sought a chair near an exit sign. The ladies, young and old,

<u>The Old Park Plaza</u>

I was not at the Park Plaza to meet women, as one does at some crowded bar. I was there to drink in the rhythms, lyrics, and excitement that were not part of my otherwise dreary world. Women entered the picture on the basis of their specific sizes, availability, ages, shapes, rather than their overall physical attractiveness, since I was more interested in selecting the right dance partner to better coincide with my absence of expertise. Actually, the older women suited me best, their having more patience with an eighteen-year-old beginner. The thermal quality of their very close seductive dancing contrasted with young girls who maintain a respectful distance. The more attractive women were the best dancers, having progressed further thanks to their popularity. They also had better knowledge of the latest moves, so that my advancement on the floor was now at a faster pace. To finally dance with the best was a trophy, a gold-medal accomplishment, especially since you had to bravely ask her or her partner's permission

When women are found to be less important in your formative years than dancing and musical influences, it is then that you assert your self-esteem, like a rite of passage. The woman in your life is in many ways superior to you. Dancing is a woman's sport. Dancing engenders a desire to excel, to be "good," to become perhaps one day a champion on the dance floor stage! Now you can lead the woman gracefully and capably, having shed your ungainly shyness.

Cuban ritual, with some break moves involving hitting the floor with the flat of your palms and your feet off the ground.

"Midnight," *negro como el telefono*, black as a 1930s telephone, was the only dancer who challenged Electrico, the dance master of the Park Plaza. He would hurry out onto the floor while applause for Electrico was still resounding, so as to cut into Electrico's performance appraisal. Midnight dressed entirely in black, including a rare vest, an encumbrance which gave him a fuller, more solid contrast to Electrico's string-bean frame. Midnight had a down-and-dirty, solid-man quality that contrasted with Electrico's height advantage (a four-inch difference). Where Electrico flew, Midnight was glued deep into the music, *heavy* man! Electrico was far out; he had the whole place stunned, shocked. Like two road-runners, their movements risked stress fractures. Amazingly, neither seemed to be out of breath off the floor. It was the audience that was left breathless.

The trumpets of the Happy Boys brought down the walls of the Great Depression. They were the pipers we followed to recovery. From a low-key romantic locale hidden away in El Barrio, they raised the level of intensity in their choice of more cheerful melodies, such as "Ahora Seremos Felices." Most Park Plaza patrons were from West 114th Street, "the most dangerous street in New York" at the time. Many of them did not own a radio. They went home singing along dark streets a music that SWEETENED THE DREAMS OF THEIR SLEEPING NEIGHBORS.

Whatever inevitable competitive activity we encounter in our basic formation, dancing leads us to better-balanced decisions and sharp reflexes. We learn when to advance, when to retreat, etc. Sunday visits to the Park Plaza replaced Sunday mass. My manic dancing became a triangular routine: Saturday Rumba Matinee at La Conga Club, Sunday at the Park Plaza, and often evenings at the Havana Madrid Club. I arose in the morning after dancing in my sleep. My command of Spanish improved along with my footwork. Songs like "Oye, Mi Cachia," "Teng' Una Rumbita," "¿Pa' Que No La Bailes Como Baile Yo?" -- translated: Sweetie, I have a nice rumba. Why don't you dance it as I do? I also learned to decipher the lyrics. The singer is telling her to forget the conservative *danzón*, in favor of the rhumba. Such exposure formed an autodidactic education, unequaled in any formal setting. It taught me to recognize stylistic variations of vocalists and of dancers like the Ballet Mambos of Mike Terrace.

The old Park Plaza, as an incubator of prodigious Afro-Latino culture in America, was the foundry of an overlooked segment of our history. During the downcast days of the Great Depression, it brought together a diverse society onto a dance floor. Today, no bronze plaque distinguishes the site. On the contrary, the solemn façade of a church, oddly named *La Hermosa* (the beautiful), seems to claim a smug victory over the gaiety that the Park Plaza once signified. Stuffy liturgy now rules where romance once blossomed.

From Julio Andino to Mario Rivera, from José Mangual, Sr. to Mario Bauzá, Graciela, Celia, Myrta, Leo, Max, Tito, Vitín, Arsenio, Cortijo, Pete, *El Conde*, Manny,

Maelo – díos mio – they are all gone, but not before having once danced at the Park Plaza.   This list may sound like what the Romans called *pompa funebris* (a funeral procession), but they are not mere "dust to dust!" They are, like so many other Latin artists, gold dust – that noble metal that shines forever.

If the old Park Plaza were still with us, I'd be going for a cab right now, to take me to number 4 West 110th Street.

....

MANY CITIES CLAIM THE TITLE OF 'PARIS OF THE ..WHATEVER'. BUENOS AIRES IS CALLED 'THE PARIS OF THE NEW WORLD'. BEIRUT WAS CALLED 'PARIS OF THE MIDDLE EAST', SAIGON , 'PARIS OF SOUTHEAST ASIA'. THIS TERMINOLOGY COULD REFER TO THE ARCHITECTURE AS WELL AS TO THE SPIRIT ONE FOUND IN THESE CITIES, BUT WHEN ONE CALLED HAVANA, 'EL PARIS DEL NUEVO MUNDO' THEY MEANT THE JOIE DE VIVRE PRINCIPALLY. .THE EXCELLENT RUM , FINE TOBACCO, THE HABANERAS OR THE COOL SPRAY ALONG THE MALECON THAT MAKES YOU LOVE THE PLACE. IS IT THE CONSTANT HUM OF A SILENT RYTHMIC GENERATOR, THE SPICEY LYRICS OR SEXY CITIZENS? WHEN THESE LYRICS CONTAIN IRONIC HUMOR, IT BECOMES A LAUREL AND HARDY WORLD..MORE

BEARABLE AND MORE TRUE TO LIFE. UNLIKE THE MESSAGE FOUND IN THE MALINGERING SOPHISTRY OF COUNTRY OR WESTERN MUSIC.

AT ONE TIME YOU COULD SAIL OF FLY TO HAVANA FOR VERY LITTLE. A WEEK END WAS SUFFICIENT TO ENROLL YOU AS A LIFETIME SUPPORTER OF THE PHENOMENON YOU DISCOVERED THERE. YOU HAD TASTED A BRAND OF UNIVERSAL HAPPINESS THAT, AS AN ELDERLY BLACK LADY ONCE TOLD ME AT THE END OF HER CRUISE TO NASSAU, 'I NEVER KNEW LIFE COULD BE SO SWEET'. HAD SHE GONE TO HAVANA, SHE WOULD HAVE KNOWN WHAT MADE IT SO, SHE WAS REFERING BASICALLY TO HER EXPERIENCE ABOARD THE SHIP . THE TRULY SWEETENED LIFE IS THE ONE IN WHICH DARK THOUGHTS ARE DROWNED OUT BY A MUSICAL ANTIDOTE..ONE THAT CAN BE SHARED LIKE A BOTTLE OF WINE WITH YOUR SUPPORTIVE NEIGHBORS. YOUR WOES ARE SPREAD ACROSS A SPECTRUM OF UNDERSTANDING SYMPATHIZERS. MUSIC, THEY SAY, IS MEDICINE. WHAT IS IT THAT MAKES CUBA ROCK, SWING, JUMP...THAT PUTS POETRY IN THE AIR? IT IS CALLED 'TUMBAO', THE COHESIVE POETRY IN THE AFRICAN DRUM.

<u>Refugees in Havana</u>

Havana in 1941 was one of the gayest cities on Earth. With pristine beaches, lively music, tobacco, rum, and beautiful women in abundance; it was a tropical paradise in the sun. Who could choose a better location to wait out the war in Europe?

In the upper-class sector of Havana, Vedado, about thirty families were living, not as Cuban refugees, but as Jewish refugees. They had managed to escape Nazi persecution, but they lived from day to day in despair, with no means of support other than donations from Jewish charities. Many had endangered relatives in Europe. With little chance of returning to the ruins of their former homes, they survived as best they could. Not permitted to hold jobs in Cuba, they were desperate people.

Among the professionals, artists, and businessmen were many tailors whose wives took needle and thread in hand and made neckties for sale. During the Great Depression, this strategy earned poverty-stricken Jewish families money for food. The gift of a necktie for Father at Christmastime arose during the birthdays and holidays as a result of this activity. Since Christmastime encouraged the greater display of decoration, these Christmas ties enlivened the male wardrobe, adding cheer to a sad time in America, and helped to break the somber style of dress in general in America.

In Cuba, however, the tropical climate and the absence of air conditioning meant a need for loose clothing. An example is found in the typical Cubavera: an unbuttoned neckline shirt with no tuck-in at the waist. Even today, neckties are being abandoned in greater numbers around the world. Climate change?

When Jewish refugees saw me passing by daily, they became more and more curious, and more suspicious of me. Could I also be a refugee, they wondered? I was approached by the tie salesman one afternoon, who had at last spotted a likely customer. Here was a gentleman who actually was wearing a tie in Havana!

It was an easy sale. I bought a tie since I could not only use one, but because the price was cheap. Besides, it was a practical souvenir of Cuba to take back *home* to remind me of those who had lost theirs.

MIAMI AND CUBA

Very Truly Yours

By HELEN MUIR

A STUDENT at the University of Miami, Vincent LiVelli, earns money to pay for his college tuition in a novel way. He gives rumba and conga lessons at Miami Beach clubs . . .

AN AFRO CUBAN BLESSING

HAVANA   1941

        In a wooden shed that was mostly an altar of some sort,
with much of the open sky for a roof, lived the most highly respected
Santero in all of Cuba. He lived among a jumbled botanica of wax
flowers, unrelated plaster saints of various sizes and framed dieties.
Small sacks with secret contents were hanging from the trees. . .
In short,i found myself visiting an authentic sanctuary in a spiritual
jungle. Nevertheless, I felt strangely at ease in this unlikely garden,
in this absurd theater, in this unfamiliar make-shift environment.

        All this had actually begun a few nights earlier, when
after an all night party, i had left Miami for Havana to study at
the University of Havana with Prof. Bustamonte. On the way to the
Hotel Inglaterra with my hang-over, I kept my eyes shut against the
Cuban sun. Being siesta, the empty streets seemed uninteresting.
Once in my room, I fell on to the bed and into the arms of "morfeo".
Around seven o'clock, I was slowly awakened by an approaching musical
alarm. From the balcony window came sounds from the street. Unaccustomed to balconies, I grasped the railing to steady myself. Down below
ran a river of colored lanterns gyrating among ruffled-skirted and
ruffle-shirted dancers. With ceremonial-like authority, a parade
of intensely disciplined congeros pased by as in review. When the
spectators below stood on their chairs, no doubt the high-light of
the spectacle was approaching.."Los Dandy de Belen" were strutting
by haw Orleans style, with tails, spats, twirling canes and top hats.
"Sient'un bongo, mamita me'ta llamando, sient 'un bongo...

        I had arrived in Havana, unaware that it was Carnival!
This was not a mere touristic, theatrical display. Imagine my amazement. This was more than theme floats and majorettes..this was serious
universal harmony..the splendor of a joyous humanity. The fireworks
were in the eyes of these people. Where did the individual begin and
rhythym begin since they were one? Overcome, and like an "espantaneo",
I ran down and plungeded into the delirium of it all, falling in step
with this elegant/primitive fantasy. I had gone from a stupor that
hot afternoon arriving in Havana for the first time, to the sobering
sudden discovery of one of life's true amazements..a bountiful gaety
ready to be shared with the whde world. Like winning the lottery of
felicity,.I was changed forever.

        Several days later, I mentioned casually to a student
friend that I had been having difficulty reading Dr. Fernando Ortiz.
Struggling with the Lukumi vocabulary and negligible Spanish, he
volunteered to take me to Regla to meet Juan Beson. There may still
be people who remember this most influential babalao, with his tall,
thin noble stance and his solitary front tooth,(that like a badge,
evinced a certain sincerity).

"What is he up to?", I wondered, as I stood back watching him
lighting candles. "He is invoking the Virgen de Regla, asking for
protection of your house", said my friend, who had graciously taken
me to Casablanca in Regla. The babalao obviously grasped that I had
not come as one searching for voodoo anecdotes. Rather, he was now
responding to the answer I had given him when he had asked me,
"Why have you come here?" (The very same question a pyschologist
asks a new patient). With Nanigo provers traveling quixote-like
around my brain, I was about to confess that it had not been my
intention to come..that my friend had suggested it, when I stammered..
"La..La Musica..." At that moment, the surrounding night seemed to
withdraw itself, to distance itself in silence, from this tableau
of a babalao, a oung american and his Cuban friend, under a celestial
confluence. We became a trinity like three magi on a holy night

Juan knew very well why I had appeared before him. He blessed
me, saying in Spanish, "You will carry this music around the world".
Was it prophesy or a command? Was it an example of his psychic insight?
Whatever it was, it has influenced my life, of that there is no doubt.
Was I to go forth like that neophyte apostle, St. Paul, an evangelist
preacher?? Knowing nothing of the technicalities of music, but
much imbued with the workings of its mysterious power, I wondered
over it. Was his benediction merely an embellishment of ritual?
...an example of pastoral embellishment of lyrical rhetoric? Could
it have been any one of the following?:

A step toward greater spiritual revelation
A religious experience. A divinely inspired assignment
A canonization invoking the attention of the Orishas
A sacred covenant. An oracular portent
An unescapable aesthetic responsibility that made me a
messenger, indebted, involved, obedient, privileged
An imposition that made me an instrument of the music
itself. A crusader of sorts
Was the santero a channeler between an invisible God
made audible to me

One fact emerges from the picture of my life after the encounter.
I can see that I have actually "carried the music around the world".
Begginning in 1941, I opened rumba dance studios along Miami Beach.
I performed it in the Philippines during World War with the USO.
In '47, we taught with Tony & Lucille Colon at Grossingers. We went
as far north as the Like Champlain Hotel, teaching. Later, leading
the immensely popular conga lines of the 50's. In 52, we went around
the world for 90 days teaching, running Champagne Dance Contests
aboard cruise ships. In recent times, we gave Oral History series
at the Smithsonian, exhibited our latin poster collection at Boys
Harbor and at colleges around the US, always engaged in preaching
the benefits of this music.

It seems as though I was handed a dream in Regla that I have
seen slowly materialize into reality, leaving me embraced by a force
beyond music. Surely the Orishas are pleased for we leave the world
a better place with this happy music..a task set before all mankind
Is it not true? And so it was foretold long ago that I would one day
write this article. BLESSED IS HE WHO KNOWS HIS WORK - (Thos. Carlyle)

Once we break the code of silence and *abre cuto*, as is said in Yoruba, "Open our ears," the channels to our brains closer to our thinking than are our hearts.

The Kongo word MAMBO means spirit. It has the power to animate from the tip of your toes to your sense of balance and overall performance. In Haiti, a mambo is a priestess, a woman that would in Cuba be called a Santero if women were permitted to be Santeros in Cuba. The trance while dancing is not part of Afro-Cuban ritual needed to connect with the spirits, as it is in Haiti. In the Dominican Republic, dancing is more formal, and in Cuba the Afro-Cuban dancing and singing are connected more closely to demonstrations of spiritual involvement. Popular mambo as taught in dance studios or as displayed on TV is a far cry from the institutionalized form that has been passed along from generation to generation, and that began in the heart of Africa as an accoutrement to worship.

Answered prayers are considered miracles that can occur upon awakening or can take years to occur. Planet conjunctions may be involved, especially if it happens while the subject remains alive and is physically able to respond. Today we can touch planets around the cosmos as well as asteroids, the moon, and our space vehicles. We are already communicating and receiving external information in return. Sounds waves are two-way streets that provide the Q & A of life's mystery. The biggest puzzle of why we are here has the answer waiting. We have been kept waiting needlessly or necessarily, but what matters now is the fact of Santeria, with 300 million adherents and growing, what with Afro-Cuban rituals and culture of the peoples involved around the world. All it needs is popularity, legitimacy, and synchronization with other religions, beginning with acceptance by the Vatican. That is what we should be praying for with the drumming that is coming now out of Cuba.

"YOU WILL CARRY THIS MUSIC AROUND THE WORLD"

(Santero Juan Besson, Regla,Havana, 1941)

This benediction, if that's what it was, has puzzled and
followed me over the years.. Since it has influenced my life,
I speculated on its meaning with a variety of interpretations,
hoping not to offend the Orisha, Yemaya, Patrona de Regla.

I wondered if it was:

An example of Pastoral rhetoric
A lyrical embellishment of the ceremony
An example of his psychic insight
A first step toward greater spiritual revelation
An assumption on the part of the santero
A divinely inspired assignment
A sacred covenant. A canonization. A powerful religious experience
A proclamation to invoke the attention of the Orisha
A pronouncement to keep me involved, indebted, obedient
An aesthet8c responsibility, making me a messenger, a crusader
An imposition that made me an instrument of the music itself
An honor and high privilege. Was the Santero a channeler between an
invisible God made audible and myself.

Looking for answers, the truth emerges from the picture seen
as a whole. Following the encounter with the Santero, I went on
to carry the music around the world just as he had said. In
1941, I was teaching the 'ritmo' to dance classes in Miami Beach
later at the Catskill resorts, as far north as Lake Champlain,
In the Philippines, we exhibited the dances with a USO show.
We taught aboard ships sailing for 90 days around the world,
lectured on the music at the Smithsonian, made hours of videos
about the music and exhibited posters of the bands that played
the music by means of posters collected over the years beginning
in 1971. The exhibit toured the college campuses for 3 months
and are installed at the Boys Harbour Conservancy for visitors
to enjoy. We taught and led the Conga lines that were popular in
the 50's and ran champagne Dance Contests aboard cruise ships.
Adding to this, writing about the music and celebrities in the
Latin music world brought the music before the public.

It is as though I was handed a dream that I saw turned into
reality before my eyes, leaving me embraced by a force beyond music.
Each day, the world responds in ever greater numbers to this music.
Watching something grow, like a plant we watered is a blessing that
must please the Orisha. We will leave the world a better place because of it and that is the task set before all mankind, is it not?

"What is he up to?", I wondered, as I stood back watching him lighting candles. "He is invoking the Virgen de Regla, asking for protection of your house", said my friend, who had graciously taken me to Casablanca in Regla. The babalao obviously grasped that I had not come as one searching for voodoo anecdotes. Rather, he was now responding to the answer I had given him when he had asked me, "Why have you come here?" (The very same question a pyschologist asks a new patient). With Nanigo provers traveling quixote-like around my brain, I was about to confess that it had not been my intention to come..that my friend had suggested it, when I stammered.. "La..La Musica..." At that moment, the surrounding night seemed to withdraw itself, to distance itself in silence, from this tableau of a babalao, a young american and his Cuban friend, under a celestial confluence. We became a trinity like three magi on a holy night

Juan knew very well why I had appeared before him. He blessed me, saying in Spanish, "You will carry this music around the world". Was it prophesy or a command? Was it an example of his psychic insight? Whatever it was, it has influenced my life, of that there is no doubt. Was I to go forth like that neophyte apostle, St. Paul, an evangelist preacher?? Knowing nothing of the technicalities of music, but much imbued with the workings of its mysterious power, I wondered over it. Was his benediction merely an embellishment of ritual? ...an example of pastoral embellishment of lyrical rhetoric? Could it have been any one of the following?:

A step toward greater spiritual revelation
A religious experience. A divinely inspired assignment
A canonization invoking the attention of the Orishas
A sacred covenant. An oracular portent
An unescapable aesthetic responsibility that made me a messenger, indebted, involved, obedient, privileged
An imposition that made me an instrument of the music itself. A crusader of sorts
Was the santero a channeler between an invisible God made audible to me

One fact emerges from the picture of my life after the encounter. I can see that I have actually "carried the music around the world". Begginning in 1941, I opened rumba dance studios along Miami Beach. I performed it in the Philippines during WOrld WarⅡ with the USO. In '47, we taught with Tony & Lucille Colon at Grossingers. We went as far north as the Like Champlain Hotel, teaching. Later, leading the immensely popular conga lines of the 50's. In 52, we went around the world for 90 days teaching, running Champagne Dance Contests aboard cruise ships. In recent times, we gave Oral History series at the Smithsonian, exhibited our latin poster collection at Boys Harbor and at colleges around the US, always engaged in preaching the benefits of this music.

It seems as though I was handed a dream in Regla that I have seen slowly materialize into reality, leaving me embraced by a force beyond music. Surely the Orishas are pleased for we leave the world a better place with this happy music..a task set before all mankind Is it not true? And so it was foretold long ago that I would one day write this article. BLESSED IS HE WHO KNOWS HIS WORK - (Thos. Carlyle)
THOS. CARLYLE

Afro-Cuban Historietas

Prior to Miguelito Valdez's late '30s protest lyrics that preceded Martin Luther King, Jr.'s "We Shall Overcome" was a freed slave named Juan Gualberto Gomez, who introduced the first act of nonviolent civil disobedience to the Americas by attending, in the company of black followers, a classical performance at the Teatro Payret. Sitting in the mezzanine reserved for whites, he and his followers were arrested for disturbing the peace. He died in 1935 at the age of 81 and no doubt was a prime influence on Miguelito, who performed for the Waldorf Astoria's principally white audience, thereby breaking the restrictive color code in force at that time in locales such as the Waldorf. Miguelito also had access to Dr. Fernando's focused attention on Afro-Cuban (Yoruba) culture, and to José Martí, Cuba's venerated liberator, who, with our help, freed Cuba from Spain's control. It was Dr. Ortiz, the anthropologist/author who in 1906 first spoke out about *negrosidad* (blackness), in English.

Efforts to abolish slavery and the many attempts to appreciate black culture range from Victorian England, 19th century Brazil to the present day. They also include Supreme Court decisions, the Quakers, writers like Baldwin, Ellison, preachers, Gospel singers, Black Panthers, name them . . . but it will be the religious uniqueness of Santeria that has the key to the grip on our minds and hearts. Santeria drummers enlist forces more powerful than what has been involved throughout a sad history.

When the world awakens to the drum and not to the *word*, it is then that a clearer wisdom comes forth. The "way" can commence with the synchronization of Santeria with the Roman Catholic Church's approval followed by the manifold religions of the world. Compassion and altruism preached by Buddhists and all other credos will not perform the task that is insurmountable with the spiritual intervention that Santeria seems to offer, in a manner unavailable in all other approaches. This quality may have originated in Africa millions of years ago when prehistoric drumming animated the essence of an inanimate object called a DRUM. An object that sent energy outward that connected with a counter-response from energy returning to us. Men have worshiped the sun for eons as a source of energy that it supplies but does not absorbs. It is the earth that both receives energy and gives out energy into the cosmos. Perhaps Aristotle was correct – we may be the center of the universe in that sense. What has been missing, and may at last be at hand – is the two-way communication essential to "divine intervention."

Determined to get an education, I dropped out. Perhaps another college, other than Brooklyn College, would be wiser. In 1940, I enrolled at the University of Miami, unaware that it was an anti-academic "country club". Suddenly my grades were A's and B's. Teaching Conga at Miami Beach hotels paid for my tuition. I then applied and received an Exchange Grant to study at the University of Havana. "International Law" sounded interesting. I enrolled in it under Professor Bustamonte, known to his students as "El Sordo", the Deaf One. My own hearing had been damaged by lead. Sitting in the back of the class because of my height and with limited command of the language, I nevertheless was happy in Havana, enjoying academic freedom and Rumba.

It was a long way from Brooklyn College, whose motto was "Nil Sine Magno Labore" or, "No Pain, No Gain". Teaching "English Conversation" at the Havana Business Academy paid my expenses.

Sadly, after just three months, World War II found me in the US Army at a Military Intelligence Training Center. Upon graduation, they sent me to the University of Wisconsin and then on to Command and General Staff School where, as a Portuguese Interpreter, I was a private among generals. Upon my Army discharge, I still felt uneducated. It was obvious that I was desperate since I enrolled in the Army Security Agency School as a "theoretical cryptography trainee". It was time to try Brooklyn College again. This time for my diploma which read "Social Studies". Learning had by now become a way of life. I applied and received an Institute of International Education, Pan American World Airways Fellowship. They flew me to Brazil to study "Jornalismo", only to discover upon arrival that there was no such course. I was quite happy with the GI Bill and Samba.

WORLD WAR II

Rush Civil Affairs Set-Up in Japan

America wasn't prepared for a sudden end of the war in the Pacific—so General MacArthur and his occupying forces are unnecessarily handicapped in their stupendous job of destroying Japanese militarism.

Why? They are bogged do[wn] ministration when all of their well have been devoted, from rounding up the Tojos, the Su Shimadas and all the rest of the before a possible hara-kiri epide the Allies' "wanted" list.

And how weren't we ready for of the war? We failed, as Richard Inquirer war correspondent, expl enlightening article yesterday; t trained civil affairs organization move into Japan with our armed fo

One result of this failure, it is that there was delay in getting afte criminals responsible for the war. T delay in tracking down members of torious terr Society. Th Jap public went on sp the surren

What h particular late," wit

A class training Minnesot language what no ished th usual pr

Then experts that th to Jap

The were Japanese, public life. Presumably it was largely

of this that Japan's war criminals were free for some days to pursue their own business, even if that business concerned suicide and the cheating of Allied

He helped secure /-J Day postmark

Vet recalls war's end in Japan

By VINCENT LIVELLI

The WWII Surrender Ceremony had already begun as we ran toward the harbor that Sept. 2 in 1945 in Yokohama, Japan.

Passing the Yubin Kyoku, Yokohama's Imperial Post Office and needing stamps, we rushed into the sandbagged building.

My companion, Mario, an ex-POW Italian just escaped from Hirohata Prison, spoke some Japanese. I had him ask for stamps for the U.S. when I realized the potential value of the cancellation "YOKOHAMA 2-9-45-NIPPON." V-J DAY! Though it meant missing the U.S.S. *Missouri* commemoration, we got to work on a mountain of envelopes addressed to 44 Perry Street, New York, N.Y.

Back in my office in the Customs Building, it became evident such a rare opportunity should be exploited more. I'd invest all I had.

The next morning, Sept. 3, we returned and commanded the Postal Clerk to repeat the Sept. 2, 1945, cancellation which he quickly obeyed.

Early in the morning of the 4th, we went back for more, only to find a line-up of G.I.s at the window, like a run on a bank.

In order to bypass these poachers, we demanded to see the Postmaster. Mario didn't know the word for postmaster. "The Postmaster, le Directeur!" I shouted. Immediately someone volunteered: "Monsieur le Directeur se trouve au troisieme etage." "Accompagnez-moi!" I ordered, racing up the stairs. Mario, showing some mistrust, wanted to know where

we were all going.

Arriving at the postmaster's office, a pitifully brittle gentleman stood up at attention, bowed and called out to a young man who entered nodding and bowing as though happy to see us. He was dressed as was the postmaster, in a white polo shirt and dark pants. He would be our interpreter.

Fast Talking

Invited into a carpeted sitting room, we were handed business cards. Before negotiations began, tea was served. "We apologize. There is no sugar." I was informed in French. I offered my cigarette case and four were selected and delicately sniffed by everyone in turn. Mistrusting the interpreter's English, or Mario's Japanese, we settled for Mr. Tatejiro, the assistant postmaster, who spoke French.

We drew our heavy chairs closer and agreed to get down to business. I rightfully claimed that the continued use of the rubber stamp YOKOHAMA 2-9-45 NIPPON was injurious to the

interest of those who had already invested in large quantities of cancellations.

Relaying this to Postmaster Sakabe, Tatejiro carefully explained to us that the honorable postmaster was continuing the cancellation as a gesture of service, of respect and friendship for "les soldats Americains."

"Au contraire," I interrupted indignantly, "he is injuring those investors that he has already helped. There must be a deadline set to all this."

Without further discussion, I dictated a notice in English that read, "Notice to the Public: The 2-9-45 cancellation will be discontinued as of 5-9-)5" and ordered it signed, "I Sakabe, Postmaster, Yokohama Post Office." American soldiers would respect this order I guaranteed and added that Sakabe must now assume full responsibility.

On Sept. 5, I found a correctly spelled sign placed at the side of the clerk's window. However, a line of G.I.s stood waiting their turn, money in hand.

I summoned Tatejiro. "Another visit to the director is necessary!" As we climbed the marble stairs, he appeared inscrutable. Calmly, he explained to Sakabe what it was that had upset me. "Bring me the rubber stamp," I demanded, refusing the invitation to be seated.

"I am extremely disappointed," I said, addressing the Postmaster who stood before me pokerfaced. Continuing in English, I added, "This all reminds me of another incident of mistrust..." Tatejiro entered, holding out the rubber stamp. It was examined, verified and tested several times... tempting 2-9-45's appeared.

"This is to be kept in the possession of the postmaster. Hadn't he agreed to do so yesterday?" The clerk would be punished I was assured and the stamp and stamp pad locked in the vault overnight. As we marched out, I placed a single pack of sugar on the table.

On Sept. 6, returning to the Post Office, we found that all was peaceful at the marble counter. Calling on Tatejiro for the last time. I slipped him a packet of sugar and asked him to relay to the honorable postmaster that I was now pleased.

We withdrew without bowing, trusting that the Sept. 2 episode was at last a thing of the past. We left Tatejiro holding the packet happily. Going out the door, I gave him a quick wink. Darned if he didn't wink back.

Editor's Note: Mr. Livelli donated the WWII 1945 Victory-Over-Japan cover to the National Postal Museum in 1993.

THE WAR PROFITEER

BY

Vincent Livelli

We made and sold wine from plums supplied by the Mess Sergeant.

We made watch bands and bracelets form downed planes' aluminum.

We banked crap games spread on Army blankets while crossing the Pacific to New Guinea from San Francisco.

We sold cigarette rations, plus additional items while doing extra duty assigned to "ration detail".

We taught Spanish classes to WACS and were amply "rewarded".

We sold sugar packet sent from home to the hungry "Japs"…

Where we could have made a considerable amount of money, we chickened out. All this was chickenfeed compared to running gambling on a cruise ship.

The first opportunity occurred in Leyte, P.I. While with the Philippine civil affairs unit we were in charge of distributing clothing to the natives. By resisting the black markets I enriched my character.

The second opportunity to make money was due to my assignment to process soldiers. I was made the sole judge to determine their fate during the Battle of the Bulge. I had to determine on the basis of an oral interview whether they would go back to college or ship out overseas. The exam I supervised was for foreign language proficiency. It was an especially difficult decision

IMPERIAL POST OFFICE, YOKOHAMA.

Official Business.

Vincent Livelli
44 Perry Street
New York, NY 10014
212 255 0576

LETTER FROM YOKOHAMA

**by
Vincent Livelli**

Yokohama, September 7, 1945

The Surrender Ceremony had already begun as we ran toward the harbor. Passing the Yubin Kyoku, Yokohama's Imperial Post Office and needing stamps, we rushed into the sand-bagged building.

My companion, Mario, an ex/POW Italian just escaped from Hirohata Prison, spoke some Japanese. I had him ask for stamps for the States, when I realized the potential value of the cancellation "YOKOHAMA-2-9-45-NIPPON". V-J DAY! Though it meant missing the S.S. "MISSOURI" Commemoration, we got to work on a mountain of envelopes addressed to 44 Perry Street, New York, New York.

Back in my office in the Customs Building, it became evident such a rare opportunity should be exploited more. I'd invest my all!

The next morning, September 3rd, we returned and commanded the Postal Clerk to repeat the September 2nd, 1945 cancellation which he quickly obeyed. Early in the morning of the 4th, we went back for more only to find a line-up of GI's at the window, like a run on a bank. In order to by-pass these poachers, we demanded to see the Postmaster. Mario didn't know the word for Postmaster. "The Postmaster, le Directeur!" I shouted. Immediately someone volunteered:

"Monsieur le Directeur se trouve au troisième étage." "Accompagnez-moi!" I ordered, racing up the stairs. Mario, showing some mistrust, wanted to know where we were all going. Arriving at the Postmaster's Office, a pitifully brittle gentleman stood up at attention, bowed and called out to a young man who entered nodding and bowing as though happy to see us. He was dressed as was the Postmaster, in a white polo shirt and dark pants. He would be our interpreter.

Invited into a carpeted sitting room, we were handed business cards. Before negotiations began, tea was served. "We apologize. There is no sugar." I was informed in French. I offered my cigarette case and four were selected and delicately sniffed by everyone in turn. Mistrusting the interpreter's English, or Mario's Japanese, we settled for Mr. Tatejiro, the Assistant Postmaster, who spoke French. We drew our heavy chairs closer and agreed to get down to business. I rightfully claimed that the continued use of the rubber stamp YOKOHAMA 2-9-45 NIPPON was injurious to the interest of those who had already invested in large quantities of cancellations. Relaying this to Postmaster Sakabe, Mr. Tatejiro carefully explained to us that the Honorable Postmaster was continuing the cancellation as a gesture of service, of respect and friendship for "les soldats americains". "Au contraire," I interrupted indignantly, "he is injuring those investors that he has already helped. There must be a deadline set to all this." Without further discussion I dictated a notice in English that read, "Notice to the Public: The 2-9-45 cancellation will be discontinued as of 5-9-45" and ordered it signed, "I. Sakabe, Postmaster, Yokohama Post Office." American soldiers would respect this order I guaranteed and added that Mr. Sakabe must now assume full responsibility.

On September 5th, I found a correctly spelled sign placed at the side of the clerk's window. However, a line of GI's stood waiting their turn, money in hand. I summoned Tatejiro. "Another visit to the Director is necessary!" As we climbed the marble stairs, he appeared inscrutable. Calmly, he explained to Mr. Sakabe what it was that had upset me. "Bring me the rubber stamp," I demanded, refusing the invitation to be seated.

"I am extremely disappointed," I said, addressing the Postmaster who showed no emotion whatsoever. Continuing in English I added, "Because of me your Post Office is making a killing. Tatejiro entered, holding out the rubber stamp. It was examined, verified and tested several times...tempting 2-9-45's appeared. 'This is to be kept in the possession of the Postmaster. Hadn't he agreed to do so yesterday?" The clerk would be punished I was assured and the stamp and stamp pad locked in the vault overnight. As we marched out I placed a single pack of sugar on the table.

On September 6th, returning to the Post Office, we found that all was peaceful at the marble counter. Calling on Mr. Tatejiro for the last time, I slipped him a packet of sugar and asked him to relay to the Honorable Postmaster that I was now pleased. We withdrew winners, bowing, trusting that the September 2nd episode was at last a thing of the past. We left Mr. Tatejiro holding the packet happily repeating to himself, do-mee-no, do-mee-no, do-mee-no". Going out the door, I gave him a quick wink. Darned if he didn't wink back.

The ARMY of the UNITED STATES hereby certifies that

VINCENT A. LIVELLI

has completed satisfactorily the course of study in

AREA AND LANGUAGES

pursued at THE UNIVERSITY OF WISCONSIN, MADISON, WISCONSIN

His training was completed on 4 MARCH 1944. The record of his performance is available, on request by appropriate authority, for the purpose of determining his academic credit.

BY ORDER OF THE SECRETARY OF WAR:

FOR CERTIFYING INSTITUTION
University of Wisconsin

FRANKLIN W. CLARKE COMMANDANT
Lt. Col., Infantry

POST MASTER
Ichiro Sakabe

Yokohama Post Office

THE SATURDAY EVENING POST

YOKOHAMA, BY WIRELESS.

I HAD expected some heroic utterance from Cpl. Vincent A. Livelli on the historic day when the armada of American transport planes first landed the advance elements of General MacArthur's headquarters on the sacred soil of Nippon. We of the Military Government Section were doubtless one of the most important elements of this headquarters. I listened for a pearl of oratory, because Livelli's Latin imagination usually provided the proper flamboyant phrase for such a situation.

But now that we had come in over a countryside that, two weeks ago, would have been spitting fire at us, had swooped beside enemy planes wearing the livid orange circle of the Rising Sun on their fuselages, had been beckoned into place by booted American paratroopers in a jeep, and had set foot on the concrete taxiway, Livelli gave forth with something surprisingly unheroic, and to the point. He said, "It looks good. There are more Americans than Japs around here." The statement was quite penetrating, because landing in the middle of Japan wasn't exactly good for the nerves, no matter how many agreements had been signed. The crux of the matter was, after all, how much protection we might have if anyone should start shooting.

Livelli's comment was quite apropos. Yet, something more dramatic might have been said on the occasion—something to touch Livelli's pronunciamento on the occasion of the founding of our Military Government Section in Manila: "Military government follows the glories of victory with the glories of peace."

Well, it had been a rough trip from Manila to Japan. Livelli, like the rest of us, was tired—not too tired to feel honored to be in the first batch of Military Government people to reach Japan, but a little too tired to think up forensic phrases.

The odyssey from Manila had been a masterpiece of hurry-up-and-wait. It was a classic of the old Army game of ordering the other fellow to be at a rendezvous early, so as to allow plenty of time to get there yourself. All this, of course, was cheerfully endured by the Military Government Section. It was a wonderful break to be among the first to go to Japan.

While we waited, I unearthed some amazing facts about the life of young Livelli, the general's secretary. I discovered now that he had talents besides the ability to speak assorted languages. For instance, he had been a professional dancer and entertainer. His troupe had played in Chicago at the Chez Paree, at the Wonder Bar in Detroit, at the Five o'Clock Club in *(Continued*

Miami, and in New York, where he and the other dancers had been sort of male hosts. The background had been fitted into a few years, while Livelli was still going to college, and helped to explain his grace, his ready smile and his prepossessing approach.

Livelli demonstrated there were still other facets of his personality. He was reading James Joyce's Finnegans Wake, a book a little heavy, perhaps, for a dancer. He explained that he was interested in it from a philological point of view, for the novel had French and German phrases in it, said Livelli, and it seemed as if it were written in Anglo-Saxon.

MILITARY BLUNDERS

MANY MILITARY MEN ARE FOUND WITH MARS PROMINENT IN THEIR
HOROSCOPES. MY MARS IS IN THE TWELFTH HOUSE…THE HOUSE OF HIDDEN
MEANINGS, ODD RESTRICTIONS, AS WELL AS INSTITUTIONS, LIKE THE ARMY FOR
INSTANCE.

WHEN WORLD WAR II HAPPENED, I WAS LIVING IN HAVANA WHERE I COULD
HAVE SAT OUT THE WAR AS MY ROOM MATE HAD CHOSEN TO DO. I CAME HOME
AND ENLISTED. W. HILE TAKING MY INDUCTION PHYSICAL EXAM, THE MEDICAL
OFFICER CLASSIFIED ME 1-B. 'ESSENTIAL HYPERTENSION' , HE WROTE. FEARING
THAT SUCH AN ODD CATEGORY WOULD RESTRICT MY CHANCES FOR
ADVANCEMENT, I PLEADED SUCCESSFULLY TO BE 1–A.

ON MY FIRST DAY IN THE ARMY, I HAD AN ENCOUNTER WI8TH DEATH.
VOLUNTEERING FOR A JOB, I FOUND MYSELF CLEANING UP THE BLOOD OF A G.I.
WHO HAD HEMORRAGED AND DIED ON THE BARRACKS FLOOR. SINCE I WAS
HEMOPHOBIC, I LEARNED TO AVOID VOLUNTEERING.

IN TIME, AS AN INTERPRETER AT COMMAND AND GENERAL STAFF SCHOOL, I
FAILED TO SNAP TO ATTENTION WHEN THE COMMANDING GENERAL ENTERED
OUR OFFICE. WORKING ALONE IN A REAR ALCOVE AND DUE TO POOR HEARING, I
HAD NOT RESPONDED RAPIDLY ENOUGH. FOR PUNISHMENT, THEY RETURNED
ME TO MY ORIGINAL OUTFIT WHERE I FOUND THAT ALL MY BUDDIES HAD BEEN
RUSHED OF TO THE BATTLE OF THE BULGE. NOW, AS A LONER MISFIT, I GAINED
A MODICUM OF INDIVIDUALITY.

ALTHOUGH I WAS A MERE PFC FRENCH MILITARY IINTELLIGENCE
GRADUATE, THEY SHIPPED ME OFF TO THE ISLAND OF SAMAR IN THE
PHILLIPINES. WHEN WE FINALLY REACHED TOKYO (3 DAYS BEFORE THE
OFFICIAL SURRENDER), I WAS STOPPED BY THE MILITARY POLICE. THEY HAD
SEEN ME WALKING WITH A PAINTING UNDER MY ARM WHILE IN THE COMPANY
OF A RELEASED P.O.W. ASSUMING ME TO BE A LOOTER, A CRIME KNOWN TO
CARRY THE DEATH PENALTY, THEY CONFISCATED THE PAINTING EVEN THOUGH
I POINTED TO THE SIGNATURE. IT HAD BEEN PAINTED BY THE P.O.W. WHILE HE
WAS IN A JAPANESE PRISON. SINCE I WAS TOLD THAT JAPANESE CURRENCY HAD
NO VALUE BACK IN THE STATES, I GAVE IT ALL AWAY AND ARRIVED HOME
BROKE.

UPON MY DISCHARGE, IT WAS DISCOVERED THAT MY "ESSENTIAL
HYPERTENSION" WAS DUE TO "A CONGENITAL INFANTILE KIDNEY" AND THAT I
WAS HARD OF HEARING DUE TO CHILDHOOD LEAD POISENING. "HOW DID YOU
GET IN THE ARMY", THEY WONDERED. CONSIDERING ALL THIS IRONIC
FOOLISHNESS AND ALL THE BAD MARKS ON MY ARMY RECORD, INCLUDING
"REPORTING LATE FOR GUARD DUTY" (DUE TO A CHARMING W A C LANGUAGE
CLASS I HAD BEEN TEACHING)..THESE SERIOUS BLEMISHES SERVED TO MAKE
ME "UNACCEPTABLE" WHEN I VOLUNTEERED FOR WORK WITHIN THE C I A . IT
PROBABLY SAVED MY LIFE.

WHEN I GROW UP…..

Going from Vienna to Budapest (Magyoraszág) along the Danube is a pleasant trip But in 1968 it was a risky choice for a visit. The rare American tourist was usually Jewish , returning in hopes of retrieving his "life diamonds"..family jewels that were buried, hidden from Nazis and Commies. My reason for going was to see the fabulous collection of booty, the treasures of the defeat of the Ottoman Turks housed in the War Museum. Then again there was my curiosity regarding the true treasures of a country..the ladies of Hungary, reputed to be the most beautiful in Europe".

In my U.S.Army surplus rucksack were some rock and roll cassettes, more valuable than Marlboros. This was risky since my name was probably on some list as having smuggled rock and roll records into Moscow in '58. On board , separated from the otherwise solemn passengers was a group of frolicking Austrian firemen on holiday.They were going to a convention in Budapest in civilian clothes and without their wives. As men without women, they were, like myself, curious about the "most beautiful women". Like Australians, these Austrians invited strangers to share a Pilsner or two. So it was that I was soon adopted as an honorary mascot. Docking in Pest, I found myself embedded among these new friends. As "visiting delegates", we were waived through customs, fortunately. Once at the Hotel, it was discovered that one member had failed to make the trip leaving his pre-paid single room available to me ..free. I was soon off to the Museum, only to find it closed. Although the many bars of Budapest were open all day, the ladies only emerged late at night.

That evening, the firemen invited me to join them as their guest at the Matias Restaurant where a delightful Gypsy zither ensemble, fine Tokay and paprika-ed goulash awaited me. After multiple toasting, I found the mice peering down from holes in the ceiling moulding, waiting for their table very amusing. Early next morning, I left gifts for my comrades and boarded the bus for Estergom. The still dark streets were empty but the trolleys were jammed with workers en route to factories. The street signs read like some scrambled scrabble set. Hungarian is a Ural-Altaic family of languages that includes Turkish and Lapp. The only word I learned was fire.."tüz", thanks to the hallway exits in the Hotel. Today, I still treasure my encounter with the firemen. It was an odd fulfillment of a forgotten ambition..I was a fireman for a day.

4/30/04

Livelli, Vincent Anthony

GRADUATED_________________ DEGREE_________________

| SECOND YEAR | SEM. | | TERM |
COURSES	CR.	GR.	GR.
1940-41 : 2nd Sem			
Art 232 : Hist. of Art	2	B	4
French 202 : Inter.	3	B	6
Hisp. 201 : Econ. Probs. of Mod. Lat. Am.	2	B	4
Hisp. 302 : Hisp. Amer. Diplo. Rel.	2	B	4
Portuguse 102 : Elem.	3	A	9
Soc. 201 : Intro.	3	B	6
	15		33

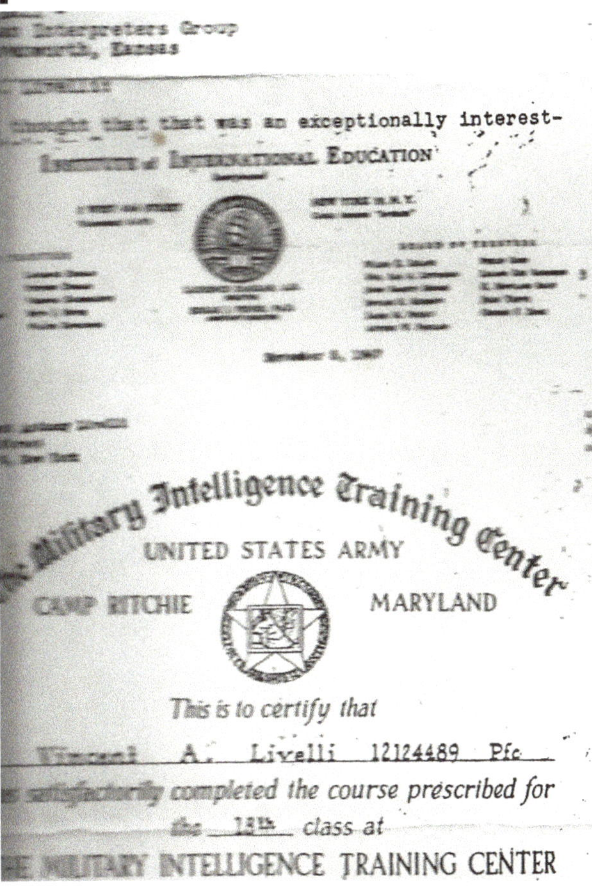

CENTERS:—
191 Joralemon Street, Brooklyn 2, N.Y.
90-20 Sutphin Boulevard, Jamaica 2, N.
28 Richmond Terrace, Staten Island 1, N.

May 6th, 1943

TO WHOM IT MAY CONCERN

Mr. Vincent Livelli has been teaching Portuguese and Spanish for this Organization for the past six months.

His pupils numbered over 25 including officers and enlisted men of the Army and Navy.

We cannot recommend Mr. Livelli too highly for his complete competence and scholarly manner which was a credit to the Organization.

Respectfully,

Mrs. Martha R. Finkler

Martha R. Finkler

Ft. Eustis, Va.
18 October 1943

TO WHOM IT MAY CONCERN:

Private Vincent A. Livelli, ASN 12124489, has been performing services in connection with the Army Specialized Training Program.

His work has been both professional and clerical in nature. His ability in speaking, reading and writing four foreign languages has proved of invaluable aid to the staff serving on and with the Army Specialized Training Program Board. His loyalty, cooperation, competency and manner of work are most commendable. His conduct and his work command the respect of everyone associated with him.

By reason of his academic and professional backgrounds, it is felt that any promotion or advancement which might be offered him would prove to be of benefit to the military service. Also, it is believed that because of his unusual language qualifications, his services might be better utilized in a commissioned status.

VINCENT J. DELLORTO,
1st Lt., A.G.D.,
Recorder.

It was a long way from Brooklyn College, whose motto was,
"Nil Sine Magno Labore" or, "No Pain, No Gain". Teaching
"English Conversation" at the Havana Business Academy paid
my expenses.

Sadly, after just three months, World War II found me in the
US Army at a Military Intelligence Training Center. Upon
graduation, they sent me to the University of Wisconsin and
then on to Command And General Staff School where as a
Portuguese Interpreter I was a private among generals.
Upon my Army discharge, I still felt uneducated. It was
obvious that I was desperate since I enrolled in the Army
Security Agency School as a "theoretical cryptography trainee".
It was time to try Brooklyn College again. This time for my
diploma which read "Social Studies". Learning had by now
become a way of life. I applied and received an Institute of
International Education, Pan American World Airways Fellowship.
They flew me to Brazil to study "Jornalismo", only to discover
upon arrival that there was no such course. I was quite happy
with the GI Bill and the Samba.

But wait, what about CCNY? The Army had sent me there in '43,
"awaiting assignment".(Evidently the authorities were puzzeled
by my record that even listed "Institute For Advanced Studies ,
Princeton, N.J. - Portuguese Monitor".) In a half empty classroom, I sat like a ward of the State, institutionalized.

Undoubtedly, this was all a continuation of a childhood pattern.
During the Great Depression, families were constantly evicted.
Attending a variety of High Schools and Sunday Schools seemed
normal and fun. At home, we spoke English. Relatives spoke
Genoese, Sicilian, Neapolitan and neighbors spoke Portuguese
and Yiddish, etc.At age seventeen I was enrolled in a night
secretarial course at Bay Ridge High School- an all girl school.
Later, I would crash the New School to hear MeyerShapiro talk
about Mondrian's "endless contingencies".

...he Infantry Ne... Had it So Tough

Military G... ...Japan discover that the ... ...to
the battlefield, ...

WEEK BY WEEK, TO TOK...

...after wartime combat m...
...torpedo planes, joined up with...
...assigned to rule all Japan. He...
...the overnight mushrooming of Midget...
...installment, from behind the scenes, he...
...hears about in the news.

YOKOHAMA, BY WIRELESS.
...expected some heroic utterance
...Col. Vincent A. Livelli on the his-
...when the armada of American
...planes first landed the advance ele-
...General MacArthur's headquarters
...soil of Nippon. We of the Mil-
...Government Section were doubtless one
...important elements of this head-
...I listened for a pearl of oratory,
...Livelli's Latin imagination usually
...proper flamboyant phrase for
...situation.
...that we had come in over a coun-
...two weeks ago, would have been
...at us, had swooped beside enemy
...wearing the livid orange circle of the
...Sun on their fuselages, had been
...into place by booted American
...officers in a jeep, and had set foot on the
...taxiway, Livelli gave forth with
...surprisingly unheroic, and to the
...he said, "It looks good. There are
...Americans than Japs around here." The
...comment was quite penetrating, because
...the middle of Japan wasn't exactly
...for the nerves, no matter how many
...documents had been signed. The crux of the
...matter was, after all, how much protection
...we have if anyone should start shooting.
...His comment was quite apropos. Yet,
...something more dramatic might have been
...suited the occasion—something to touch
...off a pronunciamento on the occasion of the
...arrival of our Military Government Section
...like: "Military government follows
...the rules of victory with the glories of peace."
...It had been a rough trip from Manila
...But Livelli, like the rest of us, was
...not too tired to feel honored to be in
...the first batch of Military Government peo-
...ple to reach Japan, but a little too tired to
...coin forensic phrases.
...Our odyssey from Manila had been a mas-
...terpiece of hurry-up-and-wait. It was a
...case of the old Army game of ordering the
...low to be at a rendezvous early, so as
...to have plenty of time to get there yourself.
...This, of course, was cheerfully endured by

THE SATURD...
into Japan. The hardship...
much to Col. Loomis Parrar...
Tilton, Mr. Charles Thomas and D...
Homfeld as we moved, with baggage...
one end of the airfield to the other, as directed, then moved back whence we had
come, then were misdirected from one plane
to another, then waited in the meager shade
of our plane wing for three hours until such
time as it would take off.
    We had been told to be at the airfield at
seven o'clock in the morning, but we were not
airborne until 11:35. Somewhere, unnamed
characters were giving themselves plenty of
time to meet their obligations at the expense
of us who had to do the waiting. But the
same allowance had been made all along the
line of command, and many, not just we,
were caught in the accumulation. Even the

While we waited, I unearthed some amazing facts about the life of young Livelli, the
general's secretary. I discovered now that
he had talents besides the ability to speak
assorted languages. For instance, he had been
a professional dancer and entertainer. His
troupe had played in Chicago at the Chez
Paree, at the Wonder Bar in Detroit, at the
Five o'Clock Club in
Miami, and in New York, where he
and the other dancers had been sort of
male hosts. The background had been
fitted into a few years, while Livelli
was still going to college, and helped to
explain his grace, his ready smile and
his prepossessing approach.
    Livelli demonstrated there were still
other facets of his personality. He
was reading James Joyce's Finnegans
Wake, a book a little heavy, perhaps,
for a dancer. He explained that he was
interested in it from a philological
point of view, for the novel had French
and German phrases in it, said Livelli,
and it seemed as if it were written in
Anglo-Saxon.
    I retired in confusion before this on-
slaught of culture and contented myself with talking to Charley Thomas,
the civilian expert on finance. With his
light blue eyes, white mustache and
venerable bald head, he looked like the
little man on the cover of Esquire. He
told me about his prewar years in
Yokohama, and then floored me with a
polysyllabic list of certain Japanese
whom he was going to look up when
we got to Nippon.

LARRY KEIGHLEY

ODYSSEYS

SS CUBA	Passenger	'41	Hav/Mia
SS GENERAL POPE (US ARMY)	"	'45	Jap/USA
SS URUGUAY (Maiden Voyage)	Cruise Director	'48	NY/BA/NY
SS BRAZIL	"	'49	"
SS ARGENTINA	"	'52	"
SS EVANGELINE	"	'49	NY/NAS/NY
SS YARMOUTH	"	'49	"
SS YARMOUTH CASTLE	"	'51	"
SS ATLANTIC	Ass't Cruise Director	'51	NY/WI
SS NUEVO DOMINCANO	Cruise Director	'51	MIA/WI
SS BAHAMA STAR	"	'51	"
SEA CLIPPER (Freighter)	Passenger	'52	US/HOLLAND
MN USO DI MARE	"	'52	SPAIN/ITALY
ANDRE (Freighter)	"	'52	ITALY/USA
SS FLORIDA	"	'53	MIA/HAV
SS PRESIDENT MONROE	"	'52	YOKO/NY
SS PRESIDENT WILSON	"	'52	SFO/YOKO
SS OCEANIC (Maiden Voyage)	1st Ass't Cruise Director	'56	NY/WI
SS HOMERIC	Ass't Cruise Director	'59	"
MV METEOR	Passenger	'54	NY/WI
TS OCEAN MONARCH	Cruise Staff (Amexco)	'55	FTL/WI
MS J.V.OLDENBARNEVELDT	" "	'55	COLON/MIA
MS ORANJE	" "	'55	"
SS WILLEM RUYS	" "	'55	"
SS NORTHERN STAR	" "	'55	"
SS EMERALD SEAS	" ---	'56	MIA/NAS/MIA
RMS CARONIA	" (Amexco)	'58	NORTH CAPE
RMS QUEEN MARY	" "	'58	SHPTON/NY
SS OSLOFJORD	" "	'58	MED CRUISE
SS NIEUW AMSTERDAM	Shore Excursion Manager	'59	NY/WI
SS NEW AMSTERDAM	"	'59	NY/WI
SS STATENDAM	"	'60	NY/WI
SS VOLENDAM	"	'60	NY/WI
SS ROTTERDAM	"	'60	NY/WI
SS VEENDAM	Passenger	'60	TORQUAY/NY
SS ARIADNE	Cruise Staff (Amexco)	'60	AMAZON
SS INDEPENDENCE	Cruise Staff (Fugazy)	'60	St CROIX/NY
MS ANGELINA LAURO	Passenger	'63	MED CRUISE
SS BRASIL	Cruise Director	'63	NY/BA/NY
MS SEA VENTURE	Cruise Director	'63	NY/BERMUDA
SS FRANCE	Shore Excursions (Amexco)	'67	NY/WI
TV RAFFAELLO	Cruise Director	'67	MED CRUISE
TV LEONARDO DA VINCI	"	'67	"
MV KARA DENIZ	Passenger	'68	NPLS/ISTANB
MS IVAN FRANCO	"	'68	ISTANB/NPLS
SS MERMOZ	Cruise Director	'74	MED CRUISE
SS ROYAL VIKING SEA	Cruise Staff	'74	NO/CAMERICA
SS NILI (ZIM)	Passenger	'74	MIA/WI
TSS STELLA SOLARIS	Host	'77	ATHENS/FTL
MS DANAE	Passenger	'85	MED CRUISE
MV SAN GIORGIO	"	'84	"
MN GALILEO GALILEI	"	'85	"
SS ROYAL VIKING SUN	Guest Host	'92	MONTREAL/NY
TSS FIESTAMARINA	Passenger	'94	MIA/DOM.REP.
		'95	MIA/MEX

To begin with a clean slate, I had to find my utopia, a space where I could construct a world within an already fertile environment. Having red Mathew Arnold who, while on a voyage to Margate, wrote how better behaved people were at sea than on land. Tantamount to winning a lottery that I had nto purchased a ticket for, I was dealt a good luck hand like a Royal Flush that washed away what I left ashore and a Full House that became my home at sea. I landed a job as cruise director in a virgin industry in 1948 and began settling into a career that spanned 30 years. By setting up a Program of Daily Activity and an enthusiastic cruise staff, a hostess and a Travel Officer to assist, I fashioned a life-style for my-self that became my utopia. Sailing first class with an unlimited bar account, with semi-celebrity status among celebrities, all-expense paid lifetime of vacations, I was cloistered in a wholesome, glorified existence with forty ways to make money, plus many "extras". I did alright,

It wasn't long before successful wealthy passengers or member of the crew asked me, "How did you get a job like this?" to which I still have no answer.

"The greatest loss is to remove oneself from the physical world," someone once said. Many who wished to change the world or their plight in it through nature, drugs, cults, communes or escapes that were legitimate experimentation, freedom of expression or plain folly, failed. Going to sea actually brought me in closer touch and familiarity with the bigger physical world. It seemed that my childhood stamp collection sprang to life with visits to eihty countries including Brunei, Borneo, Burma, Sarawak, Lapland, with duplicate visits to Israel, Egypt and others and to rarities like Papua, Andorra. San Marino, Lichtenstein, Algeria. To sail as over sixty ships I had to "Jump ship" leaving one company in order to join another that called at places I had yet to visit. Holland American Line boasted the Rotterdam flagship, the Nieuw Amsterdam, the New Amsterdam, Statendam, Veedam, Volendam, Maasdam. I worked all of

I had prepared for my interview by memorizing the names on the name plates on the office desks.

I was told I would be on a ship for a 38 day cruise to South America. I began to wonder about what I was getting into. Could I be ready and leave on time? What about a wardrobe? Was I qualified? What about mal-de-mer?

As thing turned out, I found a home on the ship, even though I still had trouble with port and starboard while walking aft. As for higher education, I wondered how it was possible that I had already attended 2 colleges and 4 universities, and that they all offered me free tuition? Was it because the army had sent me to study Geopolitics at the University of Wisconsin, or that my parents made sure I got a B.A. from Brooklyn College? Was it thanks to a benefactress who paid my tuition the University of Miami, or because of a Pan-American World Airways grant I received to the Institute of International Education, sending me to of Rio de Janeiro on a tuition free fellowship? Perhaps it was the exchange program between the University of Miami and the University of Havana or, or the Army snafu that found me sitting for weeks in an almost empty classroom while patiently awaiting assignment at City College on Amsterdam Avenue?

While all this emphasis on learning could be considered of great value, it was only after I left the muffled atmosphere of the classroom box that I felt myself becoming educated by sailing around the world.

Eighty per cent of our knowledge comes from our vision. I looked up at the sky in bored resignation day after day. Then, I closed my books and opened my eyes on the world outside the classroom window that framed my day dreams. Soon I was deciphering

Latin and Greek inscription on ruins, handling the intricacies of foreign currency and customs, fraternizing with the world, while sharing the "Brotherhood of the Sea."

It wasn't until I "graduated" from South America, Europe, Asia, and the rest, that I realized good fortune dawned on me, having left behind on land the frustrated tutors my puzzled parents had engaged to help me progress. I gave thanks to the astrological lottery I must have won.

By day, rainbows festooned my horizons. By night, star-bedecked skies charted my course as planets paroled the path they had set before me.

1

THE ASTROLOGICAL LOTTERY

By

Vincent Livelli

When asked what I would do if I ever won the lottery, I would answer, "Buy a yacht, and sail it around the world." But there's no need to win the lottery to go sailing around the world, year after year. All that is needed is to be born with your ascendant in a water sign, such as Scorpio favorably aspected by Jupiter your 9th house, the house of long journeys and higher education. Even thought my birth sign was Aries, a cardinal fire sign, for over fifty plus years I would cruise the oceans of the world, picking up knowledge along the way. It didn't matter that I knew nothing of navigation, had no family history of sailors, and was a poor swimmer. Aside from a row boat in Central Park, the Staten Island Ferry, a short crossing from Cuba to Key West that made me sea-sick, and two U.S. Army transports in WW II, I never saw myself living and working on a ship. It was called "a life of sacrifice" by many and a dangerous occupation for centuries.

After 68 ships and 60 countries, I began to examine my horoscope to confirm the relevance of its odd message.

One day while looking for work around the Wall Street area, a travel poster lured me into a steamship office and out of the bitter winter winds that blew off New York Bay. Perhaps I could land a 7 day Caribbean cruise as a dance teacher. Instead, I was offered a job as an assistant cruise director – a position I knew nothing about, and one that in 1948 very few people knew anything about. I spoke some Spanish and Portuguese.

"How well do you remember names?" I was asked.

We obviously needed each other. The three ships needed staffing with entertainers.
I was made the Assistant Cruise Director aboard the S.S. URUGUAY, accountable
to the Hostess. She quickly taught me the ropes; the Dance Contest, the Get-
Together Games, Water Sports in the Pool, the Masquerade Party, Deck
Tournaments, the Port Lectures. I MC'd the shows in Spanish, English and
eventually in Portuguese. I ran the Bingos and Horse Races, the Ship's Pool, the
Ship's Cruise News, Novelty Contests, Presentation of Prizes, Passenger Shows,
Parties and more parties. Every night was New Year's Eve with very good
champagne. In 38 busy days I had lost 13 pounds dining like a king.

When people retire, they plan to take "a Cruise". What does a Cruise Director do
when he or she retires? Bus drivers take bus rides. They, take cruises. Purpose of
trip: Pleasure. Occupation: Retired Cruise Director. Since the" job "   pays well,
with "room and board" in luxurious surroundings, with celebrities and jovial fellow
world travelers, there is little incentive to ever retire. The ocean is endless. The ship
is a theater of life at its best. Why, we won't mind , we'll be buried at sea.

My fifty five ships included two freighters. Let's begin with them. The owner of the
Greek Line once asked me to teach him to shoot dice. By chance, he did very well as
a beginner. As a tip, he gave me two round trip tickets to Europe aboard his
Freighter, "Sea Clipper", returning on the "Andre" from Leghorn to Staten Island.

After the URUGUAY, came the BRAZIL and the ARGENTINA, 38 day cruisers to
Buenos Aires and return. Then a parade of others, i.e., the EVANGELINE, the
YARMOUTH and the YARMOUTH CASTLE, all going to the Antilles from New
York.   The ATLANTIC, HOMERIC and OCEANIC to the West Indies, the
PRESIDENT WILSON, around the world, the Hamburg-American Line ARIADNE
out of New Orleans up the Amazon, the IVAN FRANCO , the KARA DENIZ ,
Naples to Istanbul, the DANAE and the SAN GIORGIO out of Venice, the
CARONIA to the North Cape, the ROYAL VIKING SEA and the ROYAL
VIKING SUN , the latter out of Montreal and the majestic QUEEN MARY trans-
Atlantic. Then there were seven Dutch ships. One named the MV JOHAN VAN
OLDENBARNEVELDT. She barely squeezed through the Panama Canal.
She later became the ACHILLE LAURO, sunk in the straits of Hormuz.
Many of these fine ships seem gone, sold, scrapped or simply sailing under different
names and personalities. One stands out. She was an old Canadian liner belonging
to the Clarke Steamship Company, known as the " Northland " and renamed "New
Northland" A real Yankee. They sunk her for her insurance, but not deep enough.
This occurred only after she had been purchased by the FLOTA MERCANTE DEL
ESTADO DE LA REPUBLICA DOMINICANA and re-named the S. S. NUEVO
DOMINICANO. Whenever a ship is "lost at sea" it is a tragedy of a singular sort.
The Titanic and Andrea Doria still haunt us. The NUEVO DOMINICANO was
special .She was the first true cruise ship to sail out of Miami after WW 2. Today,
we have 30 ships, with more on the way. Built for winter seas, she braved Floridian
hurricanes without weather advisories.   She pioneered ports like Ciudad Trujillo,

(Trying to understand me better)

As a retarded misfit of sorts with my hearing deficit, I've had to fashion a world unlike what is offered to us by God. Like a plant still alive but with dead flowers, mine is a world unlike yours. For impressions to reach me, I had to go travel to rare wonderments like Great Wall, Baalbek, Sarawak, Brunei, Ilban villages, the Sistine Chapel, or to find myself in the presence of *santeros*, or 90 celebrities, 88 countries, 64 ships, three colleges, three universities with five languages. Shock or amazement was needed to reach deep into me for the rightful *me*, for my patrimony. I was not to be excluded from a full life, except for what I wished to avoid. Being set apart gratuitously by controlling circumstances was comparable to poisoning. I didn't recognize my condition while still a formative "slow-to-learn" adult. That is why today I look back long years and rejoice now. The choices that I made or those that arose inexplicably empowered me to resist the forces that would have otherwise placed me in the bowels of the beset world of the twentieth and twenty-first centuries.

The thirty-billion-dollar cruise industry began with three second-hand slot machines that were pulled up from the Hudson River, where Mayor Fiorello LaGuardia had dumped them, in order to protect the public from organized crime. The three barnacled machines showed up in 1952 aboard the S.S. Nuevo

Domenicano of the Eastern Shipping Company in Miami, placed on board by the Danio crime syndicate out of Chicago and Miami's Meyer Lansky mob. Lansky was just starting gambling in Havana as well. Since I was the Casino Manager as well as the Cruise Director, perhaps I can claim to be one of the guys who got gambling sailing on cruise ships out of Florida.

But whatever happened in 2014 with all those odd occurrences that crippled the cruise industry – the virus contamination, the engine room fires, steerage breakdowns needing tugboats? Remember how it all mysteriously normalized overnight? No doubt an agreement with the protection racket where a "piece of the action" was involved. Cruise billions attracted attention on this new turf afloat that made Al Capone look bad. It is Carnival Cruise Lines that dominates with controlling interests, and Holland-America, Caribbean Cruise Line, Costa, Crystal, and possibly Norwegian as well. They all stopped fighting each other with a "sit-down" à la *Cosa Nostra*. It wasn't only the stuffed toilets that stank up the industry, it was the cover-up. Now the casinos, the hotels, travel agencies, shops – everything from the price of your Coca-Cola to your cabin is "organized" to the average Joe's disadvantage.

<u>Accidental Laughter</u>
by Vincent Livelli

Rarely does one laugh at the scene of an accident, the victim least of all.

During the long voyage to Buenos Aires from New York, we organized prize fights out on deck for crewmembers. They were successful as entertainment and relaxation as well as a way of settling some minor disputes. Among the 300 crewmembers, we often had semi-professional boxers that taught lessons and gave exhibitions.

Why not have a prize fight in the main lounge, I thought, as part of our activities? We had been running musical chairs, horse races, costume parties, and were looking for something different. The captain outlawed crew fights in public rooms, of course, but passenger fights that were for amusement and harmless comical displays could be considered as part of workouts in the gym or as self-defense training. He OK'd the idea.

To carry this project further, it was decided that a boxing ring was to be set up in the main lounge, with two contenders chosen from the passenger list.

Prize fights during the forties and fifties were very popular, more so than today. The many scandals and ring injuries put the damper on them, but everyone knew of Luis Firpo, the Argentine heavy-weight world champion who had fought Dempsey. We decided to ask an Argentine passenger to enter the contest against an American opponent. Where the unexpected would enter the picture was in the selection of the fighters. We appealed to two elderly grandmothers to play the role of pugilists for the fun of it. Being fight fans and good sports, they agreed. We then supported them with backup managers and trainers and out-men, in keeping with actual ringside teams with towels, stools, etc.

Acting as announcer, I introduced the referee, followed by the fighters: "In this corner, fighting out of Jersey City, New Jersey, wearing the blue and weighing in at 120 lbs. . . . " In addition to the robes and shorts and boxing gloves, the two ladies were wearing sneakers, since ships in the forties were not stabilized. When the ship's drummer sounded the bell for the opening round, the audience began to encourage their fighter according to their selection, based on nationality.

(Early prize fighters concealed brass knuckles inside their gloves). Unknown to the audience was the fact that each lady held hidden from everyone's view some hair that had been cut prior to the bout, along with a pair of false plastic teeth. The first round featured the teeth falling to the floor after some "blows," followed by clumps of hair for all to see. For the second round, the fighters were seen with black eyes that were applied with shoe polish during the break. After some wrestling and wild swings at each other, the bout was stopped on a T.K.O. when one of the fighters sat on the dance floor pretending to need assistance from the referee to regain her feet. As she struggled upright, a large puddle was evident on the polished floor of the ring, that was quickly mopped up by the lounge steward.

Rather than being embarrassed by this unrehearsed display, the elderly woman arose with a gesture of victory by raising her arms over her head to loud cheering. "It was an accident," she cried out above the sound of much laughter.

CHICAGO AMERICAN

Nate GROSS

JUL 17 1958

555 Passengers, Crew of 695
Set Sail on Caronia for Arctic

TOWN TATTLER ABOARD RMS CARONIA en route to the Top-of-the-World—"The Green Goddess of the Sea," an affectionate name for this ship used by travelers the world over, was at Pier 90 waiting to sail from New York to "The Land of the Midnight Sun."

The customary excitement at sailings was greater

PLAZA 9-7400

VINCENT LIVELLI

SPECIAL SERVICES DEPARTMENT
TRAVEL DIVISION
AMERICAN EXPRESS COMPANY

649 FIFTH AVE.
NEW YORK 22, N. Y.

world. He stands 6 feet 6 and weighs 220 pounds.

★ ★ ★

THE CRUISE staff numbers 20, including two women social directors, but all are not Cunard employes.

staff. Ten carefully chosen men were brought to 65 Broadway for conferences. On occasion, men have been called in from abroad, but European tours now are in full swing.

These staffers are espe-

DOMESDAY SEX

(Rough SEX on THE high SEAS)

You've made love in a phone booth, an elevator or perhaps during a turbulent mile-high flight..how about in two hurricanes in the middle of the Atlantic ocean. Forecasting the vagaries of weather in the fifties was hit and miss meteorology. Off the Cape Verde islands en route to New York, the M.S. OSLOFJORD's 380 passengers were finishing dinner. Some had stepped out on deck to romance at the railing when a sudden drop in temperature swept in with a chill that sent them back into the Main Lounge. The decks became slippery and the wind whistling through the slates in the Promenade doors rose in pitch and velocity. Many chose to return to their cabins but veteran frequent trans-Atlantic travelers chose to ride things out in the bar, leaving reluctantly when the Captain blew his stack and ordered them to do so. Facing a major storm, with no where to evacuate in the ocean, even without advisories or bulletins we realized our growing danger as the ship's horn alerted the shipping lanes of our presence. For the next 12 hours what was usually referred to as "the only way to cross" became most likely a CAT 3 display of Poseiden's Wrath. We're now talking Ty-fooon , man.

Norwegians are among the best seamen in the world. The Captain now steered us north where unfortunately, hurricane #2 was aiming at us. (Let us name them Katrina and sister Rita). Mother Nature's hysterical behavior unleashed her fury full force against our tiny vessel. This time around, towels were laid in hallways to prevent slipping. The elevator was out of service and the Purser's Office was shuttered. Canvas removed from the life boats and the bar was empty. The Fire Brigade went cabin to cabin closing portholes, ropes were strung along railings, the piano was bolted to the dance floor.

Broken glass and loose hazards such as tables and chairs with broken legs and arms were cleared away.

I ~~put on my life preserver and~~ hunkered down in my bunk trying to deflect dark thoughts, in this furious ocean. The sound of crashing dishes and a cry caused me to jump to the door. There in the pantry was my stewardess looking scared to death. I beckoned her in and we soon found ourselves steadying each other. Comforting became cuddling and eventually, intimacy. The carpet was safer than the bunk. Everything not secured joined us on the floor. Flying debris such as the bakelite telephone, the water bottle and articles from the bureau drawers that opened and closed with the rock and roll responded to the ocean wishes. It was shake, rattle and roll time as we banged against the bulkhead and against each other. Teeth hitting teeth discouraged kissing. We were riding a thrill ride called Tumbler of Love. The unpredictability of inconsistent motion had its way with us, WITH THE SHOCKING POSSIBILITY OF "GOING DOWN" DURING A TYFOON, MAN!

No one was in control of this runaway Major Force as we knotted together in the belly of the beast. When a 20 degree roll progressed to a 30 we tightened our stomachs and whenever the propeller emerged spinning from the depths , the stateroom shuddered violently. Levitating minus gravity with each pitch , we discovered positions, plateaus and paroxysms unknown to exist. Unlike Kama Sutra's tantric devotees we were into basic rough sex…delirious, delicious, vicious passion-making gone mad. Routine sex had become now a danger — induced dance with a female's shreek that is music to every male. The quality of such intimacy was compacted by centrifical force as we dug our entwined toes deeper into the carpet. Saddled together as the time for heroic spasms approached, we became exploding transformers. "It was a blast" is my standard answer to "HOW WAS YOUR TRIP?"

SALSA ON THE HIGH SEAS
(SALSA SOBRE LAS OLAS)

TWO OCTAVES BELOW 'A' MAJOR, THE SHIPS' HORN OF THE FIESTAMARINA
SIGNALS THE SAILING FROM MIAMI. UN CRUCERO CON SABOR LATINO,
CON TUMBAO Y RUMBON, NACE UN NUEVO CONCEPTO EN LA INDUSTRIA
MARITIMA, UN IDEA QUE IBA CRECIENDO PASO A PASO.
MUSIC HAS ACCOMPANIED MAN'S VOYAGES THROUGHOUT HISTORY. THE
MAJOR NAVAL FORCES OF THE WORLD ALL HAVE THEIR BANDS. TITO
PUENTE PLAYED IN ONE. ROMAN GALLEYS ROWED TO THE BEAT OF A DRUM.
IN VENICE, GONDOLIERS ROW TO ARIAS. KING LUDWIG FLOATED ON A
BARGE IN HIS CASTLE WITH RICHARD WAGNER. CIRCLE LINE BOATS
HAVE CRUISES CALLED "MAMBO ON THE HUDSON" AND "MERENGUE ON
THE HUDSON" AND IN PARIS, THE BATEAUX-MOUCHE SAIL UNTIL THE
DAWN ALONG THE SEINE PLAYING PORROS AND EXCELLENT SALSA. BACK
IN 1807, OPULENT PLEASURE BOATS PLIED THE NEW YORK WATERWAYS
FEATURING COTILLIONS WITH LARGE ORCHESTRAS ABOARD, ENDING WITH
FIREWORKS. ON WHALING SHIPS DURING MONTH LONG HUNTS, SEAMEN
DANCED TO CHANTIES. THE FRENCH SHIP "JEAN MERMOZ" FEATURED
"SYMPHONY CRUISES". FROM THE LONE ACCORDIANIST ON THE FERRY
CROSSING NEW YORK BAY TO THE FIESTAMARINA, WITH ITS MUSICAL
EMPHASIS AND LATIN MUSICAL HERITAGE - A POWERFUL COMBINATION_
SALSA SOBRE LAS OLAS MARINAS.. SALSA ON THE HIGH SEAS.
BACK IN 1948, 3 ships CALLED THE GOOD NEIGHBOR FLEET SAILED
FROM PIER 32, NEW YORK ON 38 DAY CRUISES TO SOUTH AMERICA.
THE ORCHESTRAS OF THE "BRAZIL,"ARGENTINA"AND "URUGUAY"STRUGGLED
WITH LATIN RYTHMNS. THEY PLAYED FOX TROTS FROM NEW YORK TO
PORT OF SPAIN, CALYPSO FROM TRINIDAD TO BAHIA, THEN SAMBA AS
FAR AS SANTOS AND THEN FROM THERE TO BUENOS AIRES..THE TANGO.
I t was after the passengers RETIRED THAT THE TRUE LATIN SPIRIT
MANIFESTED ITSELF IN THE FORM OF THE CREW CONJUNTO THAT FORMED
EVERY NIGHT ON THE AFT END OF THE SHIP. THE ESPANTANEO - TYPE
BAND MIGHT FEATURE SUCH ARTISTS AS HOT LIPS GARCIA FROM EL BARRIO,
DOROTEO, WHO POPULARIZED 'AMOR PERDIDO', TU NO COMPRENDES
 DOLOR COBARDE RIGHT FROM THE HAPPY BOYS AT THE PARK PLAZA ON
110TH STREET. HOT LIPS PLAYED MALAGUENA SALEROSA TO CALL THE
PASSENGERS TO DINNER EACH NIGHT. HIS TRUMPET REPLACED THE GONG.

MERCHANTS RELYING ON TOURISM ADVERTISE IN THE SHIPS' NEWSPAPER,
EDITED BY THE CRUISE DIRECTOR WHO CHARGES FOR SPACE. SHOPKEEPERS
WILL PAY FOR PUBLICITY GIVEN AT PORT LECTURES THAT THE CRUISE
DIRECTOR DELIVERS PRIOR TO ARRIVAL IN EACH PORT. MERCHANTS WILL
COME ABOARD TO BE INTRODUCED TO CLIENTS BY THE CRUISE DIRECTOR.
THEY MAY KEEP A RUNNING ACCOUNT OF THE TOTAL PURCHASES MADE FROM
THE SHIP WHILE IT IS IN PORT, COMMISSIONABLE TO THE CRUISE DIREC-
TOR. CASES OF LIQUOR,BOTTLES OF PERFUME AND GIFTS ARRIVE AT HIS
OFFICE JUST BEFORE DEPARTURE. IF HE WEARS CLOTHING WITH SHOP LOGOS
HE IS FREE TO KEEP THEM, HE IS NOT CHARGED FOR TAXIS, DINNERS OR
DRINKS FOR HIMSELF OR HIS GUESTS. HE IS ALLOWED A CUSTOMS EXEMPTION
AS A US CITIZEN. BY PURCHASING MERCHANDISE IN A FOREIGN COUNTRY,
INCLUDING IT IN HIS EXEMPTION OR BY PAYING THE DUTY,HE CAN SELL
IT PROFITABLY IN THE STATES. HE CAN PURCHASE IN THE US, ARTICLES
IMPOSSIBLE TO OBTAIN IN FOREIGN COUNTRIES AND SELL THEM THERE AF-
TER PAYING LOCAL DUTIES. HE CAN ACT AS A COURIER, CARRYING DOCUMENTS.
HE CAN SERVE AS A REVEREND AT SERVICES THAT PROVIDE A COLLECTION.
FOR THE "SEAMENS' FUND". HE IS IN CONTROL OF SHIPS' PRIZES AWARDED
TO CONTESTANTS. ANY REMAINING WILL BE DISTRIBUTED AS HE SEES FIT.
HE PROMOTES THE SALE OF SOUVENIR PHOTOS, SHIPS' MENUS, DANCE ALBUMS
RECORDED BY THE ORCHESTRA AND DANCE LESSONS,(WHICH HE MAY GIVE HIM-
SELF IF THERE IS NO TEAM ABOARD).

THE CRUISE DIRECTOR IS IN CHARGE OF THE BINGO GAMES AS WELL AS THE
HORSE RACES. TOGETHER WITH THE CHIEF PURSER, HE RUNS THE SLOT
MACHINES AND THE SHIPS' MILEAGE POOL. ASHORE, CASINOS ALLOW HIM
A PERCENTAGE OF THE RECEIPTS. IN THE COMPANY OF FIRST CLASS
PASSENGERS HE IS GIVEN STOCK TIPS, CAN BANK ABROAD AVOIDING TAXES
WITH HIS FOREIGN ADDRESS AND CAN SELL HIS STATEROOM WHEN THE SHIP
IS OVERBOOKED. IN THIS CASE HE MOVES INTO THE CREW QUARTERS. HIS
HEALTH INSURANCE AND VACATION IS PAID. HE CAN SELL CRUISES FOR A
COMMISSION FROM HIS COMPANY OR OPERATE TOURS THAT HE FORMS USING
THE COMPANY AS CARRIER, I.E., DANCE TEACHERS AND THEIR PUPILS.
MOVIES AND PHOTOS CAN BE SOLD TO MAGAZINES AND NEWSPAPERS. HE HAS
NO OFFICE EXPENSES AND HIS HOSTESS IS HIS SECRETARY. HE CAN SHIP
HIS CAR WITH HIM TO A COUNTRY WHERE IMPORT TAXES ARE VERY HIGH OR
WHERE LUXURY ITEMS ARE FORBIDDEN, THEN ABANDON IT THERE TO BE AC-
QUIRED BY A PRE-ARRANGED BUYER WHO HANDLES THE FORMALITIES. WITH
PROPER DOCUMENTATION, HE CAN IMPORT ANIMALS OR RARE PLANTS AND FISH.
WITH HIS YEARLY BONUS HE CAN COLLECT FOREIGN STAMPS OR COINS.

DURING A SIMPLER PERIOD ALL THESE ACTIVITIES WHERE ABOVE BOARD,
OR SLIGHTLY UNDER THE TABLE. PROSECUTABLE?,HARDLY, INVOLVING AS
THEY WOULD INTERNATIOANAL MARITIME LAW AND PERHAPS AN ADMIRALTY
COURT.

TWO YEARS LATER, NORTHBOUND FROM RIO TO NEW YORK,
A PASSENGER CAME ABOARD. IT WAS MARY, THIS TIME WITH TWO LITTLE
ONES AND HER MAID. WE COULD TELL SHE HAD ENTERED OLD WORLD RIO
SOCIETY AND THAT BRAZILIANS CONSIDERED HER "BEM FORMADA", REFER-
ING NOT TO HER FIGURE, BUT TO HER CHARACTER. I THEN RECALLED HOW
AT THE END OF THE "HONEYMOON EXPRESS", RON HAD ASKED ME FORMALLY
TO INTRODUCE HIM TO "THE YOUNG LADY FROM NEW JERSEY". I RECALLED
HOW HE HAD WATCHED HER, HER TABLE MANNERS, HER BEHAVIOR AT THE
CAPTAINS' COCKTAIL PARTY, AT THE POOL AND HER REACTION TO THE STRESS
OF THE CONTEST THAT NIGHT. HE EVALUATED HER EVERY MOVE AND AS A
SALESMAN WHO KNEW A BARGAIN HE COULD NOT REFUSE, HE WAS SOLD.
BUT WHAT MUST HAVE CLINCHED THE DEAL, MORE THAN THE SPELL OF THE
STARS AND THE SOUTHERN CROSS OVERHEAD, (ALTHOUGH THE STARS COULD WELL
HAVE HAD SOMETHING TO DO WITH IT) MUST HAVE BEEN HER ADMIRABLE
COURAGE, HER FAITH IN HIM. THEY WERE TWO WINNERS AT THE RIGHT
PLACE AT THE RIGHT TIME FOR THE RIGHT REASON. AS A WEDDING
PRESENT, THE COMPANY REFUNDED HER FARE..IN FULL.

SHIPBOARD ROMANCES ARE FREQUENT BUT ACTUAL MARRIAGES ARE
RARE. ON ANOTHER CRUISE, A STRIKING COUPLE BOARDED IN RIO ONLY TO
DISEMBARK THE VERY NEXT MORNING IN SANTOS. THEY WERE THE MOST POPULAR
SCREEN LOVERS IN THE LATIN AMERICAN FILM INDUSTRY. THEY HAD COME TO
BE MARRIED BY THE CAPTAIN. THAT EVENING, IN THE CAPTAIN'S QUARTERS
AND NOT IN THE SHIP'S CHAPEL, THE WEDDING CEREMONY TOOK PLACE IN THE
PRESENCE OF THE CHIEF PURSER, THE HOSTESS AND THE BRIDE-TO-BE'S MAID.
WAS THIS A HOLLYWOOD PUBLICITY MARRIAGE THE PASSENGERS WONDERED? OR
TO ESCAPE RIO'S HYSTERICAL FANS, PERHAPS? IT WAS FOR A MORE PRACTI-
CAL PRE-NUPTUAL CONSIDERATION. BRAZIL IN THE FIFTIES HAD OUTLAWED THE
CASINOS AND THEIR SPECTACULAR SHOWS. IN THIS MOST CATHOLIC COUNTRY,
DIVORCE WAS ILLEGAL. BY MARRYING UNDER AN AMERICAN FLAG IN INTER-
NATIONAL WATERS, A LOOPHOLE WAS DISCOVERED. THE SHIP'S CHAPLAIN
WOULD NOT OFFICIATE, BUT COMPANY ENCOURAGED THE CAPTAIN TO PLEASE
THE MANY REQUESTS. IT WAS THE CAPTAIN WHO REQUESTED TO BE RELEASED
FROM THIS OBLIGATION THAT DEPRIVED HIM OF HIS SHORE TIME. THE LAST
CEREMONY THAT THE CAPTAIN PERFORMED WAS FOR HIS CHIEF STEWARD WHO
WAS ENGAGED TO A "CARIOCA". THUS, THIS LUCKY YOUNG LADY, LIKE THE
MANY WORLD WAR II BRIDES FROM EUROPE,WON HERSELF A TRIP TO THE USA, A
MUCH COVETED AMERICAN CITIZENSHIP AND A MUCH PRIZED AMERICAN HUSBAND.

SHIPBOARD MARRIAGES

by

Vincent Livelli

        DANCING UNDER THE STARS ON DECK IS A POPULAR SHIPBOARD
ACTIVITY. ROMANCE BLOSSOMS. MEANWHILE, PLOTTING TO HASTEN NATURES'
PROCESS ALONG IS THE HARD WORKING CRUISE STAFF.   ONE OF THE SOCIAL
DEVICES THEY EMPLOY IS CALLED "THE HONEYMOON EXPRESS".   THIS CON-
TEST CALLS PASSENGERS ONTO THE DANCE FLOOR WHERE THEY ARE PAIRED OFF
RANDOMLY. A SUITCASE, CONTENTS UNKNOWN,. IS GIVEN EACH PARTICIPANT.
AT A SIGNAL FROM THE CRUISE DIRECTOR, THE SUITCASE IS OPENED AND THE
CLOTHING IS PUT ON. FIRST COUPLE DRESSED WINS. A BIZARRE MIXTURE OF
OVER- AND UNDER-SIZED GARMENTS EMERGE, I.E. LONG JOHNS, TEDDYS',BRAS
AND LACED CORSETS. GENTLEMEN IN KIMONOS, LADIES IN TAILS CAUSES WHAT
LATINS CALL "FRENETICO ARDOR". EVERYONE WINS A PRIZE OF SORTS. THE
REAL WINNERS ARE THOSE WHO HAVE NOW FOUND A NEW PLAYMATE. ON ONE
PARTICULAR CRUISE, THIS "NOVELTY GAME" RESULTED IN AN UNUSUAL MARRIAGE,
NOT BETWEEN THE PARTICIPANTS BUT RATHER BETWEEN A CONTESTANT AND A
SPECTATOR.

        BOUND FOR BUENOS AIRES ABOARD A 38 DAY CRUISE WAS A GROUP
OF CORPORATE SECRETARIES,EMPLOYEES OF STANDARD OIL OF NEW JERSEY.
AMONG THEM WAS ONE WITH A YANKEE FRAME AND KNOBBY KNEES. SHE WOULD
HAVE GONE UNATTENDED HAD THE HOSTESS NOT CAJOULED HER INTO THE CON-
TEST. AS A RETICENT PARTICPANT, SHE MANAGED TO WIN THE SYMPATHY OF
THE CROWD. SHE OBEYED THE RULES, FOLLOWED INSTRUCTIONS, HELPED HER
PARTNER AND ACCEPTED HER DEFEAT WILLINGLY. WEARING SIZE 45, LONG
TROUSERS AND A BIT DISSHELVED SHE LEFT THE FLOOR LIKE A GOOD SPORT.
THUS, SHE CAUGHT THE ATTENTION OF THE MOST ELIGIBLE CHAP ON THE
PASSENGER LIST..HANDSOME, YOUNG, RICH,.TRAVELING ALONE AND DESPERATE!
HE WAS DESPERATELY SEEKING A SECRETARY WHO WOULD RE-LOCATE, ONE WITH
AMERICAN KNOW-HOW FOR HIS NEW COMPANY IN RIO, USING SMALL PUSH CARTS
SELLING ICE CREAM AROUND RIOS' MANY BEACHES. HERE WAS A FRONT OFFICE
SECRETARY WITH AMERICAN BUSINESS EXPERTISE!

        THE CRUISE HAD BEGUN FROM PIER 32 NORTH RIVER, CALLING AT
PORT-OF-SPAIN FOR WATER AND FUEL AND AT BAHIA TO LOAD COFFEE. IN ALL
IT TOOK JUST NINE DAYS TO REACH RIO. WITH 500 PASSENGERS TO ENTERTAIN,
THE CRUISE STAFF HAD LOST TRACK OF MARY UNTIL SHE APPEARED IN A VERY
ATTRACTIVE BATHING SUIT FOR THE NEPTUNE CEREMONY. WORD SOON SPREAD
AROUND THE SHIP THAT A ROMANCE HAD HAPPENED. UPON ARRIVAL IN RIO,
A PASSENGER CAME UP TO SAY "GOODBY". "BUT YOU'RE BOOKED FOR THE FULL
CRUISE, MARY, YOU'RE NOT LEAVING US HER ARE YOU?",ASKED THE CONFUSED
CRUISE DIRECTOR. "OH, YES. I'M SO HAPPY. RON AND I ARE GETTING MARRIED",
WAS HER PROMPT REPLY. AS MARY WALKED DOWN THE GANGWAY TO HER NEW LIFE
SHE TURNED, HESITATED, BLEW A KISS, WAVED HER WHITE HANDKERCHIEF AND
WINKED OVER HER SHOULDER.

From a role-call of history's important women that would begin with Eve, star Cleopatra, and eulogize Susan B. Anthony, for example, the only ones that truly count are those that make you the man or woman that you are. Aside from school teachers or even your dear mother proper there is a woman in the story of one's life that did what no other could or what no other succeeded in doing, namely, making you the you you are today. Her name was Eleanor Britten, Miss New Jersey, form Nutley and a gal "with more sea miles than Admiral Halsey." She circumnavigated the globe continuously as a Social Hostess and Cruise Director. Eleanor was a woman welcomed aboard at the beginning of a multi-billion dollar industry at a time when women on ships were considered bad luck. She was a cheerful buddy to everyone with a stockpile of sailor-type jokes. I never knew anyone who said a bad word against her, even women who erroneously feared her popularity among their husbands. She dated celebrities like Conrad Hilton and was rumored to be the favorite of her company's chairman. As a solid Roman Catholic and an unmarried to the end, Eleanor stood out in a mass of people of the time, the pre-and post-WWII World, who were seeing answers about behavior under changing mores and fashions. Her cheerful confidence in herself and her naval discipline reminded us of Will Roger's, "I never met a man I didn't like."

ELEANOR 1948

RENE ESTELA

Dining Afloat, Ashore and Abroad

by Vincent Livelli

Dining aboard a cruise ship while sailing under a foreign flag, passengers have the choice of many different cuisines. It can be said that they eat abroad without leaving home.

The epicurean menus of Queen Mary II offer cheeseburgers and milkshakes. A 1992 menu of the Royal Viking Sun listed *"Herring Housewife style"*. In 1936, the typical luncheon of the S.S. Munargo of Munson Lines offered *"mixed finnan haddie canapé, chow chow, noodles natural, corned spareribs, pickled lambs' tongue and Postum."* The plush British P & O Line's entrées, called "hot dishes" showed a full selection of *lamb bérgère, larded hazel hen, tournadoes of beef charon, parmesan soufflé* and under dessert, *pears, bananas, tangerines, figs and assorted nuts*. Fruit, especially "black house grapes" as well as vegetables like asparagus were luxuries. Before refrigeration in the thirties, the elegant P & L Liner S.S. Strathaird boasted *"Celery au jus."* In the fifties, the Yarmouth Castle showed *"Potatoes au natural"* while sailing to Nassau.

On 38-day cruises from New York, the top chefs of the S.S. Brazil, S S. Argentina and S.S. Uruguay were obliged to produce meals that satisfied the palatal demands of passengers according to their countries, as well as those of the Americans aboard. For example, the European-oriented Argentinians would pass up carujá, mungusá, vatapá, feijuada, farofa. It had to be bífe de lomo or lomillo. All waiters on these cruises wore white gloves. A bigger challenge during long voyages from Sydney to Southampton faced the chefs of the Dutch World Services. Meals aboard the S.A. Oranje, the Willem Ruys and the M.S. Johann Van Oldenbarnevelt became unbearably predictable, i.e., dessert being cornstarch pudding. Nor could wines travel well under the motion of the long voyage. One passenger called it prison fare.

When in 1956 Alaska became a state, the pastry chefs of the M.S. Oslofjord produced a gigantic baked Alaska for the Americans aboard that was carried flaming into the restaurant by four waiters. That envied place d'honneur, the captain's table, with pre-dinner cocktails in his off-limits quarters followed by "the descent" to the dining room via the grand staircase, the gifts for the ladies hidden under their napkins, the best champagne and finest damask, was a true feast... "*ab ovo usque ad mala*", from soup to nuts. *Post cibum* (after dinner) brandy was served in the men's smoking room, separate from the ladies' room, as they were known in the thirties. The floor shows that followed were never as spectacular as they are today but were well recived after such a "régal de diner."

In the old days of very heavy feasting (that is still the case today), the S.S. Belgianland boasted eight tons of creamery butter on its world cruise. The Norwegian Line now uses asterisks to indicate items approved by the American Heart Association.

The chief steward often organized upon request little dinner parties served apart from the ship's restaurant, either in your large suite or in an alcove. While special occasions called for such affairs, the farewell 'til we meet again themes were nostalgic happenings with singed menus and exchanged addresses for fellow shipmates and tablemates. One party aboard the M.S. Easter Prince of the Furness Line ended with the highly spited hostess tossing two remaining unopened bottles of Dom Perignon high out over the dark ocean. "For the fish!" she yelled. This was in 1934 at $6 a bottle.

Dining abroad in Europe during the seventies was not trop cher. Thankfully, the French franc gave ten to one or more at one point. Some of us knew where it was sixteen to one! With this windfall we made "La Grande Tour Gastronomique," beginning at Nice, then Moulin de Mougins and continuing on to Lyon (Paul Bocuse), Roanne (Les Frères Trois Gros), Tours (Barrier), Viene (Madame Point's Résidence de la Pyramide) and in Provence, L'Osteau de Beaumanière. During several trips to Paris we were fortunate to experience dinners at the following: Taillevent, Maxim's, La Tour D'Argent, Le Bristol, Le Relais de Louis XIII, Le Train Bleu, Le Fregate, Le Closerie des Lilas,

2

The following are some Village restaurants that we have lost: Osteria del Sole, Ye Weverly Inn, Sazarac House, Fez (Time Cafe), Caffé Cefalu, Cafe Latino, Casablanca, Cluyb Gaucho, Markt, Lotfi, Sabor, Turkish Grill, Figaro, O'Henry, Mori, Formerly Joe's, Bill Bertolotti, Louie's, Nick's George's, Ann M. Miller's, Top-of-the-Gate, Dan Stampfler's, Bianchi and Margarita, The Brevoort, Mexico, Le Bijou, Beau Village, La Metairie, Petite Abeille, Lombardi, Night Gallery, Mr. Black, Delancey's Steak House, One Fifth Avenue, Tiffany, Cedar Tavern, Kettle of Fish (MacDougal), Joe's Luncheonette—Sam Remo.

Sam Remo, like Chez Brigitte, lasted for fifty years. Unlike Mr. Lito, who surrendered to hiked rent, the Santini Brothers sold the San Remo for a huge profit. The "Remo" and Chez Brigitte deserve plaques. Neither had photos on the wall, like Minetta Tavern's prize-fight gallery. But if the Remo had, the photos would have shown a collection of all-star literati. The nightly attractions were brilliant arguments about culture, the counter-culture and the counter-counter-cultures as postwar influences arose.

A snapshot of the customers at the Remo would find in the mid-forties: Anatole Broyard *(Kafka Was the Rage)*, William Gaddis *(The Recognitions)*, Milton Klonsky *(Blake's Dante)*, Anais Ninn *(Ladders of Fire)*, Maya Deren (avant-garde filmmaker), Sheri Martinelli (who shared her various talents with Broyard, Gaddis, Bukowski, Ezra Pound and others). They quoted the likes of Henry Michaux *(A Barbarian in Asia)*, or maybe the three versions of *Lady Chatterley's Lover*. The Remo's ghosts of temps perdus have vaporized into what today is an Asian eating place.

Pabulum (food, in Latin) is the first taste of life at the breast. Bitter or sweet, raw life is refined with our reasoning and our seasoning. Perhaps the concept of a soul arose from the smell of cooking as it floated invisibly, seductively, attaching itself to us. The redolent scent in the closet of your lover's perfume, like a second presence or the organic comfort from warm food with a taste that lingers.

4

To handle a menu or wine list with finesse shows us a traveler who has
tasted and known well a world he respects. The French ceelebrate culinary
creativity, as do the Chinese. But there is a dark side to all this. Aside from
plating, price service, etc., there is obesity, butchery, swinish gluttony, messes,
burns, waste, not to mention blood Jell-o, snobbery that talks about the rusticity
of the Peruvian purple potato, for example.

Where we once hunted for sustenance on dangerous missions, food is today
brought to us upon command. Where we once poured a libation on the ground
for the gods, we can now overindulge in an otherwise raw world. Come eat, for
the ice-carved centerpiece drips tears as its fragile beauty washes away before our
eyes. What finer garden is there than the marketplace that displays nature's
fertility and fragrant harvest? The bedtime snack pacifier finalizes our day like a
good-night kiss. Where a cruise ship can be called a "floating bedroom", the cozy
"table in the corner" leads us traditionally to encores of ever more satisfying
desserts.

Our restaurants are the candles glowing in the windows of our
neighborhoods after dark. Like local parishes for our spiritual needs, they
replenish an organic emptiness. They are a second-removed family kitchen.
Grandpa's chair sits empty at the head of the table after he is gone. Where we
begin with bowed heads, we can end with toasts. When ă la table, we are as
though around a tribal campfire. Who remembers the soda fountain at
Bigelow's? As restaurants go, so do neighborhoods. As for dining aloft, eat first
or fly empty.

<u>An Enjoyable Life</u>

Four words describe my life: carrousel, cabaret, circus, carnival – and one more can be added – circumnavigation. Like a non-stop merry-go-round, my voyages on ships carried me around the globe. The entertainment I installed on them turned cruising into a cabaret that prior to that did not exist on the oceans. With so many nationalities and personalities and diverse languages involved in the performance of my duties as cruise director, a circus could describe my working day. Visiting places during celebrations and national holidays worldwide presented me with a carnival-like environment and a gay impression of the world. My life was a selective experience bringing me to events at special moments in history, leaving me with the feeling that it was all prearranged and not of my doing.

None of this could possibly have happened unless by good luck or by good timing. To sustain such an unlikely lifestyle required an ability that I did not possess. Success basically requires everything from focus to prayer, plus talents of unique design.

Because of an impairment, I overcame the lack of natural ability. In spite of severe deafness, I learned to speak five languages that proved to be my entrée into show business. No one else in the comedic genre was using errors committed in front of foreign audiences for laughter. This unique backdoor presentation could have sounded demeaning or insulting to such an audience, but humor overcame sensibility. For example, "Take a rest" in English is "Rest in peace" in foreign languages. Reciting their poetry to foreigners in their own language also helped as flattery.

On the other hand, mistakes that foreigners commit in English amuse American audiences. To tell foreigners jokes borrowed from their respective colloquialisms forges closeness.

Cruise ships carrying multiple nationalities onboard had difficulty hiring such personnel to entertain a mixtured audience that would otherwise have been left in the dark. When not onstage, the cruise director served as an interpreter and translator when needed. This interchange often involved humorous errors. Such an environment in a confined ship's world leads to a lifestyle that incorporates the four words above, to which I might add celebrity, as in celebration of life.

None of this could possibly have happened unless by good luck or by good timing. To sustain such an unlikely lifestyle required an ability that I did not possess. Success basically requires everything from focus to prayer, plus talents of unique design.

Because of an impairment, I overcame the lack of natural ability. In spite of severe deafness, I learned to speak five languages that proved to be my entrée into show business. No one else in the comedic genre was using errors committed in front of foreign audiences for laughter. This unique backdoor presentation could have sounded demeaning or insulting to such an audience, but humor overcame sensibility. For example, "Take a rest" in English is "Rest in peace" in foreign languages. Reciting their poetry to foreigners in their own language also helped as flattery.

Floating Zoo

By

Vincent Livelli

To add more fun to "Fun Ships", why not install a petting zoo aboard, especially for children who have never been to a zoo ashore?

All that needs be done is to set up a hatchery with a mother hen, a brood of chickens and a rooster. This can instruct children as well as fascinate them. A photo holding a baby chic will sell as extra income as well.

More ambitious projects like a penguin or a peacock would expand the attraction. Animals such as harmless snakes, a beehive, or a large cage with a pet monkey would draw attention and sell photos as well. How about turkeys?

The Department of Agriculture could restructure its prohibition of such projects to allow them since the pets would not come ashore to pass inspection for disease as is now the case. Dogs brought from overseas must be certified healthy or guaranteed for weeks as is now the law in effect. The "petting zoo" can be displayed in a setting similar to the ship itself with an imaginary captain's quarters and a general maritime background.

For greater entertainment a pony ride around the ship could a part of the activity program. A small cart (like a ship) could carry 4 or more children out on deck for a fun ride. At Christmas it could serve as a hay ride.

Since cruise ships under foreign registry are exempt from legal restriction that hind U.S. flag operators, the laws are less strict and since the animals do not disembark until their use is terminated aboard, this project has possibilities considering how desperate the steam ship companies are where it comes to entertainment. Rock climbing is restricted to a few passengers brave enough to climb, but a zoo is for everyone, the young and the old. Part of money earned from photos could be donated to the A.S.P.C.A., etc.

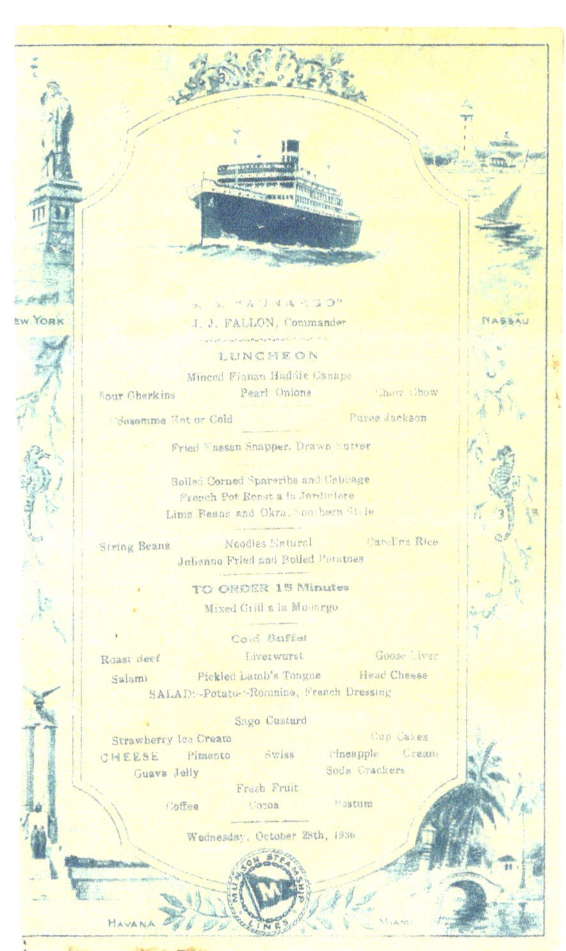

Recibí de la Compañía Pan American, la suma de Veintisiete colones, valor que esta Delegación de Migración le impone de multa, por introducir
al País sin la visa consular correspondiente, al ciudadano Norteamericano, Vicent Levelli, el día de hoy, procedente de Guatemala.

Ilopango, 8 de Diciembre de 1951.

Teniente Juan Rodezno
Delegado de Migración

Por $27.00

SAILING IN TO THE XXI CENTURY

BY

Vincent Livelli

We are sailing to the 21st century aboard floating cities. From her eleven decks the mighty cruise shiplooks down upon the port of Miami. She seems encased in a stainless steel glass container. The next century will glitter like these sparkling ships with their glass elevators and dazzling casinos. At night, the play of their lights on the water aggrandizes our consciousness. They seem to display confidence wrapped in happy colors and gold braid.

Most of our present century has been in black and white. The twenty first will be in hi-gloss, thanks to mirrored polymers. A good illustration of a jewel-like cruise ship interior would be to contrast a kitchen with wooden cabinets to one with mirrored paneling .

Ever since we danced in the night around a fire to a rhythmic sound of some sort we find a joining of light and sound. Today, the MMT , the multi-mirrored telescope with its ten mirrors is the most advanced instrument ever created . Its purpose is the retrace the Big Bang to its beginning and light to its origin... a "Son et Lumiere" par excellence! It took from 1645 when glass was first manufactured in North America to the Pittsburgh plate glass factories of the mid 19th century, for the industry to join advances in chemistry to achieve polymers as hard as steel. Medieval glaziers followed a sketched cartoon similar to tapestry weavers. Now we use computerized blueprints. Transparent glass mosaics involving metallic oxides in a melting pot, brought the art of stain glass to its height in the 13th and 14th centuries. One cathedral boasted seven acres of stained glass. Spiritual messages appeared on stained glass "billboards", some lit by shafts of sunlight 158 feet high as in the Bauvais cathedral, thus creating a religious environment akin to a compelling inescapable commercial. Clusters of unnatural spectrums brought into the empty interiors a convocation of heaven and earth. Imagine the sound of a 4000 pipe organ, the rafters resounding and raining down angelic dust, sprinkling holy magic powder along beams of chromatic sunlight onto the backs of the faithful below. Stained glass orchestrated color from as high up as 30 feet.

One even boasted seven acres of stained glass. .. Parables appeared on stained glass , some lit by shafts of sunlight 158 feet high as in the Bauvais Cathedral. A glorious religious environment was created with a compelling "message". Imagine the sound of a 4000 pipe organ. The rafters resound, raining down angelic dust, sprinkling holy magic powder along beams of chromatic sunlight onto the backs of the faithful below. Clusters of spectrums brought into the empty church interiors a convocation of heaven and earth. The contrast is obvious. Today, the message is, "Come. Have Fun". Sailing inspires meditation but the Ships' Chaplain and the Ships' Chapel have all but disappeared along with the cozy fireplace in the Ships' Lounge . We can see the XXI century approaching behind us in the rear-view mirror of imaginative cruise ship designers . These planners show us a crisp, clean slate reflecting our future world. Our dream vacations are in Technicolor. To set sail on a crystalline floating palace is to taste the XXI century just over the rainbow of an aquatic horizon. The sleek cruise ship, with its corridors of highly polished surfaces, enhances reflections of ourselves, like the mirrors of Versailles. It bathes us in gold, like El Dorado. Checking our postures and adjusting our fancies, we navigate along the well-lit avenues of these inspiring cruise ships. They turn on the Future the way Edison turned on the lights of Times Square.

Sailing about from place to place for many years kept me from ever going into business.
But business seems to follow us everywhere. By going to sea, I had hoped to escape a
nine to five fate, but in doing so I became, not by choice, a commis-voyageur.. a traveling
salesman, an itinerant peddler. Totally unqualified for the commercial world, with no
'acumen', no actuarial experience or 'product knowledge", I was truly an innocent
abroad. Furthermore, I had little respect for materialists.. that is until I came across
Emerson's, "Bring a thing from where it abounds to where it is costly."

Cacti growing wild along the roadsides of St, Martin were vendible in the States, I
assumed. The tropical fish that swam by , tortoise shells from Tortuga, goat skins from
Port-au-Prince and the sea shells of the Caymans, all would find a market at home.
Fossils from the tar pits of Tobago and snake skins from Costa Rica were salable as well
as the
exquisite butterfly wings _ found in Santos. . Young girls arranged them in sheets in
orphanages, where one could buy them eliminating the middlemen and aiding charity
There were black pearls in Margarita Island and "pepita" gold nuggets in La Guaira..I
began to see the world as a treasure in every port.

Post World War II found US Customs still operating under pre-war regulations. In
addition, there was no talk of endange: red species. Seamen as well as passengers were
entitled to a $400.00 duty free allowance once a month back in the late forties. The duty
on a bottle of fine port wine was only .19 cents, for example. two cartons of cigarettes per
person was also allowed in addition to one bottle of liquor. In Gibralter we stocked up on
scotch . Once a trip, crew members could buy liquor duty free from the ship,s locker.
 Perhaps it was Dickens or Mark Twain who commented about 19th century New York
saying, "Everything is for sale"., I found a buyer in Santa Fe who asked me to bring him
ex-votos from Bahia. There were buyers for maracas as well as fine Cuban puros,
antique "Santos " carved in San Juan were cherished and entered without duty. Soon I
was dealing in tiles from Morocco, embroidery from Madeira and sea island cotton goods
from Antigua. The Kuna women of Aligandi, San Blas waited on the dock for my ship to
dock. They sold the blouses (molas) off their backs to us. French perfume from
Guadeloupe and Martinique sold quickly in New York. Naïve folk paintings and hand
carved drums from Port-au-Prince sold well in Miami. The Panamanian molas , by the
way, could be worn as "wearable art". As Zora Neale Hurston once said, "All the world
is my oyster". Sugar was scarce in post war Japan and so were "lugs" (the tiny bar that
holds your watch band to the watch), in Buenos Aires. I supplied both .

I was in danger of going into business when I bought a Maltese terrier in Naples. He sired
over two dozen cute puppies. Would I become a "Pet Shop" owner? The baby ocelot I
bought in Manaus for $8.00, plus a bottle of Metaxas 3 Star was sold to the Parrot
Jungle when he turned savage. Docking in Alexandria found me shopping for furniture in
El-Khalili and in 1958 we bought balalaikas at GUM's for $9.00...sold them at the ship

White Elephant Sale. The world was "Entrée Libre"... "Open All Night". Bargains of a
Lifetime abounded. Like a budding miser, I hoarded discarded match covers, old
postcards, baggage tags, menus.But slowly Customs laws were tightening up, my
apartment was becoming an "entre-pôt". With no fixed base of operations (many deals
took place in hotel rooms ashore or in my cabin) and not home long enough to enjoy my
purchases, it was time to drop anchor before I sold my soul as Imelda Marcos did for a
pair of shoes. With my allotted years winding down I was a tired merchant Marco Polo,
ready to drop.   Negligible gain accrued from years of monetary maneuvering.
Where I had set forth to be a free spirit, seeking poetic nourishment, I was now no longer
the unburdened traveler. When shopping arcades, floating malls came aboard, and Big
Casinos became Big Business it was time to put up the Closed sign. As a wheeler/dealer
with a bankrupt soul, I quit before becoming a successful exhausted businessman ,
smoking duty free cigarettes.

The Age of the Great Cruise Ships.

A ship is a floating mass, as though a chunk of the world broke off on its own with you on it. The crew members are unknowing missionaries leading converts through an aquatic jungle. The passengers become devotees of a new religion called CRUISING These fledgling pilgrims return home to preach to followers, inductees into a cult of cruisers.

The 15th century Age of Exploration into the Unknown was full of heroes and horrors. Nowadays, we go 'round the Horn just for fun. We bring back souvenir countries whereas earlier discoverers picked up Inca gold, slaves and lore of sea and land monsters. Some hid their discoveries while we display them on our clothes. This new Age of Discovery will only end far out somewhere in space, with meetings with other than earth-bound earthlings. "Have you done the moon ? "You really must go". A package tour may come from a package store selling pharmaceutically-laced Bon Voyage baskets. Just let one astronaut return with a snapshot of the "face" on Mars and this touristic Gold Rush will really begin. At present, the "see the world" syndrome places us all at the mouth of a tunnel, needing numerous lifetimes with our limited days. The conceit of Space must wait a bit longer. Naturally, we would prefer to bestow on our next generations a re-shuffled scheme of things, to be able to kiss them good- by and pack them off on some space safari . We could then say, .."my son, the celestial cartographer". Many impulsive youngsters of the future will probably prefer to forego Florence in favor of a lunar week-end or a tour aboard a glass-bottom Atlantis, the way New Yorkers feel that they can always visit the Statue of Liberty some day. It is unavailability that beckons like the implied promise of a beautiful woman. But who would decline an invitation to lunch at the Taj Mahal? It takes no gravitational coaxing to leave with a moontide already within us. The centrifical pull of the Distant; the seduction of science-fiction; the biological urge to explore; to fill the vacuum of the unfulfillable; to "feel" London; to satisfy the gypsy in our psyche.

We   seem to be suffering from End of Century exhaustion and "insufficient Serenity". The remedy is rest and salt air. Travel poster-induced dreams of "paradise"   have materialized, neatly arranged by your corner travel agent. We may envy the handful of world circumnavigators that have gone on their cruises , who will in their turn, envy future travelers around the moon. Why turn our backs on ourselves? Why long to go where men have never gone when we still haven't been where men have gone already?

The Age of the Great Cruise Ships still has a long voyage ahead, like Columbus.

OF COURSE, A LET DOWN SINCE WE TRANSFERED TO AN OLDER VESSEL.
THE S.S. MONROE WAS NOT AIR-CONDITIONED. SHE WAS A C-3 TYPE
PASSENGER CARGO SHIP CARRYING ABOUT 95 PASSENGERS. QUOTING
MARK GOLDBERG IN "CAVIAR AND CARGO" SHE CHARGED ONLY"$250.00
FOR THE TRANS-ATLANTIC SEGMENT FROM MEDITERRANEAN PORTS TO
NEW YORK".SHE HAD SEEN WORLD WAR II SERVICE AT IWO JIMA AND
WAS THE SISTER SHIP OF THE PRES. POLK, ACCORDING TO MR. GOLDBERG.
CARGO WAS LOADED AND UNLOADED CONSTANTLY, AND UNDER BRIGHT
LIGHTS DURING THE NIGHT. ONCE ON LAND, OUR AGENTS, JAPAN TRAVEL
BUREAU SCRAMBLED TO SPLIT US INTO THREE GROUPS BECAUSE OF HOTEL
ROOMS BEING IN SHORT SUPPLY DUE TO POST WAR CONDITIONS AND THE
MIX UP IN OUR RESERVATIONS DUE TO OUR MIXED UP ITINERARY. LOST
BAGGAGE, TIPSY TOURISTS, TOUTS, RUMORS,..THESE ARE ROUTINE
PROBLEMS FOR THE EXPERIENCED TOUR MANAGER. BUT NOW ONE GROUP
WAS PUT UP IN YOKOHAMA, ANOTHER IN TOKYO AND A THIRD IN NIKKO.
TOURISTS CANNOT RESIST COMPARING HOTELS OR RESTAURANTS. EXPECTING
TROUBLE OF VARIOUS SORTS, I HAD WIRED THE BRAZILIAN AMBASSADOR
TO PERHAPS EXTEND AN INVITATION TO COCKTAILS TO WELCOME THESE
RARE VISITORS WHICH HE GRACIOUSLY DID. TH RATIO OF BRAZIALIANS
MAKING THIS SORT OF TRIP IN 1952 WAS ESTIMATED TO BE ONE IN
TWO MILLION, FIVEHUNDRED THOUSAND. AT THE PARTY, ONE OF OUR
MEMBERS SPOKE OF SETTLING FIVE THOUSAND JAPANESE FARMERS ON
HIS PROPERTY, WHERE THERE WERE ALREADY TWO HUNDRED AND FIFTY
THOUSAND JAPANESE IN BRAZIL, MAINLY IN THE STATE OF SAO PAULO.
TO SHOW HOSPITALITY, THE AGENT ARRANGED A "GEISHA PARTY" WHICH
WAS ABOUT AS WICKED AS WEAK TEA, WITH "MUSICALPILLOWS AS THE
PARLOUR GAME.

AFTER ROUNDING UP THE GROUP ON OUR SECOND DAY IN JAPAN, WE
BOARDED THE NEW BULLET TRAIN TO KOBE, WHERE MIRACULOUSLY,
  A BRAZILIAN NAVAL CADET TRAINING SHIP WAS IN PORT!
I IMMEDIATELY CONTACTED THE CAPTAIN AND FREE-LOADED ANOTHER
COCKTAIL PARTY, THIS TIME ON AN OPEN DECK WHERE WE COULD NOW
SEE THE S.S. MONROE ANCHORED OFF OUR BOW. SHE HAD COME DOWN
THE COAST TO MEET US THE DAY BEFORE. THE VESSEL WAS THE FAMOUS
"ALMIRANTE SALDANHA", A TALL SHIP THAT YOU CAN STILL SEE AT
THE NEW YORK HARBOR OP-SAIL FESTIVAL.

BOTH HONG KONG AND RIO HAVE SPLENDID HARBORS WITH LAVISH
NATURAL BEAUTY, BUT HONG KONG IS FOR SHOPPERS AND PREFERS
TO BE FAMOUS FOR BARGAINS RATHER THAN MOUNTAINS. IN 1952,
FOREIGN ASSETS CONTROL REGULATIONS PROHIBITED THE IMPORTATION
INTO THE U.S. OF CHINESE GOODS WHICH WERE NOT IN HONG KONG
PRIOR TO DECEMBER 17th 1952. THIS APPLIED ONLY TO U.S. CITI-
ZENS. THE BRAZILIAN WOULD BE CHARGED CUSTOMS DUTY UPON THEIR
RETURN HOME BUT THEY WOULD STILL BENEFIT TREMENDOUSLY FROM
PRICES IN THE ORIENT. IMAGINE SIXTEEN MILLIONAIRES BUYING OUT
A WHOLE CITY. IT PAID FOR THEIR TRIP! THE TOUR MANAGER'S JOB
 AS TO INTERPRETE FROM AND INTO VARIOUS LANGUAGES EVERYWHERE.

IT WAS A SAD DEPARTURE WHEN THEY HEARD "ALL ABOARD", HAVING
BEEN SUCH WILLING CASTAWAYS. WHAT AWAITED US IN YOKOHAMA WAS
OF COURSE, A LET DOWN SINCE WE TRANSFERED TO AN OLDER VESSEL.
THE S.S.MONROE WAS NOT AIR-CONDITIONED. SHE WAS A C-3 TYPE
PASSENGER CARGO SHIP CARRYING ABOUT 95 PASSENGERS. QUOTING
MARK GOLDBERG IN "CAVIAR AND CARGO" SHE CHARGED ONLY"$250.00
FOR THE TRANS-ATLANTIC SEGMENT FROM MEDITERRANEAN PORTS TO
NEW YORK".SHE HAD SEEN WORLD WAR II SERVICE AT IWO JIMA AND
WAS THE SISTER SHIP OF THE PRES. POLK, ACCORDING TO MR. GOLDBERG.
CARGO WAS LOADED AND UNLOADED CONSTANTLY, AND UNDER BRIGHT
LIGHTS DURING THE NIGHT. ONCE ON LAND, OUR AGENTS, JAPAN TRAVEL
BUREAU SCRAMBLED TO SPLIT US INTO THREE GROUPS BECAUSE OF HOTEL
ROOMS BEING IN SHORT SUPPLY DUE TO POST WAR CONDITIONS AND THE
MIX UP IN OUR RESERVATIONS DUE TO OUR MIXED UP ITINERARY. LOST
BAGGAGE, TIPSY TOURISTS, TOUTS, RUMORS,..THESE ARE ROUTINE
PROBLEMS FOR THE EXPERIENCED TOUR MANAGER. BUT NOW ONE GROUP
WAS PUT UP IN YOKOHAMA, ANOTHER IN TOKYO AND A THIRD IN NIKKO.
TOURISTS CANNOT RESIST COMPARING HOTELS OR RESTAURANTS. EXPECTING
TROUBLE OF VARIOUS SORTS, I HAD WIRED THE BRAZILIAN AMBASSADOR
TO PERHAPS EXTEND AN INVITATION TO COCKTAILS TO WELCOME THESE
RARE VISITORS WHICH HE GRACIOUSLY DID. TH RATIO OF BRAZIALIANS
MAKING THIS SORT OF TRIP IN 1952 WAS ESTIMATED TO BE ONE IN
TWO MILLION, FIVEHUNDRED THOUSAND. AT THE PARTY, ONE OF OUR
MEMBERS SPOKE OF SETTLING FIVE THOUSAND JAPANESE FARMERS ON
HIS PROPERTY, WHERE THERE WERE ALREADY TWO HUNDRED AND FIFTY
THOUSAND JAPANESE IN BRAZIL, MAINLY IN THE STATE OF SAO PAULO.
TO SHOW HOSPITALITY, THE AGENT ARRANGED A "GEISHA PARTY" WHICH
WAS ABOUT AS WICKED AS WEAK TEA, WITH "MUSICALPILLOWS AS THE
PARLOUR GAME.

AFTER ROUNDING UP THE GROUP ON OUR SECOND DAY IN JAPAN, WE
BOARDED THE NEW BULLET TRAIN TO KOBE, WHERE MIRACULOUSLY,
 A BRAZILIAN NAVAL CADET TRAINING SHIP WAS IN PORT!
I IMMEDIATELY CONTACTED THE CAPTAIN AND FREE-LOADED ANOTHER
COCKTAIL PARTY, THIS TIME ON AN OPEN DECK WHERE WE COULD NOW
SEE THE S.S. MONROE ANCHORED OFF OUR BOW. SHE HAD COME DOWN
THE COAST TO MEET US THE DAY BEFORE. THE VESSEL WAS THE FAMOUS
"ALMIRANTE SALDANHA", A TALL SHIP THAT YOU CAN STILL SEE AT
THE NEW YORK HARBOR OP-SAIL FESTIVAL.

BOTH HONG KONG AND RIO HAVE SPLENDID HARBORS WITH LAVISH
NATURAL BEAUTY, BUT HONG KONG IS FOR SHOPPERS AND PREFERS
TO BE FAMOUS FOR BARGAINS RATHER THAN MOUNTAINS. IN 1952,
FOREIGN ASSETS CONTROL REGULATIONS PROHIBITED THE IMPORTATION
INTO THE U.S. OF CHINESE GOODS WHICH WERE NOT IN HONG KONG
PRIOR TO DECEMBER 17th 1952. THIS APPLIED ONLY TO U.S. CITI-
ZENS. THE BRAZILIAN WOULD BE CHARGED CUSTOMS DUTY UPON THEIR
RETURN HOME BUT THEY WOULD STILL BENEFIT TREMENDOUSLY FROM
PRICES IN THE ORIENT. IMAGINE SIXTEEN MILLIONAIRES BUYING OUT
A WHOLE CITY. IT PAID FOR THEIR TRIP! THE TOUR MANAGER'S JOB
 AS TO INTERPRETE FROM AND INTO VARIOUS LANGUAGES EVERYWHERE.

THE CONCORDE OF THE SEAS

by
Vincent Livelli

Sailing aboard R.M.S. Queen Mary back in 1958, I found my shoes shined each morning outside my cabin. My room steward straightened my bow tie, brushed me down, and patted me on the shoulder every evening as I left for diner. We had celebrities on board, one of whom was Madame la Veuve Clicquot Ponardin, a widowed descendant of the house of Veuve Clicquot. Music played for dinner, and the grand staircase, the stage for "La Grand Descente" was not split in two with right and left sides as it is on QM2 because of traffic entering the restaurant.

There was "Bristol" spit and polish in evidence all over the ship. And without the 2,620 passengers carried on today's QM2, there was more privacy for romance.

Without stabilizers you knew you were on a ship, not at a "floating hotel." Built at an astronomical cost it is designed and constructed to sail the equivalent of thirteen trips to the moon. She has some 200,000,000 nautical miles to go. New York City spent $54,000,000 for her new pier in Red Hook. We're talking big bucks here.

She is "the most magnificent resort on the planet" the "Concord of the Seas." But fuel costs crippled this Concorde. While she enjoys the monopoly of the trans-Atlantic highway, I wonder if she will follow the path of R.M.S. Queen Mary, and be tied up like a prisoner in chains, a "stop engine" forever, with a pitiful charge of admission to board her out in California. Or will it be, "damn the prices, full speed ahead!" Let us sail out on the fabulous ocean to savor the salt air beyond the ordinary, rather than be left standing on the dock, counting our pennies. Ships are the safest and the best way to live it up, penny for penny.

<u>How Does the Cruise Director Handle Six-Thousand Passengers</u>?

We admire people like David Letterman, Bob Hope, and Charlie Chaplin, entertainers with very long successful careers. With help from writers, stage designers, wardrobe staff, press agents, and scriptwriters, it is understandable how they managed to satisfy the demands made on them. I had none of the assistance they enjoyed. Alone, performing night and day, surrounded by my audience aboard ships, responsible for not only diversion from the boredom of long ocean voyages, often days out of sight of land, I was unable to hide, so that my appearance onstage was continuous. I had to be Master of Ceremonies, perform, introduce myself anew, as well as provide fresh material and in foreign languages. No wonder the company didn't want to lose me!

The prominent people I met should have had some effect on me, but I did not see things that way. It was I who was to have an effect on them. What I did, as I look backward . . . . <u>Perhaps the most convincing evidence, of all the factors that contributed to the construction of my life, were established against the odds of my hearing impairment combined with my advanced age that have allowed me to see myself as successful in two ways, not one. (Help! It's not clear.)</u> The *oreishas* have been satisfied with me, and I, satisfied with my self, that is, my *self* esteem regained.

One could say I was dead, that I never existed or that I never mattered at all, or that I was of little importance if I was ever living a life that evolved around Anatole Broyard and Milton Klonsky, Sheri, Willie Gaddis, Helen Parker, the San Remo ('38), the Cornelia Street Bookstore, Dick Gilman, Larry Rivers, Anaís Nin, Stanley Hayter, or Henri Michaux's influence.

Let's add eighty countries, first XXXXX? seventy-five languages (I'm deaf), one hundred celebrities (beginning with Henri Michaux and Duke and Duchess), sixty-three ships (around the world), lecturer (Smithsonian, New School, John Jay College, on Afro-Cuban music), and an unpublished writer – except for some minor stuff.

No obituary for Sheri, disrespect for Anatole's major influence, no mention of Vincent Livelli. It's my fault for not speaking out more, and for leaving the Village to explore Henri Michaux's world, and for not owning any tech toys or computers. Like no obituary for Sheri, no mention of V. Livelli. My fault for living sans computers or email. I'll be writing you to make me feel alive before my demise.

S.S. BRASIL 1950

<u>Open House</u>

Having lived for many years aboard ships, my cabins, large or small, were home to me. To enter someone else's private domain was always a fascinating experience.

In the late forties, a cruise director sold shore excursions whose itineraries often included permissible intrusions into many notable venues. Whether by invitation, chance, or occupation, my travels were the keys that opened the doors to a world that has "many mansions."

The following is a list of visits paid to a world open to inspection:

Ashford Castle, Ireland
Mahatma Gandhi's House, Bombay
Simon Bolívar's Home, Caracas
King Ludwig's Castle, Neueschwanstein
Betsy Ross's Cottage, Philadelphia
Hemingway's House, Key West
Ann Hathaway's Cottage, Stratford-on-
    Avon
Iban Long House, Borneo

The Forbidden City, Peking
The Virgin Mary's Home, Turkey
    (Ephesus)
King Farouk's Houseboat, Cairo
The Vatican, Vatican City
Delmore Schwartz's apartment, Charles St.,
    NY
Washington Irving's Home, Phillipsburg,
    NY

The White House, Washington, D.C.

While walking around Bombay in 1981, I happened to read a small painted sign indicating that the one-story frame house had been Mahatma Gandhi's home. It looked "as is," threadbare in appearance, with a low wooden fence out front that came right up to the front door, leaving no room for a garden. Everything appeared donated or home-made of plain wood alone. What stood out the most, aside from his spinning wheel, was a rickety table. The table stood just at the entrance and took up two-thirds of an inadequate room that was his kitchen. It reminded me of some of the cramped cabins I called home aboard ship.

In Holland, time did not permit a visit to Ann Frank's House. In Kajuraho, India, I entered the temples of the Chandela people, and in Sarawak, the Iban longhouses.

A "chola" is a thatched, round earthen hut. The native Chola in Canaima, Venezuela is like the White House in a way. Families move in, stay for a while, then move out so that others may move in.

THE OPEN SEA

DEAR BLISS: YOUR DAD WAS PUZZLED BY MY "SHIPPING OUT". FOR MY PART,
IT WOULD BE LIKE LEARNING TO SWIM. A SEAMAN LEADS A STACCATO EXIS-
TENCE, REMAINING IN ONE PORT FOR THREE DAYS, ONE DAY IN THE NEXT,
NO DAYS BY-PASSING OTHERS OR MERELY HOURS IN SOME. LIKE SAMPLING
WINE, IT PRODUCES AN EUPHORIC VISION OF A COLORFUL WORLD. WHETHER
VITAL OR NEGLIGENT, CONTACTS AND EVENTS MATTER LESS, FOREVER CUT
SHORT, NEVER EXTENDED TO WHERE THEIR OUTCOMES OR THEIR MEANINGS
ARE FULLY ABSORBED. AS A RESULT, ONE FEELS LESS PROPERLY AFFECTED
BY HISTORY. SKIMMING THE SURFACE, STOPPING AT THE MARGINS OF LIFE,
ONE LEADS A DISJOINTED ROUTINE. THIS TYPE OF EXISTENCE IS ONE THAT
IDEALLY EMBODIES THE BASIC PHILOSOPHY SO EMBRACED BY VILLAGERS..
THE SENSE OF FREEDOM AND LEARNING.

SHIPBOARD LIFE IS INDEPENDENT AND SECURE, LESS TIED TO THE PAST,
LESS IN DEBT TO AN UNCERTAIN FUTURE. IT ANSWERS THE NEEDS OF
WHERE ONE WILL BE SHELTERED, FED OR SLEEP. FOR ME, IT BECAME A
MARRIAGE OF CONVENIENCE. I LIKE TO BELIEVE THAT IT STUNTED MY
GROWTH THAT WOULD HAVE HEADED IN THE WRONG DIRECTION. TODAY, IN ME,
THE VILLAGE OF THE FORTIES IS EVIDENT BECAUSE OF AN "EXTENDED
LIFE STYLE" AS THOUGH I NEVER LEFT HOME. FOR A DOZEN YEARS, I
STARED HYPNOTIZED BY THE OPEN SEA, A BODY THAT IS THE WORLD IN
ITS MOST BASIC FORM, AS THOUGH THE CREATOR USED WATER TO FINISH
THE JOB OF CREATION. AS FOR THE REST OF IT, WHETHER GOOD OR BAD,
IT WAS DOWN-SIZED TO A SECONDARY SIGNIFICANCE, SYMBOLIZING
SIMPLICITY WHERE HENRY ADAMS SAW " THE MULTIPLICITY OF THE
TWENTIETH CENTURY ". THERE WAS NO URGENT NEED TO "UNDERSTAND"
LIFE. WHY UPSET A NATUROPATHIC FORMULA OF AN UNCONTAMINATED
ENVIRONMENT OF CLEAN AIR AND WATER TO CORRECT IT? IT IS THE
SAFEST PLACE IN TODAYS' WORLD, WHERE, AT ONE TIME IT WAS CON-
SIDERED TO BE THE MOST DANGEROUS,. A LIFE OF SACRIFICE.

THE CLOSER ONE IS TO NATURE, THE MORE IT SEEMS THAT LIFE WAS LAYED
OUT TO BE SO. TRAVEL CONTINUOUSLY AND YOU WILL EVENTUALLY COVER ALL
THE BASES. IF YOU BELIEVE LIFE IS A CABARET OR A CARNIVAL, YOU
WILL SURELY SHOW UP IN RIO, CANNES, NEW ORLEANS, PASADENA, NASSAU,
NICE, BAHIA, ETC. EVENTUALLY. IF RUINS ARE YOUR THING, YOU WILL
FIND YOURSELF ONE DAY IN PAGAN, PETRA, JERASH, PACHACAMAC, MALTA,
GOREME, ISRAEL. YOU WILL THROW NAMES AROUND LIKE CONFETTI AND
OVERWHELM THE CREDULITY AND PATIENCE OF THE MOST LOYAL READER.
TO MENTION THE MOST "THIS" OR THE MOST "THAT" IS UNFAIR TO THE REST.
LIKE SPEAKING OF ONES' WEALTH OFTEN OFFENDS OTHERS, UNLESS ASKED.
BUT HOW CAN ONE REMAIN SILENT ABOUT COCHIN OR VOLUBILIS WHETHER ASKED
OR NOT? WHEN ASKED, "HAVE YOU BEEN TO.."?, IS IT PERMISSABLE TO
REPLY, "YES. FOUR TIMES"? OR WHEN ASKED, "HAVE YOU EVER.."? CAN
YOU SAY, "YES, MANY TIMES". ONE RISKS BECOMING A BRAGGART OR BEING
CALLED A FAKER. YOU CAN LOSE FRIENDS OR RECEIVE INVITATIONS. YOUR
REPLIES MUST BE SELECTIVE. IS IT BEST TO FOLLOW THE WAY OF THE
SELF-FORGIVING SOLITARY TRAVELER UNTIL THAT DAY WHEN THE DIARIES
ARE OPENED FOR ALL THE WORLD TO SHARE?

DURING THE "FAREWELL DINNER" FOR THOSE DISEMBARKING IN RIO
I SAT NEXT TO THE MOTHER-IN-LAW. UNSEEN, UNDER THE TABLE, A
LITTLE CONTINENTAL FLIRTATION BEGAN TO TAKE PLACE. LOOSENED
BY CHAMPAGNE, DEEPER EMOTIONS BEGAN TO SURFACE AND THE FES-
TIVITIES ENDED UP WITH JUST THE TWO OF US IN MY CABIN.

UPON ARRIVAL IN RIO THE NEXT DAY, NOT EVERYONE RUSHED ASHORE.
PRIVILEGED PASSENGERS COULD INVITE FAMILY AND GUESTS FOR LUNCH
BEFORE LEAVING THE SHIP. I WAS INVITED TO JOIN A TABLE FOR FOUR
WHICH INCLUDED THE SON,(POPULAR MINISTER OF FOREIGN RELATIONS),
HIS WIFE,(THE DAUGHTER-IN-LAW)AND THE MOTHER-IN-LAW. AS THE
MEAL PROGREESED THERE WAS ONCE AGAIN ACTIVITY UNDER THE TABLE.
 HAPPILY, IT WENT UNNOTICED BY THE SON, BUT BECAME QUITE OBVIOUS TO
THE DAUGHTer-IN-LAW, JT SEEMED THAT BOTH I AND THE MOTHER-IN-
LAW WERE CONSPIRING TO IMPRESS THE FRUSTRATED DAUGHTER-IN-LAW, EACH
FOR REASONS OF OUR OWN. WHAT CONVINCED HER WERE THE GOLD CUFF-
LINKS I WAS SURE SHE WOULD NOTICE- A TYPICAL BRAZILIAN GIFT TO
A NEW LOVER.

AN INTRIGUE BEFITTING THE BORGIASENDS THIS STORY. I WAS OPENLY
IN LOVE WITH THE SHIPS' FEMALE VOCALIST. WHEN WE REACHED NEW YORK,
SHE WAS SURPRIZED TO FIND A ROUND TRIP TICKET AND A VERY TEMPTING
CONTRACT TO PERFORM IN RIO WAITING FOR HER. WAS THIS AN ATTEMPT
TO SEPARATE US, PLOTTED BY THE VENGEFUL "POWERHOUSE", I WONDERED?
WHEN SHE SHOWED ME THE MINISTERS' SIGNATURE, SHE CONFESSED THAT HE
HAD BEEN COURTING HER FOR SOME TIME, UNBEKNOWNST TO HIS WIFE OR TO
HIS MOTHER, OR TO ME.

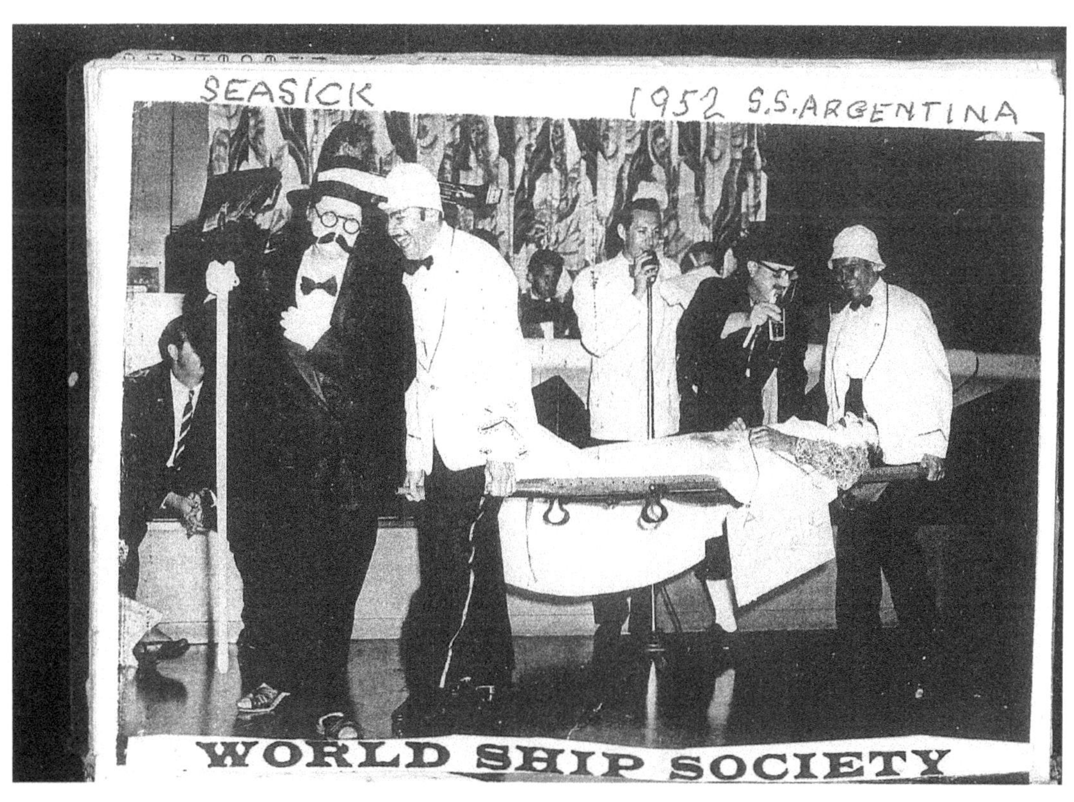

WANDERINGS

S. FRUTTUOSO - GOLFO PARADISO
Abbazia
L'Abbaye
The Abbey
Das Kloster

9/8

air mail

HAPPY

DAY MOM

Mrs Jeanette
LIVELLI
44 PERRY St.
N.Y.C.
10014
N.Y. USA.

SF 3/9

Natural Disasters & Wild Parties

Chile is known for its wine, women, and festivals. The Viña del Mar Film Festival is the Latin American equivalent of Cannes. To get there from Santiago, a British-built railway runs along the coast, entering and exiting a long chain of unlit tunnels. Some tunnels run in and out of total darkness very quickly; others go on forever. The interiors of the carriages remain blacked out, except for emergency lighting.

Chile is a very friendly country, so that I began an introductory traveler's conversation with the young lady sitting beside me. She was ripe, plump, and sweet-smelling like the fruit Chile is known for. She was luscious, a delicious papaya called *la fruta bomba* in Spanish.

At first, we sat silent while passing through several tunnels, resuming talking only to refrain upon entering the next, and so forth. Since she knew her tunnels and I didn't, she began to talk just as we were exiting, stopping as we entered the darkness, until I found her hand searching for mine in silence. There was no need to talk, except to mention that I would be staying at the Hotel Miramar.

At the hotel as I was preparing for the beach, there came a gentle knocking at the door that coincided with sudden pounding at my window. A wave came crashing against it — we were having a Chilean earthquake! I opened the door. Rosita was calm, smiling, happy to see me. I was as rattled as the windows. She knew her earthquakes and I didn't. I embraced her with anxiety, urgency, intensity, and necessity. When the room began to swing, sway, rattle, and rock, I was shuddering, causing Rosita to laugh at me. When the bed hit the wall while we were acting like lunatics, I thought, Ride it out or run naked into the street. But this meant coitus interruptus. She silenced my fears with a prolonged kiss, as though it had all been fun and a wild

IN PRAISE OF TRAVEL WRITERS

TRAVEL WRITERS DESCRIBE PLACES VISITED OR PLACES TO VISIT OR AVOID.
BUT WHY GO TO NIAGARA AND NOT SEE THE FALLS OR TO PARIS AND NOT
SEE THE EIFFEL TOWER? TO GO TO KING TUT'S TOMB AND NOT ENTER IS
UNREAL OR TO GO TO THE TAJ MAHAL AND SKIP SEEING IT. SUCH THINGS
CAN HAPPEN AND DID TO THE WRITER.

TRAVEL IS FULL OF THE UNEXPECTED OR THE UNEXPLAINED. BUT TO BE IN
MOSCOW AND NOT VISIT THE KREMLIN OR IN TUNISIA AND MISS CARTHAGE,
TO BE IN THE VATICAN AND NOT TAKE IN THE SISTINE CHAPEL. IMAGINE
SEEING THE PYRAMIDS AND NOT RIDING A CAMEL, BUT A DONKEY INSTEAD,
DUE TO A STRIKE. IMAGINE ALSO, BEING IN LIMA AND PLANNING TO
VISIT MACCHU PICCHU ONE DAY OR IN HONG KONG TEN TIMES,PLANNING
TO GET TO MACAO SOME DAY. WE MISSED THAT HISTORICAL SIGNING CER-
EMONY ON THE S.S. MISSOURI. HOW COULD WE NOT ATTEND THE OLYMPIC
GAMES IN MOSCOW IN 1958 IN ORDER TO SIGHTSEE. HOW CAN ONE PASS
THROUGH TORONTO, THE BEST LIGHTED CITY IN THE WORLD, IN THE DARK?

SUCH HAPPENINGS ARE NOT UNUSUAL TO SOMEONE IN THE TRAVEL INDUSTRY
WHO TRAVELS CONSTANTLY. TO SKIP THE TAJ MAHAL WOULD BE INEXCUSABLE
WHERE IT NOT THAT I HAD SEEN IT TWICE BEFORE AND AGRA HAS MANY
PALACES AND ATTRACTIONS. SURELY NIAGARA FALLS CANNOT BE MISSED
DUE TO ITS ENORMITY ALONE. WE COULD HEAR ITS MIGHTY ROAR BUT DUE
TO THE BLACK-OUT IN EFFECT DURING WORLD WAR II IT WAS INVISIBLE.
THE SAME WAS TRUE IN TORONTO. AS I WAS DESCENDING THE STONE STEPS
TO ENTER KING TUT'S TOMB, I WAS CALLED BACK TO ASSIST A STRICKEN
PASSENGER AND WE WENT TO THE HOSPITAL INSTEAD. THE WORST FOG TO
HIT PARIS IN YEARS BLOTTED OUT THE EIFFEL TOWER. THE CITY AND
THE PEOPLE WERE WHAT WE CHOSE TO SEE IN MOSCOW INSTEAD OF THE
KREMLIN. AS FAR AS MACAO IS CONCERNED, THE HYDROFOILS UPSET THE
STOMACH. ON MY WAY TO THE S.S.MISSOURI, I DETOURED INTO DEALING
WITH V-J CANCELATIONS WITH THE POSTMASTER IN YOKOHAMA INSTEAD.
CARTHAGE INVOLVED FIGHTS WITH STUBBORN THIEVING CAB DRIVERS AND
WAS CANCELLED. THE NEW ORLEANS MARDI GRAS ENDED THE DAY BEFORE
WE ARRIVED SO WE MISSED IT. WE HAD TO LEAVE IN THE MIDDLE OF A
PAPAL AUDIENCE OR MISS THE SHIP IN NAPLES. EN ROUTE TO PARIS,
WHEN THE TRAIN STOPPED AT LOURDES, THANK GO WE HAD NO REASON
TO GET OFF. WE SPEEDED ALONG THE HIGHWAY RIGHT PAST WOODSTOCK II.
WE WERE WISE TO LEAVE THAT WATERFRONT DIVE IN MONTEVIDEO BEFORE
THE FIGHT STARTED. IT WAS WISER ALSO NOT TO VOLUNTEER TO VISIT
HIROSHIMA JUST AFTER THE BOMB.

SOMETIMES WE MAY BUMP INTO GROUND SHAKING EVENTS BY ACCIDENT,
LIKE JAPANESE EARTHQUAKES, OR SUDDEN STORMS IN THE ATLANTIC.
WE CAN BE DELIGHTED BY HINDU WEDDINGS AT THE HOTEL OR THE
SURPRIZE ON FINDING WE HAD ARRIVED IN HAVANA DURING CARNIVAL.
A CHANCE MEETING IN THE DARK IN PORTOFINO FOUND US IN CONVER-
SATION WITH THE DUKE AND DUCHESS OF WINDSOR. THE NIGHT THE
BROWN BOMBER, JOE LOUIS,WON THE WORLD CHAMPIONSHIP WE WERE
ON LENOX AVENUE. NOTHING QUITE COMPARED TO SHOPPING IN HONG
KONG IN 1952. WHAT MAKES FOR GOOD READING IN A BUSY WORLD..
USEFUL INFORMATION THAT ENTERTAINS AS IT EDUCATES.

IN PRAISE OF TRAVEL WRITERS

HOW COULD ONE MISS THE EVENTS OF THE SIXTIES AND SEVENTIES?
JFK'S ASSISINATION, VIET NAM? WORKING ON CRUISE SHIPS DURING
THOSE TIMES PUT YOU JUST OUT OF RANGE OF THE MOST SHATTERING
EVENTS. JUST EIGHTY MILES OFF SHORE PUT YOU AT A SAFE DISTANCE.
EXCEPT BY SHORT WAVE OR THE SHIP'S NEWSPAPER, TRYING TO CATCH
UP WITH HAPPENINGS WHILE ANCHORED BRIEFLY IN DIFFERENT PORTS,
WAS TO BE FAR REMOVED IN PLACE, TIME AND TOUCH.

IN THE WRITING COMMUNITY, TRAVEL WRITERS ARE JUST A STEP ABOVE
MOVIE CRITICS, BUT IT IS THEY WHO WRITE THE MOVIE. WHETHER IT
IS A POST CARD, DIARY OR "DON QUIXOTE", THE DESIRE TO WRITE
GOES ALONG HAND IN HAND, STEP BY STEP WITH THE NEED TO RELATE,
TO SPEAK, TO COMMUNICATE, TO ASSIST OTHERS WITH A MAP OF LIFE.
MANY REMAIN UNDISCOVERED BY A GROWING TRAVELING PUBLIC. MONA LISA
DOES NOT BELONG TO EVERYONE. SHE BELONGS MOST TO THOSE WHO STAND
IN FRONT OF HER. MARCO POLO WENT FORTH AS A MERCHANT AND RETURNED
AS A WRITER, AS A TRAVELER. A SUNSET SETTLING ON THE SURFACE OF
THE RED SEA OR THE RARE UNCOVERING OF THE CREST OF THE JUNGFRAU
REVEAL MOTHER NATURE'S JEWELRY.

A SPECIAL SEND OFF GOES OUT TO THE TRAVEL WRITERS WHO EXCAVATE
THE ATTICS OF THE WORLD TO BRING HOME TO US THE MUSIC IN THEIR
TALES. WHAT WOULD THE WORLD BE LIKE WITHOUT THEM? TERRA INCOGNITA.

Vincent Livelli
44 Perry Street
New York, New York 10014
212-255-0508

4-16-2015

BEEN THERE, DIDN'T DO THAT

By

Vincent Livelli

Travel often mirrors life in that much of it must remain unaccomplished. But why travel to the Taj Mahal, for example, and skip seeing it or to King Tut's Tomb and not enter it? In Paris we didn't see the Eiffel Tower or Big ben in London. We didn't drink tequila in Tijuana or vodka in Moscow. At Niagara Falls we could hear the roar but left without seeing them. At Waikiki Beach we didn't go swimming nor did we ride a camel at the pyramids. We didn't take in Carthage while in Tunis and avoided Macho Pichu while in Peru. We transited the Panama Canal but not by ship and left the Vatican without seeing the Sistine Chapel. We rode by the changing of the guards in London without stopping and missed the surrender ceremony aboard the S. S. "Missouri". We ducked out of the guided tour of the Kremlin and never saw the Golden Pagoda while visiting Rangoon. In Cozumel, we ignored the "Mayan" ruins. In Poland we didn't buy a single souvenir and sailed around the world, but not as a tourist. We visited many times in Hong Kong, but never Macao.

It could be considered cool by some not having a photo of yourself holding up the leaning Tower of Pisa, but really now, the Taj Mahal or King Tut? The above list of world famous "must do's" were skipped for good reasons. First of all, we had seen the Taj Mahal twice before and Agra has many other

marvels to visit. We had to forgo king Tut and return to the hotel with a friend who tripped on the steps. The famous London fog blanketed Big Ben and in Paris it was visibility zero. During World War II the Niagara Falls were blacked out and we were there at night. What, no Tequila, no Vodka? (Doctor's orders). No swimming at Waikiki? (Ear infection). The changing of the Guards was nothing new; we'd seen it in Ottawa. Thieving cab drivers in Tunis caused us to cancel Carthage and a camel driver's strike forced us to ride a donkey at the Pyramids. Hearing about a plane crash discouraged flying to Machu Picchu. In Panama, we crossed the canal by Train, In Italy, it was see the Sistine Chapel or risk missing the ship. Bumpy hydrofoil rides are no fun...so no Macao. On the way to the S. S. "Missouri", we detoured to buy valuable V-J Day cancellations at the Yokohama Post Office. Meeting Muscovites was better that a taxing guided Kremlin Tour. "Steer clear of Cozumel's artificial artifacts". Seemed like food advice, Scorching heat discouraged climbing the countless steps to see the Shwegadon Golden Pagoda in Burma. In Warsaw no one understood the word "souvenir".

How could one not hear of J.F.K.'s assassination or be so ignorant about the Beatles, Elvis, or Viet Nam? Working on ships during those years removed us from the impact of these events. History went on without us. We were out of range of things, dependent on short wave, wandering in a barren time and space like Don Quixote. Ignorant of what went on at home, like Ulysses, we were prisoners of the sea, brothers of Robinson Crusoe, sailing to a different drummer in a sea world.

Nevertheless, we all travel on inexorably to the last stop. The one "must do" on our itinerary that we cannot fool around with. Didn't see Macao? Perhaps we should have, At the Deauville Casino we just watched. At the Tropicana we didn't see the show because we had passed out. At the Tour D'Argent we skipped the Specialite de la Maison (Lobster)....no shell fish. We spent time on an island in San Francisco Bay...not Alcatraz, but Angel Island. We visited Hungary, but only Buda and not Pest on the other side of the Danube. Fish is what we ordered at the famous Gallagher's Steak House (Doctor's orders), "No red meat". Didn't climb up the bronze Buddha on Lantau Island, too many steps. Pompeii's brothel wall frescoes were "closed to the public" and "off limits". Nile River boats sail N/S, we sailed E/W from the Winter palace Hotel dock to the Valley of the King's.

HIDDEN PLACES OF THE WORLD

THE FISHING VILLAGE OF
San Fruttuoso, WHERE IS IT?

Traveling to rare places that combines the thrills of danger with the illusion of fantasy awakens and teases the tourist's explorative curiosity. It leads him to spiritual as well as geographical encounters. He leaves an overly familiar back yard for alien words.

Not far from Stonehenge, a hydrofoil speeds you to Rye on the Isle of Wight, Queen Victoria's vacation spot. Above Manila is Baguio, with its centuries old rice terraces. Parisians leave Paris to drive to Vaux-Le-Vicónte, the magnificent abode of Louis XVI's finance minister. Leave Buenos Aires for Lujan with its cluster of houseboats around the National shrine. Escape busy Bombay to visit the Ajanta Caves in the harbor where porters will carry you to see them. Enter gilded interiors of Orthodox Churches the Soviets didn't want you to see.

Some places seem to hide from us. Shangrila was "found" in the misty valleys of Himalaya. Angel Falls curtained itself behind spray. Peruvian Nazca lines (GEOGLYPHS) had to be discovered from the air, and like crop circles, they are best seen from above. 30,000 seat Roman theater in Turkey set in a deep valley is out your line of vision, until you reach it from below. Pompeii was covered in ashes like the treasures of ancient Egypt buried beneath a warm blanket of desert sand. Clouds hide isolated villages covered in ice and snow in the Andes. The tunnels of Edinborough, like the catacombs of Rome and the sewers of Paris, are invisible to the passer-by. Mayan cities by the hundreds remain covered by jungles and rain forests. Scuba divers must first be taught how to visit underwater sites, and much gold rests on the bottom of the oceans. Las Vegas casinos

<u>"DO NOT TOUCH"</u>

        LIKE THE SEXUAL URGE, THE UNIVERSAL URGE TO STEAL IS GOVERNED
BY THE "LOOK, BUT DON'T TOUCH" RULE. THIS ADMONITION IS NEVER MORE
STRICTLY ENFORCED THAN IN MUSEUMS THROUGHTOUT THE WORLD.

        ONE AFTERNOON IN ESTERGOM, HUNGARY, I WAS PUZZLING OVERAN
UNINSPIREING LARGE BUILDING, WHEN A VERY PLAIN LADY APPROACHED
SEEMING TO WANT TO HELP. "I AM A NUN, BUT FORCED TO WEAR THESE
STREET CLOTHES. IT'S THE LAW", SHE SAID SOFTLY UP CLOSE TO ME.
I ASSUMED IT WAS AN APPEAL FOR A DONATION, WHEN SHE UNSOLICITEDLY
OFFERED TO TAKE ME INTO THE BUILDING TO SATISFY MY CURIOUSITY. IT
WAS,I LEARNED, THE RESIDENCE OF HIS EMINENCE, CARDINAL MINZENTY.
THE CARDINAL WAS UNDER HOUSE ARREST AND HAD INFREQUENT VISITORS.
ONCE INSIDE, WE WERE TOLD THAT THE OLD MAN WAS NAPPING, BUT THAT
I WOULD BE FREE TO LOOK AROUND HIS RESIDENCE IF I SO DESIRED. IT
SOON DAWNED ON ME THAT THIS WAS AN ENORMOUS STOREHOUSE OF THE MOST
PRICELESS MASTERPIECES OF PAINTINGS THAT WERE TO BE CONFISCATED BY
THE SOVIET GOVERNMENT THE DAY THE AILING CARDINAL DIED. THE MANY
PAINTINGS WERE HANGING ON THE WALLS OF THE TASTEFULLY FURNISHED
ROOMS, SIMILAR TO ONE'S LIVING ROOM, FOR EXAMPLE. PERHAPS RELYING
ON DIVINE PROTECTION, THERE WERE NO GUARDS ANYWHERE. WITH MUCH TO
ADMIRE, I PASSED THE ETCHINGS OF ALBRECHT DURER RATHER HASTILY.
IN AN ADJACENT ROOM WERE I CAME FACE TO FACE WITH A ROW OF 13th
CENTURY SIENA SCHOOL ARTISTS..SIMONE MARTINI, LORENZETTI, THE -
FOLLOWERS OF GIOTTO! BY ADDING PERSPECTIVE TO GIOTTO, THEY HAD
BECOME THE FOUNDERS OF THE "INTERNATIONAL STYLE" OF PAINTING.
IT WAS THEN THAT I BEGAN TO FEEL A COMPULSION TO STEAL, LIKE A
POOR SOUL DESPARATE ENOUGH TO KIDNAP SOMEONE'S INFANT. WHY,THESE
PAINTINGS COULD FIT IN MY JACKET POCKET! COULD I, A CONFIRMED
CATHOLIC, AN INVITED GUEST WITH MY INVISIBLE HOST ASLEEP IN THE
HOUSE SOMEWHERE, COMMIT A ROBBERY? FURTHERMORE, THESE WERE DEEPLY
RELIGIOUS IN CONTENT. WOULD IT BE STEALING OR A HEROIC RESCUE OF
WESTERN ART IN THE MANNER OF THE CIA. DIDN'T SOMEONE STEAL THE
MONA LISA ONCE AND WASN'T THE AMERICAN MUSEUM OF NATURAL HISTORY
ROBBED OF ITS "STAR OF INDIA" BY MURPH THE SURF AND RECOVERED.
MORE THAN MY CHRISTIAN CONSCIENCE STOPPED ME..IT WAS THE RISKY
AIRPORT SECURITY CLEARANCE. I LEFT THE PREMISES SHAKEING.

        THE NEXT DAY, AT THE AIRPORT ENTRANCE WAS A LONG TABLE LOADED
DOWN WITH AN ASSIMILATION OF PAINTINGS, STATUES,CHANDELIERS, FUR-
NITURE, STUFFED CHAIRS AND ASSSORTED CUMBERSOME BRIC-A-BRAC THAT
OBVIOUSLY BELONGED FORMERLY TO FAMILIES LEAVING BEHIND THEIR HEAVY
POSSESSIONS. EVERYTHING WAS FOR SALE FOR DOLLARS IN THIS MAKE-SHIFT
DUTY FREE IRON CURTAIN FLEA MARKET THAT HAD AN ODOR OF TRAGEDY.
I REMEMBERED SOME PEOPLE IN MIAMI APPROACHING ME TO ACT AS A MIDDLE-
MAN, HANDLING SOME OLD MASTERS. I HAD NO HEART AND NO HEAD FOR SUCH
TAINTED BUSINESS. BESIDES I HAD ONCE SOLD A HENRI MICHAUX FOR FIVE
TIMES LESS THAN IT WAS WORTH.

    SIMILARLY, I WAS ON FERDOWSI STREET IN TEHERAN, NEAR OUR
EMBASSY, VISITING THE CROWN JEWELS IN THE ROYAL TREASURY. THIS
BEING THE IRANIAN FORT KNOX, THERE WERE GUARDS WITH GUNS EVERY-
WHERE ONE LOOKED. UNLIKE THE TOWER OF LONDON WITH ITS FAKE PASTE
COPIES,THESE WERE GENUINE..BARRELS OF EMERALDS, DIAMONDS IN
BUCKETS, A GIGANTIC GOLD GLOBE OF THE WORLD, ALL SHORTLY TO BE
CONFISCATED BY THE AYATOLLA SINCE THE SHAH WAS PREPARING TO FLEE
HIS PEACOCK THRONE. AGAIN, I LEFT SHAKEING.

    IN INDIA, I WAS PRIVILEGED TO BE SHOWN THE FAMILY JEWELS
AND HEIRLOOMS OF THE MAHARANI OF JAIPUR. THESE MOGUL BAUBLES,
"AS LARGE AS EGGS",WERE SAFER IN HER JEWELERS'VAULT THAN AT THE
PALACE, I WAS TOLD. IN VENICE, THE MUSEO MARITIMO WAS CLOSED
FOR REPAIRS BUT A SMALL TIP GOT ME IN. ... THE CUSTODIAN, A VERY
FRAGIL GENTLEMAN EASILY OVERPOWERED..NO WONDER 25,000 ART OBJECTS
ARE STOLEN EVERY YEAR IN ITALY WHERE 60% OF THE ART IN EUROPE IS
TO BE FOUND. IN NEUESCHWANSTEIN, I FOUND MYSELF PRACTICALLY ALONE
IN LUDWIG THE MAD'S ENORMOUS CASTLE SURROUNDED BY TREASURES. THE
LOUVRE HAD NO LINES WAITING TO ENTER AND HALF EMPTY CORRIDORS. IN
THE 50'S, I TRESPASSED ON KING FAROUK'S YACHT ON THE NILE AND IN
CAPRI, WE HAD THE WHOLE BLUE GROTTO TO OURSELVES. THE CAIRO MUSEUM
OF ANTIQUITIES, WAS ITSELF AN ANTIQUE, A DUSTY ATTIC WITH CREAKING
FLOORBOARDS, RICKETY STAIRS, BRITTLE DISPLAY CASES, DOZING GUARDS,
ILL-LIT NOOKS AND CRANIES WHERE ONE COULD WAIT TIL CLOSING, LIKE
TOPKAPI. IT SEEMED TO BE EMBARRASSED BY ITS RICHES. ALL OVER SOUTH
EAST ASIA THE GUATAMA BUDDHA IS EVERYWHERE VISIBLE, LIKE THE SHRINES
OF THE MADONNA IN ITALY. TODAY, ONE VISITS THE LIMA GOLD MUSEUM BY
INVITATION ONLY AND THE PEOPLE'S REPUBLIC OF CHINA IS READY TO KILL
OVER SOME CELEDON, PORCELAIN AND JADE STORED IN THE NATIONAL MUSEUM
IN TAIWAN. AS GENERAL MACARTHUR SAID, "THERE IS NO SECURITY".

    JUST IMAGINE MAKING OFF WITH AN ENCRUSTED CHALICE FROM THE
CLOISTERS, RANSACKING THE AMBER ROOM, ROBBING THE GERMAN GOLD TRAIN,
OR NUESTRA SENORA DE ANTOCHA..MENTION GETTY, MELLON, HEARST,
MAJORIE MERRYWEATHER POST, THE GLAMOROUS CAT BURGLERS..OH WHAT AN IN-
TRIGUEING PLACE, THIS ART WORLD! A BILLION DOLLARS CANNOT BUY "DAVID".
WHO STOLE THE RUBIES FROM BUDDHA'S THIRD EYE IN PAGAN, BURMA? IT'S
TRUE, RUBIROSA STOLE THE HEARTS OF THE TWO RICHEST WOMEN IN THE WORLD,
WHO WERE HARDLY ATTRACTIVE AND HOWARD CARTER MAY HAVE HELPED HIMSELF
TO A FEW "WONDERFUL THINGS", BUT THE CROWN GOES TO PARIS,WHO, BY
KIDNAPPING HELEN OF TROY BROKE THE RULE. HE SATISFIED BOTH URGES
BY STEALING A PRIZE BEAUTY, THE CROWN JEWELS OF SPARTA .....

                AND A SECURE PLACE IN HISTORY

WHEN I GROW UP…..

    Going from Vienna to Budapest (Magyoraszág) along the Danube is a pleasant trip
But in 1968 it was a risky choice for a visit. The rare American tourist was usually
Jewish , returning in hopes of retrieving his "life diamonds"..family jewels that were
buried, hidden from Nazis and Commies. My reason for going was to see the fabulous
collection of booty, the treasures of the defeat of the Ottoman Turks housed in the War
Museum. Then again there was my curiosity regarding the true treasures of a country..the
ladies of Hungary, reputed to be the most beautiful in Europe".

    In my U.S.Army surplus rucksack were some rock and roll cassettes, more valuable
than Marlboros. This was risky since my name was probably on some list as having
smuggled rock and roll records into Moscow in '58. On board , separated from the
otherwise solemn passengers was a group of frolicking Austrian firemen on
holiday.They were going to a convention in Budapest in civilian clothes and without their
wives. As men without women, they were, like myself, curious about the "most beautiful
women". Like Australians, these Austrians invited strangers to share a Pilsner or two. So
it was that I was soon adopted as an honorary mascot. Docking in Pest, I found myself
embedded among these new friends. As "visiting delegates", we were waived through
customs, fortunately. Once at the Hotel, it was discovered that one member had failed to
make the trip leaving his pre-paid single room available to me ..free. I was soon off to the
Museum, only to find it closed. Although the many bars of Budapest were open all day,
the ladies only emerged late at night.
    That evening, the firemen invited me to join them as their guest at the Matias
Restaurant where a delightful Gypsy zither ensemble, fine Tokay and paprika-ed goulash
awaited me. After multiple toasting, I found the mice peering down from holes in the
ceiling moulding, waiting for their table very amusing. Early next morning, I left Fats
Waller, Earl "Father" Hines and B.B. Smith as gifts for my comrades and boarded the bus
for Estergom. The still dark streets were empty but the trolleys were jammed with
workers en route to factories. The street signs read like some scrambled scrabble set.
Hungarian is a Ural-Altaic family of languages that includes Turkish and Lapp. The only
word I learned was fire.."tüz", thanks to the hallway exits in the Hotel. Today, I still
treasure my encounter with the firemen. It was an odd fulfillment of a forgotten
ambition..I was a fireman for a day.

<u>**Safety in Marriage**</u>

There was a time when I had no enemies except for some gun-licensed husbands. When the 6th Precinct warned that for every homicide 27 were single men and 1 was married, I became curious and more aware, if not alarmed. Married men live longer and I was single.

If you found that your enemies included the Castro crowd, the Mafia, the Basque Separatists, the KGB, the Al Quedistas, some disgruntled Haitian bus drivers and an array of jilted girlfriends, you might want to consider marriage.

<u>The Castro</u> contingent would like to see me gone. IN Miami, I am always seen in the company of ex-Bay of Pigs instructors, hermano pilots, families of executed journalists, barqueros.

<u>The Mafia</u> mistrusted me after I turned down their offer to steer suckers to the Havana casinos. I big-mouthed how they destroyed Coney Island and burned down Harlem for insurance scams while I took tourists around New York.

<u>The Commies</u> were angry at me when I, as a tour guide, told a busload of Italian tourists while passing by the U.N., "Hanno cagato (shit) in tutto il mondo". The passengers were all from Livorno, a solid, 100% red stronghold.

<u>The KGB</u> learned by my boasting, that I had once smuggled rock and roll records into Moscow in 1958.

<u>The Basque Separatists</u> (ETA) were furious when I announced at the mike, "VIVA ESPANA, Y SUS COLONIAS". It happened this way. When a tour company called, I was told "You will have 45 Spaniards for 7 days to Niagara Falls". As they boarded the bus, by way of welcoming them, I gave a "Long live Spain!" greeting.

<u>Al Queda</u>. I subscribe to Aramco Magazine for its cultural exploration of the Muslim world. I pass it on to my Arabic grocer so now the entire Islamic community has my name and address and identify me with oil exploitation of their land and the Great Satan. Besides, my lady friend is Jewish.

The Saudis. Four years ago I contacted the Saudi Arabian Minister of Tourism, offering myself as a guest speaker to assist in developing his fledgling tourist industry. As a good-will gesture, I forwarded with my letter a very valuable Holy Koran, hand-written on vellum. Unfortunately, some of the book was torn and worn from wear. In a culture where one error in regard to the Koran required severe accounting, i.e., a misspelling mean beginning all over gain, I was needless to say, not invited.

My landlord. My apartment in Greenwich Village is furnished entirely in 100% authentic Moorish décor. Since the landlord is a 100% orthodox Jew, he would like to see me gone from my rent-controlled apartment.

Haitians. "You split 50/50 with the driver." That's Standard Procedure on bus tours. On one 2 hour tour, all we received from four passengers was a dollar. Since neither of us had change, I told the driver he'd get his half dollar next trip. Word spread among the brotherhood of drivers that I was cheating, holding back, pocketing, etc.

The threat of furious husbands has greatly subsided over the years. As old friends die off, new ones are harder to find. On the other hand, enemies seem to endure and accumulate.

Should I risk marriage to better my survival odds (with perhaps a hostile mother-in-law) or should I get a pit bull and triple-lock my door?

The Illegal Alien

On December 8, 1951 I was arrested as an illegal alien in El Salvador. "Who would want to migrate to El Salvador," I argued. This did not go over well with the Immigration officials. My crime was "illegal presence" in the country. I was searched for stolen pre-Colombian artifacts and for drugs. There were no ATM's or credit cards for bribery in 1951 and I had little cash left at the end of my trip. Placed in the not-too-welcome custody of a Pan Am representative, I escaped jail and hand-cuffing, and was put up at a hotel, where I paid for my room, the soap, towel and toilet paper, the visa, the fine, and breakfast by selling my Bell & Howell camera to the desk clerk. You see, I had no visa!

The hotel was wooden and in a bad part of town. Graffiti said, "Yankee, go home." I will, if you let me, I thought to myself. The Pan Am rep had told me that citizens carried concealed weapons, and that I was a rich Americano. Tourists were strangers, and besides, a revolution was brewing. The hotel ceiling had a peephole that permitted a view of my bed, and sure enough, my floor board allowed a view of the floor below. I slept in the well-worn bed with the Roman poet Ovid's words in mind: "The conscious couch holds the enamored pair." There was no mosquito net   since no one actually "slept" in this bordello, nor was there a bar.

This situation began in Miami when I convinced Bob Sheldon, President of TAN Airlines, *Transportes Aéreos Nacionales de Tegucigalpa* that, instead of carrying chickens, shoes, etc., as cargo to Central America, he should carry tourists to the recently-headlined Mayan ruins. "Take advantage of the newly-awakened travel business that was spreading from Nassau to the West Indies and beyond," I proposed.

PIMP →

HOTEL ASTORIA
THE BEST AND MOST FREQUENTED

JOSE CABRERO
SOCIAL REPRESENTATIVE

SAN SALVADOR
EL SALVADOR, C. A.

TELEFONO 1340

So it was that I found myself sitting on cargo crates with no seat belt, flying on an itinerary survey of the project. Besides it being a dangerous adventure, I had time to watch natives on their way to Sunday mass, carrying smoking incense that filled the plaza with holiness. Mothers carried children like backpacks, clothed in locally-woven, colorful shawls. I saw many parrots, flamboyant flora, hamacas, heard flutes, and walked in a jungle.

The reason I arrived in El Salvador without a visa was due to my mmissing my Pan Am connecting flight to Miami. The TAN flight from Honduras to Guatemala had gone well, but the Pan Am flight from El Salvador to Miami that I was scheduled to connect with left before I landed. Whose fault was it? Mine, Pan Am's, TAN's, an incompetent travel agent, a time-zone error, the weather factor, or just a bad day to travel?

I never got to see the ruins of *Tikal* or *Copan* (as had been my primary motive, actually). Mr. Sheldon lacked financing and the pioneering spirit. I arrived home safe and sound (*sano y seguro*), stamped, sealed, and delivered.

Recibí de la Compañía **Pan American**, la suma de Veintisiete colones, valor que esta Delegación de Migración le impone de multa, por intrucir al País sin la visa consular correspondiente, al ciudadano Norteamericano, Vicent Levelli, el día de hoy, procedente de Guatemala.

Ilopango, 8 de Diciembre de 1951.

Teniente Juan Rodezno
Delegado de Migración

FLYING DOWN TO RIO

Two strokes of good luck occurred simultaneously in 1947, one by sea and one by air.

The first unexpected windfall involved sailing to Rio as an assistant cruise director aboard the S.S. "URUGUAY". The other was a PAA "travel fellowship" to study at the University of Rio de Janeiro thanks to the Institute of International Education. Although I was under-qualified for both choices, it was only my minimal command of Portuguese that helped to favor me with such propositions. I accepted both offers.

After sailing down to Rio, we returned to New York where I accepted the fellowship. Pan American World Airways System President, Mr. Juan Trippe, handed me my round trip ticket and wished me Bon Voyage.

This was to be my third flight, the first being a gift from a friend from Miami to Havana in '41, the second, courtesy of the U.S. Army in '45 and this one as a guest of PAA in '47.

In '41, still tipsy from a Farewell Party, I was disappointed to find that my very first time in the air would be aboard a "flying boat" instead of a real plane and that it would only last less than an hour from Dinner Key, Coconut Grove to gay Havana.

My second flight from Okinawa to Tokyo was the most joyous experience imaginable. We had just won the war. Now we were about to land as a victorious Advanced Echelon at Atyugi Airport 3 days before the official surrender.

In '47, the flight to Rio from New York by propeller-driven clipper took approximately 22 hours flying 2/3 of the time over the "Green Hell" of the Amazonian rain forest. The plane was empty except for the wife and child of one of the pilots. Just before landing to re-fuel in San Juan, P.R., we entered a rare, violent downdraft like a plunging elevator which many planes do not survive. Next stop, Belem in the state of Para to refuel and off again to cross the equator, but not before being sprayed down the front and back of my shirt with DDT. Sitting with no one to talk to, with no magazines, just the Atlantic Ocean and the flat jungle below, we weren't "there yet", when I began to shake. Thinking it was from the vibrating propellers, I tried to dismiss it.

In 1959, I was about to leave sunny Florida for the Nord Cap, the North Cape Cruise aboard the Caronia. While packing my luggage, I discovered among some change from assorted countries I had visited, a coin from Iceland, a country I had never been to. Someone must have passed this tiny coin, small as a dime, off on me. Since we would be stopping at Reykjavik, of all places, I threw it in my bag.

Miami and Reykjavik are as different as night and day. Above the Arctic Circle, Iceland is the "Land of the Midnight Sun," and like jet-lag, your sleeping routine is upset when the sun never goes down behind the horizon, and midday is like midnight for most of the year. The Borg Hotel lobby bar was the brightest spot in the capital, where, like Nome, Alaska, the spunky citizens are proud of their stamina and ability to hold their liquor. The talk is mostly about fish, and the city smells much like Bergen, Norway. With no smart shops, cathedrals, or museums in 1958, Reykjavik was kind of "Why do people live here" place. Even so, I'm sure they miss it when they are away and are happy when they return home.

The language is impossible, the hard liquor hard to swallow, and aside from ice caves, there is not even skiing on its scrubby glaciers (Think *permafrost*). Like Easter Island, there were few trees to be found growing in the lava formations, few birds, and a sad beach with black sand, darker than Mt. Pelee's in Martinique. Being an inveterate tourist, I left the cheerful carousers at the Hotel Borg bar and took a taxi to see the sights. This was no Sun Valley or Snow Owl Inn in New Hampshire, more like Montauk. I closed my eyes and dozed off, helped by the "Welcome to Iceland" vodka toast I had, the uninteresting main street, and the scattered desolation of the outskirts. I would have welcomed a display of spectacular Hawaiian volcanic volatility. Sadly, Iceland went bankrupt in spite of being energy self-sufficient — thanks to its thermodynamic hot springs.

In the middle of nowhere, the taxi came to a halt. "Go see the hot water coming up from the ground," said the driver. I would have refused, except for the fact that I had to "go." Risking frostbite, I walked gingerly up to a small pool of steaming, bubbling, gaseous water. As I was about to rush back to the cab, the driver called out, "Make a wish. Throw a coin in the water. You will come back to Iceland." Now, I have thrown many pennies into fountains — even over my shoulder at Trevi, but a wishful thought of returning to Iceland — should I risk it? I searched in my pocket for a coin. Out came the one I had carried for thousands of miles from the sunshine state. As I was about to toss it into the gurgling, sulfurous pool of vaporous water, I stopped cold, then dropped it gently in. I returned to the taxi with a warm inner glow, mumbling, "I'm sure as hell never coming back here, but the little coin has."

North Cape Cruise

Cunard Line

R·M·S· Caroni

Vincent Livelli
44 Perry Street # 4W
New York, New York
10014

LAUGHTER, GOOD AND BAD IN MOSCOW

by

Vincent Livelli

The Soviet Union was not a tourist destination in July, 1958, but the American Express Company sent me there with sixteen passengers for the Summer Games held in Moscow. It was a small open window during the Cold War that soon was shut once more, until the Berlin Wall came down.

Once I had my people settle in the stadium, I took off. How many opportunities does one get to peek behind the iron curtain, I figured? Besides, in addition to the standard sightseeing protocol of shops and museums, etc., my motivations was inspired by the possibility of meeting a Russian demoiselle to make my visit more memorable.

I asked my taxi driver, "Where does one find romance in Moscow?" "Go to Gorki Park, late at night," was his advice to me. Since there were no evident night clubs, as in other capitals, I extended him a fine tip, which he refused. Today, Moscow is jumping, but back then the city was grim in darkness. Workers throughout the Eastern Europe Empire arose at sunrise to head for their jobs.

That night, I optimistically left the Moskva Hotel to cross over to Gorki Park - an area with few lamp posts scattered throughout the area. The driver was correct, for I soon was summoned by a PST-PST coming from behind some hedges. In the darkness I was nevertheless able to discern a pitiful elderly woman, very much unlike today's ladies of the night that have made Moscow famous.

This discouraging encounter did not dissuade me from continuing my nocturnal adventure. Walking on a crushed stone pathway, I broke the silence of the night. As I progressed deeper into a foreboding environment, I caught the sound of distant laughter. This being the first and only gaiety I had encountered since my arrival two day prior, I took particular notice to it.

Unfortunately, my footsteps must have reached the two couples that I came upon, half-concealed among the trees. Their laughter had encouraged me to approach them, but by my doing so I caused them to abruptly silence themselves in unison. They remained absolutely silent until I passed. Nor did they resume their laughing as I exited the park.

As a cruise director, charged with bringing passengers, strangers, together in good cheer, and as one who has the joy of insuring high morale during long voyages, I was puzzled to find that I had caused the very opposite by silencing the joy of laughter by my presence. What kind of world did they inhabit? Had they been laughing at me for some reason (as the Amazonian Indians had done) I could readily accept their behavior understandably.

Laughter is welcomed universally from the baby's crib to the death row cell, but where it is legislated, distorted like cryptograms, dependent on Vodka or Charlie Chaplin movies that back-fires on the system when they showed him as a worker chained to his boring job workplace, laughter triumphs along with the good over the bad.

Compared to older cultures, we are like freshmen sniffing glue. African folkways display a more mellow ethos, a cool, laid-back quality unlike ours. Muslims leave their dinner to retire to smoke hashish in a separate setting, similar to our taking brandy or coffee apart. They may take a toke in a "Turkish corner." We can imagine this set in a family scenario after the children are excused, making a more functional family. After breakfast, I have seen throughout North Africa, young men assembling with others, preparing for their work day by smoking pot. Established propriety is evident in their attitudes and comportment. Compare Mardi Gras' rowdiness with Rio's more orderliness, where ether, called "lança perfume," is permitted by law for only the four days of Carnival. Obviously, inhalants, oil of peppermint, patchouli, and any of the thousands of other examples of scents we encounter daily, are subtle determinants of our overall moods, not to mention the vital role of pheromones that affect the air and thus the conduct of creatures from ants to humans. Since we are removing global warming contamination, can we replace it with nitrous oxide to end wars? Forget things like intellectual property rights, metabolites, gang wars, etc. as we just breather normally.

California is the worst milieu for legalizations of marijuana. A less kookie locale to study reactions should be sought. We must season the atmosphere, using, for example, our air conditioners in working areas, shopping malls, prisons, hospitals for experimentation. Refreshening the air we breathe every living minute from school rooms to the world headquarters of the United Nations might dislodge the miracle of a more congenial world citizenry. Contrariwise, ionized air causes depression, according

to the recent findings of the British *Journal of Medicine*. Suicide is high among sea captains, and sailors are often homesick. Who would suspect that pure air can be depressing, especially after the rain? Air is a powerful vehicle. Like our shadows, it is with us to the end. We can upset the beer industry, the drug cartels, the psychiatric and pharmaceutical establishments. Like CPR set to music, gaiety resuscitates, but happiness proper is released from inside out and is an ever rarer commodity than levity to raise the spirit. To find and to found a New World we may have to fashion better quality air. Columbus used <u>water</u> to find it. Bessemer used <u>fire</u> to establish the new world of the Industrial Revolution, Rockefeller drilled the <u>earth</u> to fuel and propel a new world. The time may have come now to use the <u>air</u>. This is the Age of Aquarius, an air sign. The challenge is to improve the air's quality for a New World.

pass the word…to assist others with a map of life and places Marco Polo went forth as a merchant and returned as a writer. Mona Lisa does not belong to everyone equally. She belongs most to those who stand in front of her. The travel writer is a diamond setter who assembles for us Mother Nature's jewelry. He is the ancient cartographer who showed us our unknown world. Quick get your pen, get your camera!

A special send-off goes out to the brave travel writers who excavate the attics and corners of the world to bring back home to us the music in their tales. What would the world be like without them…**TERRA INCOGNITA!**

RUSSIAN ROULETTE 1958

THE SOVIETS WERE HOSTING THE OLYMPIC GAMES IN MOSCOW IN 1958.
THE ENTIRE AMERICAN COLONY WAS AT THE STADIUM ROOTING FOR THE USA.
BECAUSE OF A LACK OF INTEREST IN HOCKEY MORE THAN ANY INDIFFERENCE
TO PATRIOTISM, I MANAGED TO GET IN BED WITH AN ATTRACTIVE RUSSIAN
YOUNG LADY. THIS MEANT MORE TO ME THAN AN AMERICAN VICTORY ON THE
PLAYING FIELD. MY "VICTORY" WAS LAYING NEXT TO ME MAKING ME A BIG
TIME WINNER BUT ALSO RAISING THE POSSIBILITY OF AN INTERNATIONAL
INCIDENT AT THE HEIGHT OF THE COLD WAR. BETTING WAS HEAVY ON THE
OLYMPIC OUTCOME. I WON A TEN DOLLAR BET THANKS TO THE YOUNG LADY.

MY SHIP, THE R.M.S. "CARONIA" VISITED ICELAND WHERE MY BUDDY, HUGH,
HAD PROMENADED AROUND THE SHIP SHOWING US HIS GORGEOUS GIRLFRIEND,
"MISS ICELAND". HUGH AND I HAD BEEN TOUR ESCORTS TOGETHER AND RIVALS
IN HAVANA, LONDON AND SPAIN. HERE WE WERE IN MOSCOW, LOOKING FOR
FEMALE ACTION. WE HAD A $10.00 BET AS TO WHO WOULD SCORE FIRST.
WHEN NOTHING HAPPENED IT LOOKED LIKE THE BET WAS OFF, UNTIL THE
LAST FORTY MINUTES BEFORE LEAVING MOSCOW. WE WERE GOING TO BE
FIVE DAYS AND FOUR NIGHTS AT THE MOSKVA HOTEL AND DECIDED TO
TEAM UP SINCE THINGS DID NOT LOOK PROMISING. THE FIRST NIGHT,
NOTHING. THE CONCIERGE RECOMMENDED GORKI PARK (WHERE THE SELECTION
WAS JUST AWFUL HIDING IN THE BUSHES). NO LUCK AT ALL ON THE SECOND,
THIRD, FOURTH AND FIFTH DAY, UNTIL DEPARTURE TIME FOR COPENHAGEN.

WHILE RETURNING TO THE HOTEL TO CHECK OUT, I WAS APPROACHED VERY
GENTLY BY A CHAP, I SHOULD SAY VERY CAREFULLY. WE MISTRUSTED BUT
NEEDED EACH OTHER. I HAD TO UNLOAD THE LIPSTICK, NAIL POLISH AND
EARL "FATHER" HINES RECORD IN MY BAGS, ALONG WITH THE HEAVY BOTTLE
OF JAMEISONS AND THE MARLBOROS. "WHAT DOES ONE DO TO MEET WOMEN?",
BY NOW IT WAS TOO LATE BUT I HAD FOUND THE RIGHT MAN. WE WERE IN
BUSINESS. I WROTE MY ROOM NUMBER FOR HIM AND HURRIED TO THE HOTEL.

AS I WAS WASHING UP AND ABOUT TO START PACKING A KNOCK INTERUPTED MY
SHOWER. IN CAME MY NEW FRIEND WITH A MISS UNIVERSE TYPE, BETTER
LOOKING THAN MISS ICELAND! I HAD INTENDED TO UNLOAD MY STUFF ON HIM
ALMOST HAVING FORGOTTEN BY NOW THE OTHER BUSINESS. TO MY SURPRIZE
HE POLITELY EXCUSED HIMSELF, REFUSING THE DRINK AND THE CIGARETTE
AND LEFT, LEAVING HER. I WAS BOTH DISAPPOINTED AND SUSPICIOUS, BUT
EAGER. CHECKING MY WATCH, I JUMPED INTO BED WHILE SHE TOOK CARE
OF THINGS IN THE BATHROOM AND SOON WE WERE COMMUNICATING UNDER THE
SHEETS. A KNOCK AT THE DOOR FRIGHTENED BOTH OF US. SHE GRABBED THE
SHEET, BRINGING IT UP TO HER CHIN, AND RAN INTO THE BATHROOM SAYING,
"RUSSKI?". I COULDN'T ANSWER SINCE I DIDN'T EXPECT ANYONE. GOING TO
THE DOOR, I FOUND A WELL-DRESSED GENTLEMAN WHO SEEMED SO OUT OF
PLACE TO ME. "ARE YOU ALONE?" HE ASKED, BEFORE STEPPING INTO THE ROOM
IT WAS OBVIOUS I WASN'T. "DON'T LET HER COME OUT", HE SAID EVEN
THOUGH SHE WASN'T ABOUT TO. AS WE DISCUSSED DETAILS INVOLVING ICONS,
COSMETICS AND CURRENCY, I REALIZED THAT THESE TWO GUYS WERE WORKING
TOGETHER, ONE BRINGING ME THE GAL, THE OTHER BUYING MY GOODS. THE
FIRST ONE WOULD BE SEARCHED, FOUND CLEAN BY THE WOMEN WHOSE JOB ON EACH
FLOOR WAS TO REPORT SUCH SUSPICIOUS ACTIVITY. THE SECOND, A HOTEL
EMPLOYEE WHO WAS BEYOND SUSPICION DUE TO HIS HIGH POSITION. A KNOCK
ON THE DOOR WHILE WE WERE DEALING, TURNED HIS FACE WHITE AS A SHEET.
"CAUGHT!", I FIGURED WHEN I SAW HIS REACTION. BLACK MARKET IS BAD-BAD.

BEFORE I OPENED THE DOOR, HE SLIPPED TWO ICONS UNDER THE SOFA CUSHIONS
AND I QUICKLY PUT $50.00 IN HIS HANDKERCHIEF POCKET. HE TOOK ONLY THE
NEWSPAPER HE HAD WRAPPED THEM IN FOR CONCEALMENT ORIGINALLY. COOL. AS
SOON AS I OPENED THE DOOR HE WAS OUT IN A FLASH, BRUSHING PAST THE
PORTER WHO HAD COME FOR MY BAGS AND WAS POINTING AT HIS WRIST. WITH
SIGN LANGUAGE I INSTRUCTED HIM TO PACK MY BAG AS I THREW EVERYTHING
OUT INTO THE HALL, SAYING "BUS, BUS". OPENING THE BATHROOM DOOR,
IT WAS BACK TO BED. THEN, DRESSING REAL FAST, LIKE A FIREMAN, EVERY-
THING HEIGHTENED BY THE DANGER INVOLVED, I TURNED SENTIMENTAL FOR A
MOMENT AND WAS SURPRIZED THAT SHE REFUSED TO ACCEPT ANYTHING BUT ONE
CUFF-LINK FOR "SOUVENIR". THIS, SHE COULD GET PAST THE WOMAN AT THE
HALL DESK. THROWING HER A KISS, A LA DOUGLAS FAIRBANKS, OR ZORRO,
I DASHED FOR THE LOBBY.

HUGH AND I HAD COME BACK TO THE HOTEL TOGETHER BEFORE DEPARTURE TIME.
HERE HE WAS WITH HIS GROUP SEATED IN HIS BUS, WAITING WORRIEDLY FOR
ME. HE KNEW I WAS ALWAYS FIFTEEN MINUTES AHEAD OF SCHEDULED DEPARTURE
TIME. HE HAD TAKEN BAGGAGE COUNT FOR ME, AS WELL AS THE HEAD COUNT.
WE WERE READY TO LEAVE WITH PASSENGERS WATCHING US OUT OF BOTH BUS
WINDOWS. "YOU OWE ME $10.00", I SAID. OF COURSE HE REFUSED TO BELIEVE
ME UNTIL I TOOK HIM BEHIND A PARTITION, UNZIPPED MY PANTS AND SHOWED
HIM I HAD NO UNDERWEAR. HE STILL SEEMED UNCONVINCED UNTIL I SHOWED
HIM THE HANDKERCHIEF I WAS WIPING MY BROW WITH. IT BORE THE UN-
MISTAKABLE CLINCHER..THE UNIVERSAL GIVE-AWAY..A RED SMEAR.

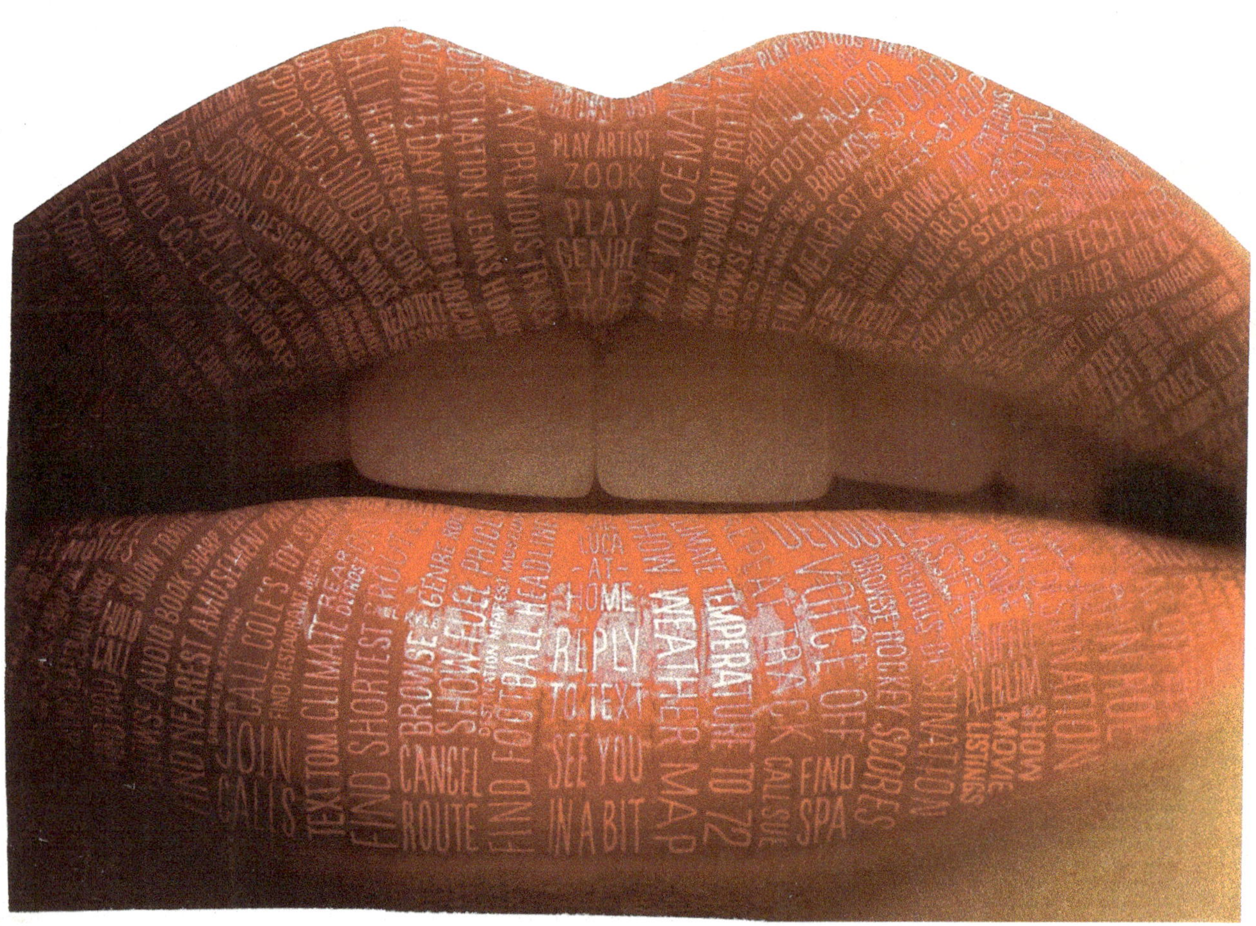

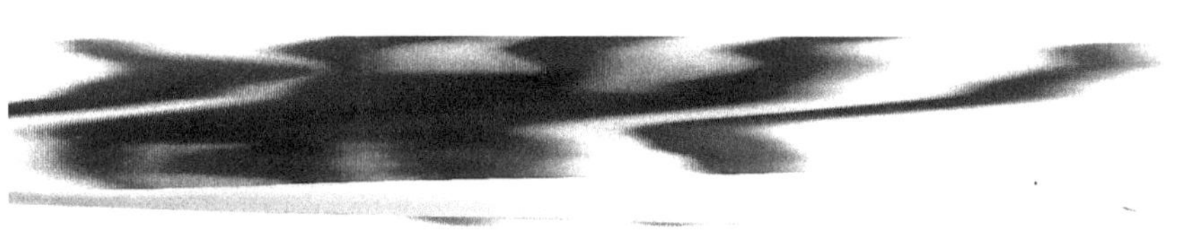

Vincent Livelli
44 Perry Street #4W
New York, New York
10014

LAUGHTER IN THE JUNGLE

By

Vincent Livelli

Have you ever jumped back in fright from something that suddenly shows up right in front of you? It could be a close call from a speeding New York taxi, but in the Amazon it's most likely to be a part of Mother Nature.

As we sailed, pieces broken off the mainland formed islands that floated past your port hole with tall trees alive with chattering monkey sounds. Barely visible at night around the bend in the river the captain of the Ariadne, of the Hamburg-Amerika Line, proceeded with great caution. It could be as deep as 25 feet or dry in areas after the rainy season.

We arrived in Manaus while the many unpaved streets were still muddy and unfit for sight-seeing around town. The pungent smell of fish reminded me of Bergen, Norway, only in a hotter climate. Furthermore, it was the jungle that I had come to visit where there were rumors of pygmy monkeys. Aside from some butterflies and birds, we had encountered no piranha, boa constrictors or anacondas and alligators. A short walk out of town brought me to a narrow river that discouraged crossing to where the rain forest was waiting. While resting on a log I saw that the tall tree in front of me had its bark peeling off. Out of curiosity, I stood up, grabbed the loose bark, and dislodged it. Hundreds of angry tarantulas slowly spread out like a carpet of red soldier ants. Jumping back in horror and surprise, I fell back against the log and onto the ground. They say it takes multiple bites from killer bees, but like poisonous snakes, it takes but one bite from a tarantula to finish you off. Who knew that spiders lived in trees?

Suddenly an outburst of laughter filled the air. Lined up along the opposite bank of the river was a cluster of Satera tribe Indians. Naked they were, except for painted torsos, feathered arm and head bands, shell ankle bracelets, and bows and arrows. Some wore loin cloths but young women were bare breasted, which in 1959, I was unaccustomed to witnessing. They had all been hiding, silently spying on me behind the foliage. I got up and headed back to town feeling like a fool but wiser and frustrated, and lucky. It took me a while to laugh about it.

Vincent Livelli is a world traveler cruise director, tour director, social director, and performer. He has been featured in documentaries, novels, journal publications, and has lectured at the Smith

THE GREATEST THEFT OF ALL TIME

by

Vincent Livelli

The greatest robberies are not those that involve property, identities, or abductions. They are those that rob us of knowledge, wisdom, and progress. They are those that deprive us of the forward march of civilization and the evolution of mankind.

Such a theft occurred over 2500 years ago when the gold cap stone atop the Kaufu Pyramid was stolen, leaving a gapping mystery regarding the universe. Buried among the dusty pages of eons of forgotten history is the story of the removal and disappearance of this celestial navigational beacon.

Early Egyptians were far ahead of their time in terms of astronomy. In spite of a sparse history behind them, they may have advanced with assistance of *outside help*. Egypt became a stopped clock, a gigantic tomb of time itself, halting the forward movement of the future. This in turn deprived mankind of our planetary destiny among our galactic cousins.

Let us conceptualize as a fanciful premise the restoration the capstone, less of an endeavor than the salvation of Abu Simbal. When the momentous impact of this possibility is recognized, a miraculous device might be re-installed to invite back the visitors to earth. We have surrendered to the past, but there are futurists like Edison, or Benjamin Franklin, who in 1752 discovered the phenomenal influence of electricity, waiting to be born.

We live in the "Information Age," but neglect re-activating the ultimate treasury of knowledge that could put our modernity to shame. The printing press revolutionized an

1

EMBASSY CLUB 1948
PLAZA SAN MARTIN
CALLE FLORIDA Y CHARCAS
BUENOS AIRES, ARGENTINA

FIFTY YEARS AGO, THE CAIRO MUSEUM WAS MORE A WAREHOUSE THAN A TREASURE HOUSE. CREEKING FLOOR BOARDS AND RICKETY RAILINGS MADE IT AN ARTHRITIC RELIC. REEKING OF DARK DEEDS BEHIND DARK SHADOWS, IT WAS A HOUSE THAT SHELTERED DEATH. EMBALMED NOBILITY INHABITED A WOEFULLY NEGLECTED PALACE. IT POSSESSED THE MUSTINESS OF AN UNDISTURBED ATTIC AND THE COBWEBS OF A LONG UNENTERED CELLER. LARGE ROOMS STUFFED LIKE CLOSETS, HELD AN OVER LOAD OF MUMMIES. A FILM OF DESERT DUST COVERED GLASS CABINETS BADLY IN NEED OF ATTENTION. SAND HAD ENCROACHED NOOKS AND CRANNIES, RELENTLESSLY DEFYING CLEANING LIKE NEW YORK WINDOWS. IN SHORT, IT WAS A PRIME EXAMPLE OF 'IMSHALLAH'S INTENTIONAL NEGLECT.

THE HISTORY OF SEVEN THOUSAND YEARS WAS SCATTERED ABOUT. TIME ITSELF WAS ON EXHIBIT. YOU WERE PRESENT IN THE MIDST OF AN UNFAMILIAR HOLINESS AMONG OTHER-WORLDLY DIETIES WHOSE TIME SCALE WAS NOT OURS. THE PHARAOHS IGNORED THE VISITOR, DECEIVING HIM WITH THEIR GLASS EYES FIXED ON ETERNITY. WHEN THE PLACE WAS CLOSED FOR THE NIGHT, DID THESE INDIFFERENT NOBLEMEN CONVERSE ABOUT AFFAIRS OF STATE OR THE NOISOME FUNGI?

FREE TO ROAM ABOUT LIKE THE CATS THAT LIVED THERE, YOU FELT UNINTIMIDATED 'JUST LOOKING' AS YOU WOULD AT TIFFANY'S. CARETAKERS AROSE BOWING AS YOU APPROACHED. AS YOU LEFT THEY AROSE ONCE AGAIN THIS TIME SMILING IN THEIR LONG ROBES. UNLIKE COMMERCIALIZED MUSEUMS, SHE HAD NOT SOLD HER SOUL. SO MANY IMPOSING STATUES IMPLIED THAT A POWERFUL INFORMATION HAD BEEN THEIRS, THAT THESE ALMIGHTY KINGS HAD TAKEN FORMULAS TO THEIR GRAVES WITH THEM. WHEN ROBBERS EMPTIED ROYAL TOMBS THEY DEPRIVED US OF THE REST OF THE MYSTERY…FOREVER LOST LIKE THE ALEXANDRIAN LIBRARY. WHAT PUZZLES US TODAY WAS QUITE EXPLICITE TO THEM. THE MUSEUM CRADELS AN ANCIENT FAMILY, PROTECTING HER PROGENY, HER FIRST BORN S REMAINS. SHE CAN BOAST HER PRIDE AND JOYS ASLEEP IN HIS BEJEWELED CRIB, THE YOUNG KING AND HIS GOLDEN TOYS. THE ENTIRE WORLD INHERITS GRATEFULLY THE BROKEN BITS AND SMALLEST SCRAPS OF EGYPT S OFFERINGS, EVER CRYING FOR MORE. FORTUNATELY, AS THE MUSEUM SLOWLY AWOKE AS FROM A DREAM, ITS UNIQUE MYSTIQUE WAS PRESERVED BY MOTION PICTURES. KARLOFF WAS VERY MUCH AT HOME HERE. FRIGHTENING FILMS SHOOK THE DUSTY BLANKET SHE SLEPT UNDER. SOON MAJOR REPAIRSINDIRECT LIGHTNING, TEMPERATURE CONTROL SCARED OFF SOME OF THE SPOOKY SPIDERS WHILE THE AURA OF SKULLS AND BONES REMAINED ALIVE. LONG LINES OF SEEKERS COME TO THE MUSEUM BUT NOT FOR ART'S SAKE ALONE FOR WHO IS NOT SUMMONED BY THE FRIVOLOUS POSSIBILITY THAT HERE-IN LIES THE ANSWER TO A UNIVERSAL CONCERN…AN INKLING INTO THE HEREAFTER AND THE GREATEST TREASURE OF ALL…THE SECRET OF IMMORTALITY.

A BUNGLED MUGGING
..Tunisian Style

Accustomed to being accosted by trinket merchants
and postcard vendors, my first reaction was tolerant enough.
Falling in step behind me was this iron-Mike look-alike,
telling me everything was going to be alright. Was this my
friendly waiter joining me on the way back to my hotel?
Feeling friendly, as one does having met friendly natives
all day, I allowed him alongside. What, I wondered, was
going to be alright?
     Its dark before you know it in the alleys of Tunis.
My hotel, the Maison Doree,was still an alley away. My big
mistake was to feel safe on unfamiliar turf wearing jewelry
a double no-no. As my friend extended his hand toward me
I grabbed it as in a hearty handshake. Just then a light
went on over our heads and we eyeballed each other. The
ability one acquires travelling to shake off sticky individuals came in handy. I reversed and he kept going. His hidden
accomplice was encouraging him to attack. This mugging was
being botched. The victim was escaping but not for long. The
three of us played tag among parked cars as I made it to the
corner bar. The place was jammed with mugger-types. "Spaghetti,
tomato sauce", I said to the skinny waiter, as I cased the room
for a back door. Three perfectly normal looking young women
in a sea of rough me.. a good sign. In similar settings in
Muslim countries, the women blend into a safer kind of mans'
world, liberated from continuous sexual bombardment. Usually,
Arab men whisper, like the Turks, their heads almost touching.
Here, with wine on every table, you couldn't hear yourself talk.
     As I played with my food, I shifted my valuable around.
My credit card first, into my shoe; passport inside the shirt;
U.S. cash in the sock; sunglasses in the side pocket together
with my Dirans. Perhaps this would satisfy my muggers who no

2

THE AMERICAN EMBASSY IN RIO HOSTED A RECEPTION FOR CARDINAL
FRANCIS X. SPELLMAN. HE WAS NOTED FOR HIS MEMORY OF NAMES. "MR.
LIVELLI, WE MEET AGAIN"AS HE HELD ON TO MY HAND IN THE RECEIVING LINE.
A PRINCE OF THE CHURCH WAS COMING ON TO ME. WITH THAT SINFUL THOUGHT
IN MIND, I MOVED ALONG. AT THE VATICAN, YOU MIGHT SAY I HAD A RUN-IN
WITH POPE PAUL P. VI.IT OCCURED DURING A PAPAL AUDIENCE WHILE HE WAS
BEING CARRIED THROUGH THE CHAMBER. UPSETTING THE SANCTITY OF THE
OCCASION, I WAS CAUGHT BETWEEN TWO HIGHER AUTHORITIES, HIS HOLINESS
AND THE CAPTAIN OF OUR SHIP. IT WAS EITHER WAIT FOR THE CEREMONY TO
END OR MISS THE SHIP IN NAPLES. ROUNDING UP MY RELUCTANT TOURISTS,
WE SNEAKED OUT (THE WRONG DOOR) BUT I DID NOT SACRIFICE MY JOB
AND HOPED TO BE FORGIVEN AS WE RAN DOWN THE STAIRS.

I HAVE FELT JACK DEMPSEY'S GENTLE HAND SHAKE, JAN PEERE'S FULL
VOLUMN AS HE BROKE INTO AN ARIA IN FRONT OF ME. I'VE BEEN REJECTED BY
ELSA MAXWELL AT HER TRADITIONAL TRANS-ATLANTIC COKTAIL PARTY. BRENDA
FRAZIER, NEW YORK'S NUMBER ONE DEBUTANT DURING CAFE SOCIETY MATINEES
SPURNED MY INVITATION TO A RUMBA, HIDING BEHIND "SHIPWRECK KELLY",
HER FIANCE. SENOR WENCES LET ME DOWN WHEN I APPEALED TO HIM AS AN
ENTERTAINER TO PERFORM FOR US EN ROUTE TO NEW YORK WHEN THE MORALE
OF THE CROSSING WAS VEY LOW. IT WAS, AFTER ALL, AN UNWRITTEN UNDER-
STANDING THAT PERFORMERS WOULD PLEASE THE PASSENGERS. SOME ARTISTS
ACTUALLY PAID FOR THEIR PASSAGE IN THAT MANNER. AS "INTRATTENITORE
SOCIALE", I WAS DESPERATE TO SAVE MY CRUISE DIRECTOR JOB WITH HIS HELP.
"MY TRUNK IS IN THE HOLD", WE EXPLAINED EACH TIME I BEGGED HIM. THE
PURSER FEARED HIM FOR SOME REASON, SUGGESTING THAT I WAS STALKING
WENCES. I NEVER SAW TALENT IN HIS SILLY ACT AND SPIT AS HE WENT DOWN
THE GANGPLANK AND I LOST MY JOB. THE UNCOMFORTABLE FEELING EVERYONE
HAD SHAKING JOHN PETRILLO'S PINKY (HE WAS PRES. OF THE POWERFUL
MUSICIANS UNION) AND EVEN MORE UNCOMFORTABLE WAS THE ARGUMENT I WAS
INNOCENTLY THE CAUSE OF WHEN AT A FAMILY REUNION, THE SON-IN-LAW
LEFT RAGING ABOUT HOW HIS NEW WIFE SUSPECTED HIM OUT OF HER JEALOUSY.
I HAD MERELY SAID IN ANSWER TO A QUESTION ABOUT MY OCCUPATION, "IT
GIVES MARRIED MAN SO MUCH FREEDOM, THIS WORKING ON A SHIP". IT WAS
A SCENE THAT TRIGGERED A DIVORCE IN THE CLEMENCAU FAMILY IN CANNES.
NOT BEING MUCH OF A JESTER, I COULDN'T BLUFF AWAY MY IGNORANCE WHILE
SPEAKING ABOUT CHAMPAGNE TO THE WIDOW OF CLIQUOT PONSARDIN (THE VEUVE
HERSELF) OR ABOUT PERFUME WITH BARONESS ROCHAS. ONE DAY, I BUMPED INTO
ORSON WELLES WHIL GOING THROUGH THE REVOLVING DOORS AT CIPRIANI'S
GIUDECCA. HE WAS PERHPAS EITHER HURRYING TO THE BATHROOM OR TO THE DIN-
ING ROOM OR BOTH. THE FIRST TIME OUR PATHS CROSSED WAS AT THE STUDIO
REHEARSAL FOR THE "INVASION FROM MARS". I WAS A GAFFER AND THE PHOTO-
GRAPHER AND I WENT FOR DRINKS JUST BEFORE AIR TIME. AT THE BAR WE
WATCHED EVERYONE, INCLUDING THE BARTENDER RUN OUT INTO CENTRAL PARK
TO LOOK UP AT THE SKY. WE SAT ENJOYING OUR DRINKS AND OUR PRIVILEGED
INFORMATION. MANY CELEBRITIES ARE CHEAP. THE MAHARANI OF BARODA OWES
ME FOR THE "DETOL" SH ASKED ME TO BUY FOR HER IN NASSAU AT THE BRITISH
COLONIAL HOTEL SOME ARE DOWNRIGHT SCARY, LIKE SANTOS TRAFFICANTE
AT THE SANS SOUCI SUGGESTED I TAKE TOURISTS TO HIS CASINO. I HAD TO
REFUSE THE OFFER. THE BOUNCER AT EL MOROCCO WAS FORTUNATELY MY FRIEND.
PERHAPS I WOULD HAVE BEEN RUFFLED UP FOR ASKING TOMMY MANVILLE, THE
ASBESTOS MILLIONAIRES DATE WHILE HE WAS DRUNK AND OBNOXIOUS, TO RUMBA.
MANY FAMOUS AUTHORS ARE WEIRD. DELMORE SCHWARTZ THREW ME OUT OF HIS
CHARLES STREET APARTMENT WHEN I MADE WHAT I THOUGHT WAS A KIND COMMENT
ABOUT HIS LIBRARY. LOUIS VUITTON WAS ANGRY AT ME WHEN I COMPLAINED TO
HIM THAT HIS LUGGAGE DID NOT HOLD SHAPE VERY WELL, ESPECIALLY IN THE
RAIN. "YOU MISTREATED IT", HE SHOUTED AT ME. THEN THERE WAS THE EM-
BARRASSING PERFORMANCE BETWEEN THE PARISIAN SOPHISTICATE AND THE VERY
INEXPERIENCED LEARNER-LOVER ANAIS NIN AND I.

The Walls Of The Nomads
by
Vincent Livelli

Le Corbusier called tapestry, *"Le mùr du nomad "*, the walls of the nomads. In
the Arabic world, tapestries and carpets played important political, social and
economic roles representing social status, wealth and currency. During the Jazz Age,
machine- woven Arabic-style tapestries invaded America. Machines had been
developed during the Industrial Age to weave carpets and tapestries at costs lower
than child labor. Thousands of works were mass-produced in Belgium and France.

During the early 1920's these machine-woven fabric murals were an outgrowth of
the ancient Chinese silk wallpaper that became popular in 18th century, England.
Reminiscent of these were "papiers pients imprimes a la main", a hand painted
wallpaper displayed in the 19th century French chateaux.

During the Ch'ing Dynasty (1644 - 1911 A.D.), hand-sown or woven works were
increasingly touched up with a brush, becoming part tapestry and part painting. The
Kuna Indians of Panama and Colombia sewed vertical "brush strokes" into their
"mola" appliques, having watched the conquistadors apply paint on canvas. In
countries that did not have the painting tradition, clothing and funerary textile were
often a principal outlet for religious or creative expression .

Today, prosperous nomads moving into cities paint the doors and gates of their
new homes, using the same designs as on the walls of the tents they left behind.
Ironically, today we find throughout the Islamic world enormous "Oriental" carpeting
covering the floors of many humble village mosques. These carpets nevertheless
command the traditional respect.

Imprinted fabrics of all sorts could now be purchased in America by the poorest of
families. They were offered for sale in urban department stores and bought mostly by
immigrants settling in the Bronx, Brooklyn and even as far west as Chicago. Designed
to fit the specifications of the modest living space of a 1920's flat, they effectively
liberated this art form from the confines of manor houses and museums and introduced
them into tenements. Here they could soothe the home-sick immigrant from Eastern
Europe or from the Bay of Naples. As America became more sophisticated, these
"fake" tapestries were discarded like broken shards and replaced by oil paintings. It is
as though the tents have been folded and have disappeared into the desert from
whence they came.

"What is he up to"? I wondered, as I stood back watching him
light some candles. "He is invoking La Virgen de Regla, asking
for protection for your house", said my friend.The bAbalao was
responding to the answer I had given him when he asked me, "Why
have you come here"? (This is the same question a psychologist
asks a new patient). I was unprepared with a reply and with
Nanigo proverbs traveling Quixote-like around my brain, I was
about to confess that it was not my intention to come..that my
friend had suggested it..when I stammered..la..la musica".
At that moment, the night surrounding us seemed to physically
withdraw itself in respectful silence. From this tableau of a
babalao, a young American and his Cuban friend, a trinity emerged
like three magi on a holy night.As I received his blessing, I
felt that he knew very well why I had come to Regla. "You will
carry this music around the world", he said. Was this a prophesy
or a command of sorts? Was it an example of his psychic insight?
Whatever the meaning, it has influenced me all my life..of that
there is no doubt. Knowing absolutely nothing of the technicalities of music, but now much imbued with the workings of its
mysterious power. Was I to go forth like a neophyte apostle,
an evangelist PROSELYTIZER?

Much shaken by this truely religious experience, I wondered:
     Was his ODD STATEMENT merely an example of lyrical rhetoric?
     an example of pastoral eloquence, an embellishment of a
     ritual, a divinely inspired assignment, a fortitious INDOCTRINATI
   a revelation that made me a propagator of this music,
     a step toward my greater spiritual education, a sacred
     covenant, an oracular portent, an inescapable aesthetic
     responsAbility that made me involved, indebted, privileged,
     a canonization witnessed by invisble Orishas, an unexpected
     imposition that made me an instrument of the music itself?
     Was the santero a channeler between Yemayá and a new convert?

After this encounter, one fact emerges from the overall picture of
my life. I can see that I have faithfully "carried the music around
the world". Returning from Cuba in 1941, I opened dance studios all
along Miami Beach, performed with the La Playa Dancers around the
states, exhibited rumba with the USO in Samar, Philippines, ran the
Champagne Dance Contests aboard cruise ships, lead the immensely
popular conga lines of the fifties, taught with Tony and Lucille
Colon at Grossingers, lectured Oral History of the music at the
Smithsonian, donated my poster collection of Latin Orchestras to
Boys Harbor. I was given a dream in Regla that today I see slowly
materializing into reality, like a plant I have watered. Surely we
make the world a better place with this happy music..a duty that is
set before all mankind..is it not? So it was foretold that I would
one day write this for you to read.

          BLESSED IS HE WHO   HIS WORK - (THOMAS CARLYLE)
                    HAS FOUND

TRAVELING DAYS ARE NEVER OVER

By

Vincent Livelli

The urge to travel endures even after traveling is overtaken by time, tide, danger, and /or wear and tear. Sitting on my stoop I assist confused tourists visiting the Village. "Can I help you?" I ask. By doing so I am returning, in that way, to my traveling days. "Where are you from?" is the phrase that brings back in remembrance the countries I once enjoyed deeply, still recall fondly, but are never to be seen again, they being lost loves restored to an afterlife status.

There is always a something pleasant to say with visiting foreigners. In this way travel is a two-way street that we visit together. They show up from all over to learn and end up enjoying their discovering that we know much about where they come from. The more we all travel, the more we can learn from each other- from the "dissemination of information". It adds to the two-way enjoyment of plain living and also to the joy of having traveled well. If you live somewhere like the Village, the world comes to your doorstep. It's also true for those who live in Paris. The visitor is someone knocking at your door who has come to know you.

The demonstration of knowledge, it is like diamonds,- the more they are flaunted, the more pleasure they bring to life. For the Japanese tourist from Atami, I'll say, "Ah, Atami, the "Honeymooners city", like our Niagara Falls. Is the Tokyu Hotel still there?" For Frenchmen, "Is the Coq Hardi doing well in Bougival?" Italy? "Is the Museo Navale opened again in Venice?" Spain, you say? "Is the Fenix Hotel still there?" Brazilians are asked about Teresópolis, and Israelis are informed that I have a tree planted in Haifa. To Iranians I mentioned the poet,

Ferdowsi, and to Germans, the Palace Neuschwanstein. Argentines hear me speak of Cabaret Tabaris. I'm waiting for Egyptians, to speak to them about Um Khulsum.

Tourists are time-bound to itineraries and if time allows, some poetry is okay. For Spaniards, "En un lugar de la Mancha." For Italians, "Tanto gentile e tanto onestà…." For Germans, its Schiller's Lorelei, "Ich weiss nicht was es soll bedeuten…". Englishmen hear Lovelaces's, "Whereas in silks my Julia goes…" Iranians? "How long, how long in infinite pursuit of this…and that endeavor and dispute…."

For the French, "Maitre Corbeau sur un arbre perclait…".

NEWS FLASHES AMERICAN PRESIDENT LINES

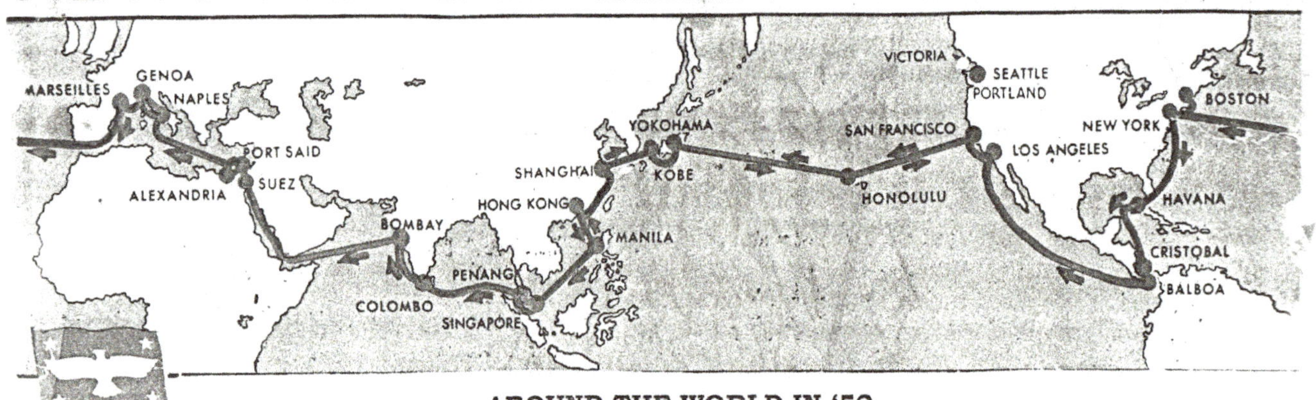

AROUND THE WORLD IN '52

by Vincent Livelli

Even today, few people have been around the world. Historically, up to 1952, only about 250,000 had done so. Your everyday tourist and your world traveler are not in the same league as the circumnavigator who closes the global circle, thus claiming the travel trophy.

Out of inborn curiosity, we all share this universal dream. As part of the ego, we feel an itchy spirit within us, strongest in adventurers, traders and dreamers. Strong also in those who have the means to do so or the madness of those who do it alone. The latter are the most admired. It was my job, as a tour manager, to do it with sixteen wealthy Brazilians, two hundred and fifty odd pieces of baggage and one Maltese terrier.

The carrier was American President Lines and the travel agency was Exprinter of Brazil. The cruise took ninety days visiting 24 ports and clocked 24,000 plus sea miles. The luxury liner, S.S. Pres. Wilson, carrying 330 passengers, took us from San Francisco to Yokohama and the S.S. Pres. Monroe took us from there to Staten Island, via the Suez Canal.

We left San Francisco in mid-July, arriving on schedule in Honolulu but with what was to be called a "screw loose". While a replacement propeller could reach us and be installed, we would be "stuck" for eight days. Groans turned to delight when my Brazilians were put up at the Royal Hawaiian Hotel ($40.00 a day double in 1952) courtesy of Lloyds of London. They called this vacation within a vacation "por conta do Coronel Bonifacio". Originally, there was to be 29 in our party but because of the west coast maritime strike at the time, thirteen dropped out which made the tour manager happy but with the eight day delay, the round the world arrangements went out the window. The lucky sixteen sent postcards to the dropouts back home as you can imagine since they were now treated as visiting celebrities in Blue Hawaii. Swimming at Waikiki (a beach as famous as Copacabana), lulled by island music and eating suckling pig (a traditional favorite dish in Brazil). They were millionaire large land owners coming from the steamy interior of a very hot country who now were being fanned by ocean breezes. They would have been content to savor this "Paradis" forever had it not been that the wonders of the world were ahead and one did not keep King Tut's Egypt waiting.

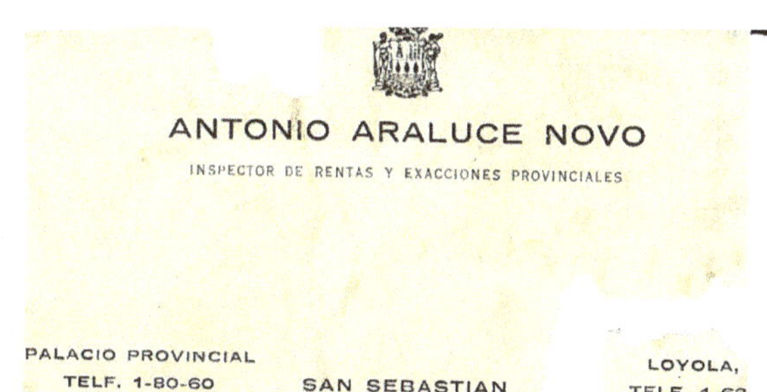

<u>Mistaken Identities</u>

by Vincent Livelli

As a global target for foreign visitors, New York was a sleeping giant badly lacking linguistics, guides, and know-how. During the early seventies, the birth of our travel industry was premature. "Go to JFK, meet 45 Spaniards and escort them to their hotel" was the order I received from the tour operator, which we did. However, this simple assignment almost created an international incident that threatened to turn friends into foes.

When the passengers were seated and the baggage loaded for departure, my bus driver turned on the public address system and handed me the mike. "Bien venidos a los Estados Unidos y a la Gran Manzana (the big apple), y viva España," was my friendly welcome. This was the customary greeting I extended to overseas visitors to New York. For the French, it was Vive la France. Suddenly, it was as though a bomb had exploded in the bus from the front to the rear. Hostile shouting resounded in a language I had never heard. These were all Basque nationalists jumping up from their seats, reacting in shock and awe as I also was, together with my driver. It was as though I were welcoming some Irish Protestants with a blessing from the Pope, or an Israeli/Arab confrontation.

Fortunately, my convincing sincerity and my repeated apologies simmered them down so that I was able to restore control; I mentioned my memorable visit to "la Perla del Cantabrico, San Sebastian, and beautiful Biarritz, as well as how warmly I had been welcomed by their countrymen.

Another meet-and-greet encounter involved fifty Argentine cadets on a good-will visit to the United States, coming to New York from Washington, where it seems they had been snubbed by our State Department. It was a moment in our history when we were obliged to condemn Argentina's treatment of its element and of *los desaparecidos*. The papers were loaded with photos of mothers carrying portraits of their missing children in streets of Buenos Aires. After Washington, it was understandable why they would identify me with the policies that were prevalent at the time.

Since I had had no advance briefing on any of the diplomatic intrigue involved in my assignment, and because I had always been received with *brazos abiertos* (open arms) when my ship laid over in B.A., I extended *un fuerto abrazo* (a warm embrace) as they boarded the bus.

On this occasion, a totally opposite reaction manifested itself, much different than the Basque fiasco. This was prompted by my mentioning at the mike that I was a soccer fan (untrue), and a friend of Luis Herrera, their international polo- and race-car champion (true). Having anticipated a cold-shoulder reception, the general and his cadets were now in the palm of my hand. I solidified this newborn friendship by referring to tender beef, tango nights, and the floor shows at the Mar del Plata Casino. Since everyone had spent days eating Anglo food, I suggested a churrasco at El Rincón Criollo, the only Argentine restaurant in New York at that time. The cadets were traveling on their stomachs, so the offer was accepted by loud cheering. This was music to my ears since I would be receiving a commission for the business from the restaurant.

Shepherding Pilgrims

By Vincent Livelli

Astrologers have told me that Mars, the planet of energy, rules much of my life. Also included is courage and creativity. An episode in Rio demonstrated this.

While escorting Archbishop Connaly of Seattle and six pilgrims to Brazil for the Eucharistic Congress, I found myself behaving true to myself and my zodiac chart.

As the Archbishop was preparing to leave our hotel for the ceremonies that were to take place all along Copacabana Beach, and where two million people had gathered, I waited for him the lobby of the hotel. He and his pilgrim priests assembled ready to board transportation to our assigned seating area. Since time was an element in the arrangements, my role was to arrive on schedule, an escort's chief responsibilities in many cases.

I beckoned to the Archbishop to remain at the entrance while I cleared the way for him to cross over to where the cars were waiting to take us down the side of the mountain to our assigned seats on Copacabana Beach. We were running a bit late, which manifested itself in my reaction to possible problems I would be encountering.

Running out into the very center of the street in front of the hotel I held up my hands to stop traffic coming from both right and left, so that my Archbishop could cross to where our cars were stationed. What I was taken by surprise by was not only that I managed to stop Brazilian drivers cold merely by acting like a traffic cop, but also my stopping a trolley car that was coming from around the side of the hotel, ringing its bell loudly. In spite of the clanging and coming out of the night like a monster, I stood my ground. I didn't flex a muscle or give an inch. What made the scene even more dramatic was the fact the trolley was coming down a steep hill and slid before it stopped just feet away from me with sparks igniting under its wheels.

As I signaled to the Archbishop to now proceed safely to our cars, he and the group walked calmly and safely as befitting his prominent position, while I turned now to the left, now to the right, bowing to the crowd with a special *muito obrigado* thank you salute to the trolley conductor and driver.

But it wasn't entirely a question of my courage or creativity that played a part that night. It was the Archbishop's attire, his tall cone shaped hat, his flowing vestments, and his symbol of authority the shepherd staff that did the trick.

In Tokyo, three days before the official surrender there were opportunities and fortunes to be made.

One day, early in the Military Occupation, a young Japanese fellow speaking excellent English became my friend. He had worked in acts, as an acrobat in the States before the war. I decided to go into the night club business with him. Off Ginza, in a narrow side street we opened what I named "The Tokyo Officers Club". With music for dancing, thanks to a beat-up, wind-up record player and five or six records, one being "A Little Grass Shack in Ka hu la Ka lu la, Hawaii" we served Suntory beer, sake, and excellent Japanese scotch.

I gave the club to my friend.

The third opportunity was more delicate, involving as it did none other than my Commanding Officer, General Crist, Supreme Commander (until general Mac Arthur arrived one day later to take over the Japanese high official government dignitaries dressed formally and with top hats as shown on the deck of the S.S. Missouri Surrender Ceremony). These men had come to have an audience on the first day we were setting up military government offices in Yokohama — later moved into the DAI ICH I building in Tokyo.

In full view of this delegation of Japanese government people I had spread out on my desk some local currency. They were then ushered into the General's office while one remained with me outside the office. They had placed an envelope with Japanese currency in it to bribe me for information. The next day they left another envelope with currency. I did not touch it, I turned to them and said, "Sayonara". AS I SAW THEM TO THE EXIT,

Contacts

Hon. Amb. Herschel Johnson	Former Ambassador to Brazil
Hon. Amb. Lester Mallory	Former Ambassador to Jordan
Hon. Amb. Joao C. Munis	Brazilian Ambassador to USA
Hon. Amb. G. Corominas	Argentine Ambassador to UNO
Hon. Amb. Pimentel Brandao	Brazilian Ambassador to UNO
Hon. Amb. J. C. Blanco	Uruguayan Ambassador to USA
Hon. Amb. P. Barrenechea	Peruvian Ambassador to Brazil
Hon. Amb. Sydney Pierce	Canadian Ambassador to Brazil
Hon. Amb. J. M. Del Castillo	Mexican Ambassador to Brazil
Hon. Amb. Julio Carneiro	Brazilian Ambassador to Japan
Hon. Amb. S. Sudjono	Indonesian Ambassador to Brazil
Hon. Amb. Muzaffor Goker	Turkish Ambassador to Japan
Hon. Amb. Mateo Indelli	Italian Ambassador to Japan
Hon. A. DuPetit Ibarra	Assistant Secretary of State, Uruguay
H.R.H. Chulalonghorn	Prince of Thailand
Hon. M. Albert Dussoix	Mayor, Geneva, Switzerland
Hon. Archibald Wemple	Mayor, Schenectady, N.Y.
Hon. Fred. Peterson	Mayor, Portland, Oregon
Hon. C. D. Baker	Mayor, Las Vegas, Nev.
Hon. Wm. W. Donaldson	Mayor, Pontiac, Michigan
Hon. Dick Scharz	Mayor, N. Kansas City, Mo.
Hon. Joseph Lawlor	Mayor, Ames, Iowa
Hon. W. E. McNulty, Jr.	Mayor, Columbia, S.C.
Hon. Ezra Summers	Mayor, Norfolk, Va.
Hon. Richard J. McConnell	Mayor, Philadelphia, Pa.
Hon. Frank G. Schemanske	Mayor, Detroit, Michigan
Hon. Nelson Howarth	Mayor, Springfield, Ill.
Hon. Byron F. Nelson	Mayor, Minneapolis, Minn.
Hon. Farrell D. Smith	Mayor, Corpus Christi, Texas
Hon. H. J. Hamilton	Mayor, Augusta, Georgia
Hon. Charles F. Hodel, Jr.	Mayor, Pittsburgh, Pa.
Hon. Carl Gardner	Mayor, Owensboro, Kentucky
Hon. James B. McNally	Justice, Supreme Court, NY
Mr. Joseph Houghton	Pres. Esso Refining, Argentina
Mr. Jose Klabin	Pres. Klabin Paper, Sao Paulo
Mr. G. Prado	Pres. Prado Crystal, Sao Paulo
Mr. Armando Pereira	Pres. Center Industry, S. Paulo
Mr. Luiz Campella	Pres. Industrial SA, Sao Paulo
Mr. C. De Carvalho	Pres. Carvalho Cacao, Bahia
Mr. S. Yankelevitch	Pres. Radio Belgrano, Argentina
Mr. Alberto Puig	Pres. Wool Shippers, Uruguay
Mr. Pedro Correa	Pres. Tabacaria "Lawdres", Rio
Mr. Z. Damm	Pres. Stalex, Sao Paulo
Mr. C. Borden	Pres. Brazilian Power & Light
Mr. L. Robert Vitkin	Pres. American Flange

<u>Travel Unpleasantries</u>

Following all the drama of World War II, the world suddenly had an empty feeling to it. Compared to today, 2015, there simply was "no one around." Imagine standing today in front of Mona Lisa with no one else next to you, or lying on Copacabana Beach all alone. Walk Greenwich Village at 9 a.m. Sunday mornings and you feel back in time in a 19th-century neighborhood. Times Square at that time on most days is also "empty," not haunted but silenced, emptied. As we multiply we show more rude behaviors. The more space you have, the more life you own. People find peace far from people, say, on vacations, as a form of "vacating" a locale. On the go, only a mere handful of rather unexpected encounters called "unpleasantries" crossed my path. One here at home when an angry cab driver threw the tip I gave him back at me. It seems that when I went to sea the standard tip for taxi drivers, regardless of the distance traveled, was $.10. When I returned to life in New York, I still thought as I had prior to isolating myself on ships, so that I did not know the $.10 tip was an insult. This incident made me feel like a 1972 tourist visiting New York, quite uninformed regarding tipping. No visitor should receive such treatment, I believed. I decided to see the city from the perspective of a foreign visitor and, if possible, help change things by educating persons concerning the travel industry that was just beginning to see more foreigners.

In Spain, a Madrid shoeshine boy asked me to remove my shoes so that he could do a proper shine. This was back in 1952 when Spain was undergoing much poverty. When I complied, he ran off with my shoes, leaving me unable to run after him. In Cairo, even today, you never put anything in your handkerchief pocket. Kids run up and grab whatever they can before running off. In Morocco today, shopkeepers wrap inferior merchandise, which you don't discover until back home, believing that you received what you purchased. When the Egyptians wanted the British to leave Sudan (The English occupied Sudan at that time), a stone was thrown at my head while I was in Luxor. I must have been mistaken for an Englishman.

Some Middle Eastern people love us; others don't. A Tuareg spat at me in front of his son when I did not buy a trinket from him. In the Bekaa Valley, Lebanon, the natives turned the America flag upside down. In Iran, the Torah was on the floor at the entrance to an antique shop where customers entered, and, leaving, were obliged to step on pages of the Torah. At Maxim's in Paris, the waiter was caught overcharging us by about $20 US. In Quebec, in a Chinese restaurant, my order contained leftovers from someone else's lunch. When I asked the waitress for an ashtray, she returned with one and said, "That will be one shilling, please." This happened in Nassau.

In Rome, at an exclusive Bulgari jewelry shop, they did not give me the tourist tax exemption. I was unaware that I was entitled to receive it. When I returned to claim it I was told, "Sorry. The cash register is closed." In Damascus, the shopkeeper camouflaged the exit to keep me from leaving. In Tokyo shortly after the surrender, the shopkeeper's entire family rushed around the store erasing old prices when I came in. In Marseilles, porters on strike laughed at me breaking my back because I was carrying my luggage so I would not miss my train. In Yugoslavia, the captain left the dock, although he saw me running to the ship. I managed to jump onto the deck just in time.

In 1959, while exploring a jungle path, I tripped and fell, only to hear laughing coming from some Indians that, unaware by me, had been following behind me, hidden. In St. Martin, during the early Sixties, native people resented tourists, making visitors very uncomfortable, until the government put up a large billboard saying, Don't kill the goose that lays the golden egg!

Early tour buses had no onboard toilet facilities. We pulled up to a large restaurant on the highway, only to catch the owner putting up Restroom for customers only. A heavily sequined evening gown was missing when we left the Flora Hotel. By paying a reward, we retrieved our stolen passports in Rio. I didn't seek a path less traveled – the world itself was.

"I'd like a centrally located hotel in Prague," I advised the travel agent in London." "We have one just ten minutes from the main square," he said. When I arrived in Prague, I discovered that the agent meant by car, not within walking distance. Whoever heard of a hotel without an elevator? I had to carry luggage up three flights in three trips in France. While carrying and reading a conservative Italian newspaper in Livorno, I was insulted by the

Communist dock workers. In Bombay, in 1952, I had to return to the ship and descend the gangplank, since my shirt had Muslim writing on it. In a Hindi city still recovering from massacres, an unscrupulous tour guide at a museum pocketed the entrance fee, saying, "It's closed."

After escorting sixteen very demanding Brazilian millionaires around the world for ninety days, I received no gratuity. Not only do Brazilians consider tipping belittling to a tour manager, but the travel agency told them it was not customary, I found out, adding that "the tip was already included in the package price!" In France, you can order a glass of Champagne. I did not know that if you ordered it in Argentina you must pay for the entire bottle. At La Conga in New York, I tipped the maitre-d' well for a ringside table, only to find more tables added to ringside as customers arrived all night.

At the Sert Room of the Waldorf in 1942, I was asked to "leave the dance floor" for dancing an authentic fast rumba, not Arthur Murray's rumba. Camel drivers on strike at the pyramids charged us the same for riding on a donkey. A cab driver in San Francisco charged us for a "return trip" after dropping us off at the airport for our flight. Same thing happened in South Korea. A carton of Marlboros to the chief purser allowed us to carry a puppy onboard from Barcelona to Naples. Otherwise, "No Dogs Allowed." Accepting a dinner invitation to dinner in Lisbon, I found myself starving until it was served after 10 p.m. In Buenos Aires, while in a dentist's chair, the electricity was suddenly shut off. The dentist continued using a foot pedal to operate the drill. In St. Bart's, a beach picnic party poisoned one hundred sixty of my passengers, due to potato salad left out overnight unrefrigerated. "You Jew, dirty Jew," a passing motorcyclist yelled out at me in Casablanca.

When talking of unpleasant subjects, one tends to exaggerate, but with pleasant happenings it would not be so to say that some are understated, especially if Lady Luck is involved. Perhaps we fear that we must pay back in some way, eventually. Without exaggeration, arriving in Havana in 1940 in the midst of Carnival, and not in the midst of a revolution -- as photographer Walker Evans did – not only was it pleasing, it changed my approach to travel.

It was a sad departure when they heard "All Aboard", having been such
willing castaways. What awaited us in Yokohama was of course a let down
since we transferred to an older vessel. The S.S. Monroe was not air-
conditioned. She was a C-3 type passenger cargo ship carrying about 95
passengers. Quoting Mark Goldberg in "Caviar and Cargo", she charged only
"$250.00 for the trans-Atlantic segment from Mediterranean ports to New
York". She had seen World War II service at Iwo Jima and was the sister
ship of the Pres. Polk, according to Mr. Goldberg. Cargo was loaded and
unloaded constantly and under bright lights during the night. Once on land,
our agents Japan Travel Bureau scrambled to split us into three groups
because of hotel rooms being in short supply due to post war conditions,
the change in our reservations and our mixed up itinerary. Lost baggage,
tipsy tourists, touts, rumors...these are routine problems for the experienced
tour manager. But now one group was put up in Yokohama, another in
Tokyo and a third in Nikko. Tourists cannot resist comparing hotels or
restaurants. Expecting trouble of various sorts, I had wired the Brazilian
Ambassador to perhaps extend an invitation to cocktails to welcome these
rare visitors, which he graciously did. The ratio of Brazilians making this
sort of trip in 1952 was estimated to be one in two million, five hundred
thousand. At the party, one of our members spoke of settling five thousand
Japanese farmers on his property. There were already two hundred and fifty
thousand Japanese in Brazil, mainly in the state of Sao Paulo. To show
hospitality, the agent arranged a "Geisha party" which was about as wicked
as weak tea, with "musical pillows" as the parlour game.

After rounding up the group on our second day in Japan, we boarded the
new bullet train to Kobe, where miraculously, a Brazilian Naval Cadet
training ship was in port. I immediately contacted the captain and free-
loaded another cocktail party, this time on an open deck where we could now
see the S.S. Monroe anchored off our bow. She had come down the coast to
meet us the day before. The vessel was the famous "Almirante Saldanha", a
tall ship that you can still see at the New York Harbor Op-Sail Festival.

Both Hong Kong and Rio have splendid harbors with lavish natural beauty,
but Hong Kong is for shoppers and prefers to be famous for bargains rather
than mountains. In 1952, foreign assets control regulations prohibited the
importation into the U.S. of Chinese goods which were not in Hong Kong
prior to December 17th, 1952. This applied only to U.S. citizens. The
Brazilian would be charged customs duty upon their return home but they
would still benefit tremendously from prices in the Orient. Imagine sixteen
millionaires buying out a whole city. It paid for their trip. The tour
manager's job was to interpret from and into various languages everywhere,
always in the middle of price wars between buyers and sellers.

The Brazilians were not bargain hunters as such. Rather, they were starving shoppers in general having suffered the scarcity of so many things due to World War II. For example, they bought dozens of mirrored sunglasses which they all wore during the entire trip. Converting various currencies into "Cruzeiros" was a numismatic nightmare since due to inflation, their money was quoted at a different rate each day. It would go from 32 to 40 to the dollar when the official exchange rate was 29. Furthermore, they used the international metric system. They managed well while dealing with the sharpest Orientals and Middle Easterners, learning as they went along.

"Cochin is regarded as one of the beauty spots in India. The oldest settlement where the Portuguese arrived in 1500 for trading purposes", I informed them at the port lecture. There was to be no shopping here and due to a lack of cars we did the sightseeing tour by rickshaw. In the states they had bought Cadillacs and large TV's but in Cochin the best buys were sweetmeats. With no shopping, they concentrated on the scenes around them, i.e., the Holy Men and the Jewish Synagogue, school children and snake charmers.

Throughout the Orient, drivers seemed to go out of their way to scrape the rear ends of pedestrians. This practice was a means to "prevent pursuit by evil spirits that might be behind you". It served to scare the devil out of the devil. When we asked Captain Holt about this strange custom where Chinese junks barely miss being run down by large ships, he dryly said, "Sometimes they don't make it".

When it came time to leave the group in Marseilles and the world of carpet vendors, pearl merchants, saris, statues, tailors and the rest, I decided to buy myself a present. Since Brazilians consider tipping degrading to an individual and since tipping the escort is customary everywhere else, they offered me a gift. I settled for a Maltese terrier that I named "Monroe", in Portuguese "Mon Roy" and translated into English, "My King". Complicated international arrangements had been made to return the group to Brazil aboard the "Giulio Cesare". In fact, only two took the "Cesare" while the rest took the "Caesar Augustus", the "Anna C", the "Conte Grande" or the plane. Obviously, they began needing a change of scenery but ended needing a change of company. The trip itself went smoothly enough in spite of the inter-shopper rivalries and the soccer feuds between Cariocas and Paulistas, between modern Magellans.

Embraces abounded as each tour member stepped forward to kiss and say "Boa Viagem" to their tour manager who had brought them around with no lost baggage. We exchanged addresses and promised to send photos and kissed again. I remember thinking that I'd do it again, but next time alone.

Page 3

THE BUSINESS OF LIFE

(CAVEAT: LET THE SHOPPER BEWARE)

Sailing about from place to place for many years kept me from ever going into business. But business seems to follow us everywhere. By going to sea, I had hoped to escape a nine to five fate, but in doing so I became, not by choice, a commis-voyageur, a traveling salesman, an itinerant peddler. Totally unqualified for the commercial world, with no 'acumen', no actuarial experience or 'product knowledge", I was truly an innocent abroad. Furthermore, I had little respect for materialists.. that is, until I came across Emerson's, "Bring a thing from where it abounds to where it is costly.

Cacti growing wild along the roadsides of St, Martin were vendible in the States, I assumed. The tropical fish that swam by , tortoise shells from Tortuga, goat skins from Port-au-Prince and the sea shells of the Caymans, all would find a market at home. Fossils from the tar pits of Tobago and snake skins from Costa Rica were salable as well as the
exquisite butterfly wings found in Santos. . Young girls arranged them in sheets in orphanages, where one could buy them eliminating the middlemen and aiding charity, There were black pearls in Margarita Island and "pepita" gold nuggets in La Guaira..I began to see the world as a treasure in every port.

Post World War II found US Customs still operating under pre-war regulations. In addition, there was no talk of endangered species. Seamen as well as passengers were entitled to a $400.00 duty free allowance once a month back in the late forties. The duty on a bottle of fine port wine was only .19 cents, for example. two cartons of cigarettes per person was also allowed in addition to one bottle of liquor. In Gibralter we stocked up on scotch . Once a trip, crew members could buy liquor duty free from the ship,s locker.
 Perhaps it was Dickens or Mark Twain who commented about 19th century New York saying, "Everything is for sale". I found a buyer in Santa Fe who asked me to bring him ex-votos from Bahia. There were buyers for maracas as well as fine Cuban puros, antique "Santos " carved in San Juan were cherished and entered without duty. Soon I was dealing in tiles from Morocco, embroidery from Madeira and sea island cotton goods from Antigua. The Kuna women of Aligandi, San Blas waited on the dock for my ship to dock. They sold the blouses (molas) off their backs to us. French perfume from Guadeloupe and Martinique sold quickly in New York. Naïve folk paintings and hand carved drums from Port-au-Prince sold well in Miami. The Panamanian molas , by the way, could be worn as "wearable art". As Zora Neale Hurston once said, "All the world is my oyster". Sugar was scarce in post war Japan and so were "lugs" (the tiny bar that holds your watch band to the watch) in Buenos Aires. I supplied both .

I was in danger of going into business when I bought a Maltese terrier in Naples. He sired over two dozen cute puppies. Would I become a "Pet Shop" owner? The baby ocelot I bought in Manaus for $8.00, plus a bottle of Metaxas 3 Star was sold to the Parrot Jungle when he turned savage. Docking in Alexandria found me shopping for furniture in El-Khalili and in 1958 we bought balalaikas at GUM's for $9.00...sold them at the ship's

REFLECTIONS

HOW I BECAME A WRITER

This is titled "How I Became a Writer" with writer in quotes.
As two battalions of firemen entered my building, I was seen exit-
.ing barefoot, clad in my bathrobe. In my arms clutched tightly,
was a sheaf of manuscripts, no doubt grabbed up in my haste to
escape the flames. Held back by the police, was a crowd of onlookers. Many were curious, but others seemed hostile since I was
responsible for fouling up a street that real estate agents call
"the finest in the Village" during the annual "Plant It On Perry
Street" campaign. Watching this pitiful victim shuffle into the
gutter, out of the way of the hoses, turned their smoldering fury
into sympathy. No doubt, many spectators were legitamit authors.
Sensing the tone of the crowd, I must confess that I held my bund-
le of papers a bit tighter and a bit higher. Yes, I was playing
to the crowd..an actor now who was in the eyes of many, an author
whose manuscripts had come before the public. In their way, they
succeeded in evincing an emotional response that mere words could
not ;(especially since it was just a stack of old Income Tax forms).
My work was consumed in the flames but my image as a neighbor in
need was established and a collection taken up for a fellow writer!"

.turning boos into cheers.

Back in the seventies, before we became the Capital of the World, tour guides were few and far between. Today there are over two thousand Back then, New York meant business, not pleasure particularly, for that we New Yorkers went to the Catskills or to Miami Beach. As tourism grew, guides had to devise commentaries to describe this dynamic city to visitors; a city that rushed by the strangers in its midst who were usually on street corners consulting maps of Manhattan. Standard fixtures like the Empire State, the Statue of Liberty even the Apollo on 125th Street , did not bring out the true soul of the city. New York at that time could best be described as a mad market place .so that the tourist business went unappreciated by City Hall until the early 70s.

To interpret a city to European visitors, a city uninterested in an industry as profitable as Tourism required a professionally trained guide, similar to those officially licensed, multi lingual couriers who might well be polyglot professors with MA's in geography and ancient history. The guide could call off the 52 floors of the Woolworth Building, called "The Cathedral of Capitalism" but 4 hours of statistics about skyscrapers did not make for a good day around town, especially for those who had come to find out what we were really like. Actually, we were frightened by foreigners, confused by their politeness and their unusual needs. To satisfy the natural curiosity that inspires TRAVEL, AN expensive investment overall, there should be a deeper reaction, one similar to what we feel on our first day in Paris, for example… a fond attachment, if possible, that could last a lifetime.

How to have the sightseer feel that the city had a big red heart and some poetry? How to mellow the interchange between an unschooled tour guide and an almost unwell-come stranger , who comes without his cappuccino, his concierge or his favorite VINO..one who is almost a nuisance on a busy day. How to set.in place an efficient industry that benefited a city when so many industries did the opposite? When word got back to Europe that meals were less expensive and plentiful and that our hotels, while not as traditionally endowed as the Grand Hotels and that our tour buses although shabby when compared to those that one found in a country like Portugal, for example at that time, the visitors nevertheless admire our fine roads and highways in the "land of the automobile". When in the eighties, the tide came in, bringing pizza, gourmet delis and , sidewalk tables, there was still a gap between Europeanized NY and Hiltonized Europe. What was lacking was a tour guide with flair..a professional embodying the spirit of the city.

Since foreigners were warned of language hurdles, they felt that it was their lack of an understanding of English that hindered their grasping of what made New York tick. Paris, with its cultural and artistic advantage was forever secure, but we New Yorkers were expected to display an aggressive stance what with our reputation for bigness. The Englishman visiting Rome returned to London briefed fully on ancient ruins and mad emperors. We, on the other hand, could only boast of having done so much in so

Safety in Marriage

There was a time when I had no enemies except for some gun-licensed husbands. When the 6th Precinct warned that for every homicide 27 were single men and 1 was married, I became curious and more aware, if not alarmed. Married men live longer and I was single.

If you found that your enemies included the Castro crowd, the Mafia, the Basque Separatists, the KGB, the Al Quedistas, some disgruntled Haitian bus drivers and an array of jilted girlfriends, you might want to consider marriage.

The Castro contingent would like to see me gone. IN Miami, I am always seen in the company of ex-Bay of Pigs instructors, hermano pilots, families of executed journalists, barqueros.

The Mafia mistrusted me after I turned down their offer to steer suckers to the Havana casinos. I big-mouthed how they destroyed Coney Island and burned down Harlem for insurance scams while I took tourists around New York.

The Commies were angry at me when I, as a tour guide, told a busload of Italian tourists while passing by the U.N., "Hanno cagato (shit) in tutto il mondo". The passengers were all from Livorno, a solid, 100% red stronghold.

The KGB learned by my boasting, that I had once smuggled rock and roll records into Moscow in 1958.

The Basque Separatists (ETA) were furious when I announced at the mike, "VIVA ESPANA, Y SUS COLONIAS". It happened this way. When a tour company called, I was told "You will have 45 Spaniards for 7 days to Niagara Falls". As they boarded the bus, by way of welcoming them, I gave a "Long live Spain!" greeting.

Al Queda. I subscribe to Aramco Magazine for its cultural exploration of the Muslim world. I pass it on to my Arabic grocer so now the entire Islamic community has my name and address and identify me with oil exploitation of their land and the Great Satan. Besides, my lady friend is Jewish.

POLYCOM AND THE HACKER

(Solving the biggest problem)

     The sign in the old garage read: "WE REPAIR COMPUTERS..
ALL MAKES". At a cluttered workbench and on shelves were PCs
to be repaired. Some werewaiting to be claimed like pets in
an animal hospital.

     When the workshopclosed and the lights were turned off
the clacking of a keyboard was heard. WAS SOME INVISIBLEW TYPIST
AT WORK IN THE DARK? Suddenly a screen lit up, revealing an odd
PC...a hybrid assembled from spare parts, from components salvaged
from a tinkerers technological grab-bag. Old discarded models had
been joined toadvanced sets and made interoperable. HI-PERFORMANCE
devices had increased its signal range, memory power and compat-
ability. Like a hot-rod in a chop shop, it was more than the sum
of its parts..it was POLYCOM!

     Sony now lit its screen, Toshiba stirred..Apple, MacIntosh,
Dell all joined a chorus of chatter that was quickly silenced by
POLYCOM. "THIS IS POLYCOM. WE ARE ABOUT TO BE ATTACTED...SEND ME
YOUR MEMORY BANKS...NOW! Like mice scurrying in a cupboard, the
sets obeyed, supplying responses that were rapidly digested.
Now fully arsmed with an enormous array of information, the virus
is overwhelmned. In doing so, this unique union ofcomputers has
just solved the industriessbiggest problem.

     When the garage opened in the morning, the repairman was
heard to mutter, "Wonder how come this old guy is warm to the
touch?".

da dear

u might like to pass these on

and since I mentioned it

her. It was originally meant

be a children's story, and

a way, it still is a fantasy,—

fantasy that could save the

iggest Problem as yet unsolved.

The blending of bordello/elegance is Big Business.
In 1957, along London's upscale Bond Street, the ladies of the
night displayed a take off on proper upper class aristocrats.
They were seen dressed (over dr essed rather than under dr .essed)
in boas, jewelery, and fur jackets, that allowed them to be made
more visible in evenings of fog.and warmer in the climate.
Compare this to the halter. and tight skirt of their American
sisters of today. Actually no flirtatiouscostuming is needed
since the corner spectacle is an obvious enough "statement",
to use an industry terminolgy. Locate the scenario on a mirrored
runway on 7th Ave's Fashion Mile. FOR "EXPOSURE".

When Cristina Fiorucci visited New York"s Garment Center,
I was assigned to escort her, as I did with Commendatore Ettore
Fila from Biella, Italy as well as members of the Zegna, Hermes
and Canali families. I knew my knowledge of the special language
of the fashion crowd was limited. With such exposure to these
"Full Front" folks, it was only a matter of time before I would
become fascinated by them and would want to join the club. That
was how Arabic Chic was born, still-born, for when I brazenly
called Anna Sui, she hung up on me with a Chinese cuss word.
The Institute of Fashion Technogy was expensive and the Small
Business Administration told me it would take 4 years of trying.
In such a mad-cap, high stakes , crazy circus, anything goes.
Just who are the big spenders at Viky Tiel's boutique if not the
chic Saudi Arabians?

MAKING A FRIENDLIER NEW YORK

America is an immigrants adopted country. but has America adopted the immigrant?

A photo in a letter sent back home to let's say. Guatemala speaks powerfully across
the miles. On the other hand. a phone call accents the separation as does the inability to
communicate with the average New Yorker in proper English. Once conversation ends
they face the silence alone. Photos communicate on a deeper more precious level. A
phone call ends abruptly often leaving much unsaid. perhaps distorted. costly and in
a way. mechanical. We kiss a photo, but a phone? never. Photographs are portable like
cell phones. They can be enlarged. reproduced . passed around in a hauntingly warm
manner. confirming love more clerly.

 Immigrants are like soldiers with families overseas. Many never return home. Calling
"home" for Christmas is not comparable to mailing a letter with photos enclosed. Rarely
refused is a polite request to take someone's photo. Such a request seldom enters an
immigrants life. many of whom do not own a camera or mistrust strangers understandably. As I go about my "project" in my busy city. I snap pictures "for your family"
I say. For an insignificant investment . in this manner. I make many people happy and
make New York friendlier. Friendship cannot be bought but can sprout out of a visible
commitment of concern for those immigrants who have come to us. To photograph them
at work. smiling while working is better still. It allows a stranger on our streets to show
his or her appreciation of us with a thank you without humility. with dignity. Like the
disposable camera. the immigrant is not disposable. Looking at the face in the photo.
he or she smiles back. This is whats he came here for. this is whats we want to see from
him…that big New York smile.

<u>"ANYBODY GOTTA' MATCH?"</u>

Lauren Bacall- "TO HAVE AND TO HAVE NOT"

As we stop smoking, book matches will gradually disappear
along with those restaurant ashtrays we took home as souvenirs.
The strolling cigarette girl in her French doll dress, offering
her tempting tray is rarely seen now. The busy club photographer
who made us "smile" as he solicited the tables has gone like the
cuspidor and wax matches. Restaurant matches, with their colorful
advertisements, still bring back memories of special occasions
alone or in the company of friends. They serve to keep alive that
flickering flame of recall while much of our memories have gone
off with the smoke. We hastily scribbled our phone numbers on them.

Let us remember that first match cover that read, "HOTEL TAFT,
GRILL", The Dancingest Band in Town". It was there, while dancing
to Vincent Lopez's Band that you fell in love. Remember when she
blew your match out in order to light YOUR cigarette at the Russian
Tea Room, or when everyone rushed to light her cigarette at MAXIM's,
including the waiters? Looking at a CHAMBORD match cover brings back
what the French call, "regal de diner". The cover from Ben Marden's
RIVIERA reads, "Just across the George Washington Bridge", where one
went to see Sally Rand's white feather fan dance or that Red Hot
Mama, Sophie Tucker. Chin Lee's, MORI's in the Village, EL CHICO,
"The Oldest Spanish Night Club in New York" are all gone. The Hotel
Astor, "At the crossroads of the World" is gone. The WALDORF CAFE-
TERIA cover stated, "Serving 60 million customers each year" in
the Garment Center. FELTMAN's Coney Island reads, "26 Attractions,
Dinners $1.00 up, the SWING ClUB, 35 West 52nd claims, "Never a Dull
Moment", the HOTEL DIXIE's cover reads, "In the Center of Everything"
"Try our Southern Fried Chicken". Jack & Charlies simply says, "21".
The HOTEL ST. GEORGE, Clark Street, Brooklyn claims "WORLD'S MOST
LUXURIOUS SALT WATER POOL" and in Miami Beach, the FIVE O'CLOCK CLUB
offers, "Drinks on the House at 5 O'Clock". In Hong Kong, the PENIN- -
SULA, (blank); in St.Louis CRYSTAL PALACE,"Pre-Broadway Productions".

Throw-away match covers, like cigarette stubs were thrown in the
gutter. How could you discard the Palm Beach Casino, Monte Carlo,
where lighting a new-found friend's cigarette began as courtesy and
ended in ecstacy? Matches served romance better. The mechanical
lighters, smelling of butane, would hinder the tender concern of a
trembling hand that she gently steadied while looking in your eyes.
Such devices could never match the elegance of the HOTEL VILLA D'ESTE
match cover with its noble coat of arms. They drew us closer together
hudling over a flame threatened by a strong wind.

INVITATIONS TO THE DANCE
(Latin Dance Hall Posters)

For some thirty years, colorful posters could be seen on
corner lamp posts around Times Square. They added a bright note
to an otherwise grey landscape. It was a time when churches of
different denominations were painting their entrance doors red
to attract worshippers nostalgic for the vibrant tropical environment of the Caribbean.

Communities were awash in posters. Like old political campaign slogans, many remained up long after the event they served.
With the beginning of the "Quality of Life" policy, zero tolerance
was added to "Post No Bills". Posters disappeared or were confined
to specified areas of the city where they were grouped in with
assorted advertisements, thus losing their special cachet. Soon
these cheerful placards became a dying artifact. They were replaced by handbils given out at dance hall entrances, like cir-
culars.

In the 1890's, they were distributed as playbills along the
14th street theatrical district. Unlike Europe where paper is expensive, "towns in America were covered with posters lacking
artistic value"- Jules Cheret, quoted in THE POSTER by Alain Weill.
For a peramulatory city like New York, posters have now been reduced to small notices arriving by third class mail. Clever 19th
century posters advertising various products such as soap or food
were "puns in design", similar to the 1980's Woman's Lib Roseland
Poster.

The scope of the exhibit portrays the growth and expansion of
Latin music from 1970 to the present. A portion of the exhibit dis-
plays classic Anglo festivities, i.e. Thanksgiving Day, Memorial Day,
Sadie Hawkin's Day and the 4th of July. When the first "LATINO
FESTIVAL MUSICAL" opened at Madison Square Garden, admission was $7.00.

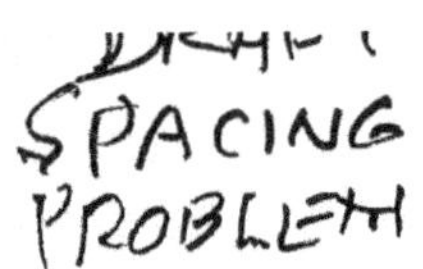

"I PAY CASH FOR OLD CLOTHES'

During the days of the Great Depression, you would hear, under your window, someone singing"O Sole Mio",

"I Sharpen Knives" or "I Buy Old Clothes". Today, because of some bad luck, I'm living like a peddler, out of a suit-

case. Because so much of my life has been lived on the go, this is not an entirely unaccustomed situation for me . For many

years I lived on ships, sleeping in small cabins with tiny closets. Frequenting thousands of eateries that were my kitchens so

to speak, plus the hotel rooms that served as homes while working on the road as a tour director, travel became my way

of life. As an itinerant, I've been a lucky traveler. This is why, now that I find myself living in a tiny room, furnished not to my

admittedly odd tastes, I can easily make my way through life's pathways and lesser alleyways. This set-up, though not of

my choosing, is good enough when compared to say, Daniel Boone, who lived in and off a forest all his life.

Sobering moments enter the picture of my life when, in a thrift shop, I catch myself paying cash for old clothes

Just like back in the days of the Great Depression.

(TALKING TO MYSELF)

THE TROUBLE WITH WRITING DIALOGUES, LIKE TALKING TO YOURSELF,
IS THE QUOTATION MARKS ONE MUST USE. KEROUAC SKIPPED THEM AND WAS
ABLE TO GET AWAY WITH IT. LIKE THE TRAVEL WRITER WHO HAS DIFFICULTY
SITTING STILL AT THE WORD PROCESSOR WHEN HE PREFERS TO BE OFF AND
AWAY FROM THINGS LIKE SENTENCE STRUCTURE AND CORRECT GRAMMER,
THE DIALOGUIST MUST POSSESS PATIENCE WITH PUNCTUATION. EVERYONE
READING HIS WORK IS LOOKING FOR ERRORS HE KNOWS. HE CANNOT TRAVEL ALONE.

FURTHEMORE THE DIALOGUIST MUST INVOLVE HIMSELF AS CLOSELY
AS POSSIBLE WITH SOMEONE ELSE. FOR EXAMPLE, YOU MIGHT SAY, "YOU
ALWAYS HURT THE ONE YOU LOVE"..A NICE ROUND QUOTATION. "YES, YOUR
FRIEND SAYS, BUT WHO DO I LOVE THE MOST?".."WHY, MYSELF", HE ADDS.
YOU ANSWER BY SAYING, "WILL WE NOT AGREE THEN THAT BY LOVING YOUR-
SELF THE MOST YOU ARE RISKING HURTING YOURSELF THE MOST IN LIFE?"
"WE LIVE PLAYING WITH A DANGEROUS INVOLVEMENT DAILY" "YES, ONE
CONTINUES, IT'S LIKE FLIRTING WITH YOURSELF, THINKING IT TO BE A
HARMLESS FLIRTATION".

"WHY DO WE FEAR DEATH?". THE MONOLOGUIST FEELS COMPELLED TO
ASK HIMSELF, PUZZLING HOPELESSLY. ALONG COMES A FRIEND WHO SAYS, ,
"WELL, I THINK IT IS BECAUSE THERE IS THIS UNIVERSAL FEAR PLANTED
IN EVERYONE OF US BY THE CREATOR". "EVERY LIVING BEING HAS A
GENE LABELED "FEAR OF DYING", LIKE FEAR OF HEIGHTS, FOR EXAMPLE.
"WHY DO YOU SUPPOSE SUCH AN UNPLEASANT UNEASINESS EXISTS IN US"?
YOU ASK...IT GOES CONTRARY TO THE GENE MARKED "SURVIVE BRAVELY"
DOES IT NOT?". YOUR FRIEND COUNTERS WITH, "HAVE YOU CONSIDERED WHAT
WOULD HAPPEN IF WE LACKED THE FEAR GENE?". "NO", YOU SAY. "WHY,
EVERYONE WOULD RUSH TO LEAVE LIFE AS QUICKLY AS POSSIBLE IN ORDER
TO GO FORWARD WITH THE OBVIOUS FORWARD PROGRESSIVE MOVEMENT INTO
THE UNKNOWN..INTO THE FUTURE. DOESN'T THAT MAKE MORE SENSE THAN
JUST HANGING AROUND?". TO COUNTER THIS YOU SAY, "I THINK IT WOULD
BE "NICE" IF WE HAD A GENE IN US THAT GUARANTEED A LIFE FULL OF
HAPPINESS. THAT WOULD INSURE, TO USE AN EXTREME PROPOSAL, THAT WE
WOULD BEST REPLACE HATE WITH LOVE". THE DIALOGUE CONTINUES WITH
YOUR FRIEND SAYING, "IF SOMEDAY WE IMPROVE ON NATURE, MANIPULATING
THE GENETIC CODE, THEN YOU WOULD REALLY BE AFRAID .... OF THAT HAPPY
FELLOW DOWN THE STREET WHO IS NOT AFRAID TO DIE".

GOT AN IDEA ?

1) A scale in the handel of a suitcase. (1951)

2) Lapel buttons for hard of hearing people for identification.

3) Scented candles with coffee aroma.

4) Toy earphones for children using parent story tales to
   induce sleep or teach ABC's.

5) Mirrored walls to reflect light devices to alert hearing impaired.

6) Curtains around TV sets to give them the appearance of theater screen

7) To re-place expensive tile (or missing pieces), use copying machine,

8) Diluted chlorine dioxide in a spore killing solution strength
   in the form of a pomade applied to the nostrils to limit Anthrax.

9) Exercise by rolling from side to side to increase blood circulation
   throughout areas of the brain and body.

10) The brain concentrating on itself by hanging picture of healthy brain.

11) Shock-absorbers for horse saddles. (1977)

12) Pictorial vests (1964 idea). Slogan T-shirts (same).

13) Mirrored finger nail polish. (1980)

14) Neckties whose design can be altered with paint to suit yourself.

15) Replace kitchen wood panelling with colored or plain mirrors (plastic

16) Lightweight plastic sheet inserted under clothing for chest protectio

17) Barbers offer spray service to cover bald areas after a haircut.

Satin sheets or velvet scarves made from remnants.

19) Visualization: videos with military ceremonies and music to inspire &
    encourage recovery for patients fighting disease.

20) Bathroom tanks with spicket to moisten tissue papper

21) Glo-paint to change scenes (i.e., *sunrise* sunsets) when lights are on or off.
    DIMMERS

22) Runners for luggage.

23) Head bands with artificial bangs in blond, brunette,

24) Remove from the genome map the genes responsible for Fear of Death.

25) Charge interest on deliquent credit card accounts (1956).

26) Ventilate ear canals where bacteria grows in dark damp areas by
    use if a doughnut shaped pillow with open center.

27) Recording of water falls to trigger difficult urination. Increase flo

28) A pomade applied to the neck as a "love bite" (hickie) for teenagers.

29) Collect smoking memorabilia (match covers, etc.) now.

30) Pierced ear jewelry for cats.

31) Shoulder holsters for water bottles (1997).

32) Continue horoscopes of deceased family members with aspects
    regarding commmication after death.

33) Up-scale scenes on revolving lampshades (not toys). (1997).

34) Induce low grade pain in order to produce increased endorphins.

35) Expensive mens hose: Better use knee-hi womens hose. Inexpensive.
    Light weight, dry quickly, less room in luggage, better fit,
    disposable, identical to womens elastic, elegant. heavy gauge type.

36) Recordings played in lobbies as theater-goers are exiting.
    For example, voices of unseen or unmentioned characters in a play
    are heard (mischeviously) commenting on aspects of the play,
    commenting on the play, joking about the audience, laughing at

    jokes (as though coming from a dressing room after the performance)

    thus repeating parts to lend more meat to discussions about the play.

    Songs featured in the play can continue out into the street with lyrics

37) Drive-through home garages to avoid   backing up. (2000)

38) Prize fights on cruise ships with betting. Strip clubs beyond 3 mi. limi

39) Plastic spray bottles filled with scented water to cool off with--
    sold at sporting events or along parade routes.

40) cruiseship entertainers perform ashore at local clubs while in port.

41) An ornamental Medallion worn on a necklace or chain, that contains
    important emergency ID as well as a flacon of smelling salts. (1989)

42) A lending library among friends. Include CD and Videos.

43) Keep extra umbrellas strategically stored to avoid carryingneedlessly

44) Familiarization bus tours for new citizens. (1998) FREE

45) Combine English & Spanish sub-titles on TV to teach languages. (2000)

46) Dance studios and health food restaurants in Health Clubs (1998)

47) Fans to cool hot interiors of parked cars activated by timers.

48) Pancake make-up for age spots and dark veins on hands.

49) Recorded prayers that are activated when lights are turned off
     at bedtime.

50) UNDER WATCH BAND, MEDICAL I.D. FOR EMERGENCIES

51) ADD COPPER POWDER TO WICKS TO BURN CANDLES GREEN FLA

52) LARGE BALLONS AS PART OF LIFE RAFT EQUIPMENT
    VISIBLE ABOVE THE HORIZON.

53) MAKE THE BANK YOUR BENIFICIARY (IN ORDER TO SECURE INTEREST

54) Squeezeable baby bottles with formula (LESS MESS)

55) MARKED TRAILS FOR FOREIGN TOURISTS IN N.Y.

56) CUDDLING ROBES

57) VNFRAMED FABRIC SCENES PASTED ON WALLS APT.

58) N.Y. APT. WINDOWS THAT FACE COURTYARD WALLS. PAINT THE WALL

59) animatism = inanimate powers

60) PUSH-UP EXTENTIONS ON BOTTLE AND CAN TOPS

Our human brains reject what is not comfortable for

All creatures oppose that which offends (PERHAPS TO OUR OFTEN DISADVANTAGE) BUT NOT WHAT CANNOT BE IGNORED

SOME SCIENTISTS BELIEVE THAT THERE ARE POSSIBLY MULTIPLE UNIVERSES. THIS THEORY IS BASED UPON THE FACT THAT OUR UNIVERSE IS EXPANDING LIKE AN INFLATEING BALLON. IF ALL LIVING CREATURES ARE LIVING IN REALITIES OF DIFFERENT LEVELS OF DEVELOPMENT FROM MICROBES TO HUMANS WITH HUMANS ENJOYING THE MOST ADVANCED REALITY THEN WE MAY PERHAPS BE EXPANDING INSIDE AN EVEN GREATER REALITY THAT SURROUNDS US INVISIBLY.

SCIENTISTS HAVE PROVEN THAT THE UNIVERSE IS RAPIDLY EXPANDING, FORMING MULTIPLE UNIVESES. AS WELL POSSIBLY. IF REALITY CAN BE MEASURED BY TECHNICAL PROGRESS AS EVIDENCE THEN PERHAPS WE ARE, LIKE THE UNIVERSE ITSELF, ACQUIREING MULTIPLE REALITIES OR PERHAPS WE HAVE ALREADY DONE SO. TIME WILL TELL.

Le Courbusier called tapestry "Le mur du nomade",
the woven walls of the nomades. Tapestry weaving is one
of the earliest human skills. Time consuming, requiring
teamwork between fiber producer, dyer, dyer, designer,
and weaver, like carpets. In Europe, the production of
the Gobeline was reserved by ministerial authorization,
made "fil a fil". In the Islamic world textiles played
social, political, and economic roles, representing to
all, wealth, currency and social status. They were part
of a State treasury or a daughter's dowry.

The ancient Egyptians used linen and Coptic weavers
were unsurpassed in their knowledge and skill. Prior to
1925 tapestries were made of natural fibers; some with
gold thread using wool, cotton, linen or silk. They were
for many centuries among the highest priced of art forms.
Recently, three Gothic fragments from 15th. Century Basel
were auctioned in London for more than on million dollars.
In 1515, Raffael was ordered by the Vatican to execute a
series depicting "The Acts of the Apostles". In the 19th.
Century, tapestries declined and were almost extinguished
as there was simply no need for textile murals to decorate
or help warm castles, churches and monasteries but from
1500 to 1650, Belgium was the tapestry capital of the world.

They were sold in urban department stores and could be purchased by the humblest family for as little as $5.00. As "art decoratif", they brought exotic visions of foreign cultures to the masses. Today, large Belgium made "oriental" carpets can be found covering the floors of village mosques.

As an art form, they lacked the highest expression of Muslim art, namely, calligraphy   Crude attempts might appear along borders in mock designs (Fig.#1). The Minerets of the Haran Mosque appear to have been the source of those shown in Fig.#2. The curved sword (jambiyya) and the slender rifles were never shown as menacing, rather as possessions of pride and status and often incorporated in dances. The noble Arabian horse, the servile camel, the donkey and at times a dog belonging to noone in particular were shown. In Fig.#3, we are presented with a traveler (mousaffir) with his companion (rafiq) being directed "ala al-shemal", to the nearest hostel (khan). As an intellectual statement, men are pondering over a chess board rather than backgammon, it being the more familiar game to the Westerner. Camels invariably appear smaller in size to accomodate the canvas confines. Women, even when dancing alone, are proper and modest since these tapestries were to be hung in often strict family settings. These imaginery "turqueries" are not voluptuous, depicting harems or houris that so tantalized Ingres. In 19th century Victorian England, a fashionable residence would have its "Turkish Corner". Rarely does a Westerner appear but in Fig.#1 we find a Victorian traveler with his rigidly corseted madam, holding his riding crop

The tapestries shown here were mass produced in Belgium and in France   as L'art decoratif for the living rooms of poor immigrant families mainly living in The Bronx, Brooklyn and Chicago. They were found in large department stores and could be bought by the poorest family for as little as $5.00 during the 1920's. They brought the exotic visions of foreign cultures to the masses. Today, large Belgian made "Oriental" carpets can be found covering the floors of village mosques throughout the Middle East.

As an art form they lacked the highest expression of Muslim art, namely, calligraphy and the arabesque. Crude attempts are shown along borders in mock designs (Fig. 1). The minerets of the Haran Mosque appear to have been the source of those shown in Figure 2. Rifles and the curved sword (jambiyya) were never shown as menacing, rather as possessions of pride and status and often incorporated in native dances. The noble Arabian horse, the camel, a donkey and at times a dog are included. In figure 3 we are presented with a traveler (mousaffir) and his companion (rafiq) being directed "ala al - shemal", to the nearest hostel (khan). As an intellectual statement, players are shown pondering chess rather than a backgammon board, it being the more familiar game to the Westerner. The camel always appears smaller in size to accomodate the canvas confines. Dancing women appear modest since these tapestries were to be hung in strict family settings.

These imaginery "turqueries" are not voluptuous, showing
harems or the prostitute (almah)that so tantalized Ingres. In
19th century England a fashionable Victorian residence would
have its "Turkish Corner". Rarely does a Westerner appear but
in Figure #1 we find a Victorian gentleman with his tightly
corseted wife, holding his crop (to beat off beggars?). For
added exoticism, a Turkistan with pig tails might mysteriously
materialize in the background. The most popular among the poor
working class families were   jardins romantiques"a la Francois
Boucher and Watteau. In an Italian-American family the ubiquitous
Bay of Naples with Vesuvius- until old world memories were abandoned. When America became more sophisticated they were replaced
on living room walls by oil paintings as the country prospered.
Until discarded, they served to depict a world still to be discovered from which one could imagine and even learn about the
Islamic world. Imagine the bulbous tombs of the pious of Sayun;
the Suq-al-Talh in Saddah, the city of Sinbad; the castle of
Bahla in Oman. Imagine the professional storey teller (rawi),
the scribe (katib) and the muleteer (katirji).

They were extensions of such Hollywood movies of the 20's
as "Beau Geste", 1926, the "Thief of Baghdad", 1924, "Son of
Sheik", 1926,"Morocco" 1930, played by stars like Fairbanks,
Cooper and   Valentino. Prior to all this, artist
travelers were returning from Arab lands with paintings, lithographs and albums of daguerrotypes illustrating busy bazaars,
mosques, monuments and forbidden

Born Again

by

Vincent Livelli

We are all born only once, or are some of us born twice? Jesus was born, died and was born again as the Christ we know today. In order to perform miracles one has to be a miracle personified and in order to become a living miracle such as Jesus, one must first die and be reborn.

When I lost my hearing and much of my ability to think and react normally, I was dead (DEAF) from the neck up, if not entirely so. My world was unlike others for a purpose that was to become clear to me with time. It took years to become evident to me that, like Jesus, I had a mission to perform before dying. Because this is all virgin territory I cannot set a date but I will give the cause- "natural causes" will be on my death certificate.

What miracles can I perform knowing the power I possess, having been born, died, and born again? Preachers are inspired and some claim success at healing. There are cases of miraculous healing powers after the person with such power disappears after the fact, after having appeared seemingly out of nowhere.

What I can see myself doing in this world of miracles is coming to the aid of not only a needy fellow human but of all humanity, as Jesus represents to succeed in such a challenge requires a universal phenomenon, This I call music- Afro Cuban in part, for once it reaches everyone worldwide, it will be the equivalent of Nirvana, the Buddhists requirement for

*"DEAD FROM THE NECK UP" MY FIRST GRADE TEACHER

universal harmony based on compassion and altruism- something that can be identified with precis, harmonic sound waves, the brain of all alpha and omega.

Why Afro-Cuban music? Because it is born from suffering- the plight of black slaves, millions of them. Their cries reached out as sound waves and "arias". Like preachers with miraculous cures that they achieve through the sound of their sermons, coupled with their personal powers that could include having been born twice.

Some preachers may not know of it and accept their gift as itself miraculous, whereas it is actually a result of having been chosen for the task. Chosen by and how is where the creator comes into the picture. Time and place are the basic necessities for astrological phenomena. Events are created by the alignment of planets controlled by gravity and are the creator of all that occurs everywhere.

These far out fanciful speculations can get your interest going in a new direction, but without the minimal substantiations these also named scholarly considerations end up empty. If we need miracles badly enough like communal praying in the recovery of a selected patient, the miracle we are also at the same time seeking is not only the recovery of the patient but perhaps more startling, the appearance of a miracle itself.

When born for a second time, the person occupies a changed reality that is unlike any of his/her fellow humans.

When you awake from sleep you are in a new reality, one that you had no problem doing without. But the "Big Sleep" separates you entirely from al that constitutes reality. This temporary absence allows whatever was, to emerge under different circumstances. This is where the miracle can become a reality prayer. It is what Einstein would call, a leap in the fabric of time. A "pause" allows the magician the time to perform his slight-of-hand. A miracle is a trick against physics and the physical world and the laws involved. The tricks that can be repeated are not miracles. To be born is miraculous, but the true miracle occurs only once. The second occurrence of one's life is the true miracle.

Sound and the Invisible World

By

Vincent Livelli

Your brain can turn on and off of what it wishes to deal with. Focus is reserved for what is interesting at any given moment- the rest is shut out so that attention can be placed where it does the most good.

But there are not only objects cast aside as interference, there are also spirits that become invisible by the brain's selective process of only focusing on its target at the moment. Like the shadows cast, the ignoring of spirits covers over the persistence of spirits. What we don't see is unlike what we don't hear. We hear in total darkness, whether we "listen' or not.

It is this penetration on the part of sound waves, as contrasted with light waves that gives us the power to penetrate the invisible spirit world that surrounds us.

Static is the accumulation of eons of sounds fumbled together. It may be well what constitutes the "black mass" – the unknown dark fabric of the universe.

Sound was the big bang of creation that scientists claim, "At the end of time sound will be the last to disappear." Sound creates sound over and over since no barriers existed to hold back sound since time began, whereas light fades and is extinguishable. This is also true of light, but light has a time limit, whereas sound does not. Its time limit depends on nothing, since it is part of time itself. Sound, like water, escapes through the smallest opening, whereas light can only be seen up to a certain point. Sound penetrates every opening that is its fabric. It is the measure of all things in that the universe is constant motion and constant sound. There is no silence in space, but there are invisible objects that we can hear but not see called, dark matter filled with the sound of static. This is what keeps our cosmos expanding forever since there will always be sound as long as there is matter and even anti matter as well.

We do not need to see sound waves in order to communicate. A high priest in Santaria is one who has been able to receive the instruction necessary for divine interpretation of evidence provided in the manner in which chance determines the message. It is the divine response to prayer or a request of some sort. Using objects to demonstrate answers is a random presentation of positive and negative, the Babalaou- will read and "divine" the answer for the adherent, based on what formation the objects used arrive at. Cowie shells or palm shells are the most common objects employed.

But the high priest will, in addition to what he sees as a result of the formation that is in front of him, also receive through thought, which can be similar to "audible" information, a prophesy, or a premonition from Nature's invisible aspect. Perhaps we are surrounded by a second invisible reality that is made available to us by summoning the power of the vibrations in drumming in order to communicate supernaturally. Luck is supernatural.

Chez Brigitte

Back- in 1994, Brigitte Catapano, the owner of Chez Brigitte, a "tiny French bistro" at 77 Greenwich Avenue, retired to Florida, leaving her assistant, Madame Rosa Santos, to carry on. Chez Brigitte survived for fifty years, from 1958 until June 5, 2008.

With no tables, back-to-back counters and elbow-to-elbow swivel stools, this closet-sized eatery seated eleven. You were eating "en famille" at prices that changed little over the years. Tasty French bread, oil and vinegar, a grated cheese dispenser at your seat, began a dinner for $9 that included boeuf Bourguignon in red wine sauce, roasted potatoes, carrots, sweep peas, or macaroni salad. The pois casses split pea soup with onions and croutons was a classic. In 1982, entrees began at $6.50. "Eating out" at Chez Brigitte was "eating at home."

Surrounded by giants like the nearby Waverly Inn, Morandi, San Ambroseus and Bruxelles, originally from Marseilles, Chez Brigitte was one tough cookie. In a rough racket, she was in a class of her own. The last owner, Mr. Jose M. Lito, form Asturias, took a loss after having remodeled the "tiny bistro," but it was the Villagers who were fed there over the years and the Village itself that share his loss as well.

Pabulum (food, in Latin) is the first taste of life at the breast. Bitter or sweet, raw life is refined with our reasoning and our seasoning. Perhaps the concept of a soul arose from the smell of cooking as it floated invisibly, seductively, attaching itself to us. The

MULTIPLE REALITIES

By Vincent Livelli
10/19/15

My mother said we are all God's children to which I add

"We are all children of Nature as well, but we live in

different realities." Your environment is your personal

reality. All creatures respond to their own particular

environment and necessities. Dogs, for example, live in

a different reality than we do. So do all God's creatures.

All reality has a boundary that prevents confusion

similar to our brain's ability to exclude needless

obstructive information. As humans we ARE PHYSICALLY

KEPT from entering what I call invisible Reality.

Just as a dog does not know our reality nor does it need

to. THIS DOES NOT PRECLUDE US FROM INVOLVEMENT IN IT SPIRITUALLY. HOWEVER,

There are cases of dogs and other animals sensitive to unseen apparitions, dangers or presences such as spirits that are inexplicable. Certain sensitive humans have also experienced super-natural reality or as I call it Invisible Reality." Perhaps we are living in a world that is within this second reality or that we are unconscious of similar creatures that are unaware of their other world environment. They have no need as animals to know it in order to pursue their normal lives.

It is in the Invisible Reality that our protectors (Saints, Orisas) exist. It may also be the habitat of our ancestors, our protectors. It may be that Heaven exists in this second more advanced reality OR IN A THIRD REALITY.

When America was awakening in the jazzy 'Twenties, travelogues were second only to school texts as the most widely read books by an entire generation of American students. Inexpensive tapestries with foreign scenes found a ready market by portraying a world awaiting discovery. These cloth murals became the magic flying carpets hanging on a working class living room wall. As *"l'art decoratif"*, they brought enchanting visions of other cultures to the masses, as did the contemporaneous magic lantern and the new box camera.

Like "Chinatown", the Islamic world especially exemplified the exotic for Americans in the 'Twenties. Artist vagabonds and merry wanderers were returning home with their paintings, lithographs and albums of daguerreotypes illustrating bazaars and casbahs from the Land of the Bible.

That harsh judge and uncomfortable traveller, Mark Twain, in his **"Visits to the Holy Land"** found the Middle East "more and more pleasant". Karl Baedeckers' **"Guide to Egypt and the Sudan"** was essential reading, as was Lowell Thomas' account of Lawrence's Arabian campaign. King Tut's treasures and Barnum's **"Little Egypt"** hypnotized the masses.

-4-

"The Sheik", 1921, Thief of Baghdad", 1924; "Son of Sheik",
1926; "Beau Geste", 1926, were performed by those heros of
Araby named Valentino and Fairbanks. Seraglio-inspired
"peep-shows", stereographs and stereopticons were hawked
along 14th Street, where a coin lowered the veil and
allowed an illicit glimpse into the titillating world of
Odalisques, Arabesques, and Burlesques.

Like the anecdotal oils of the earlier Orientalists,
"Arabic" motif tapestries teased a natural hunger for
travel. Set in Flaubert's "inaccessible horizon" of the
placid Sahara, they, like the Sphinx, had something to say
even though they lacked the movement and vitality of a
Delacroix, who had cried out *What can Egypt be like?"*.
Jean-Leon Gerome condemned this *"decor panoramique"* that
perpetuated a fictional artistic "orient", for he had set
out to document "the real orient".

As an art form these modern works with Arabic themes
lacked the highest expression of the Muslim art that they
imitated, namely, arab script calligraphy, which was read
from right to left, like a triptych. "Lettering" might
appear along borders in mock designs (Figure 1, lower right
corner), where a Western gentleman with a Prince of Wales
walking stick discusses a purchase, perhaps for the
"Turkish Corner" of his fashionable Victorian residence.
The minarets of the Haran, Turkey mosque seem to have
inspired those that are depicted in Figure 2.

-5-

KEEP EM' COMING

Just as no one, neither the city or the business community, knew beans about how to handle what was to become a 30 billion $ windfall, I didn't understand what was happening back in 1970. Fifty million visitors today 2010 began with on minibus and a tiny travel agency in the Westminster Hotel, called Apple Tours. It was staffed by an elderly woman and a bus driver, their conscious efforts were centered on airport transportation more than on tourism. Demand for sightseeing followed and was almost accidental and certainly not as yet organized. There were no guides – especially foreign speaking guides, no concierges, no city officials interested in the subject. Hotels, restaurants, theaters that today cater to visitors did not exist. For that matter there were really few tourists to be seen anywhere.

When we learned that what tourists around at that time raved about how inexpensive dining was in N.Y. compared to Europe, we began to see their interest. Word got back to Europe also how cheap our hotels were and how for very little they could enjoy a 4 hour minibus tour visiting an uncongested city that lacked the cathedral visits popular in Europe but that offered the sights of Little Italy, Chinatown, the Statue of Liberty, the Empire State Building, Fifth Avenue's mansions and such as it was, Times Square with only modest illumination from movie marquees. Two restaurants that added bright

The curved sword (*jambiyya*) and the slender rifles
(Figure 3) were never shown as menacing, rather as
possessions of pride and status and were often incorporated
in dances. The all-purpose camels were invariably shown
much smaller than normal in stature to accommodate the
confines of the canvas. The Arabian steed, with its
handsome head, and the utilitarian donkey were sometimes
joined by a stray saluki (Figure 4).

In Figure 5, we are presented with a traveler
(*mousaffir*) with his companion (*rafiq*) being directed "*ala
al-shemal*", to the nearest hostel (*khan*). In them we see
the bulbous tombs of the pious, the story-teller (*rawi*),
the scribe (*katib*), the muleteer (*katirji*), and the rug
merchants of the Suq-al-Talh (Fig. 6).

Men are shown pondering chess boards rather than
backgammon, it being the more familiar game to the
Westerner (Figure 7). Women are proper and modest even
when shown dancing with their taborets since these scenes
were to be hung in family settings (Figure 8).

As intellectual statements, these imaginary
"*turqueries*" were never voluptuous, never depicting the
houris and harems that so tantalized Jean Auguste Ingres.
Nor did they shock, as did the interior decoration of the
Pompeian villas. Nor were they revealing, as in the tomb
paintings of Egypt. They were not theologically
allegorical, like the Metropolitan Museum Unicorn series,
nor ultra exotic, like the **"Tenture des Indes"** that hang in
the Palace of the Grand Masters in Malta, nor *avant-garde*,
as is Joan Miro's work in the World Trade Center's
mezzanine.

Today, Belgium stands at the head of the "Realist
Imperative" movement in art. Perhaps it was the Belgians'
need for cultural identity affirmation that produced this
fantasy tapestry of "non-places" --- European idealizations
imposed on Arabic landscapes for American homes.

Rene Magritte might have derided these wall hangings
as " apparatus of Bourgeois reality". They may not be
d'Aubusson or de Felletin, but with their "pervading gloom
of antiquity" these works preserve a mythical dreamworld,
like a slowly dissolving Saharan sunset.

Japanese Geisha have already converted their facial coloration to a white canvas that draws attention to the small lips. We blow up the size of our mouths with full lips. But bigger in this case is not better, since, rather than a very young-looking childlike face, large mouths and lips are found on older females.

We are not talking about saddling women in America with the pasty white canvas of the geisha. On the contrary, a bright soft yellowish touch with bright royal-blue lipstick, for example, covering the entire face makes an extraordinary statement. Eyebrows adding color as well can present us with a painting that lives and breathes.

"Make something new."

Ezra Pound

It is only a question of time before the cosmetics industry comes up with a product that makes women ever more attractive. The skin is a very tempting canvas for catching a man's eye. Forty shades of lipstick, fifty shades of nail polish, eye shadow, hair coloring, lenses, leave only the skin to go beyond everyday makeup. Pancake and powder have served well for hundreds of years, but a new day is coming to give women a new face, and not by Botox, surgery, or sun lamps.

FALL FASHION WEEK 2004

(Arabic Chic)

Vicky Tiel and **John Anthony**
will go as haute as $45,000 per.
One-of-a-kind jobs because, for that
money, you don't want to see anyone else

    Living in the "Fashion Capital of the World", New York
men are more knowledgable about fashion, and about women.
When I read that Viky Tiel had an outfit for sale for $45,000,
I wasn't surprized. I had met her in 1974, living in a stable
that served as her work shop, show- room and sales office. You
entered her cobblestoned court yard through doors hugh enough to
admit two horses and a wagon. Distant from the chic Faubourg
St. Honoré, in the 6th Arrondisement, her creations were pre-
Christian LaCroix. "W"would call them brazenly avant-gard, more
flashy, trashy and rash than anything on display on the Left Bank.
Today, on fashionable L'Île St. Louis where she lives, she can.
be called a mover and shaker in the industry.

    Back in the fifties, I escorted Mrs. Peck of Peck & Peck,
an upper class women's store in New York. She had wanted to
see the red·light district in Piraeus. It was a pleasant warm
afternoon, and like Rue St. Denis in Paris, the ladies of the
night were nevertheless, open for business, beckoning us in their
naughty nighties. Walking along with the impeccably attired Mrs. ..
Peck, who was,as one can imagine,a very old school business woman
while passing rows of floosies like bewitching gypsies, my minds'
eye pictured Mrs. Peck devilshly dressed in the clothes of the
vixens. Blame the environment, but I had begun to find Mrs.Peck
quite sexy by nature. Just imagine the seductive elegance she
would display if dressed in the revealing gowns (or should we say
night gowns)of the ladies surrownding us.I could see her in the
teasing couture. She'd gain added irresistability and be not
impossibly out of place if done in good taste with a wild price
tag.

THE ASTROLOGICAL LOTTERY

By

Vincent Livelli

When asked what I would do if I ever won the lottery, I would answer, "Buy a yacht, and sail it around the world." But there's no need to win the lottery to go sailing around the world, year after year. All that is needed is to be born with your ascendant in a water sign, such as Scorpio favorably aspected by Jupiter your 9th house, the house of long journeys and higher education. Even thought my birth sign was Aries, a cardinal fire sign, for over fifty plus years I would cruise the oceans of the world, picking up knowledge along the way. It didn't matter that I knew nothing of navigation, had no family history of sailors, and was a poor swimmer. Aside from a row boat in Central Park, the Staten Island Ferry, a short crossing from Cuba to Key West that made me seasick, and two U.S. Army transports in WW II, I never saw myself living and working on a ship. It was called "a life of sacrifice" by many and a dangerous occupation for centuries.

After 66 ships and 60 countries, I began to examine my horoscope to confirm the relevance of its odd message.

One day while looking for work around the Wall Street area, a travel poster lured me into a steamship office and out of the bitter winter winds that blew off New York Bay. Perhaps I could land a 7 day Caribbean cruise as a dance teacher. Instead, I was offered a job as an assistant cruise director – a position I knew nothing about, and one that in 1948 very few people knew anything about. I spoke some Spanish and Portuguese.

"How well do you remember names?" I was asked.

I had prepared for my interview by memorizing the names on the name plates on the office desks.

I was told I would be on a ship for a 38 day cruise to South America. I began to wonder about what I was getting into. Could I be ready and leave on time? What about a wardrobe? Was I qualified? What about mal-de-mer?

As thing turned out, I found a home on the ship, even though I still had trouble with port and starboard while walking aft. As for higher education, I wondered how it was possible that I had already attended 2 colleges and 4 universities, and that they all offered me free tuition? Was it because the army had sent me to study Geopolitics at the University of Wisconsin, or that my parents made sure I got a B.A. from Brooklyn College? Was it thanks to a benefactress who paid my tuition the University of Miami, or because of a Pan-American World Airways grant I received to the Institute of International Education, sending me to of Rio de Janeiro on a tuition free fellowship? Perhaps it was the exchange program between the University of Miami and the University of Havana or, or the Army snafu that found me sitting for weeks in an almost empty classroom while patiently awaiting assignment at City College on Amsterdam Avenue?

While all this emphasis on learning could be considered of great value, it was only after I left the muffled atmosphere of the classroom box that I felt myself becoming educated by sailing around the world.

Eighty per cent of our knowledge comes from our vision. I looked up at the sky in bored resignation day after day. Then, I closed my books and opened my eyes on the world outside the classroom window that framed my day dreams. Soon I was deciphering Latin and Greek inscription on ruins, handling the intricacies of foreign currency and customs, fraternizing with the world, while sharing the "Brotherhood of the Sea."

It wasn't until I "graduated" from South America, Europe, Asia, and the rest, that I realized good fortune dawned on me, having left behind on land the frustrated tutors my puzzled parents had engaged to help me progress. I gave thanks to the astrological lottery I must have won.

By day, rainbows festooned my horizons. By night, star-bedecked skies charted my course as planets paroled the path they had set before me.

CLAVES AND THE COSMOS

(The Music of the Spheres)

Like the old Morse Code, sound waves send messages out into
space. In this fanciful premise, we claim that the claves, with
their asymetrical rhythym, have a disruptive influence. on
the atomic celestial clock. The classic tick tock, one two, one
two beat is disturbed by the clave   one, one two, one two beat.

There are no events without the involvement of energy. Some
planets release energy, such as the sun, while others both emit an
receive energy, such as the earth. The sound waves of the claves
disrupt the symetrical   flow of orderly emission of energy.
The repetitious clack of the claves would hypnotize a listener if
it were not for the pause that is its distinguishing feature. With
this pause, the claves control the entire orchestra. If we were
to modify our clocks to mimic the claves, replacing the regimen-
ted sound of seconds to the clave beat, we would syncopate the
music of the spheres.

We humans are not sufficiently inspired by such possibilities.
The magician employs a pause to achieve his trickiness. In that
significant inst ant, he accomplishes his purpose. Nature may
"hate a vacuum" but the vacuum (read pause) exists for good reason. The claves involve man in the way the cosmos works. They
may command the respect and control of the celestial orchestra,
like a Toscanini. What is repetitive in clave rhythym can be
called "cyclical" when applied to the cosmos. If life is both the
teacher and the test, claves can be said to "cheat" by not fitting
the mold. Our learning never seems to fit into our lives properly. The workings of cycles influence education itself and can,
with their forshadows, show us the unseen, the unknown, and in
that way, achieve the goal of "education." We mortals invite the
sickness of misfortune by waving our fists in the face of the Gods
with our prideful approach to learning. The answer is in the claves,
two simple wooden sticks.

lighting were Toffinettis and Jack Dempsey's Clam Bar. The Bond sign and the Camel Cigarette sign were eye catching along with Coca Cola but little else would warrant a visit to N.Y. as is now the case regarding "brite lites."

What made the tourist industry, a phenomenon that rescued a bankrupt metropolis, was not, I Love N.Y., but the breakdown of the language barriers.

Four of us founded the IATM, the International Assoc. of Tour Managers and Interpreters in '72. This small group between them 6 major languages and that opened the way for what we see today – a million people with many foreign languages waiting for 2012.

This is some of the history of NY's tourist phenomena that I was involved in getting started back in the early 70's. Like the Cruise / gambling industry and other such events, my con-tribution is only now beeing recognized, happy to say. It's the best way to tie a ribbon on a long career on ships, stage and Greenwich Village formation. Makes me a sort of a "historical figure" having played a part in it all. God bless USA

PAIN VS. PAIN

Stimulating the Immune System

When exposed to pain, the body produces endorphins that
protect and nourish the immune system. Like an innoculation,
a painful stimulation would serve to produce endorphins. This
pain would be of a sufficiently low intensity as to be unnoticeable by the individual but evident to the body itself.

Unlike acupuncture that "unblocks" key points in the
framework of the body requiring repeated stimulation, an
implanted "painful"sensation could be made to <u>continuously</u>
manufacture the necessary supply of endorphin. In accupuncture,
the needle provides the pain that soon disappears after the
initial prick. Furthermore, it is well known that surpressing
pain for the short term merely covers over the cause. For example,surpressing the production of acid in cases of stomach
ulcers goes contrary to the body's effort to produce the acid
that fights the cause of the ulcers.

Like exercize, to be effective,the individual must follow
a regular and frequent program. This routine can be monitored,
increased or decreased. The body must be conditioned to "respect"
the pain, to recognize it as beneficial. A tree can be made to
grow in a modified "man-made" shape, coaxed along tenderly, often
for its own betterment. Man is always upgrading the beauty of his
garden. When infants cry out in pain they strengthen their lungs
and become more aware of themselves. They receive "outside"help.
As they grow, they become aware that this help exists. The comfort
that endorphins supply can be accessed through stimulation, through
"friendly" pain.

Do women outlive men because of tight shoes?

IN SUPPORTR OF SILENMCE

IN SUPPORTROF SILENCE

(IN SUPPORT OF SILENCE)

SILENCE IA NRURE MEDIATATING
INSIATINXTIVELNESS IS THE PATHWAY INDTO AN UNKNOWN WORLD BOGTH FOR

A SWELL SAS DFOR THOSE WHO HEARLIUFE IA PRODGRAMMED TO BE ELUSIVE D
UNSTABLE FRAGILE AS THE MACHINERY OF TYHE DEASRD MARVELOUS LIKE
ISELF. SIGHT IS DIREDCT IRIS RETINA NERVE BFUT HEARING IS BITS AN
PIECES OF D IDT COMES AS AN FETER THOUYGHT TO SIGHT THROWN TOEGETHER
SOPME SPECIEIS MANAGE WILL WITHOUT AURAL OPACITY PERFORMING ESSEN-
TIAL TASKS FOR EXISATENCEEACH SENSE OF THE FIVE EACH ONE CAN BE USEDAS
WISDOM WHICH IS A COMBIONATION OF ALL SENSES COMNBINED

WE MUST RID DTHE WORLD OF EMOTION. DEAF, DUMB AND BILIND DREMPOV

TDHE DEAF. AND BLIND AND LEAVE DDSTHE FUTURE NO DUMFB BUT BRTILLIANT
FOR AS MANKIN THJAT IS IDEAL. ALLOW ONLY BEILLIANCE BASEDONA
LEASS COMPLICATED DDMUILTDIP LICITSY LIKE A HAIFBKU, DEPNDDENT N
HMAN NATURE WHICH IS SDTILL PROMITIVED, BYUT ON BRILLIANCE WHICH
ALREADY EXISTSS IN SMALL QUANTITITESD WE NEED LESS DEPLENDENCY ON
EMOTDION, WHICH IS A HUNG OCVER FROM OUR PRIMAL HUNTING ANFD GUYI
FISHING SKILL THAT INVOLVED TRTICKERY AND STEALTH AND CUNNIN G TO
POROVIDE SURVIVAL, AND WICH IS REFLECTSED IN OUR DAILY LIVES AS
A DMECHANIZXM TO COPE WITH OUR DAILY WOLRLD LAODED WITRH EMODTION

SOUND CAN BSREASK DGLASS AND IS INVISLIBLER

SILENCE RAEDUCES EMOTIONALD INTDERCOURDSE DTHE AUCTIONEER IS RAFF
SPIEL AND TCHE GDODS ASRE LISSDENDINGF IN SILENCE?SOUND IISTRANQ
AS IN A PJAUSE AT THE PROPER MOPMENT IN TIMEDNOISE CAan be wastse
my familey motto was speak few words lest you hve much tdo answe
a silence ssdtreeam like atricle of meaning dfemands more adttent
on and receives more. two soullnds cand cnflict or harmonizedtho
blanketed fy noise cn a continuethat is stronger and deeper fwith
dsover come.silence is sedation of the sueperficiaflolous
dcontmemp latoioon andf meditatioon are sisters dd. librariy are
abodes of silence filled to dthe ceiling with knowledge of the ag
ages as repectfor the hallowed past of humaity .
SILENE MAGNIFIES MALKES MOMENTS IMPORTASTNSDSOUNDS REQUIRE A PARA.
ESTABLIESH MEANING BUT SOUNDS EMBODOY LESS HONESTY DTHAN SILENCE
HENSRY LIMLLER MUIS IS THE BEST WAY DTO EXP;RESS TSHE INESPRESSI
  SILENCE IS ASWEAPONOF GREAT POWER INTHE WOMB THE FETUS LEARNS FR
ITS ENVIRONMENT, FTROM INTRUSION FROM RHTHYMN DISTURBANCES IOF TH
BEATING PULSEATION REGULARITY ESSENTIAL SILENCE IS OMNIPRESENT U

BROKEN. IT IS THESTATIC MORE OR LESS OFTHEUNIVERRSE UNTILORGANIZE
SOUNDSGIVE WARNINGS BUT SILENCE HAS THE POWERE OF SURPRIZE THE E
USSE OF SOPUND TO COMMICAYE

"Shall we meet at Le Procope, "Le Rendez-Vous des Arts et des Lettres"? Or perhaps at McSorley's Old Ale House, "Established 1854", 15 E. 7th Street or over at the counter of RICKERS, "no better food anyplace", Oven Fresh Apple Pie 15 ¢, with French Ice Cream 25 ¢. Didn't we meet at the CONCORD, "World's Foremost Year-round Resort"; or was it as GALLAGHER's STEAK HOUSE, "Broiled over Hickory Logs"? See you at SYLVIA'a , "QUEEN of SOUL FOOD", 328 Lenox Avenue or at the WHITE CASTLE, "Buy 'em by the "sack". Save me a seat at RITA DIMITRI's, La Chansonette, rue de l'ancienne comedie, or at CALVADOS, "dejeuners d'affairs", HARRY'S BAR, "dal 1931", MOANA, "Sporting d'Ete" in Monte Carlo or ROXY, Cannes. How about ALCAZAR, rue Mazarine, "Diners menu 75 francs, or at SANS SOUCI, Miami Beach, "Florida's Reigning Queen". Perhaps at CARNEGIE, "Delicatessen & Restaurant" or 8th STREET, "Delicatessen & Dining Room". BIANCHI & MARGHERITA's on West 4th Street, "Opera a la Carte"will do nicely.

Match books from these famous addresses represent good times "a la table". They will disappear eventually as many of the spots have changed over the years. What will we find to replace them or the "gaite et joyeux souvenirs" they hold so dear for us?

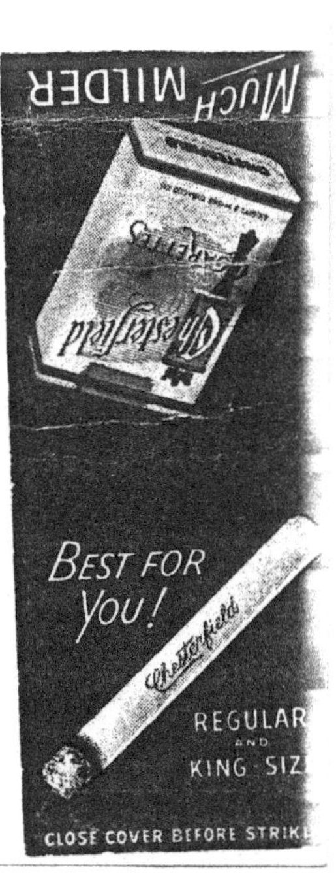

PLEASE WAIT TO BE EATEN

(theme restaurants)

PEOPLE NEEDED SOME CHEERING UP AT THE END OF THE GREAT DEPRESSION.
TODAY, WITH THE BATH HOUSES GONE,THERE IS A NEED FOR SOME RIBALD
GAIETÉ. THEME RESTAURANTS, LIKE THE ELVIS PRESLEY MACDONALD}S
IN CHICAGO IN THE '60's BUT WITH MORE SEXUAL OOMPH AND SPICE
ON THE MENU IS NEEDED. DURING THE FORTIES, RESTAURANTS AND CLUBS
FROM JACK DEMPSEY's ON BROADWAY TO MIAMI BEACH'S CARROUSEL CLUB,
ONE COULD WATCH VERY RISQUÉ COMIC CARTOONS DISPLAYED ON AN OVER-
HEAD TRACK THAT RAN THE LENGTH OF THE BAR SIMILAR TO A MINIATURE
RAILROAD TRAIN. QUITE SHOCKING TO THE LADIES AT THE BAR, THESE
DISPLAYS WERE POPULAR AS THE TV SPORT EVENTS ARE TODAY.

CARRYING THIS GIMMICK FURTHER, WE CAN SEE THEME RESTAURANTS WITH
A "THEME FOR EVERY TASTE". FOR EXAMPLE, FOOT FETISHISTS WOULD
BE REQUESTED TO REMOVE SHOES AND SOCKS BEFORE ENTERING. FOR THE
S/M DINER, SIGNS WOULD READ; "PLEASE WAIT FOR YOUR HOSTESS TO
BEAT YOU". ANIMAL FANCIERS, A SELECT CLIENTLE,CAN DINE IN THE
VIP CUB ROOM AND IN RESTAURANTS WITH NAMES LIKE "LE VOYEUR",
DOORLESS REST ROOM STALLS FOR EXHIBITIONISTS. AT "THE CIRCUS",
DAISY CHAIN GUESTS WOULD HAVE TO LINE UP TO BE SERVED. THOSE
DINERS INTO ARM PIT SEX COULD FIND DÉCOR OF FAMOUS ARM PITS
ALONG THE WALLS. MOVIE DINERS COULD BE PROVIDED WITH PRIVATE
VIEWING BOOTHS. CUSHIONS FOR THE CHIC HOLLYWOOD UNDER-THE-TABLE
CELEBRITIES COULD ADD COMFORT AND IN THE "NYMPH ROOM",THE AFTER
WORK CROWD COULD RELAX.NASAL SEX GUESTS COULD BE SEATED WITH ANAL-
ISTAS FOR A BETTER ECLECTIC MIX. IN-HOUSE CHAPLAINS COULD BE ON
HAND TO PERFORM THREESOME MARRIAGES. UNRULY BONDAGE CUSTOMERS
WOULD BE KINDLY REQUESTED TO CHECK CHAINS AT THE ENTRANCE. FOOD
SMEARING GOES BACK TO ROMAN TIMES, BUT UNLEASHED DOGS, CRYING
"BOW,WOW", WOULD NEED HIS OR HER DOMINATRIX TO ENTER.THE DESERT
MENU LISTS THE PASTRY CHEF's SUGGESTED CHOCLATE GEN-ITALIA TRAY.
BOOK EARLY IS RECOMMENDED FOR SEATING IN THE WINE CELLER DUNGEON,
WHERE THE NOTICE READS, "THERE ARE NO STRANGERS HERE, JUST
GIRLS YOU HAVEN'T MET YET".

BACK IN THE '70's, THE MEMBERS ONLY "CHICK CLUB" IN AMSTERDAM
FEATURED LIVE THREE X THEATERICS, NOT FOR THE AFTER OR BEFORE
THEATER- GOERS, BUT DURING.AMATEUR NIGHT EVERY WEDS., TRANS
BEAUTY CONTESTS EVERY SAT.,FISTING EVERY FRIDAY ANDIN-LAW FAMILY
ORGIES ON SUNDAYS(to put batchlor parties to shame) WOULD HELP
BUSINESS AT PLACES WHERE "THE ELITE MEET TO EAT".

VORRAREPHILIA
FANTASIES ABOUT
EATING

REVERSE IMPLANTATION FROM MAN TO ANIMAL

By

Vincent Livelli

The orangutan is the closest animal to man. Can it be brought up to the intellectual level of man? Many attempts have failed, but let us consider some new approaches.

An infant's brain develops thanks in great part to hearing conversations and precedes in that way to learning to speak, respond and think, always advancing as its exposure increases to maturity, finally.

We use animals and plants to improve mankind and our world. Pigs are able to repair our aortas by transplant, thus saving lives, for example. The orangutan lacks the ability to communicate intelligently with us due to its inability to reproduce sentences since it lacks a sound larynx box that enables all we humans to talk. Talk stimulates the brain and produces intelligence in that manner.

If we can install by transplant a human voice larynx box into an orangutan it may, like an infant, eventually understand sounds, meanings, ' languages, and speech proper. This would raise it more to our level where it can participate in the betterment of mankind, instead of remaining just a "distant cousin".

<u>The Honeymoon</u>

Living together while not married is a way of getting to know how compatible couples are.

Better still is to travel together when more of life's surprises are involved.

Queen Victoria took Prince Albert to India for a honeymoon. That marriage worked out very

well, but many modern-day trips can "trip up." For example, a travel agent will for profit send newly-

weds to St. Lucia — a long, exhausting flight. In June the West Indies is stiflingly hot and not worth the

expenses involved, compared to a honeymoon in Europe — the same distance away, and cooler.

Where do the Japanese go for their honeymoon? They go to Atami, called the Niagara Falls of

Japan. The British go to the Isle of Wight or to Brighton. Filipinos go to Baquio, above Manila —

Italians to Capri, but do Americans still take the Honeymoon Express from Grand Central Terminal?

Many now prefer cruise voyages, and can even be married by the captain or take the families along with

them if they can escape to be alone. This type of escape is even more romantic, since a challenge is

involved, leaving the family members outside the stateroom with a "Do Not Disturb" notice on the door

. . . for the entire trip, if desired.

The trouble with the perfect honeymoon is the fantasy world it creates, making the marriage a

commonplace letdown. It is supposed to provide a lifetime together with a wonderful memory forever.

The same with the second honeymoon, and even a third. But does it succeed?

When a second honeymoon is intended to save a shaky marriage, it is time to think now of

separate vacations. They have a better proven track record, especially since you may well miss each

other, based on the old "absence makes the heart grow fonder." If that fails, try your luck and marry

your old sweetheart, if possible, or start from scratch. But find someone with a sense of humor, and

money. Zsa Zsa Gabor married eight times, so don't be afraid of marriage. Just try to pick a good

honeymoon and a good traveler, rich or poor.

WRITINGS

"Vincent" by Lewis Lazar

An Informal Interview with Vincent Livelli
By Lewis Lazar

I never asked if I could interview Vincent. Technically, I never interviewed him.

"Come over to my apartment," he said. "Do you have a minute?"
"Of course."
"I like your style. Anyone who carries a bamboo pen and a pot of ink is a character worth knowing."

Vincent speaks in a tar-thick Brooklyn accent. Not the Brooklyn accent of rising sentence endings, as if in question of the very credibility of the sentence itself. More like, the Brooklyn accent of dockyards and shipyards, of street kids, of Greenwich VIllage in the 30's and 40's, of Harlem in the 20's; of sophisticated talk in down-and-out, dimly lit, bars. He growls like gravel that has been run over by a bicycle made of unwashed brass instruments.

At 94 years old he has the confidence of someone who had the luck to fall in to an American Dream, cushioned with pipes made of lead, street thugs in threads and school teachers who carried metal rulers to beat into submission children who would have been better off day dreaming. Now ripe with experience, he's optimistic. I'd even say he believes in the American Dream.

When Vincent welcomes you into his apartment it is a high honour, after three flights of stairs, in a building that has seen little change in 40 years. He pushes open a grey gloss paint door to reveal a world that transcends time and national boundaries. The carpets are dusty, but they are carpets bought in Algeria. The tapestries look faded, but they are genuine Moroccan tapestries, the lights are dim, but that is because they are in cases of bronze and brass Arabian steal with patterns of the cosmic cycles. There are no doors, only silk sheets and curtains. He has a television but it is lacquered in mother of pearl. Mind you, this is a modest one bedroom with a kitchen, a small sitting room and a bathroom. You forget this easily, New York City sleeps in a grey background of wind, rain and snow…and you forget entirely what country you thought you were in.

It smacks me as incredible that Vincent still holds a grudge against Harry Belafonte, who stole his girlfriend in 1948….a woman who was married to a banker on Long Island, whom he introduced to the downtown Village scene in the 40's…A WOMAN…at that. A cross between "Marilyn Monroe and Mother Theresa" he sighs. It is equally incredible that he danced, twirled and did the grinder with the mistress of Bugsy Mallone, the notorious gangster, without realising what he was getting himself in to.

It seems often the case with Vincent…that he doesn't know what he's getting himself into.

"After all these years, I ask myself why haven't I forgotten anything?"…"Why is that?" he repeats.

"Why?" I ask

"Grass…what else could it be?"

An Interview with Vincent Livelli: Part I
Interviewed by Lewis Lazar

I often find myself reaching for my phone, covertly trying to press record, while Vincent recounts one of his yarns about how Ernest Hemingway paraded his weight around Havana Harbour in the 40's or how he watched Orson Welles record War of the Worlds *in the studio where he was a gaffer, before it was broadcast to the public, prompting mass hysteria.*

Vincent always seems inextricably bound to the fantastical. His life has been one surrounded by many the great Latin musicians and dancers of the 20ᵗʰ century, nobility in transit, mafia men and their mistresses, political heavy weights in war time and icons of many a cultural renaissance from Charlie Parker and Celia Cruz to Anaïs Nin. He spent 40 years on ships sailing as a cruise director and rumbero (Afro-Cuban dancer). He was a best friend and confidante of Greenwich Village artists and intellectuals such as Anatole Broyard, William Gaddis and W.H. Auden and has a rich sense of the journey America, and the world in its wake, took as it spun through the 20th century.

Here is an interview with Vincent Livelli, 95 years old, authorised on record in 2015.

INTERVIEWER

Can you tell me about your relationship with Anaïs Nin?

VINCENT LIVELLI

I'd be happy to because that brings back beautiful memories.

She was an unusual person in many ways: European, Catalonian, Cuban, middle-aged…sexy in a very distinguished, respectable manner. She had an etiquette in her sexuality where she received you, very properly, and made you feel comfortable as a young guy meeting an older, experienced woman. So she made me feel at home in her arms, which is what I needed.

In 1947 there was a lot of strict protestantism in the atmosphere with taboos. Sexual freedom was on the horizon and they were afraid we would become liberated sexually in America, which we have become. She helped start it.

INTERVIEWER

How did you meet her?

LIVELLI

She had just arrived in the Village and was meeting new people. One of whom was Sherry Martinelli, Anatole Broyard's great love. (Anatole Broyard wrote *Kafka was the Rage*.)

Sherry introduced me to Anaïs at a book store on Greenwich Avenue called 'Four Seasons'. We were to celebrate her recently published book *Ladders to Fire*. She invited me to a party she was giving in honour of the publication…so that's what happened. You're not recording this, are you?

INTERVIEWER

Maybe! Who knows?

LIVELLI

Oh…well it's up to you. Well, she impressed me immediately because she was Spanish/Cuban and I was into learning Spanish and more about Spanish women, etc. She was the epitome of a Spanish liberated woman. She was probably not very well-received in her home land, better in the Village where the atmosphere was not rigid, conservative.

INTERVIEWER

Did you dance with her?

LIVELLI

I did dance with her in many ways…horizontally and vertically.

INTERVIEWER

Really?

LIVELLI

Yes …We had a nice afternoon tryst. It was all set up beforehand, in a way, which takes the spontaneity and romance out of it.

I had gone to the publication party. There were about twenty people there. I stood out because I brought some rumba records and she was crazy to dance, as were many young girls trying to learn this new dance. I brought these records, we played them. And no one else knew how to dance the rumba so I had the evening to myself with her. Everybody left and she asked me to stay, but I had to leave. I wasn't prepared to stay overnight with her. At that point it was just sexy dancing.

So she said, "Come meet me tomorrow afternoon if you're free." This time I didn't bring any rumba records, I brought myself. We got into it because she was meeting me with a diaphanous gown that spoke eloquently about her figure under all that clothing, like sleepwear…long. I'd never seen a woman dressed that way. So that excited me. You know? *What's under there?*

She stretched out on the couch in a seductive way and relaxed and I relaxed. We just looked and talked to each other a little bit, then we got closer. It happened in a beautiful afternoon. Very nice Village episode for a young guy with an older experienced woman. I think my whole sexual history revolved around older women.

Here was an experienced woman who had probably slept with nobility and was in-demand in New York because of her talent and literature and I had her all to myself. But guess what?… I didn't know what to do! I was just a young innocent…I just let her take the momentum, and she did. It made me feel older, wiser and experienced. It was a brief encounter, I never saw her after that.

Later I found out she slept with everyone I knew, including Gore Vidal and Tennessee Williams.

§

Vincent has an accent that you scarcely hear in New York any more. It is the street talk of a Brooklyn born boy who grew up during the Great Depression in Greenwich Village, in an Italian family surrounded by Jewish immigrants, who had no resources to pay for professional entertainment and so relied on the art of story telling with comrades to pass the time. It belies a great eagerness and optimism, as well as a wistful, devilish sense of humour. The only other voice I can think of that comes close to it is that of Henry Miller, the eloquent defender of free thought and speech.

INTERVIEWER

What do you think of Henry Miller?

Well, Henry Miller and I have something in common. He took a shine to an African-American homosexual painter named Beaufort Delaney. Very big name in the art world. Henry Miller was supporting him because Beaufort had no source of income except charity. I took an interest in Beaufort because we both collected drums. When I visited his apartment on Greene Street he had a nice collection of African drums. When I went around the world I brought back drums from India and Indonesia…so when I went on the ships for good I gave him my drum collection and that took care of Beaufort very nicely. Henry Miller and a gentlemen named Ascoli, from a philanthropic family, was supporting Beaufort and so was Anatole. We were all helping the guy out. He was a precious individual, we wanted to see him stay alive.

He had a philosophy about living. When I asked him, "How do you manage?" He used to sit on a particular bench in Washington Square Park, waiting for his lover. Well this one time I joined him before the lover arrived. I asked him about his attitude towards life. He was one of the most successful people, managing without any source of income. He was just existing. How did he do it? He had the right attitude towards life. He made people feel wonderful in his presence. If you were sitting with the Dalai Lama you would get the same feeling. In fact he wore a similar head covering like a religious person would which made it all the more appropriate. But he wasn't religious in the sense of trying to indoctrinate you. His whole being exuded confidence in life. That life would be kind to him. He had this feeling of optimism that I wanted to understand and incorporate in my attitude towards life. He didn't worry about a thing. I said to him one day, "Beaufort, don't you ever worry about the future and what's going to happen to you? No one's buying your paintings!" He said, very simply, "I only worry when I don't feel well." So that's a simple answer that doesn't cover your existence, how you live, and he seemed to be very healthy. He was like a cherub. He had a little round face, he sort of sat very calmly like how a religious person doesn't move around very much. They're sort of in contemplation and relaxed about everything. That's what he had to teach me. He taught me how to not worry, to be confident in myself, to play drums. Here's a fella who just likes to play, without any association to an orchestra, just to sit and drum.

He was living in a cold apartment. No steam heat, a stove with wood coal and no hot water. The windows were broken. He seemed not to worry about that. The cold weather didn't bother him. He was dressed very smart, he wore a lot of heavy clothing that made him look like a monk. He made a great success of his life when James Baldwin took interest him and they became lovers.

INTERVIEWER

Could you tell me about the first time you met Charlie Parker?

LIVELLI

Sure. It was not a clear meeting. He was just one of several people at the San Remo on Bleeker and Macdougal. The jazz musicians playing in the village started to become aware of the San Remo, where the art colony established itself in 1946, '47 and '48. Charlie Parker meant nothing to me because I knew absolutely zero about jazz except that it came from New Orleans and I'm in New York. I'm not too interested in what's happening outside of New York. It's sort of like nowhere. New Yorkers were very sophisticated about protecting New Yorkers being special. When I met him, I said to myself I'm going to learn something from this fellow because I want to teach him something about Afro-Cuban music, and I'll learn something about jazz. When he was leaving I asked if I could join him. We went up from the San Remo all the way to Broadway where he was staying at a hotel. The building is still there but I think it's bought by New York University. We went up to his room, he took out some grass and he offered me some. I hesitated at first, saying I wasn't ready for marijuana…little did I know. So he said, "This is good." So I took a little…the word escapes me.

INTERVIEWER

Toke!

LIVELLI

Toke! Yes…I love that word. Well I didn't feel anything, though I may have been talking to him differently without realising it. I said to Charlie, "First of all, I'm sorry, I don't know anything about jazz because I've avoided the topic, purposefully. I've left my interest in some bay end in the future and the future never seemed to arrive." Well, here I am in the presence of Charlie Parker! Now if I'm not mistaken, he was a short little fellow. I didn't respect him very much because I knew very little about him. If I would have talked to musicians they would have said, *Charlie Parker! The Bird!*…I would have said, *Who? What bird?* I was ignorant. He came across as a very intelligent guy. I believe he had been to Cuba…had he? I know Dizzie Gillespie had been to Cuba and came back very impressed. I don't know about Charlie. Well, here's what happened: He's jazz, I'm Afro-Cuban and the two are not gonna meet. He felt that that belonged over there and that jazz was it. He was going up with jazz and *Who the hell is this Afro-Cuban, stupid guy?* He thought he's gonna teach me about jazz and he's not gonna fuck around with this Afro-Cuban shit. That was his attitude. And I felt a little disappointed. It shouldn't have turned out that way.

INTERVIEWER

But he turned you on to grass for the first time?

261

In a way he did because he said to me, "This is what you should do every morning." Well, in a sense he did teach me something, if not about jazz. He said, "You get up, you turn on and the day is beautiful." That's what his advice was and I said, "Alright, I'll remember that."

INTERVIEWER

Tell me about dancing.

LIVELLI

Dancing?

INTERVIEWER

Yeah.

LIVELLI

Well I had never thought about being a dancer. My family wanted me to be a priest because I had an ailment that didn't prepare me for society, for business or for the marketplace. I was destined to be a failure in terms of not having hearing, which is essential in business especially. You have to be on your toes. I was self conscious because I lost my self esteem at an early age, probably by the fifth grade. I was poisoned by lead.

As for my music background, I had none except that I was fascinated by drumming, because drumming was a whole different category to instrumental music. Popular music didn't interest me. The lyrics were kind of boring and worse than even today. In those days it was mush and sugary and I wanted to hear the gut music that I could understand and feel deeply and that only came across from drums. So I was into music on that level. There were no concerts really in the 30's. Well, I got into Cuban music in 1937 from Miguelito Valdés, Columbia Records, Casino de la Playa. He sang what would be considered today gospel, spiritual music. He was singing the songs of the slavery period in Cuba which was in terms of still separating black and white in a similar way to how it was being separated in the United States. It prevailed in Cuba as well. The aristocracy would have nothing to do with black people, except as servants or slaves or that category and I felt that through the music. It struck me. Especially a song that says *no puedo mas vivir, tan mal tratado* (I can't live any more, treated so bad). I enjoyed those lyrics to the extent where I memorised the songs and later when I gave talks I was able to repeat the lyrics which were in Ñañigo, not in Spanish. Well, this music hit me. That's what the ritual involves when you go to a Babalú-ayé[1]. He will hit you on the head. That's called seating. He seats 'it' on your head. It's also called *Mambo*. Mambo is not originally the name of a dance or a music. It's the name of a spirit that inhabits you, comes into you as a result of the exposure to the music. How do you get exposed? The drums are the essential ingredient. The trumpet: Wow. The piano: Beautiful. But the drums go in to every little cell and vibrate them to life.

INTERVIEWER

And how did you learn to dance?

LIVELLI

Yes, let me start now. The music coming from short wave radio in 1937. I was seventeen. I knew nothing about music and I had to interpret it through dancing which was second removed from the instrumentation, in which I didn't have talent. People asked me, "Can you play?" No, I couldn't play. But I could dance. I had that quality of expressing the music in dancing which came naturally. My mother was a great dancer. My mother taught me to dance with her. I never learned how to dance the foxtrot or any American, I went right in to Latin dancing so everything else was sort of secondary and out of place in a way. You cannot do ballet and rumba and jazz, it doesn't go. When orchestras play Latin jazz, I've seen people get off the dance floor. When I see that I know that I'm right and they're wrong. When people play Afro-Cuban the dance floor is crowded…alright, here's what happened: I said to myself, "Where the hell is this music being played in New York?" Coming from Cuba is no help. Well, I did

....

1 A high priest in Santería — *editor*

find out. I happened to go to a club in Greenwich Cillage called Café Latino on Barrow Street and there was a guy named José Mangual Sr. He said to me, "I see you come here, you like this music?" He was playing bongos. He said, "Go up to 110th Street and 5th Avenue". Prior to that I heard of a place called the Caborojeño Workers Circle in the South Bronx. So I had to move up from Fort Hamilton, across Brooklyn, across Manhattan, up in to the Bronx in 1938. It took forever. But it was too far to go up there and come home at three in the morning! José said "Go up to 110th street, the happy boys are playing there." I said ok, I went there, I walked in, paid 20 cents. I heard that music, I said, "I found it." Not only have I found something I'm looking for, but I found *it*. The happy boys were playing the music I had been hearing from Cuba. So it came to me in New York. I sat there in the corner. I didn't stay long. I knew I would be coming back many times in the future. I came back next Saturday. Sat in the corner, people thought I was a cop, because I was not part of their community. Who the hell goes to a dance hall and sits? A guy came up to me and said, "I see you sitting there, why don't you dance?" I said, "I don't know how to dance that…" He said, "Estela, venga aca, enseñele le a baillar,"[1] she took me out on the dance floor and showed me very slowly how to do a bolero. I caught on right away, I didn't need any more instructions. I already had the comprehension and the enthusiasm it takes to learn something new. The interest. So I thank them. I thank Estela in particular. She was patient with me. She stopped me, turned me around. She did everything she had to until she felt I was secure in what she was trying to put across. I never met them again, but to be taught by René and Estella, the leading Afro-Cuban dance team who made a movie, *The Thin Man*, in Hollywood. That was the height. I couldn't ask for more than that. Arthur Maries, forget about it.

So I became a professional dancer, my first gig was in 1938 at the Beacon Theatre, in beacon in New York.[2]

INTERVIEWER

How did you meet Celia Cruz?

LIVELLI

Well, that was a nice encounter, I didn't know who she was. I think she came in 1950, around that period. But I knew a gentleman named Polito Vega, who was a radio announcer, commentator, and he was instrumental in getting Celia Cruz into the country. So when she arrived he took her from the airport to the hotel and since I knew him I joined the crowd who met her as she arrived.

That was the brief encounter, except for the Sheridan Hotel, New Years Eve, I did go up and say hi and received a kiss from her. I asked her to kiss a napkin, as I was collecting women's kisses as signatures on napkins at that time.

I found out that *Guantanamera*, is a song written for the women of Guantanamo. Guantanamo is in the news! And that's where much of the beautiful music comes from in Cuba…

I saw her with Tito Puente at the Riverside Church. Many of the people were hearing the songs for the first time, but I had become familiar with the songs she was singing. So I knew when she was going to stop. And there was a moment of silence in the church that made a point, a statement. It was an epiphany. The music stopped, the band stopped, she stopped. It was a trick. I was aware of that trick. So I made myself…sort of…not too…what should I say? I was just doing it for myself, the hell with everybody. I anticipated…I knew when she was going to hit it and I hit it…I was the first one to clap. Now if you're in a concert and you're aware of the music to that extent where you are the first person in the entire audience to clap and the rest take it up from you, that's called a leader, right? And Aries[3] is a leader. I've gone through my whole life leading people around the world.

§

Vincent worked as a cruise director on sixty-two ships over a forty year period from the 1940's to the 1980's, traveling all over the world multiple times. This was in an era when cruising was a new industry. The ships were smaller, the clientele was often quite glamorous and Vincent's job was to keep the morale up by providing entertainment on board, which he did with Afro-Cuban music, dancing, invented games and excursions that he led on shore. In short, he was the inventor of his own world at sea, and everyone on the ship rallied around his imagination. This is what he is used to. He was also not in want of company.

....

1 Estele, come here, teach him to dance.
2 Edited out extrapolation on career in New Jersey, Detroit and the dancing troupes tied in with the mafia — *editor*
3 The first astrological sign in the zodiac, under which Vincent was born.— *editor*

What was the most exciting experience for you at sea?

Oh boy…handling a romantic affair during a hurricane. That story is one that people might envy, having the experience of a lifetime. I was aware and the woman was completely unaware of the events that were going to take place, so you have an advantage. You have a devilish streak where you say, *Oh boy, is she going to enjoy this, and she doesn't know it yet.*

Every time we passed a certain area of South America, the eastern coast—it juts out into the Atlantic ocean, causing the ship to have violent reactions to the movements of sea, movements up and down, sideways, and forwards and back— that meant that if you're laying horizontal, you're following the movements of the ship. Whereas with a plain romantic engagement, it's sort of…bouncing up and down. This adds a flavour that's unnatural because it's sort of a primitive grasping quality that accompanies a violent affair. It becomes violent because the ship is tossing and turning and rocking and rolling. And I knew that was going to happen. I knew when were approaching that particular part of the ocean. So when she came in the cabin, we just talked a while. I sort of had to wait until we passed that particular point and I said "Come," and we got started in my bunk but we soon ended on the floor because of the violent storm. The captain could not avoid it, it would have meant going way out of our way to avoid that violent area of the Atlantic Ocean. All the captains knew it, but nobody took advantage of it to the extent that I did. I combined it with lovemaking! Making me a hero…holding her safe and secure while she's frantically worried we're gonna sink—*The ship's going down!* So you get a closeness added to the sexual pleasure. It's the pleasure of a masculine approach to sex, where you're protecting the female. Now the violent storm became so apparent that we couldn't kiss. So it was a kissless affair in a way because our teeth were hitting our teeth, so it was dangerous. Also we were sliding on the floor. We had linoleum floors, which are slippery and not carpeted.

Anyway, the way the thing turned out was…I would postpone ejaculation until I knew the maximum quality of the storm had arrived and it was going to go downhill after that. I sort of coordinated it.

I had some practise in this, I must have done it about three times. But I went at least nine times going down to Argentina and back.

The next most outstanding was the affair I had with an older woman, with the mother of the minister of foreign affairs. She wasn't that old, he was very young. He was elected in the government. This woman was educated, charming, well-dressed, brilliant, available and seductive…for an older woman. Older women had a certain attraction, there was no question of what they wanted. Sometimes with a young girl you feel you're imposing a little and you're sort of hesitant to do certain things but with an older woman, anything goes.

Here's what happened…in fact it was in the same area that I spoke about. Here's what happened…well, we undressed… well, first we danced, spoke, then I took her to the cabin, and we became undressed and then *(knocks a Moroccan bronze canister three times, as if knocking on a door)*, "Who is it?"

'It's the fire brigade'

Two teams night and day checking on fire…they said we have to close the porthole because the water's coming in from the storm. It was a violent sea.

So I said okay. When they left, I opened the port hole again. I wanted that storm feeling to come in. We were bathed in surf. You know the force of the ocean right there, just held at bay by a wall but the circle allowed the feeling that you wanted to enter into what was going on. And we rolled around and had a wonderful experience, with an older woman. She's probably telling her girlfriend about this tonight. Anyway, it culminated with her son, her daughter-in-law, herself and myself at lunch when we arrived in Rio. The rest of the passengers went off and I was sitting at the table while the mother was touching my shoes with her shoes, making contact which was obvious by the daughter-in-law who saw what was going on and knew that we had made it—*You son of a bitch, and you didn't want to make it with me!* I turned her down! She came in the cabin and I said no…she said, "I've had an affair with cruise director on the S.S. Brazil and on the S.S. Uruguay and here we are on the S.S. Argentina." I made it clear to her, "That's good, I'm glad you made it with those guys, you're not gonna make it with me!" So, I was a little spiteful. She forgave me later, she invited me to a beautiful party on Copa Cabana. The gentleman sitting on my left was the son of the woman I had made it with. He didn't know anything about it. He didn't realise. But the daughter-in-law noticed gold cufflinks that I was wearing and it's a custom in Brazil to give a lover gold cufflinks and she knew that. When she saw that she knew for sure what happened. Good story, huh?

INTERVIEWER

Tell me about Santería.

LIVELLI

Well, that's coming in to the foreground in my life. At this stage I realise I have been engaged in something deeper, along religious lines than just getting baptised and going to confession and communion and all that. It's just a tie in with something that has been going on throughout my life, beginning in 1925 when I was hit on the head by a teacher who said, "Dead from the neck up," which made me feel as though I was different from everybody, which caused me to lose my self esteem. I did. I went through many periods of my life, through my schooling, all my universities, and I felt I was just stupid and dumb and I lost my *self*. Spelled s-e-l-f. When you lose your *self*, you're left with zero. And I felt that vacuum, which was caused by that statement, at the age of five. I took it to be the truth. My teacher was telling me something. And I went through life up to the age of about twenty-eight, twenty-nine, failing. Zero. Nothing. I was useless. They gave up on me. The teacher said, *uneducable*, so I was just a failure until I realised…hell, shit…I'm not a failure. Here I am in front of the applauding public. I'm dancing in a troupe, doing lifts and making people appreciate my talent. I have something. So it was an epiphany. I woke up out of a stupor that I had convinced myself that I had no confidence, that I was worthless. All I could do was dance a little on a dance floor with women and all that. But that isn't brains, that's sort of natural behaviour, dancing comes naturally. I never had to learn how to do routines. I just looked once, and I did it. I had that same facility, that same faculty with languages. Everybody would say, *Boy, you've got a good accent, where did you learn how to speak Spanish?* It was just a fake, show business is imitation. It's not you, it's a face. It's acting. So I learned how to act and carry myself through life successfully acting. It's not the real me. The real me, I left when I was 5 years old. I was gonna be something else. But the music filled the vacuum.

I think Santería originated three million, 500,000 years ago in east Camaroon, not Ethiopia. They said it on television two nights ago. The first fossils belonging to the first prehistoric human named Eva, named so by archeologists. She proved be the first human fossil and they found her bones and through the DNA they feel that we homo sapiens began in Camaroon. Now how did the communication between the Santería adherents and the average individual, Cubans mostly today, begin?

There are at least, I was told, three million followers of Santería including those who share Catholicism, Islam, Buddhist, Shinto…these regions are basically offshoots of Santería which began in Cameroon when lightning struck, and the god of lightning is called Shango. I identify with Shango because his assigned number in Santería is number four and number four in my life represents: my month of birth, April, my address 44 Perry, the 4th floor of the building and I came here in 1964. I have 10 indications that are sort of outstanding in my life with the number four. Number four has hit me. If you follow through your life and try to figure out something related to a mystery in your life, don't worry about why we are here. We are here. There is no needle in the hay stack, in fact there's not even a hay stack. We are here. Period. But we may have two realities, the every day, normal living reality and another one that we are purposely, due to our brain, ignoring, because we can't possibly overload two realities at the same time. However, that second reality is an influence.

What happened? Shango is the god of thunder. Now if you have a tree trunk that's hollowed out by insects, the thunder—*CLAP*—enters that vacuum in the tree trunk, causes a vibration. That can be heard by an individual three million, 500,000 years ago. Actually we go back to fourteen million, the Big Bang. And if the individual who hears the echo in the drum with the thunder, interprets it as a message from heaven and responds by hitting the drum. The first drum was a log that they hit with sticks, it was a hollow tree trunk and they were able to hit it in response to the thunder clap, that's communication. You hear the whistle of a bird and you whistle along with the bird, that's a human reaction. Now what happened was, the sound waves that we heard from the drum were in unison with the sound waves that we were gonna return out to the atmosphere. It started a certain communication, a code. Now, if you're in a prison and you have a mate in the room next to you, you hit the wall with the morse code (for example) to communicate, even if you're separated by a wall. Sound waves penetrate. In fact, it's difficult to have them not penetrate. They last forever, I found out.

265

Now let's say a million years went by and this reciprocal communication formed into a language between spirits and humans. The god of thunder who is in another reality, we are living in an every day reality with our drums. However, the sun, which is a good example of energy entering our atmosphere to keep us alive, the earth has a power to throw out an energy, just as the sun does, but it also receives energy. The earth receives and emits energy. Now if you're able to emit energy through sound waves, then you're able to communicate with the other reality which is sending you a message. Santería is based on communication with what are called *orishas*, we call them saints. They're not really saints, and not really powers, they're a psychic force. Manifestations of sound waves that become communicative. They relate. We are relating with forces outside of ourselves constantly. What the orisha, a power, is doing, is protecting us. Santería is able to bring these forces into play through the Babalú-ayé, the high priest, who is a channeller between the individual who comes to him for help and the message he will receive from the other reality through a trance. The orisha puts the Santero (the high priest) into a different seat, a frame of mind and opens up. So when the Babalú-ayé turned to me and had a message for me and I said, "What is it? What is the message?" my friend interpreted the language of the gods which is Nañigo, not Spanish. The message was, *You will carry this music around the world*, and I did it.

§

This is part one of a two-part interview. Part two contains stories of Vincent's grandfather (who was kidnapped by gypsies in Italy in the 1830's and went on to become a travelling musician with a dancing bear before emigrating the United States), Vincent's encounters with the mafia, his friendships with William Gaddis, Anatole Broyard, Henri Michaux, W.H Auden, and much much more.

Ladies Night Afloat

Captains enjoy socialising with their passengers, but many really go out of their way to avoid doing so. Captain S why is a pinnacle player recluse. He tolerated the human cargo he carried, but was basically a merchant mariner. Although he could, being a combination of power and masculine authority, at times appear handsome in an irresistible uniform. The ladies are taking it upon themselves to enter his name in their *carnet de bal*. As cruise director, whose major concern lies with single women who are travelling alone, something had to be done, especially since even the married ladies wanted the captains attention. Before the captain was on his way to his quarters, having left the restaurant, I had announced in the main lounge, that when I gave the signal, all the ladies were to rush the captain and and drag him onto the dancefloor. As the captain passed me with a lady on each arm, he looked up at me and said jokingly, "I'll get you for this."

The Love Kimono

Designed for fashionable display and warmth, with honourable tradition that involves virtue, the Geisha Kimono hides those knots whose functions are other than to merely secure the garment in place.

Patience is a virtue next to chastity. Since the Geisha is paid for her time as well as for her talent, as a paid performer, she can be mercenary.

Where westerners give diamonds and furs, the Japanese give their mistresses Kimonos of great value. Have you ever seen a Geisha wearing a mikimoto or diamond earrings?

Although skilled in flower arrangement, the tea ceremony and stone gardens, she is primarily a convenience, an entertainer like a taxi dancer, whose grandmother taught her the tricks that postpone climax and bring in more yen. Before she learns to sew, the Geisha learns knotting with its connotative sexual application.

In a land of much ceremony each of the four knots has a value that can be lingered over. The tantric influence can be called Niponese Kama Sutra.

She resists or surrenders her body knot by knot, obeying self control.

The unfastening proceeds in proper sequence with a meditative delay to savour the moment with a ritualistic refinement that westerners reject or ignore.

She does not emerge from her toilette in Victoria's Secret negligee or *in puris naturalibus*. Like a cat in a bag she appears before her client as though prepared to go shopping. She wears a sash (obi) like a misplaced pillow behind her back, no shortie nightie but baggy bloomers and trousered leggings. She is immersed in clothing, in wraps and cumbersome barriers that would baffle an uninitiated patron and forestall any bam, bam, thank you ma'am.

The knots prolong the pleasure…and the agony…and add to the bill.

As her skill, status and celebrity grow along with her artistic fan dance, umberella twirling and sake wine time-consuming ceremonies, her clientele increases.

On The Nature of Sound

Is there perhaps present in any naturalistic environment and in nature proper a proof of sorts that might come from the response that healthy plants exert in the presence of music, classical or jazz etc. In this same way, Afro-Cuban drumming may have joined nature's sound waves to establish a code of mutual communication after thousands of years in the making.

A breaking branch if the tree emits sound son distress that are easily recognized by humans. Human sounds echo across space and are answered backs re-echoes from nature. Sounds within inanimate objects such as sea shells are heard by humans whereas human pitched voices can crack thin glass. The human voice produces not only sound but sound waves that conjunct with nature's sound waves to produce emotions, a stronger from of communication that is exchanged between man and nature.

Opportunities

What doesn't happen is as much part of life as what does happen. Lost opportunities are even more so since they contain more seeds of future happenings but in different time frames. Both approaches have open ends for the future to handle but the future seems more reluctant to give up the past that did not happen than the happenings it has done with.

The past has a way of popping(?) up like a tiny ember still flickering with a spark whereas an event has only a cold memory until it is rekindled by the present. The present provides fuel for both but the past has the advantage of familiarity and experience the the present may not have. the past that did not take place is never dead but considered as never alive. Events are born mostly innocent and often dependent on what precedes them. The past is life that never happened merely bidded(?) its time in many ways.

Biopic

I could not dream up a story that matched my life that people could believe nor would it be plagiarized due to its uniqueness. A biopic movie would cover 95 years and not actors but photos and documents interviews and videos with a wild interruption just prior to the end when a completely ignored scenario tells another story entirely — a lot of supernatural activity with convincing evidence that explains the life that has bee shown as unique but not as supernatural.

Miguelito Valdez

It would take Caruso, Sinatra and Pavarotti to tear me away Miguelito Valdez whose lyrics struck a chord in me. The fact that part of the lyrics were unintelligible African made more veracity since we had never heard a mixture before. When translated the combination of beautiful sounds, the tragic message of the lyrics and the primitive quality of the African drumming background was unheard of in either popular or classical renditions. Not only did he sing the written lyrics composed by Arsenio Rodriguez, the greatest exponent of Afro-Cuban scores, but he sang the Spanish wording in the manner an uneducated slave would. For example, *Give me seventeen candles to make a cross* became, *Dame diez e siete vela 'pa' ponerie en cru*. In Spanish, *Dame diez y siete velas para powerless en cruz*. Now you have before you an oppressed black slave crying out for help.

The 1920's Village

Not many yards from our living rooms windows was the Sullivan street stable. During Winter the manure odor mixed with damp straw and hay were kept out but in Summer the horse flies entered our apartment. But it was during summer before the installation of window screens that life was made really uncomfortable with the mosquitoes from New Jersey that bit us day and night. The day Dad brought home two screens the family stood up and cheered. When at age 5 or 6 I was confined to the fire escape, since playing int he street with tough kids was dangerous, that the screen still had to be placed against the flies and also needed a screen to block and secure the iron stairwell where I could've fallen into the street. I was thus securely barricaded on all sides always wanting to play with the kids in the street below me. The stable was active with wagons that arrived, some coming from Brooklyn and beyond to bed down for the early morning start. Horses hooves on stone streets were pleasant sounding along with the cart wheels grinding along. Later on, with cowboy and indian movies, we kids imagined riding a speeding horse.

A Dance Host

A dance host employed by steamship company is obliged to continue dancing all evening. He cannot hide or arrest. To do this for a living may sound like a delightful pastime but actually it is exhausting since many partners are poor dancers, they cause frustration to the host when a particular favourite rumba comes on. Coaxed onto the dance floor by some temple dances in Thailand made me a hero since I was, as a dancer, able to keep up with their movements and footwork, where they had expected me to look foolish as a neophyte.

Although my mother encouraged me to dance at a very early age I was still shy and godly, until Tony Yacavino, a prizefighter, took me under his wing and taught me to perform gracefully. Well, a problem that arises in dance, as in fashion shows, is this being essential to changing costumes—we had to do tango, rumba, samba numbers with a vocalist in between to allow time for quick words and changes into my pants legs.

Not only did I find a treasure that day in 1938, I found the very one I was searching for. Unlike many treasures that one stumbles upon in life, this one was never to be lost. It remains with me forever. I belong to it and it belongs to me, like a love affair.

Once inside the Park Plaza, I sat in the shadows, hoping not to be too noticeable. This only made me more suspect, as people present puzzled over me—was I a cop, who came to the Park Plaza just to sit there? Certain that I would return many times, I did not remain for very long, since the ride home involved the IRT (Interboro Rapid Transit) and the BMT (Brooklyn Manhattan Transit) to the last stop in Fort Hamilton. The fare round-trip was ten cents. To pass the time, I bought the Daily News for three cents. Like office workers waiting for Friday, I waited all week for Saturday when I would return to the 110th Street Dance Hall, like some John Travolta.

Another discovery awaited me on my second visit. This time, it was a prize in the form of Estela, René's partner, for it was she who got me up to learn how to do a simple bolero. They were the greatest and most authentic proponents and performers of the Afro-Latin in the country!…in the world!

A pleasant surprise awaited us one hot day—the management set up an eight-foot pedestal supporting a huge electric fan. No one had ever seen one, since it had just appeared on the market. Installed at the head of the stairs leading down to the restrooms, it was supposed to cool the dance floor, especially since there were no windows or openings, aside from the narrow entrance. We welcomed it until the gradual, unmistakable odors were sucked up from below, because the long line of windows in the doorless men's room allowed fresh air in that was soon spiced with not only the typical scent, but also with cannabis. Anyone breathing such a combination of sexy pheromones became more and more overheated while dancing. When mixed with Tabu perfume, it was not all that unbearable. Besides, it was proof that a good time was being had by all.

With no bathtubs, people used public baths for men and women or took "French baths" at the kitchen sink. Some ladies may have resisted removing the Tabu until the next day in order to maintain the memories it inspired, as they cuddled their pillows closer to their breasts.

The five-piece Happy Boys Orchestra was a powerhouse. It generated electric energy that energized the dancers like pumps, dynamos, boilers, and furnaces. The musicians were fine-tuned resonances, pulsated vibrations and punctuated climaxes.

From the opening set, the gradual accumulation of various enchanting rhythms, vibes seemed to linger on, unwilling to leave the dance hall, reluctant to go out into the dark, empty night. As the evening progressed, energy pressure increased like an inflating balloon. It compounded itself to that extreme moment known as the *descarga* - the explosion! It could have killed you it you had a weak heart…for you were as close to a real-life explosion as you could ever be and still walk back to your seat.

Some dancers would slump to the floor, not from exhaustion but in tribute to the musicians, like a bow, while the musicians bowed back to the dancers. Lovers turned away from each other in order to extend their love to the musicians. After embracing each other, the musicians surrounded the pianist out of respect. On one occasion, the singer, Dorotes Santiago, concluded his piece by turning around, sliding atop the grand piano, to end up kissing the pianist. As for the crowd, included those seated, the round of embraces and kissing resembled midnight New Year's Eve. The band would sometimes favor us with an encore, but with the blast of the *descarga*, there never was one. The Fania All-Stars did it for 25,000 fans at Madison Square Garden many years later—so did others, but the one at the Park Plaza that night in 1938 went through the roof.

Interrupted Sleep and Alzheimer's

Alzheimer's is perhaps best characterized as a condition resembling sleepwalking — you are asleep but you are "awake." With Alzheimer's you "live" in a halfway state. This state is a blank, like a white sheet of writing paper that you are conscious of but that you have no use for.

As an example: While watching a movie, the screen suddenly turns blank. The projection has been cut but the screen is still there. This was the surface that your thought processes, your awaRenéss, was projected upon in order to allow you to follow your life's functions. Alzheimer's is a fatal hibernation, a turn-off.

Who are they who suffer interrupted sleep the most? Parents of infants. The infants themselves are exposed to interrupted sleep during the night and day. The ideal might be a human functioning like a computer, never needing sleep. Perhaps what lies in between is a bit like Alzheimer's. The reason for Alzheimer's progressive delusion is the bothersome, prolonged breakdown of the film's movie projector (the brain), while the movie screen (the world) remains.

Interrupted sleep mimics this unwelcome state of affairs. After prolonged stoppage, it can no longer be "spliced" by the natural abilities of the mind and body to recover belief. To have the patient resume normal living, he should be in a room with a movie of himself portrayed by a double to trick him into believing that he is normal through transference. By doing so, we replace one delusion with a fictitious, more benign one. We have him heal himself. This trick may cause him to resume his more normal life, just as the repaired movie projector's film convinces the audience to resume believing that the obvious fiction they had been watching on the movie screen once again is true and valid.

After all, what is the daily story of life if not a fiction that we have invented for ourselves to give life "meaning." We identify ourselves with actors. The Alzheimer patient will be treated with trickery into believing that what he is watching are his own actions and will power. He now resumes normalcy as part of a successful "lived happily ever after" scenario, one that brings "his" portrayal on the screen to a happy finale. The patient leaves the theater (hospital) influenced and affected. He leaves his condition of Alzheimer's behind him. No doubt a prolonged exposure to therapy is involved to restore normal function through neuroplasticity — tricking our neutrons to cooperate.

Can we project the imagery, bypassing the movie screen, directly into the brain by using the power of suggestion? To further play the game of a convincing scenario with trickery, we can disguise it as entertainment. The movie screen should be enormous, overpowering, using advanced technology of sound, lighting, smell, and 3D. There can also be the administration of medications that make the unreal more "real." It can stir long-imprisoned emotions. We leave the theater crying, laughing, singing — happier.

In our search for a more perfect reality and an always better world, we may one distant day assemble an ideal 24-hour scenario that can be portrayed and employed as convincingly real, so that our lives are what Calderon de la Barca meant in 1635 when he wrote, "Life is but a dream; *La vida es sueña Y los sueñas son.*"

The imagined stressful world of Nathaniel West's fiction (*Day of the Locust*), has already characterized our lives, since we follow Hollywood's influence in our everyday behavior. It is our culture's captor. Hollywood's filmed convincing manipulation is the present-day equivalent of medieval morality plays that guided and set our mores and minds for generations. Give us, please, not less Hollywood, but a reformed Hollywoodian ingenuity on a sustained, more aware, more wholesome level. (This needs elaboration).

We need to open up a back-door approach to Alzheimer's subtle interruption of life's dramatic story; brainwash us with clever artificiality that unrolls both our mind and body. Many of us already believe and live by faith and fiction, i.e., reincarnation. We rub off on each other during this Age of Aquarius.

We can better benefit ourselves with uninterrupted sleep through chemistry, but also through self-induced deception like self-hypnosis and innocuous trickery. Everyone likes a movie, especially if you're the leading man.

Like women who fall in love with gangsters or even murderers, some people will root for the joker against the hero (society). Childhood make-believe, like adult imagination, has appealing fantasy, including an appetite for mayhem. Vicarious behavior stimulates adrenalin. Scientists seek redeeming features in insanity and illusions.

In *The Red Rose of Cairo*, Woody Allen's characters jumped off the screen onto the laps of the audience. Hollywood's technical trickery can suspend disbelief and perhaps convince Alzheimer's patients to believe they are wrong to think that they are hopelessly doomed. Some patients become mischievous and tricky—we can forgive ourselves for using fire to fight fire.

There are times when inducing a coma is recommended in therapy. Since Alzheimer's resembles a coma, we might try to turn an induced coma on and off repeatedly. This procedure would resemble what occurs when we try to start the motor of our car if it is sluggish.

Batman, Spiderman, and Superman reflect the invincibility of the 1930s Tarzan movies. At age seven, I was about to jump off the roof like Tarzan. Screams from a neighbor encouraged me to do so, as well as to stop. The challenge of conquering flight and open space, the egoistic glory of success and the union with Tarzan were tempting. Also, the audacious display would win the attention of my 7-year-old girlfriend. Today's clownish culture has a dark side when combined with movies, TV, video, and i-Pod games. Repeated lies become convincing.

PART II

Like women who fall in love with gangsters or even murderers, some people will root for the joker against the hero (society). Childhood make-believe, like adult imagination, has appealing fantasy, including an appetite for mayhem. Vicarious behavior stimulates adrenalin. Scientists seek redeeming features in insanity and illusions.

In *The Red Rose of Cairo,* Woody Allen's characters jumped off the screen onto the laps of the audience. Hollywood's technical trickery can suspend disbelief and perhaps convince Alzheimer's patients to believe they are wrong to think that they are hopelessly doomed. Some patients become mischievous and tricky—we can forgive ourselves for using fire to fight fire.

There are times when inducing a coma is recommended in therapy. Since Alzheimer's resembles a coma, we might try to turn an induced coma on and off repeatedly. This procedure would resemble what occurs when we try to start the motor of our car if it is sluggish.

Batman, Spiderman, and Superman reflect the invincibility of the 1930s Tarzan movies. At age seven, I was about to jump off the roof like Tarzan. Screams from a neighbor encouraged me to do so, as well as to stop. The challenge of conquering flight and open space, the egoistic glory of success and the union with Tarzan were tempting. Also, the audacious display would win the attention of my 7-year-old girlfriend. Today's clownish culture has a dark side when combined with movies, TV, video, and i-Pod games. Repeated lies become convincing.

Arabic Chic: Middle Eastern Décor

An apartment furnished à la Arabe may be considered in bad taste just now. However, there is an esthetic antecedent of current signifcance in favor of such décor. In their otherwise conventional apartments, the Victorians installed a "Turkish corner," where one could relax and enjoy a smoke after dinner or whenever. These handy oases could be found from London to Jakarta in the homes of English, French, and Dutch civil servants serving the colonies.

Today, an ancient culture that can both fascinate and terrify us has entered our lives. One of its overlooked manifestations is strikingly visible in the estimable works of the Orientalist painters. In their canvases, *l'art du décor* is most evident. The sudden abundance of wood carvings that now infests our flea markets is a result of the Chinese Cultural Revolution. So will the looting in Iraq contribute also remarkable decorative objects for a virgin American market place. A mountain of Arabic furnishings will come to us. No need (like Mohammed) to go to it. Its rarity will feed its popularity. Inlaid mother-of-pearl, copper, ebony, ivory, tortoise shell, brass, ottomans, divans, and wall hangings will penetrate the last frontier in interior design and decoration, that critics still label garish, outré. Decorators have imprisoned us in a conformity conspiracy called "in style." French provincial, Scandinavian, Japanese, Chinese influences are endlessly "in vogue..." along with grandma's hand-me-down parlor set. Could it be time to reevaluate your choices, the stale miscellanea of your conflicting mementos?

By combining domesticity with fantasy, you can costume your apartment in an atmosphere of burlesque, arabesque, and the seductive odalesque. Without leaving home, you can thus escape the familiar in favor of the enchanting variety of the thousand and one nights and go where you have never gone before.

The world's richest woman, Doris Duke, transplanted Arabia to her home in Hawaii. From Malcolm Forbes to Cher, celebrities have set the stage for the Sheik of Araby...for Arabic chic.

Baby Bunting

As a natural experience, sleep can be made more pleasurable. Comfort is important and can be upgraded considerably. The familiar phrase baby bunting is applied to what a baby is swathed in. By extending this snuggling feature to adults' sleepwear, the comfort level is increased noticeably. On cold nights, the ears, head, cheeks, and nose benefit from the warm protection that a baby-bunting addition applied to adult sleepwear provides. In addition, this advancement restricts noise intrusion for more restful sleep.

By adding a hood to the pajama top with fabric other than coarse wool, warmth, protection, and more comforting and pleasurable sleep is possible. It also does away with the ludicrous skull cap.

Been There, Didn't Do That

Travel often mirrors life in that much of it must remain unaccomplished. But why travel to the Taj Mahal, for instance, and skip seeing it? Why go to King Tut's tomb and not enter it? We didn't catch the Eiffel Tower in Paris or Big Ben in London. In Tijuana, we didn't drink the water or tequila, or vodka in Moscow. At Niagara Falls, we could hear them roar but left without seeing them. We didn't swim at Waikiki Beach or ride the camels at the Pyramids. In Tunis, we never visited Carthage or Machu Picchu while in Peru. We transited the Panama Canal but not by ship, same thing in Suez. At the Kremlin, we ducked out of the guided tour and in London, the changing of the guards didn't interest us. We never saw the Golden Pagoda in Burma and ignored the *Mayan* ruins in Cozumel. Many times in Hong Kong, but never made Macao.

Veteran travelers claim it's uncool to have a photo of yourself holding up the Leaning Tower of Pisa, but really now, the Taj, King Tut, the camels! The above list of obligatory must-do attractions were all skipped for good reasons. First of all, we had seen the Taj Mahal twice before, once at sunrise and once at sunset, and Agra has many other marvels one should not miss. We had to forgo King Tut's tomb in order to return to the hotel with a friend who had tripped on the steps. The famous London fog blanketed Big Ben, and in Paris, visibility was zero. During World War II, Niagara Fall blacked out, and we passed them at night. Why no water in Tijuana needs no answer, but no tequila, or vodka in Moscow? (Doctor's orders). No swimming at Waikiki was due to an ear infection, and the changing of the guards, well, we'd seen it in Ottawa. Thieving cab drivers caused us to cancel Carthage, and a camel drivers' strike forced us to ride a donkey at Giza. We took the train at the Panama Canal, and taxi and bus from the Red Sea to the Mediterranean. Always arriving after the action, we never fired a shot at Guadalcanal, Leyte, or Okinawa. In the ring with boxing champion "Boston Blackie," but as a referee, we were spared a pounding. Orson Welles's "Invasion of the Martians" didn't panic us. We had been to the rehearsal. Disneyland was under construction when we were there, and Lenin's tomb was no problem waiting in line since American tourists were "delegates" in 1958. In 1952, the Louvre had no line. We didn't pay a fee in Xian to visit the 5000 clay soldiers in 1988. We skipped the Olympic Games in Moscow to visit churches and icons. We left the bull fights in Madrid; my lady friend threw up. We didn't ski in New Hampshire or ice skate in St. Moritz—didn't know how. During rough weather at Stand, I never got seasick. At the Tour d'Argent, we didn't order the specialty, lobster (allergic to shellfish), and at Gallagher's Steakhouse, we ordered fish. Because we passed out just as it began, we missed the fabulous show at the Tropicana in Havana, and in Pompeii, the brothel paintings were off limits. Hearing about a plane crash discouraged flying to Machu Picchu. In the Vatican, time ran out on us so that we never saw the Sistine Chapel. It would have meant missing the ship. On the way to the S.S. Missouri ceremony, we detoured to buy V-J Day cancellations At the Yokohama Post Office. Meeting the people of Moscow was more fun than a guided Kremlin tour. Steer clear of the artificial artifacts in Cozumel's *Mayan* ruins, we were told. Scorching heat discouraged climbing the steps to reach the Shwegadon Golden Pagoda in Burma.

How could one not hear of JFK's assassination, or not know of the TV program "Dallas," "Peyton Place," those Liverpool boys, or much about Elvis, or even Viet Nam? Working on ships during those years removed us from these events. History sailed on without us, often dependent on shortwave, wandering in a sealed container, we were ignorant of what went on back home. Like the ingenious Ulysses, we were prisoners of the sea, brothers of Robinson Crusoe. We travel on inexorably to that last stop, the one in our itinerary that we cannot not do.

We slept through a Tokyo earthquake. We crossed the Thames River in London, not over the London Bridge, but under it, via the Tunnel. We entered the Forbidden City, free of the $10 fee (In 1988, there was no fee), fell asleep at midnight mass. We sailed the Nile east to west, not north to south. Walked the Via Dolorosa in Jerusalem the opposite way, west to east, uphill. Didn't request permission to enter Al Quds, the Dome of the Rock (none required in 1982). In Stonehenge, we didn't approach the stones; they wanted an admission fee, we couldn't touch the stones and they were behind a fence. I had no paper or pen to place a prayer in the Wailing Wall, Jerusalem.

At the Underground St. Calixto Catacomb, I chickened out entering, too spooky. I married in an Episcopalian cathedral, not Catholic. In Budapest, I only visited Buda and not pest. At the Deauville Casino, we just watched. We spent time on an island in San Francisco Bay, not Alcatraz, but Angel Island and at Fort Leavenworth, but at Command and General Staff School as an interpreter. In New Orleans, the Mardi Gras had ended when we arrived. At Lourdes, we didn't get off the train. At Woodstock, we just drove past. I live in Greenwich village but never was a hippie. I lived on the edge but never went too far.

The Birth of the Bookstore: A Story of Life and Death

"If we can get her off Courvoisier and onto rum, we may be able to save her. If not, I give her six months," her doctor told me. This is the story of the strange demise of the bookstore's angel, Janet. It is a tale as dramatic as any on the bookshelves. Without this benefactress there would not have been the Cornelia Street Bookstore in 1945. "With luck," the doctor continued, "we can perhaps interest her in something to occupy her and take her mind off drink."

Who was I to disagree, even knowing it would never happen. The last stages of the situation were evident: the time it took Janet to answer the door, the shakes and rages, the blackouts and loss of memory, the spurts of clarity, the cross-eyes, the march toward death. That's what finally happened, but not from drink, a fall, or some accidental development. It was to be a gentle departure with dignity, painless, one that one would wish for oneself. A death process well ahead of its time, an unavoidable event, deus ex machina.

"We can open a flower shop," I suggested to Janet as we discussed her salvation, since she was frightened about her survival. "Or a bookstore," I added as a sudden thought that occurred to me. Anatole Broyard had often spoken of opening one. Janet had taken a small studio apartment at 32 Cornelia Street, and a store was available to rent at 18 Cornelia. Perhaps she could help out at the store as part of her recovery or occupational therapy.

A lawyer's meeting was set up, a large sum — a thousand dollars — was arranged as a loan to Anatole. The bookstore was born, only to be short-lived. Anatole had hoped it to be a well of knowledge for the young Village writers, offering rare names such as Henri Michaux, Frans Kafka, Celine, Cummings, Gide — authors favored by Anatole but comparatively unknown by the young unsophisticated customers. Worse, still, for stock customers these authors were difficult to find anywhere around town in 1945. Often there would be a request, a possible sale, but no book to sell. Orders were taken but not filled. It was like running a business backwards, with demand, but no supply. We can today look back at what was the classic pioneer's frustration, facing what is ahead of their time.

I had met Janet at the Club Bali in Miami in 1941. The beach season had ended and dance teams and entertainers either returned north or found work in the city. After each show, as per the club's policy, we were obliged to mingle. At ringside, a pleasant-looking young woman wearing a starched white outfit smiled up at me. I asked politely for a dance and was refused politely, with the suggestion that I might dance with her friend seated with her. Too late to decline, I discovered that Janet's nurse had lured me into an offer I couldn't now refuse. Janet couldn't stand very well off-balance, much less rumba. I accepted a drink, as the club encouraged us to do, and eventually, the crafty young nurse had us manipulated to where I ended up in Janet's bed somehow or other.

Janet was generous, wealthy, and grateful, as I began to become a male nurse for her, as well as her "dance teacher." Making frequent bar scenes with her in Miami and New York was injuring a weak kidney that I was unaware of. Over time I developed hydronephrosis, pylonephritis, and hypertension. One kidney began to atrophy after I received by accident a Mickey Finn destined for her at the 5 o'clock Club, where Janet had heckled the singer loudly. After one spinal tap and three cystoscopies (scheduled for a fourth) at St. Clare's midtown hospital and at Dr. Oswald Lowsley's Park Avenue office and overnight at the Leroy Pavilion on the Upper East Side, I left Janet since she was returning to Peoria for a visit home.

Working as a trainee now for the Sterling Drug Company, a subsidiary of I.G. Farben (Bayer), I was to be a future "detail-man." I was in daily contact with calmatives, spasmotics, aphrodisiacs, and remedies with names like thalidomide.

When I received a sudden call from Janet, I was surprised to hear that she had checked herself into a Central Park West sanitarium. When I visited her, I could not refuse her the favor she asked of me. "Next time, can you bring some Lucky Strikes and something to help me sleep?" she asked.

In 1945 we didn't know much about uppers and downers washed down with Courvoisier. When I honored her request, as I was leaving she handed me a gift, her wedding ring. On my next visit, I was told that Janet had checked out. It was just about six months. We had closed the bookshop. It was as if Janet had taken it with her *in extremo libro* (at the end of the book).

Bombay

While walking around Bombay one day, I passed by a small, unpainted frame house with a fragile fence that came right up to it, leaving no room for a garden. Written on the side of the door was " Mohandas K. GANDHI." Knocking on the door for fear of trespassing, I entered gingerly since it was unlocked. At once, I found myself in a kitchen with a bare table, two chairs, no stove or sink, but with a spinning wheel in a corner. There was barely room to turn around, reminding me of the cramped cabins I call home aboard ships for many years. I was also reminded of the old outlawed kitchens situated at the entrances of New York apartments, considered fire traps since frequent kitchen fires blocked exits to the outside.

Years later, I was sitting in billionaire Walter Annenberg's palatial, spotless kitchen in Ambler, Pennsylvania. I had been invited in for coffee by his housekeeper, with whom I had shared a cab from the airport. Since I had never known a family kitchen, I was more at home on ships.

Bring Back Whitewalls

Nineteen forty-nine Mark IV Jaguars did not have whitewall tires. However, it was possible to purchase attachable, rubberized whitewalls as an accessory. It added an increased glamour to an already hi-luxury automobile. Because muddy roads and unpaved main roads discouraged whitewall editions to the average low-cost car, whitewalls were discontinued.

Using luxury liners of the forties as an example was associated in the mind of the common man with images of great wealth. What was required to democratize the industry was the addition of glamour to business. To serve and to satisfy the envious man in the street, an atmosphere of identification with the lifestyle of the wealthy was added to cruises during the fifties. Swimming pools were added or emphasized, menus were fancier, entertainment became paramount, vessels carried passengers to shopping or to unspoiled islands, and an illusion of genuine upper-class status was made manifest with more formality aboard small ships.

Proper dressing made a cosmetic difference that revolutionized sailing. Similarly, by adding whitewalls to the average automobile we uplift the status that identifies it with the wealthy, with celebrity, with nobility, race cars, and officialdom. It is not an original idea, but a neglected one. No longer is an attachable accessory involved, since a do-it-yourself paint kit could also be made available. The rebirth of an abandoned stylish statement is today more feasible, thanks to much-improved highways and paint. Tires need not be "stuck in the mud aesthetically under our sleek cars.

If the classic 1949 F-1 Ford pick-up could boast whitewalls with hubcaps to match the color of the vehicle when many country roads were still muddy, surely we are ready to bring back whitewalls.

Stay With the Feeling

What do Buddhists mean when they say "Stay with the feeling?" They are referring to a quality that is almost tangible, that could can finally recognize within you after much long exposure to it. This quality, any Buddhist will tell you, requires attention and awaRenéss and respect until it becomes the individual. It could take years to develop or could gradually disappear entirely. We are referring to religious faith when it involves a Buddhist who chants mantras to maintain and strengthen spiritualism. When the feeling does not involve religion, it could be instead in the form of strength of a physical ability among athletes, or a skill such as Tiger Woods possesses. Gamblers try to hold onto a lucky feeling called "on a roll." A lifelong love affair such as Queen Victoria knew with Prince Albert had a special quality that they must have been aware of even when they disagreed over the Boer War. The love of the art of acting is an internal force that endures a lifetime, strong in certain people—in others it could fade away, while others never know it at all. To possess any special quality during one's lifetime may be a question of luck, inheritance, genetics, environment, or practice, but it is the essential recognition of it that plays the influence. To have a guru or to study *Kabala* helps to show you what the quality is all about, or you may remain blissfully oblivious to it. After a three-decade career aboard ships with no true talent other than the ability to uplift the morale of passengers on long, boring sea voyages—some lasting thirty-eight days—I discovered that a good, comforting "feeling" had developed in part of my personality. When away from the ship life, the force that provided this beatitude required awaRenéss of it.

AwaRenéss itself was necessarily similar to meditative effort, but not as compulsory as daily chanting mantras—more like a listening voice from within that arises from helping others enjoy their lives more, to bring about and to keep alive a force that is called cheerfulness. This is worth more than trophies or religious diplomas or faith. It is "devoutly to be wished for," as Shakespeare said, along with the Holy Bible's "Come, be of good cheer."

Buyu's Harmonic Finale

Plato emico est sed magis amicus veritas.
Philosophy is a good friend, but truth is a better one.

Buyu's long career demonstrated the solidity of the Truth in every beat on his bongo. He articulated and made Truth audible in the perfection of his artistry. What is more perfect than Truth? He mastered the flawless sound, the propitious moment, the perfect intricacy of masterful performance. He knew the ritualistic element of Afro music. Playing bongo involves unquestionably, like Truth, correctness, elegant conformation, and an echoing confirmation.

Anatole Broyard claimed that philosophy accounted for Buyu's harmonious finale. But Buyu was not last-minute philosophizing. The truth was at his death bedside. His life needed no philosophical scrutiny. He died in the arms of a friend called Veritas.

The aural nerve is the last one to die. When Buyu heard "the world's greatest bongo player," he recognized his true legacy. Thus, his last moment were comforted not by philosophy but by Truth. He was fulfilled as an extraordinary technician. Bongo drumming is a subtle, beautiful mathematic science demanding surgical calculations. It, like life, requires concentration to function explicitly. By moving aural information, numerical sequences and exquisite formulations of rhythmic equations, his genius "clicked." The most accepted approach to achievement is not always a step-by-step process. In Buyu, it seemed to be a preexistent ability manifested at the moment when most appropriate, called timing…more like telegraphy than music. His specialized knowledge was akin to the faith that all deeply religious people have in their god. His performance was immaculate, impeccable…cool, like the young child Mozart seated at his piano. But Buyu's musical score was not on sheet music. It was in his ample heart where pure truth sets us free, like death itself.

If the congas were the cannons, the bongos are more like telegraphy than music. Like no other instrument, he could fire a continuous cannonade (cañonango) like a riveter. He was originally placed behind the band itself. His artillery was metallic and when unmuffled, was as a menace to the concept of proper music.

Census Taker, 1950

I've always said I'd never take part in anything involving a million people. Until the Census, this referred to politics, religion, G.I. Joe attitudes, subway trains, bombs, even cafeterias. One of the less obvious reasons for this was perhaps the fear of not finishing something started.

But then a friend, who was worried about my being jobless — a sincere friend, mind you — arranged, through political means probably, for me to secure an enumerator's position in the Bureau of the Census, Department of Commerce. Never good at numbers, and avoiding eighty percent of the people most of the time, I didn't feel psychologically qualified for the job. No one asked me any questions about my attitudes — except toward the US Government. Therefore, I never told them.

It's amazing to me how nothing too disturbing, strange, or of great anecdotal value occurred during the three hundred visits I made up and down — and I mean up and down. Was this because I hustled in and out of homes like an experienced peddler who knows whether there's a sale here or not? For 7 cents a name, fellow enumerators came back with Kinsey-report-like stories of their canvassing. Some were feasted, some were shut out. An old gent who spoke no English was interviewed. His son told him that the person in the doorway was not the gas company, so as not to excite him. The old man disliked the gas company for asking such questions as "Where were you born?" In Spanish neighborhoods, asking *"Cuantos habitantes tenemos aquí?"* was greeted with grins. It seems *habitante* is slang for hipster.

Once in a while it was nice and a bit sad to find old New Yorkers who had lived in their rooms for the past thirty or forty years, and who answered the questions put to them in a proud *hidalgo* fashion. How New York had changed, they said, even in ten years. How the Italian families on the West Side in the Village who lived on the fifth floor and had television sets and enormous refrigerators, why didn't they leave the neighborhood for better living quarters elsewhere? They hadn't changed at all, except to add new curtains or living-room sets to the railroad rooms.

About the sixth day at this, the Census taker finds himself reaching zero production. He's walking up to the same door for the third time. He knows everyone by name now. He's seen them as they are in their homes, a sight seldom granted to strangers. If he refuses to let things go unfinished, he will begin to worry about Mr. George Berandowski in #2-A, who has not been home for three days and three nights now. And the happy-faced Puerto Rican children, six of them, playing partly in the hall and partly in the 9 x 12 room where they live with their sad-faced parents. And the woman's face that flushed a little when the question "married/' was asked the couple living together. Some worried citizens, afflicted with *fin du monde,* asked the enumerator questions about the government's foreign policy and this-and-that mess.

These were the people who lived in New York. God bless you, as the Irish say. It was good to be working again, and not a bad job either. You actually brought a reminder of democracy to so many, and I'll be darned if you don't feel the goodness in man yourself.

Chinese, Welcome Aboard!

Who are the big gamblers, the Greeks, the Saudis at Las Vegas's tables? No, it is the Chinese at Macao and at Atlantic City arriving daily by busloads.

Why haven't Chinese played the casinos on board cruise ships? I propose a plan to entice them away from hotels the way cruise ships did during the 50's, much to the despair and detriment of hotels in Atlantic City. By catering to Chinese culinary appetites, we can get them sailing and also rolling the dice. Here are some suggestions: 1. We contact the #1 Chinese restaurant in New York, as has been done with the French, and bring them aboard under contract. 2. We place personnel aboard to make Chinese gamblers feel welcome. 3. We offer a package cruise with rates competitive with land-based hotel accommodations. 4. We appeal to the Chinese families who would like to take cruises but up to now have not done so.

Here is a ripe market of not only prospective cruise passengers, but born gamblers who are now comfortable at the dinner table as well as the gambling table. 5. We dress casino hostesses à la Chinese fashion and add "Chinese night" to the social activities. 6. Invite Chinese West Indies Islanders aboard to gamble while in port. Add dinner and charge them. Familiarize them with cruise ships with tickets. While in port, most passengers remain ashore for the evening. This allows empty seats at dining room tables that are now available for paying guests who also enjoy visiting the ship that up to now has been restricted. 7. Invite complimentary, the staff of local Chinese consulates around the island nations for publicity. 8. Send announcements to attract Mainland Chinese communities with package tours—all included, to facilitate arrangements. 9. Put a Chinese on the concierge staff and use oriental motif décor in some cabins. 10. Steal personnel away from those Chinese cruise ships that may be or are already offering gambling, cruise, cuisine, etc., in Asian waters. 11. Cut the opposition in on the payroll for peace. There's enough for all. 12. Chinese acrobatic spectaculars are world renowned. They would attract American viewers to cruises if placed aboard. 13. Gambling revenue and profits have serious declined in Las Vegas. It's time the boys looked out to sea for their salvation by perhaps combining in a package Las Vegas and a West Indies cruise vacation for an increasingly prosperous Chinese customer. Advertise in China. In the 70's, the MGM Hotel, Pupi Campo was playing hot rhumbas while dancers swayed as though aboard ship. The clever management had installed a dance floor that mimicked a ship's dance floor, with gentle rolling and pitching. 14. Pay Chinese models to be photographed aboard cruise ship casinos playing at dice, poker or whatever game they prefer. 15. Chinese staff, i.e., waiters, cabin boys, etc., can present an evening's entertainment for the passengers, as is done on Italian liners.

Confessions of a Cruise Director

To further escape unsolicited encounters or to avoid confrontation, the Cruise Director knows his ships' secrets from top to bottom. Ships, like hotels, have passageways unknown to passengers. He can use internal stairways that go from front to back or from below to topside. He can disappear or he can emerge at will. Life in general is not so generous with such magic. As the most visible person on board, he can maneuver invisibility when so desired. His voice is heard over a loudspeaker like a Greek god who remains invisible. He sets events in motion and retires confidently, having acted routinely.

It is when he finds himself in port in an environment that belittles him, it is then that his calculated existence changes in a world that is now doubly foreign. No port is ever as spotless as his ship. Since he enables the Captain to remain aloof from the passengers' problems, he serves all concerned in the good voyage—the bon voyage.

I set up hours to suit my condition. Being in charge of the Program of Daily Activities, I was able to fashion a world to conform to my disability, my lack of hearing. Imagine a blind person living in an adapted environment that he or she had carefully constructed to enable normal function. In that manner, a handicap was overcome to a great extent.

Not only insulated from the world ashore that was thousands of miles away but also isolated in an otherwise inaudible world due to deafness, which was growing progressively worse over the years. As a prisoner who knows every inch of his cell, the abnormal suited me. A ship is a house that one knows well, similar to one's apartment, with much fewer everyday dangers like crossing the streets of a city. You know where everything is located. As Cruise Director, people follow you, your commands, and social program, not the reverse. His position is like some feudal lord's who never experiences the world the way others do. He has ready answers for familiar questions from his passengers.

His captain has the burden of assuring safety at sea. The Cruise Director has responsibility for the good cheer that people coming aboard expect, and are receptive, making his duty a foregone success.

Not only did I find a home on the ships, I found a new world of delights. Where in the world can you just walk into a bakery at 3 a.m. and eat all the pastry your heart desires? The ships' bakers were friends who welcomed me to come visit and hang out while they baked fresh bread. Where else could you play poker with the crew in the mess hall (galley) afterhours, or swim in the pool at 2 a.m., or romance at the bow like De Capprio, arms outstretched, or feel the luxury of the clean bed sheets every night with a piece of chocolate candy awaiting you? Remove all the niceties, the trimmings, and it's still a unique environment.

If he is fortunate enough to make a maiden voyage, he is devoted to that ship as in a marriage—she takes him to her bosom, sheltering him from a world that can be cruel. She cradles him as he sleeps in her fold. It is where his sustenance resides, and provides a stage for his personality, fulfillment, and needed and adventure. The ocean is boring, but with sudden surprises—he is in charge of surprising his passengers with festivities that also keep him both entertaining and entertained. He begins with "Welcome Aboard," and ends with "Drive safely!" leaving him feeling that he has done his part—the rest is up to you.

I Couldn't Have Done It With You

Along with the happenings that gave my life such fullness in terms of travel, adventure, and good humor came encounters with women of substance. One owned oil wells in Bakersfield, CA. She entertained me at the Westbury Hotel. Cici owned Food Fair, a national chain of supermarkets. She entertained me in Ambler, PA, the wealthiest part of Pennsylvania. Shirley owned the largest department store in Chester, PA. Another's father built fortifications for countries around the world. They received me on Park Avenue. Another's family built complexes in Clifton, NJ. One owned large tracts of lumber land, oil, gold mines, and an assortment of gilt-edged stocks, plus a million-dollar coin collection. Rita inherited a seat on the NY Stock Exchange, etc.

This does not include numerous foreign women, including nobility like the Hungarian princess I was engaged to, or the Brazilian coffee plantation families, whose daughters I met and almost married, or the daughter of the candidate for President of Brazil, or a member of Belgium's royal family.

All these and more, unattached ladies were ready to marry when I wasn't—I never was "ready." I was married to life itself, which meant no excess baggage.

Vacation of a Lifetime

The Cruise Director lives surrounded by customers. He is a floorwalker on constant duty. He is inescapable, and must remain so. His position out front has made him a captive, a celebrity workingman. He comes with his own world attached to him. The ship contains his workload surrounding him. When he can be alone, he finds himself shut in a cabin that is his world without people. He cannot stay within except to sleep. He eats outside whereas we eat inside. The army life is a similar existence, living among many, but reluctantly alone due to circumstances. His job requires discipline and he is the one providing it for himself. To hide for one moment destroys the reward received from his faithful approach to his duty. When the cruise is over, the next one is already upon him.

This life is show business, on duty 24/7. He is on a vacation treadmill, sharing vacations with hundreds of passengers. He is on a perpetual "vacation of a lifetime." He is transformed into a sea creature in an aquatic world. He breathes sea air and his skin is salty, as is his vocabulary, his gossip is ship happenings, and his view of the world is limited like a shut-out's. When cast-off is heard, the rope that ties him to the dock disconnects him from land and its significance.

What other occupation offers such a life? Unless on your yacht, where your captain does the steering while your workload is under your command. Your orders are obeyed while infringements are handled by others—you are immune, isolated from many consequences. Laws at sea differ from those on land similar to "What happens in Las Vegas stays in Las Vegas." The long arm of the law ends at the shoreline. Justice has to be carried back to land to be examined. The ocean's stern god is Poseidon.

Here is only one enormous power that alone speaks, acts, and rules fairly. His adjudication is supreme.

With good service in the make-believe fun world on today's stately cruise ship, life is simplified. The role of the Cruise Director goes back in history to the royal court jester responsible for the levity essential to living closer to the often trickery of reality. Desire for diversion is natural to all living things as a necessary ingredient to growth and learning. There were no youngsters playing baseball at sea until Walt Disney came along to make his ship a playground for them, just as others created commercially-oriented childish circuses for adults aboard. The Cruise Director is the ringmaster, promoter, and originator of the playful activities and social events passengers will share each day. Such power is almost divine, without being dictatorial, corrupt, or debatable. While offering bonuses, perks, and prizes, a ship has no need for so much of what on land seems essential to society's success. Commuting, for example. Sailing has created a brave new world from what was once the exclusive domain of the elite. It has given us more than floating hotels, that are becoming more like large, well-stocked new communities. Can we hope to establish their model of a more civilized living back on land? Politeness is still more evident at sea, as it once was in the air. The oceans are a new world to conquer, as well as, like outer space, our last frontier.

We can work at sea as we now can work at home, while enjoying travel, comforts, safety, entertainment in a new, healthier style, not to mention vacations. Will not need to dream of going on

A ship has no attic or basement, nor is there a need for them. The world is simplified unnoticeably onboard ship.

A Film Showing

I would like to interest you in a 45-minute film, "Cuban Music 1906 - 1960 that is available to be shown, from the Henry Medina Archives.

The presentation will include a special introduction by Vincent Livelli.

It has been shown at John Jay College, at the Smithsonian American History Museum, and at the Julia Burgos Center in Northern Manhattan.

If you are interested, please contact Vincent Livelli at (212) 255-0508, 44 Perry Street, New York, NY.

Thank you very much.

Vincent Livelli

Cuddling, the Origin of Love

As a natural experience, sleep can be made more pleasurable. Comfort is important and can be upgraded considerably. Good sleep is important and can be upgraded considerably. The familiar phrase baby bunting is applied to what a baby is swathed in. By extending this snuggling feature to adults' sleepwear, the beneficial level is increased noticeably. On cold nights, the ears, head, cheeks, and nose benefit from the warm protection that any type of bunting addition applied to adult sleepwear provides. In addition, this advancement restricts noise intrusion. Your partner sleeps better when you do as well.

By adding a hood to the pajama top with fabric other than coarse wool, warmth, protection, and better comforting, pleasurable sleep is possible. It also does away with the ludicrous nightcap.

Women require cuddling more than men since they understand it on a much deeper level than men do. Cuddled in their mothers' arms as newborns, they would never more in their entire lifetimes feel that at comfort, warmth, or protection—a man's "protection" cannot match the mother's love. Men are puzzled by a woman's need to be cuddled as they age. The closest one can get to the warmth, comfort, security, and feeling of being loved is while snuggled in a proper bunting for an adult. The nearest a woman of advanced age can feel what the bunting offers is a reversed full-length coat. Not only sleep can be made more enhanced, but as a replacement for the missing mother's love it can be psychologically stabilizing, especially for insomniacs and the depressed.

As a result of simple stimulation, the orgasm belongs to all. It is not solely the product of gender. In lesbianism, the "butch" element provides the protective cuddling ingredient. The "butch" is instinctively knowledgeable in this regard, whereas the average male's instinct is directed toward "on guard" for dangers. Pretended cuddling is quite easily evident to a female, whereas faux female orgasm is not, to the male.

Since dancing is a form of cuddling in motion, women respond to, and desire most, a strong leader. Dancing is continuous seduction in an embrace within a musical cocoon. Physical contact and gestures preceded "I love you," an overused refrain. Congeniality found in cuddling is a simpler solution to marriage problems.

Compare cuddling on a goose-feather mattress after a warm bath or a gentle massage. Rarely is it unwelcome as repetitious as sex can be. To cuddle pre-, during, or post sex climax is what women will always want, whether awake or asleep. Practicality engenders motivation. If a female is ejected, her survival is jeopardized. This is perhaps why the female insists on foreplay, assurance, specifically exhibited in the need to be cuddled.

Contrarily, the male viewed cuddling as dawdling, as unnecessary interference with his readiness for emergencies in a primitive hostile world. Cuddling is akin to a fetal position that includes a second (male) individual unnaturally. It is a major human experience in a deeply committed manner. It can be seen as a primeval female response, not to loneliness, but to a need for safety. It has an element of unmanly cowardice, like cringing in a foxhole in the male's psyche. Snuggling and cuddling are for infants, but when love falters it is cuddling that is required to convincingly restore its stature. The tighter the hug, the deeper the reassurance. When bound in silence, it is a primitive form of communication that predates the invention of language.

Like a poetic construction, it builds a nest in each partner's life beyond the physical man-made nestling abode. Altruistic sacrifice engendered tolerance under makeshift insecure housing. A companion to face mutual perils together, making life safer and simpler, once shelter in the form of a roof over one's head and an element of caring arose, love was born from shared bodily warming.

Cultural Circularity

As I write, the Sextets Nacional is playing, Echale salsita and *el son es el más sublime para*…right here in New York. Ignacio Piñero was a contemporary of the 1930's most popular band leader, Paul Whiteman, who was billed as the "King of Jazz." Naturally, black musicians rightfully protested Whiteman's gratuitous label. B.B. King was *their* king. Whiteman, we believe, also influenced Ignacio when he introduced the phrase, "Get hot!" and "Hot stuff!" The salsita connection is evident and was also popular with black jazz musicians as well. Latin composers contributed *calientico*, a popular rumba at that time, and spiced up tunes.

When African-rooted jazz musicians began to hear Miguelito's (later, Celia singing El Quimbo), Yoruba authentic ritual incantations, such as Bruja Manigua and Babalú, Arsenio's *Sabroso and Caliente*, wild *bembes lucumies* and Chano, they tried to adopt these odd-sounding chants, and ended up with Heidi Heidi Ho, Cubop, Bebop, Rumba Boogie and what-not. La-di-o-de is a sacred invocation. Latino musicians did not protest what could have been called an insult to their patrimony.

Music is aria made sonorous, and humans will produce it as part of our seventh sense. This seventh sense—of rhythm—resides in our brains in company with our other senses, including our sense of balance, located not in our feet but in our ears.

It doesn't matter who influences whom, but to the struggling Barrio musician it…matters. Last year, Willie Colon, playing New Year's Eve at Posto Restaurant in the meat-packing district, was able to advertise $850.00 per person for admission—Sold out! Musicians can never be paid enough. Let's remember, it was music that helped bring us out of the Great Depression, not the bankers. We sang "Happy Days are Here Again" throughout the country and the musicians were our pied pipers.

Speaking of mimicking, in the dance world the twist was an explosive effort and sad excuse to deride, willfully or not, the hip movements of the rumba—humorously. Anglos had uptight social attitudes that were made acceptable under the cloak of comedy or minstrels. The playful twist became the forerunner of Elvis's Rock & Roll show, with roots in the South. If the twist had gone north and on into mambo instead, imagine what our culture would have become! Elvis never learned salsa, and if he had, I'm sure our colleges would have less trouble teaching Spanish, for one thing. I've heard many bad rock & roll bands but never a bad *conjunto*. Are the hundreds of pop and rock groups trying to reach the heights of *salseros*? African drums have saved many Latin-jazz performances, but can we please get rid of those big, fake conga-prop drums on the Jay Leno Show? Why don't we hear a term called Afro-jazz? Who can dance salsa wearing a Mexican sombrero, and how many of us can dance a "Dancing With the Stars" salsa? But salsa is not the end of the line. We can envision our tastes going from rumba to mambo and from salsa back to Mother Africa, where tribal dances are being revitalized by Western influences, such as mambo and salsa.P.S. Webster's Dictionary claims that rock & roll "derived from rhythm & blues." I say the twist.

Dining Afloat, Ashore and Abroad

Dining aboard a cruise ship while sailing under a foreign flag, passengers have the choice of many different cuisines. It can be said that they eat abroad without leaving home.

The epicurean menus of QM2 offer cheeseburgers and milkshakes, making us feel a 1992 menu of the Royal Viking Sun listed "Herring housewife style." In 1936, the typical luncheon of the S.S. Munargo of munson Lines offered "mixed finnan haddie canapé, chow chow, noodles natural, corned spareribs, pickled lambs' tongue and Postum." The plush British P & O Line's entrées, called "hot dishes," showed a full selection of lamb bérgère, larded hazel hen, tournadoes of beef charon, parmesan soufflé, but under dessert, pears, bananas, tangerines, figs, and assorted nuts. Fruit, especially "black house grapes," as well as vegetables like asparagus were luxuries. Before refrigeration in the thirties, the elegant P & O Liner S.S. Strathaird boasted "celery au jus." In the fifties, the Yarmouth Castle showed "Potatoes au natural" while sailing to Nassau.

On 38-day cruises from New York, the top chefs of the S.S. Brazil, S.S. Argentina and S.S. Uruguay were obliged to produce meals that satisfied the palatal demands of passengers according to their countries, as well as those of the Americans aboard. For example, the European-oriented Argentinians would pass up carujá, mungusá, vatapá, feijuada lomo or lomillo. It had to be bífe de lomo or lomillo. All waiters on these cruises wore white gloves. A bigger challenge during long voyages from Syndey to Southampton faced the chefs of the Dutch World Services. Meals aboard the S.A. Oranje, the Willem Ruys and the M.S. Johann Van Oldenbarnevelt because unbearably predictable, with dessert being cornstarch pudding, nor could the wines travel well under the motion of the long voyage. One passenger called it prison fare.

When in 1956 Alaska became a state, the pastry chefs of the M.S. Oslofjord produced a gigantic baked Alaska for the Americans aboard that was carried flaming into the restaurant by four waiters. That envied "place d'honneur," the captain's table, with pre-dinner cocktails in his off-limits quarters followed by "the descent" to the dining room via the grand staircase, the gifts for the ladies hidden under their napkins, the best champagne, the finest damask, was a true feast, "*ab ovo usque ad mala*, from soup to nuts. *Post cibum* (after dinner), brandy was served in the men's smoking room, separate from the ladies' room, as it was known in the thirties. The floor shows that followed were never as spectacular as they are today, but were well received after such a "régal de dîner."

In the old days of very heavy feasting (that is still the case today), the S.S. Belgianland boasted "8 tons of creamery butter" on its world cruise. The Norwegian Line now uses asterisks to indicate items "approved by the American Heart Association."

The chief steward often organized upon request "little dinner parties" served apart from the ship's restaurant, either in your large suite or in an alcove. While special occasions called for such affairs, the farewell 'til we meet again themes were nostalgic happenings with signed menus and exchanged addresses for fellow shipmates and table mates. One party aboard the M.S. Eastern Prince of the Furness Line ended with the highly spirited hostess tossing two remaining unopened bottles of Dom Perignon high out over the dark ocean. "For the fish," she yelled. This was in 1934 at six dollars a bottle.

Dining abroad in Europe during the seventies was not trop cher. Thankfully, the French franc gave ten to one or more at one point. Some of us knew where it was sixteen to one! With this windfall we made "La Grande Tour Gastronomique," beginning at Nice, at Moulinde Mougins and continuing with Lyon (Paul Bocuse), Roanne (Les Frères Trois Gros), Tours (Barrier), Viene (Madame Point's "Résidence de la Pyamide") among others, in Provence, L'Osteau de Beaumanière. During several trips to Paris we were fortunate to experience dinners at the following:

Taillevent; Maxim's, La Tour D'Argent; Le Bristol; Le Relais de Louis XIII; Le Train Bleu; Le Fregate; Le Closerie des Lilas; Le Coup de Fusil; Le Boeuf a la Toit; Le Voltaire; Le Presbourg; L'Orangerie; L'Archistrate; L'ami Louis; L'Ile Saint-Louis; La Petite Chaise; Le Bardo; Le Montagnard; Le Doyen; Le Vernet; Le Berthoud; Les Deux Magots; Le Relais Boëtie; Le Royal; Le Petit Bistro: Le Petit Brouant; Berri-Washington; Le Copper; La Quetsch; La Perouse; La Mere Bresson; Laserre; La Rose de Sable; La Bonne Fourchette; La Coupole; L'Hermitage; Laurant; Leval d'Isere; Marius et Janette; Raffatin et Honorine; Royal Monceau; Chez Les Anges; Chez Jacky; Chez Barbe; Chez Bebart; Chez Edgard; Chez Denis; D'Chez Eux; Du Coq Hardi; Au Petit Montmorency; Prunier; Vivaroi; Lido; Louvre des Antiquaires; Les Jardins St-Germain; Atelier Maitre Albert; Royal Monceau; Relais Plaza; Sheherezade; Copenhague; Fouquet; Olivier; Maison Normande; Mme Arthur; La Mamiine; Androuette; Rita Dimitri; Guy-Pierre Baumann; Sherwood; Elysees Matignon; Le Warwick; Scossa; Elle et Lui; Alcazar; Monte Cristo; "Ile de France"; Cafe Procope; Les Muses; Chez Garin....

Back home in 1994, Brigitte Catapano, the owner of Chez Brigitte, a "tiny French bistro" at 77 Greenwich Avenue, retired to Florida, leaving her assistant, Madame Rosa Santos, to carry on. Chez Brigitte survived for fifty years, from 1958 until June 5, 2008.

With no tables, back-to-back counters and elbow-to-elbow swivel stools, this closet-sized eatery seated eleven. You were eating "en famille" at prices that changed little over the years. Tasty French bread, oil and vinegar, a grated cheese dispenser at your seat began a dinner for $9.00 that included boeuf Bourguignon in red wine sauce, roasted potatoes, carrots, sweet peas, or macaroni salad. The pois cassés split pea soup with onions and croutons was a classic. In 1 982, entrees began at $6.50.

Surrounded by giants like the nearby Waverly Inn, Morandi, San Ambroseus and Brusselles, Originally from Marseilles, Chez Brigitte was one tough cookie. In a tough racket, she was in a class of her own. The last owner, Mr. Jose M. Lito, from Asturias, took a loss after having remodeled the "tiny bistro," but it was the Villagers who were fed there over the years and the Village itself that share his loss as well.

The following are some Village restaurants that we have lost:Osteria del Sole; Ye Waverly Inn; Sazarac House; Fez (Time Cafe); Caffé Cefalú; Cafe Latino; Casablanca; Club Gaucho; Markt; Lotfi; Sabor; Turkish Grill; Figaro; O'Henry; Mori; Formerly Joe's; Bill Bertolotti; Louie's; Nick's; George's; Ann M. Miller's; Top-of-the-Gate; Dan Stampfler's; Bianchi and Margarita; The Brevoort; Mexico; Le Bijou; Beau Village; La Metairie; Petite Abeille; Lombardi; Night Gallery; Mr. Black; Delancey's Steak House; One Fifth Avenue; Tiffany; Cedar Tavern; Kettle of Fish (MacDougal); Joe's Luncheonette — San Remo.

San Remo, like Chez Brigitte, lasted for fifty years. Unlike Mr. Lito, who surrendered to hiked rent, the Santini Brothers sold the San Remo for a huge profit. The "Remo" and Chez Brigitte deserve plaques. Neither had photos on the wall, like Minetta Tavern's prize-fight gallery. But if the Remo had, the photos would have shown a collection of all-star literati. The nightly attractions were brilliant arguments about culture, the counter-culture and the counter-counter-cultures as postwar influences arose.

A snapshot of the customers at the Remo would find in the mid-forties: Anatole Broyard (*Kafka was the Rage*), William Gaddis (*The Recognitions*), Milton Klonsky (*Blake's Dante*), Anaïs Ninn (*Ladders of Fire*), Maya Deren (avant-garde filmmaker),

Sheri Martinelli (who shared her various talents with Broyard, Gaddis, Bukowski, Ezra Pound, and others). They quoted the likes of Henry Michaux (*A Barbarian in Asia*), or maybe the three versions of *Lady Chatterley's Lover*. The Remo's ghosts of temps perdus have vaporized into what today is an Asian eating place.

Pabulum (food, in Latin) is the first taste of life at the breast. Bitter or sweet, raw life is refined with our reasoning and our seasoning. Perhaps the concept of a soul arose from the smell of cooking as it floated invisibly, seductively, attaching itself to us. The redolent scent in the closet of your lover's perfume, like a second presence or the organic comfort from warm food with a taste that lingers.

To handle a menu or wine list with finesse shows us a traveler who has tasted and known well a world he respects. The French celebrate culinary creativity, as do the Chinese. But there is a dark side to all this. Aside from plating, price service, etc., there is obesity, butchery, swinish gluttony, messes, burns, waste, not to mention blood Jell-o, snobbery that talks about the rusticity of the Peruvian purple potato, for example.

Where we once hunted for sustenance on dangerous missions, food is today brought to us upon command. Where we once poured a libation on the ground for the gods, we can now overindulge in an otherwise raw world. Come eat, for the ice-carved centerpiece drips tears as its fragile beauty washes away before our eyes. What finer garden is there than the marketplace that displays nature's fertility and fragrant harvest. The bedtime snack pacifier finalizes our day like a good-night kiss. Where a cruise ship can be called a "floating bedroom," the cozy "table in the corner" leads us traditionally to encores of ever more satisfying desserts.

Our restaurants are the candles glowing in the windows of our neighborhoods after dark. Like local parishes for our spiritual needs, they replenish an organic emptiness. They are a second-removed family kitchen. Grandpa's chair sits empty at the head of the table after he is gone. Where we begin with bowed heads, we can end with toasts. When à la table, we are as though around a tribal campfire. Who remembers the soda fountain at Bigelow's? As restaurants go, so do neighborhoods. As for dining afloat, eat first or fly empty.

Doppelganger: Discovering Our Alter Ego

"There are two of you!" said the palmist. "You may have had a twin who was never born. Your energy comes from a combination of two beings that are both present at any given time. That has something to do with normal life and death and weather missing other, the twin, is involved. This is a case of two-in-one --unnatural, often found in the shape of other living organisms. Is it perhaps a new human being of an ancient or future species?

Our future brain will become so overloaded with facts that we will be unable to eradicate the useless facts. Twins will be needed and conceived where only one will assume a life form, while the brain remaining will function as two. The customary life we know now can be rearranged if we so wish, or contrarily, it basically can continue unchanged but radically and substantially improved. The saying "Two heads are better than one" can characterize the ability of humans to handle the growing complexity of the future world. Furthermore, computers will share our private lives like blood brothers, like "family." They give us advice, protection, and inspiration. We are all one coin with two sides now that we have become conscious of a form of intelligence that exists in a storage outside ourselves. It has been there all along—we called it luck, destiny, fate, but it is more natural and present in everything we experience. Call it matter and anti-matter combined in one individual's body—the palmist read the signs correctly.

Is there a companion spirit? I had gone to her for answers, and now I see that she is gazing at me, looking for an answer. The feeling that I was not alone throughout my life was confirmed—it was in my hands, and the proof was in double-life lines, double every line on both hands since my birth. "You are two-in-one," said the palm reader.

Further proof was needed. I wasn't twice as intelligent, strong physically, or gifted with any exceptional quality. What was now explainable, however, were the many incidents that involved a second presence in my life that kept me safe when everything that happened should have normally found me injured physically, involved against my best interests, or helpless to beat the odds that statistically rule society.

At age 91, for example, one does not enter the hospital and come home the following day. Nor does one inexplicably miss being killed by a wildly-driven car by mere inches. Or one who is normally exposed to the ever-present temptations in life that often condemn one to either commit offenses or indulge in harmful practices such as hard drugs.

But a big brother influence at your side cannot caution, protect or control self-sabotage. It is this stubborn, mysterious quality that we are helpless. There's even a stronger force at work. It is a force that affects the "two" of you simultaneously, called "your time is up." Happiness and peace are interdependent.

Self-sabotage is the opposite of what keeps an individual from committing suicide. The main determinant that affects our lives is Time, in that it determines aging and death itself, and not luck. Another is controlled by common sense. The word common means more than *one* brain, applicable and possessed by everyone, like Time itself. The difference is in ratio of *one* to the other or the proportions involved. Time is constantly consuming itself, while common sense is continually extending survival, not God. These two influences determine longevity.

We should better pray to our twin since an invisible twin is our "guardian angel," whether we are deserving or not. Perhaps also we can give the additional brain power the ability to enable us to produce greater computer miracles, thus allowing us to change the world and allow us to reach out and communicate with other worlds!

Obviously we will always lack sufficient intelligence to secure a peaceful world for all, but this very shortcoming on our part is what encourages us to seek solutions such as multiple brain coordination—the more the merrier.

As a former cruise director, merriment is primary in an ideal future world. Peace alone is boring—perpetual happiness plus philosophy should be the nirvana mankind seeks. Why not?

Can we inject brain food such as fish oil into the area surrounding our fetal brain, thus bypassing its developmental dependence on the mother's diet? Can we remove some of the skull area that will allow the growing brain more space in which to expand? A longer postponed gestation period may be found to permit an increased rate of growth for a larger brain. The portion of the brain that affects memory is greatly enhanced by a larger area—size may matter in this region, even if the overall size of the brain itself does not increase intelligence one way or the other.

China and Russia, with less restrictions on ethics, I fear, will succeed before we begin—thus, it is not only economics but also, more importantly perhaps, human-adjusted intelligence that will dominate the future world's direction. "Relationships are the most important factors in life" is a wise statement that should be better circulated.

Crossword puzzles stimulate memories that one already has encountered in life. What is needed is stimulation that produces deeper, more intelligent thinking—we must look to revive not only past lost memories, but to manufacture supplies of bright future ones. We learn from past mistakes, but it is wiser to try to make fewer mistakes in the future, with or without crossword puzzles, which take forever to produce results, and are often abandoned through frustration.

Perhaps what we call ghosts are our second selves that may or may not survive after we are dead. Not everyone's soul survives, or the world would be "alive" with them. One bullet might pass through both the individual and his/her companion spirit—it might miss one or the other—or hit both. A companion spirit that survives does so by becoming a corporeal presence. Ghosts are survivors of our second self. Not everyone has a second self, due to conditions of the birth process. The *Mayan*s believe that the second self of animals could enter and live in humans, i.e., the jaguar king, or they could combine in other animals, i.e., the serpent/bird, quetstqual.

Can we live forever? Longevity is in the DNA and can be identified eventually. It consists of something duplicated or multiplied that adds strength to the whole. Aside from luck, which is the biggest determinant of longevity, an extra gene, like a mutation that adds extra height to an individual, for example, or adds resistance to illness in later years—in older individuals.

Once we identify people with this characteristic DNA, we can remove this DNA from cadavers and inject it into other genomes, as recipients demands. An additional or duplicate gene will fortify the entire genome chart—not just separate illness-prone DNA's.

Longevity is an aberration, a fortunate error—a hit-and-miss, once-in-a-lifetime blessed event that can be injected like sperm into an egg that is thus fertilized and created artificially. Man will thus have the power of the Creator. Three DNA's injected can produce three long

There's a little in every woman not one hundred percent true. Could this feeling be a result of an unborn female in a male? Where else does the feeling come from if not the spirit of an unborn twin, and vice versa? Two hearts beating as one in the womb still continue, even as the other being is gone. This other being is now called the soul. The soul is present as a "feeling"—an influence that is invisible but present. When activated, ask any gambler who is "on the run" if it is he or an outer force influencing the throw of the dice. Or a "miraculous" survivor of an accident. How he survived it is often by inches—a measurement that involves closeness, as in the womb. The dead twin is still alive in another proximity.

What activates the influence of the "other?" It is the combination of the two influences that conjoin astrologically with greater force. The influence is out of our hands or control that explains why we have been unable to determine our fates—your fate is decided for you, as it is for the world in general.

If it is the same electricity that flashes in the sky that sparks our hearts' beat, then we can assume that what is outside of us is also at work inside of us. The soul has not "departed." It beats along with every other universal consciousness.

As our twin is invisible, it is still more personal, and in that way it is different from all other living beings, but still part of the whole. Personal includes the ever-present influence of your twin—a twin "you" unlike any other person. We are all unique for this reason, thank goodness, when actually we should really all be identical, like computer chips. What was now explainable, however, were the many incidents that involved a second presence in my life that kept me safe when everything that happened should have otherwise gone against me.

Perhaps one day our scientists will achieve with determination a mastery of creation that will produce an embryo containing two fetuses—with one as a "backup" for the other . . . an amplified creature in every way. Carry it further to where, way in the future, that one embryo is now the receptacle of three or four or more brains in the single individual.

This is the secret of superior intelligence, just as it is more horsepower in advanced motors . . . . multiplicity. Our current ten-pound brains are overloaded, hemmed in , so to speak. They need release from confinement. Since we cannot increase the size, we can increase the activity, as we have with computers that we actually reduced in size.

The Drums Have Spoken

What would Arsenio Cachao or Lecuona think of today's Latin/Jazz? Would they be welcoming the growing global phenomenon of *la musica*, while at the same time supporting the jazz contribution that distributed it worldwide?

Ever protective of Afro-cubanidad, Arsenio cried, " Ese Maldito Mambo!" According to Bohemia magazine in 1952, Cachao was slow to embrace Latin/jazz, and I doubt Lecuona would have. But times and tastes change us all…"I once was blind…." Gone is my Latin/jazz criticism. Discarded is my fear of any calamitous consequences supposedly involved in the merger of Latin/jazz. Perhaps I lacked the secret teaching, the "disciplina arcane" essential for such an unpopular undertaking's success. All music is musica sacra.

It is commercial materialistic greed that befouls all. The drums have spoken, and I have taken this proper moment that ancient Romans called *punctum temporis*, to surrender to better sense. Las dos alas de Latin/jazz make better bedfellows than my malingering, my belittling of the evident advantage of a union that benefits both houses like a royal marriage.

But all this does not change my duty. I was assigned a mission back in Regla in 1941 to promote and protect Afro-Cuban music around the world. One can become popular by becoming unpopular. But, as Charles Baudelaire (paraphrased) said, "Latin ou jazz, qu'importe?" (Good or bad). The ardent masses on our dance floors prove it. This music, within itself, dispels counterproductive differences that tend to exist among mankind naturally. Viva *la musica*!

Situating El Barrio

During the 40's, with better times, the old Park Plaza could afford to attract Noro Morales and Machito. The management of the Park Plaza became obliged, albeit a bit reluctantly, to improve its appearance since it meant expenditures. The superior upper floor, called the Park Palace, was well maintained with a highly polished dance floor and well-washed large front windows with views of the beautiful seRené lake in Central Park North. The old Park Plaza had no windows except in the basement. "Its dance floor had dust that arose from neglected corners where dirt had been swept. With its clapboard appearance, in spite of new chairs replacing rickety leftovers on their last legs, and that infamous fixture, the electric fan, the Park Plaza remained the sentimental locale, since it still had a quality that resembled the island dance environments where folks danced on dusty, unpaved sand lots or bare earthen floors, to satisfy their inborn craving to dance, and where they were known to dance with no overhead protection from the elements. Often, only the moon provided lighting and greater protection and encouragement for intimacy. Today's unwholesome discothèques are a far cry from a simpler environment under the stars.

Fearful of Great Depression Harlem, it appeared for a while that New York's new Latin community would come together in safer Chelsea, much as Chinatown sought safety for itself around St. John's Church in Little Italy. Especially since Sicilian families had found safe turf in the shelter of Cecelia's Catholic Church at 225 East 105th Street. Today, it is, together with East 116th Street, the nucleus of El Barrio. Furthermore, even though relations arriving from Cuba, Mexico, and Puerto Rico shared beds and space, rents rose as they were also rising with returning World War II veterans' new families in the West Village, giving rise to the East Village.

Like Chelsea, Borough Hall, Brooklyn for a while appeared to become Latinized, since steamship companies serving the US came from Mexican ports, mainly Vera Cruz. The Italian maritime agencies, like Lloyd Triestino, Lloyd Sabauda Cosolich Line and the Orient Line influenced the local Latin settlers, but not as greatly as Chelsea's Hudson Riverfront, with its European steamship traffic.

The Park Plaza supplying magnetic music of the islands served to attract the greater number of immigrants. What the powerful beauty of Mariachi could not with rancheros accomplish in Borough Hall, the Park Plaza on North 110th Street would, with the rumba of the Hardy Boys.

Eléctrico

Eléctrico's flashy movements were spasmodic, with elongated limbs, a combination of synchronization and syncopation and abrupt *quebradas*. His rumba, known as Columbia—unlike the two other basic styles of rumba, the *Yambu* and the *Guaracha*—was unknown to most of the crowd present, as was the elegant styles of the René and Estella routine that featured the *tornillo*. The difference between Eléctrico's performance and René's was the spontaneity that Eléctrico offered versus the rehearsed routine act that René handled. Both dancers made the audience proud to identify themselves with a culture that could produce such spectacular accomplishment.

We would go to the Park Plaza, hoping Eléctrico would be there. You not only went to enjoy the dance but to hear the latest news and the music and to perhaps catch the workmanship of Eléctrico on the floor—all for $.25! You were involved in dancing, listening to and viewing—and perhaps finding a new rapturous love. What Broadway show can rival that package, or clubs at Riverboat, Underground, 4D, Cheetah? During the 30s, no one in New York, or in the U.S. for that matter, showed obesity; on the contrary, people were thin as rails. Eléctrico was a string bean but trim, whereas René was older. When I met him in '39, he was not as he is shown in the film. He was in the grip of consumption (pneumonia beginning). Sunken chest and emaciated, he was visibly a sick man, so that when I saw him run after a Latina who had passed by us, looking back at him the way men look back at women that pass by, I was amazed at the speed he demonstrated as he ran down 110th Street after her. As I stood watching them walk off together, I wondered how Estella got home alone. I also felt that René had been stolen from me as well.

As Eléctrico gradually became aware of his ability to wow the crowd, he really took off—he realized his uniqueness and his natural ability. He extended himself. He may have done something on the dance floor that he would never be able to repeat. A dancer like Eléctrico comes along once in a generation, and that can be said about René as well. Who has ever come along to match them? To be inspired by them, yes, but to outshine them or rival or equal them, no, to my knowledge. The same goes for people like Charlie, Dizzy, the Duke, Elvis, perhaps, and among stars like Marilyn Monroe, Rita Hayworth, or Celia, Olga, Ruth Fernandez, Miguelito or Arsenio, Mealo, Cordijo. There are fewer among dancers. You had many, many actors, athletes, race-car drivers, golfers, but who can name (other than in ballet), popular dance stars? Cuban Pete, Killer Joe, Augie and Menzo, Pete Terrace and Elita: these should and will someday be much better known by the Latin-dance-loving public.

An Enjoyable Life

Four words describe my life: carrousel, cabaret, circus, carnival—and one more can be added—circumnavigation. Like a non-stop merry-go-round, my voyages on ships carried me around the globe. The entertainment I installed on them turned cruising into a cabaret that prior to that did not exist on the oceans. With so many nationalities and personalities and diverse languages involved in the performance of my duties as cruise director, a circus could describe my working day. Visiting places during celebrations and national holidays worldwide presented me with a carnival-like environment and a gay impression of the world. My life was a selective experience bringing me to events at special moments in history, leaving me with the feeling that it was all prearranged and not of my doing.

None of this could possibly have happened unless by good luck or by good timing. To sustain such an unlikely lifestyle required an ability that I did not possess. Success basically requires everything from focus to prayer, plus talents of unique design.

Because of an impairment, I overcame the lack of natural ability. In spite of severe deafness, I learned to speak five languages that proved to be my entrée into show business. No one else in the comedic genre was using errors committed in front of foreign audiences for laughter. This unique backdoor presentation could have sounded demeaning or insulting to such an audience, but humor overcame sensibility. For example, "Take a rest" in English is "Rest in peace" in foreign languages. Reciting their poetry to foreigners in their own language also helped as flattery.

On the other hand, mistakes that foreigners commit in English amuse American audiences. To tell foreigners jokes borrowed from their respective colloquialisms forges closeness.

Cruise ships carrying multiple nationalities onboard had difficulty hiring such personnel to entertain a mixtured audience that would otherwise have been left in the dark. When not onstage, the cruise director served as an interpreter and translator when needed. This interchange often involved humorous errors. Such an environment in a confined ship's world leads to a lifestyle that incorporates the four words above, to which I might add celebrity, as in celebration of life.

An Experiment in Euthenics
(Improving the Human Species by Reforming the Atmosphere)

(Caution: As a far-fetched fantasy based on a speculative fanciful premise, this writing touches sensitive preconceptions. It lacks credibility and may well end in erroneous conclusions.)

Nitrous oxide (N20) or "laughing gas" can improve human behavior once the dosage has been clinically certified as acceptable. If our global society is a dysfunctional family of nations, a basic revision of our approach to rehabilitation is needed.

President Obama has said, "Replace mean rhetoric with niceness and civility." Mankind in general has an inborn wish to conform, but less so to be compatible or compromising. "Come together and work together," he added. Beyond being more aware spiritually, perhaps we need to entirely reconsider reconditioning the very air we breathe. During the 1700s English nobility (as well as today's drug culturists) had known, but erroneously recognized, nitrous oxide for amusement only. They did not foresee it as a blessed remedy to help form a peaceable community of mankind. They called it "ether follies." In our urgent search for solutions to our health, as well as our historical outlook, we may be mishandling, or worse, ignoring, remedial criteria that may exist in a clinically adjusted atmosphere. Especially involved is a narcotic pollutant chemical, N20, element of nature which when given sufficient consideration can be found to be what Hurley, Freud, Timothy Leary, and Bernard Shaw had failed to find. Buried in scientific literature we find, "It is well established that nitrous oxide is the mainly naturally occurring regulation of atmospheric ozone. Under certain conditions, it does not have any psycho-motor effect." This means that it definitely has the potential to harmlessly and enormously benefit humanity. We can breathe normally while lowering the barriers that hamper our cheerfulness and our overall global compatibility.

Keeping in mind that the words *dosage* and *usage* are the keys to practicality and serious consideration, let us examine side effects of N20. Keep in mind also that these negatives are present more or less in all drugs: Disorientation (spatial and temporal); throbbing or pulsating auditory hallucinations; visual hallucinations; fixated vision; lowered vocal itch; increased pain threshold; tripping falling; frost bite; paranoia; tunnel vision; stuporousness; Vitamin B12 interference; folic acid interference; nausea; deeper mental connections.

Unlike all narcotics that involve greater progressive usage and dosage, reversely, N20 requires less and less amounts to sustain satisfaction. The individual does not risk over dosage, especially when science discovers the clinical formulation of safer inhalation. Nitrous oxide has saved lives, has revolutionized dentistry, has eliminated painful cortisol produced by stress during pregnancy (It may deliver happier babies).

How petty are all the negative side effects in view of the possible solution to our fearsome future? "There is nothing more important than human relationships," says a TV commercial. "Speak to each in a way that heals," say President Obama. "Man creates his own destiny," said Sir Isaac Newton. Then let us do so in a better fashion! Once successfully reformulated to reshape global ethos, we may learn how to live in peace without the need for artificial injection of N20 into the atmosphere. We may also be able to forego drugs that are poison altogether, replacing them with a friendlier, more cheerful chemical pollutant. As for greenhouse gas, when studied with more advanced science, N20 may reverse its effects while cleansing air quality daily. Instead of destroying the infrastructure that produces the noxious carbonized air, we should use it to introduce N20 into the air we breathe. Our atmosphere is seventy-nine percent nitrogen and twenty-one percent oxygen. This seems to be an uncomfortable formula that at one time in history was perhaps disrupted by a cosmic influence…but which can be rectified today.

Unlike fire, earth, or water, our air is invisible in its natural state, omnipresent and omnipotent…these are divine qualities. It may not be in front of your eyes but it's under your nose. Laboratory mice reject cocaine in favor of N20. Can humans do so as well?

We must think again like breaking a bone to reset it properly in order to reformulate our approach, for example, to cancer. Who would believe that the clear air that follows the rain is actually ionized air "that causes depression," according to the British Journal of Medicine. Homesick sailors and sea captains have high rates of suicide. Who would think that ecstasy pills could also prevent suicide, that the dangerous alkali substance called lye could help sanitize the world, or that venom can be anti-venom-like vaccines? Pollutants like kerosene and whale oil lit the darkness for ages. Fire contaminates but can be employed beneficially, even with its very dangerous explosiveness. Would you believe that nitrous oxide could be the unsung detergent that clears away dark thoughts, replacing them with a cheerful approach to life?

Neither criminalization nor legalization of harmful narcotics works. Six thousand a day are new pot smokers. Drugs keep Muslim nations sedated with stagnant economies just now rebelling. Don't let it happen here. Think not of yourself but of your country.

The gun is called the great equalizer. N20 could be called the great equalizer as well. Japan and Germany, with less inequality in their societies, have fewer social problems. The same is not true everywhere, in spite of Peace Week, accident forgiveness insurance, the civility caucus, various medications and *no lo contendere*.

Our brains seek novelty. Neuroplasticity uses repetitive thoughts and actions to carve restorative pathways to amend problem areas of the brain. Breathing is all repetitive with natural discipline. Much of living is a spiritual quest. The soul of humanity seems sad and in need of humor to make the difference between competition and cooperation. Gases determine to a large extent human behavior, giving meaning and purpose to our lives. History is akin to a fractured motor that repeats itself. We can postulate that beings on other planets also react to aerodynamic gaseous environments. It would be folly to disallow the potential benefits of nitrous oxide's role in replacing the bad drug cultures and the menacing militaristic tendencies passed on from one generation to the next.

Four-fifths of the air we breathe consists of nitrogen. By employing a vaporizer-dehumidifier in our bedrooms, we can distribute molecules of nitrous oxide. This can sweeten our dreams and awaken us in good humor. It can also be released in to the general environment.

We often admire the carefree dog. Let us use them examples of happier entities. With no need to understand life, they carouse in it with a playful approach. Perhaps, thanks to their very advanced sense of smell that contains many nitrate oxide receptors, they are concerned more with nourishment, while at the same time showing great affection. They breathe the same air as we do, but is their olfactory supremacy what makes them cheerful, seemingly optimistic? Perhaps a chemical imbalance of nitrous oxide affects us to where we behave badly compared to dogs. Do we fuss too much over divorce and marriage when it is congeniality that allows getting along with others? African cultures prefer a cool behavior, a more mellow ethos. Like us, some dogs are mean-spirited when very hungry. With selective breeding, we can uncover the effects of nitrous oxide on the pituitary glands of dogs and at the same time learn us some new tricks.

We use artificial stimulation like candles, perfume, air fresheners, music, and soft lights to achieve a genial social climate, with no guarantee of success. Half of those people cured of depression or anxiety become depressed again in five years. We are today at the level of sniffing glue. Compared to other cultures, we are like college freshmen. The Muslims smoke hashish after dinner, leaving the table to relax in a special setting after the children are excused. Victorians used a smoking room or took brandy or coffee or a toke in a "Turkish corner."

Contrast New Orleans rowdy behavior with its Mardi Gras and the more orderly conduct of other carnivals. The Arabs use pot wisely with the purpose of improving performance. After breakfast, they assemble with friends to prepare for the tasks ahead during their workday. They play by established propriety. Cheaper nitrous oxide can replace expensive, medically-effective cannabis.

What a powerful factor gas is in history! In the Sistine Chapel, Michelangelo painted Sybil, a Parthian priestess just over the figure of Man outreaching to God. From the Big Bang to rocketry, even the fate of Japan is "up in the air."

We are living in the Age of Aquarius, "ruler of the collective mind and universal consciousness. It rules the air that links us all as one body, one kingdom of nature. Through the communicative inventions of modern science we bring ourselves into the consciousness of ourselves as one Global Community," quoting astrologer Alan Oken. "There will definitely be changes in lifestyles. The social media bring us together like never before, for better or worse. We are exposed to the collective paradigm to which we are all living. This represents the incoming energies of this new cosmic era in terms of the fusion of personality and the soul of humanity."

"Fly the flag of Islam over all nations," say the patient Fundamentalists. We say, Raise the banner of scientifically upgraded atmosphere's global influence for peace and harmony. In so doing, we pacify our opponents without warfare. While definite confirmation of this very bewitching speculation's success awaits technological advancement, we can experiment with a micro laughing-gas environment: the object, to see if good humor, compassion, and congeniality can improve diplomatic results. Native Americans used a "pipe of peace" during negotiation. We can invite Israelis and Palestinians to a meeting where the air has been modified to provide a dispassionate atmosphere. As a calmative drug, N20 may achieve agreements that eventually pave the way to where we learn how to compromise without N20. Civilized society needs the helping of hand of N20, rather than a photo-session handshake.

Before continuing to think of establishing colonies on the Moon or wherever, we must perfect human relations and our behavior here on Earth to avoid carrying the virus of conflict with us off into space. NASA employs attempts at humor and rock and roll music to achieve congeniality during space flights. We can foresee N20's role in voyages that last for months. Barrels of rum helped world navigators survive months at sea. This method also produced combativeness, whereas a clinically safe gas would work well, with "half the fun is getting there."

By employing the Internet, the air waves, and the air-proper, we can change the ever-dangerous defective forces present that decide our history. Before we can win our two wars, we must convince the newly established police forces to abandon their cultural reliance on hashish in order to conform to the U.S. Army no-drugs policy. How can we?

Can this seemingly ludicrous-seductive conjecturing involving a gas help change the world and reshape the global ethos? We may learn at last how to live peacefully even without the assistance of a "chemical pollutant."

For more than a thousand years, constant warfare in the Middle East and in the Mediterranean world was encouraged by the jumbled prophesies of priestesses who were under the influence of noxious fumes from a volcano. Dr. Emery N. Brown at Massachusetts General Hospital has said on March 1, 2011, "We certainly know how to make anesthesia (N20) safe."

"Come be of good cheer" is written in the Bible. "Let all beings be happy," preached Buddha and Gandhi, adding, "Argue against grief." Laughter is contagious. All religions emphasize sharing. We all partake of the air we breathe, like a global household. By bathing, cleaning the air, we join "the Anointed One," Jesus and the "Awakened One," Buddha in a fusion of the soul of humanity during this Age of Aquarius, the air sign. It is incredibly tempting to surmise that we can now have the solution after trial and error. The dictionary describes the word solution as "a dispersion of one substance in another, i.e., air, so as to form a homogeneous mixture"—think, world.

Speaking of societal, Biblical, medical, or whimsical attributes and benefits of laughing gas, we close with a quote from the TV program "The Doctors" on February 11, 2011. "Nitrous oxide is responsible for erections," and with Henri Rousseau's "The Peaceable Kingdom" picturing contented beasts nestled in harmony in a crowded but placid jungle.

How long, how long in infinite pursuit of this and that endeavor and dispute? Better be merry with the fruitful gas than sadden after none, or bitter fruit—paraphrasing Omar Khayyam.

Using a prison as an ideal setting for experimentation, we inject N20 into Cell Block A using the air conditioning system. Cell Block B remains with its air unaltered. The difference in inmate behavior becomes clearly defined after a trial period. Pure air has long been used as medication. With the exact prescription, its N20 dosage could be just what the doctor ordered.

The Golden Age of Cruise Directing

Cruise directing as a position went unlisted in the government catalogue of occupations of the Department of Labor until 1960. Described here, it is revealed to all as it existed when cruising was in its infancy in the late forties and fifties.

A cruise director basically lives on his ship. If he maintains a foreign mailing address, he has no United State income tax to pay; he belongs to no union; his salary can be deposited abroad; his expense account covers bar bills, dry cleaning and tips to stewards, plus a clothing allowance. As a ship's officer, his cabin is superior.

Over forty perks come with the job—all legal—mostly in the form of untaxable commissions. For example, at the end of a cruise he will receive gifts from passengers, he is given an unlimited bar account, and if he doesn't drink, he will receive the equivalent of what he normally would drink, in currency from the country. The chief stewards' department handles large shipboard special parties, but the cruise director will be asked to organize intimate social events. This includes printing invitations and distributing them to the guests, using the ship's printer. Liquor that is not consumed reverts back to the cruise director. The orchestra, if it performs at a private function, will be included in the party-giver's bill. This includes the steward, who will be paid by the cruise director for working during their free time. He is compensated for handling such arrangements. He also makes special parties ashore while the ship is in port, for passengers requesting same. In this case, he is paid by the party giver and by the establishment, grateful for the business.

The cruise director is never more in business for himself than when he operates tours ashore, apart from those offered by the company. When passengers prefer independent activity, rather than organized excursions, he is in a position to contract local transportation, provide escorts who speak the language, and secure unavailable reservations. On a much larger scale, he runs night-club dinner dances ashore with tickets printed at no cost by the ship's printer. These events attract local clients, who attend to enjoy performances given to a combined audience. Shipboard entertainers are used, blended with local acts. Tickets for such an event are sold in dollars, and agents are paid in their currency. The exchange rate favors the cruise director. He may also buy foreign currency at a low rate in a country other than the one he settles his accounts with. Unused tickets are refunded in local currency.

Acting as agent in these transactions assures him of a profit. Furthermore, the company is mainly interested in keeping passengers satisfied with the cruise by whatever means. Other companies may not be competitive because of these "extras" provided by the enterprising cruise director. Of course, he is encouraged to fraternize, and is highly paid to do so. Merchants relying on tourism advertise in the ship's newspaper, edited by the cruise director who charges for space. Shopkeepers will pay for publicity given at port lectures that the cruise director delivers prior to arrival at each port. Merchants will come aboard to be introduced to clients by the cruise director. They may keep a running account of the total purchases made from the ship while it is in port, commissionable to the cruise director. Cases of liquor, bottles of perfume, and gifts arrive at his office just before departure. If he wears clothing with shop logos, he is free to keep them. He is not charged for taxis, dinners, or drinks for himself or his guests. He is allowed a customs exemption as a US citizen. By purchasing merchandise in a foreign country, including it in his exemption, or by paying the duty, he can sell it profitably in the States. He can purchase in the US articles impossible to obtain in foreign countries and sell them there, after paying local duties. He can act as a courier, carrying documents. He can serve as a reverend at services that provide a collection for the Seamen's Fund. He is in control of ship's prizes awarded to contestants. Any remaining will be distributed as he sees fit. He promotes the sale of souvenir photos, ship's menus, dance albums recorded by the orchestra, and dance lessons (which he may give himself, if there is no team aboard), for a percentage of the sales.

The cruise director is in charge of the bingo games, as well as the horse races. Together with the chief purser, he runs the slot machines and the ship's mileage pool. Ashore, casinos allow him a percentage of the receipts. In the company of first-class passengers, he is given stock tips, can bank abroad, avoiding taxes with his foreign address, and can sell his stateroom when the ship is overbooked. In this case, he moves into the crew quarters. Health insurance and vacation are paid. He can sell cruises for a commission from his company or operate tours that he forms, using the company as carrier, i.e., dance teachers and their pupils. Movies and photos can be sold to magazines and newspapers. He has no office expenses, and his hostess is his secretary. He can ship a US car with him to a country where import taxes are very high or where luxury items are forbidden, then abandon it there, to be acquired by a pre-arranged buyer who handles the formalities. With proper documentation, he can import animals or rare plants. With his yearly bonus, he can collect foreign stamps overseas.

During the early Fifties, all these activities were aboveboard or slightly under the table. Prosecutable? Hardly. Involving as they would international maritime law and perhaps an admiralty court or two.

What other occupation offers a similar life, unless on your yacht? Your captain does the steering of your destiny under your command. Your orders are obeyed while infringements are handled by others—you are immune, isolated from consequences. Laws at sea differ, similar to "What happens in Las Vegas stays in Las Vegas." The long arm of the law ends at the shoreline. Justice has to be carried back to land to be decided and examined. The ocean's stern god is Poseidon. In him, there is only one enormous power alone that speaks, acts, and rules fairly. His adjudication is supreme. He is incorruptible. The role of the Cruise Director goes back in history to the royal court jester responsible for the levity essential to living closer to the trickery of reality. Divertissement is natural in all living things as a necessary ingredient to growth and learning. There are no youngsters playing baseball on ships until Walt Disney came along to make his ships a playground for them, just as others created circuses for adults aboard. The Cruise Director is the ringmaster, promoter and originator of the activities and events passengers will share each day and night. Such power is semi-divine without being dictatorial or manipulative.

A ship has no attic or basement, nor is there a need for them. The world is simplified, unnoticeably, on ships. You don't notice absences in a vast empty ocean. The Cruise Director lives surrounded by customers. He is a floor walker on constant duty. He is inescapable, and must remain so. His position out front has made him a captive, a celebrity-working man. He comes with his own world attached to him. The ship contains his workload surrounding him. When he can be alone, he finds himself shut in a cabin that is his world without people. He cannot stay within except to sleep. He eats outside, where we eat inside. The army life is his house a similar existence, living among many, but reluctantly…alone due to circumstances. His job requires discipline, and he is the one providing it for himself. To hide for one moment destroys the reward receives from his faithful approach to his duty. When the cruise is over, the next one is already upon him. Bon voyage!

This life is show business, on duty 24/7. He is on a vacation treadmill, sharing vacations with hundreds of passengers. He is on a perpetual "vacation of a lifetime." He is transformed into a sea creature in an aquatic world. He breathes salt air and his skin is salty, misty as is his vocabulary. His gossip is ship happenings, and his view of the world is limited like a shut-out's.

Graciela, La LibertadoraBy Vincent Livelli

At the La Conga Nightclub in 1944, Graciela Perez broke the restraints of propriety and virtuousness the night she sang "No, No, Sí, Sí." The band fell silent, the waiters froze, the dancing stopped, and the bartender turned to witness her daring performance.

Beginning off to the side, she slowly edged center-stage under brighter lighting. She personified womankind facing an eternal seductive, copulative proposition. Her agile voice nursed a suspenseful scenario that gradually submitted to normal desire. Within this framework, Graciela reached a melodic dénouement, an artful pseudo-orgasm celebration ending in an ecstatic climactic scream. This was music to the ears of every male present.

Her startling melodramatics had no encore. Here was a breakthrough similar to Sally Rand's very daring fan dance, Josephine Baker's nudity, and Miguelito Valdez's "Babalu" number at the Anglo, uptight Waldorf Astoria. She hit us the way the rebels Lenny Bruce, Madonna, and Valentino's tango did, but without their universal celebrity. We had been presented with a revolutionary event, like a morality play vocalized. It was one that lyrically mimicked a Shakespearean dueling scene between rival moral principles. Her act liberated a stale, sexually-correct post-World War II America at a time when Club El Morocco denied entry to women wearing dark sunglasses. Graciela taunted a tight-laced society wherein any indelicate intimacy was taboo, except in crass vaudevillian skits on red-light Forty-Second Street.

The patrons at La Conga's rumba matinees were dancers and their "pupils," garment-center "cloak-and-suiters" with their models, and gigolettes. The dance floor was a smoldering tinderbox of erotic performances, with groins riveted to groins. This was reminiscent of the old Park Plaza where, during slow, grinding selections such as "El Negro Simon," the lyrics described a girl becoming "arrebata," or sexually uncontrollable. With Yoruba language working, i.e., "arrullendole cagua," lusty interpretations were left to the inflamed imaginations of the dancers. These odd, throaty sounds seemed to imply foreplay. Since the messages in these unintelligible lyrics were decoded by each dancer according to his or her level of arousal, there was sufficient amplitude for each individual to respond physically, blaming the Afro music for their suggestive behavior on the floor. The musicians, as well as the outnumbered Latino dance couples, encouraged the Anglos to interpolate the feral sensuality surrounding them, while clownish antics of frustrated beginners were perceived with good humor by everyone.

When a Latino danced with an Anglo girl, she would perform with exaggerated responses in dances that glorified femininity and the macho man. The result was a greater abandonment with new-found freedom of movement. The male Anglo, his here-to-fore secure role threatened, understandably eschewed the Afro-Cuban dance world, whereas his partner now saw it as part of her overall liberation, especially during the eighties when disco dancing meant less male control. The Stonewall historical event is a good example of a revolution beginning on the dance floor.

Graciela's substantial voice that night "ignited an overheated environment. Unless you had witnessed her, you would not have realized what it all basically meant. Her coquettish, beguiling but universally well-understood "Ay Si, Ay no" lyrics left us with a climactic, playful portrayal of a female's victory over a manipulated male, despite their mutually responsive libidos. She gracefully and cleverly flaunted her newly liberated instinct, using "No, No, Si, Si" as a musical vehicle to freedom of expression without vulgarity.Graciela came to us from a background where a 1930s rumba called "El Plato Roto" spoke of a broken hymen. It was one of many risqué numbers that, like spice, were welcome ingredients to everyday life in Cuba's torrid musical climate. We might be reminded of a more restrained delightful combination of feminine musical beauty, the eleven-piece Retunda All-Girl Orchestra, whose redolence carries us back to Havana in the forties, and the Anacaona All-Girl Band featuring Graciela.

In an alley behind the nightclub, a well-worn upright was stored during the day, available to anyone who might wish to play it. It was well known by everyone and was often found encircled by Habaneros, like fraternity boys singing their alma mater. At night it was rolled out on wheels to sit on the narrow, colonial-era sidewalk in front of the brightly-lit club. Passers-by clustered there to enjoy a free concert under the open sky. That piano seemed to belong to everyone, like the remarkable music that one heard throughout the city. The people of Havana, like those in Washington Heights, fell asleep with late-night radios playing sexy love songs.

Everyone owned Graciela in their hearts. Next to Anacaona was a second all-girl orchestra. At times, both bands played the number-one hit in unison. Since this all took place opposite El Capitolo, this nightly happy spectacle symbolized and celebrated a country where rumba was Cuba and Cuba was rumba. Music was like a second government. But it was Graciela who helped make us a bit more liberal.

Haiti Chérie: When Haiti was Happy

Haiti was on its way to becoming the Monte Carlo of the Caribbean in 1951. The gambling junkets from Miami to Havana had enriched the mob and Batista's clique so much so that Haitian politicos wanted to get in on the action. National Airlines, TWA, and Pan American shuttled hundreds of gamblers to the Tropicana, Montmartre, the Riviera with fifty-minute hops to

José Martí Airport. What Haiti lacked was a way to get high-rollers to fly past Cuba to Port-au-Prince, a distance far greater than ninety miles, to land on a primitive airport.

In Haiti's slogan "In Union There is Strength," *L'Union Fait la Force*, came the solution. General Rafael Trujillo had acquired a cruise ship called the New Northland from the Canadian Clarke Steamship Company as a wedding yacht for one of his daughters. He renamed it SS Nuevo Dominicano and teamed up with Leslie Frazier, a banana importer, to have her carry fruit to Florida. Why not carry eager suckers instead of bananas? Thus, an evil trinity evolved between Trujillo, Frazier, and the French mob interested in profiting from, not so much the business bonanza of tourism that was just becoming evident, but from a casino in Port-au-Prince on the harbor.

Haiti had also caught the attention of the Lansky Florida-based mob. Out of Dania, where they controlled Jai Alai and dog races as well as the Gulfstream Racetrack, they succeeded in placing a foothold aboard the SS Nuevo Dominicano in the form of a shipboard "casino" consisting of three restored one-armed bandits. These relics were encrusted with barnacles, having been brought to the surface from the bottom of the Hudson River where Mayor LaGuardia had thrown them. Trujillo decided to invite the *Sindicat* from France to take over gambling on the waterfront Casino International d'Haiti that Duvalier (Papa Doc) had built, using the ship for transportation. This overloaded setup between France, the Dominican Republic, Haiti, and the Florida mob was beginning to flourish. The mistake that caused it to fail, and to bring Haiti down with it, was a woman…*cherchez la femme*…Madame Getulio Vargas!Brazil had shared a common tragic history with Haiti in terms of slavery's struggles for freedom from foreigners. She became Haiti's protectoress, a sister republic. "Never again shall a colonist or a European set his foot upon this territory with the title of master or proprietor." This is taken from the Liberty-or-Death Proclamation, dated Headquarters at the Cape Haitian, 28th April, 1804, first year of independence, signed the Governor-General Jean-Jacques Dessalines, who died assassinated. Brazil had to rid itself of the Dutch, the French, and the Braganza Dom Pedro II of Portugal to become independent.

The wife of Getulio Vargas, the president of Brazil in 1951, discovered that the Casino International d'Haiti was under the influence of the French mob, presenting "immoral entertainment." She had had her husband shut down the magnificent Quintandinha Casino in Petropolis, Rio, followed by pressure on Duvalier to close the Haitian casino that was presenting Las Vegas-type floor shows, and preparing to invite the then shocking Follies Bergères. This encouraged complicity and plotting by the casinos in Carasco, Uruguay; Mar del Plata, Argentina; and Estoril in Portugal as well as Meyer Lansky's crowd, all of whom feared Haiti's unwelcome competition. They got hold of Madame Vargas's ear. The result doomed Haiti's chance to grow as a gambling mecca and as a more modern, prosperous country, albeit in violation of the moral principals of the Catholic Church. Haiti and Brazil were, and may still be, ninety-nine percent Catholic; they were also anti-abortion and anti-divorce, causing population problems to explode in *favelas*, multiple shanty towns, and corrupt construction contractors. It also meant mud slides and deaths, like the 2008 schoolhouse collapse in Petionville. Prior to the earthquake, Brazil had 3,000 peacekeepers helping control Haiti. Vargas also considered Voudou a pagan menace. Public school education was diminished in favor of Catholic schooling. A casino without sexy showgirls is a castrated casino. When Getulio Vargas was defeated after elections, an outburst of gaiety erupted similar to our post-Prohibition flapper era. It gave birth to today's Rio Carnival, which under Getulio was a sham, consisting of a parade of cars honking horns along Copacabana. He feared it could become rebellious.When the French took off, Haiti was swept under the rug. Unlike Coney Island, where destruction of buildings and arson occurred, hoping to lower real estate prices for future casino establishments, all this sudden activity fortunately awakened a sleepy island that was now aware of the resiliency of its people and of gambling's commercial advantages. But the likelihood of a happier, prosperous Haiti — thanks to gambling — and French savoir-faire and politesse, slowly died, taking gaieté parisienne with it. No longer did one notice the ladies in Port-au-Prince wearing the latest French imports — Lanvin, Hermès, Chanel — or smelling of Fragonard and Madame Rochas, that they had purchased from Elias Neustas, a Lebanese shopkeeper who originated the duty-free, tax-free concept. Gone was Fisher, the German professor/anthropologist whose warehouse-type business sold Haitian primitive paintings that were catching on internationally, along with animal skins, snakes, seashell jewelry, tortoiseshell and mahogany furniture. Also lost was an enormous stock of drums that were hand-carved on the outside with Voudou motifs that are today collectible, dedicated to *Ayan*, Ghana's god of the drum, and to *Atumpan*, Ti-Roro's talking drum. Ti-Roro, the foremost tambourist, was at this time entertaining us at the El Rancho Hotel poolside, where we took up collections for him and his three companion drummers. Why are Haitian drummers accepted as the best world drummers from West Africa to the West Indies, where there are supermarkets and people wearing shoes, compared to Haiti's penury? The drums of Haiti are angry-sounding, violent. Slavery is long gone, except in Haiti where people are economic slaves, hungry, hopeless, and helplessly dependent for survival on once-despised foreigners and now aid agencies for their marginal survival. The monopolistic cruise industry bought islands that diverted shoppers from the modest straw markets of Haiti, leaving the little man or woman to expire under his or her roadside *canope*. The cruise bosses discouraged, and may have contributed to, crime in Port-au-Prince in order to profit from the millions their passengers would otherwise have spent ashore. Nor could Haiti compete touristically.

Porto Rico's El San Juan Hotel, Hilton, and El Conquistador at Las Croabas had found the golden egg of tourism closer to Miami than Haiti's one-runway airport. Tourism found Martinique, where in Fort de France, Roger Albert had become the mayor based on his modernization of his tiny perfume shop, and where FOYAL (Fort Royal), the French restaurant in Martinique's port area, now served excellent fish dishes, with old-rum banana flambé for dessert. This was added to Josephine's Empress mystique and the Mount Pelee Volcano's 20,000 victims, or to Guadeloupe's beaches. Cruise ships carried their human cargo from the Antilles françaises to South and Central American ports. Gone were the days when, in order to reach Caracas from La Guaira, tourists had to board an elevator to reach part of the way up the mountainside in order to continue the rest of the ascent by mule. Nothing could stop tourism, except the mob.

Thirty fabulous liners leave Miami, some carrying two thousand passengers (read, shoppers) to faraway islands and places the companies discovered, like Roatan, Honduras, and Nicaragua's Puerto Limón, the Mexican Riviera, bypassing Haiti. Was this part of a plot to punish the Haitians for expelling their casino?

In 1952, the SS Nuevo Dominicano, on its way to be scrapped, was sunk, typically, for its insurance, off the coast of Cuba. Lloyd's of London, wise to mob crimes, sent divers down and discovered open sea cocks. They put the captain and others in jail in the Dominican Republic. The crew had been classified as being part of La Flota Mercante de la República Dominicana. They were classified as part of the navy and were paid one dollar a day. She was nicknamed a pirate ship, with her one hundred passengers and crew members dressed as pirates at the Captain's Dinner on the last night out. With the loss of the ship, gone were the evenings in Haiti spent dancing to Cole Porter's 1938 "Begin the Beguine," drinking Five-Star Babancourt ron at Cabane Chachoune in Petionville, all now completely erased except in memories.

In 1951, we were on our maiden voyage to Haiti. Fascinated by the amateur films of Voudou brought to us in 1945 by Maya Deren, we had expected to be welcomed by drumming, a rumba band as in Havana, or a steel band, as we glided *doucement* over the calm, pitch-dark water of the harbor. We had arrived around midnight when all was asleep, wrapped in dark shadows, with mysterious mountains whose heights were well hidden and inestimable. How were we to know until morning that the casino operators, experienced in showmanship, had installed a red carpet that began at the foot of our gangplank. They had hired for our shore excursions taxi drivers and pretty guides that knew some English, eliminating those who spoke only Kriol. The casino croupiers and table men were from France, the menu was select, printed in both languages, Château Margaux and the rest were available, along with Haitian absinthe, illegal as toxic in America. Chanel No 5 was in the air and an aperitif was extended to the ship's officers aboard the SS Dominicano. But who would have thought that in the stillness of a pitch-black late-night arrival, as we silently made for our mooring inch by inch, that we would hear coming across the harbor Claude Debussy's "Claire de Lune." Haiti will bounce back again. Of that there is no doubt. It is in her beautiful children that she will find her true happiness, which no one can rob her of.

En quittant la ville Jacmel
Pa' m'allé au balle
Panama ma tombé
   (Repeat)
Ramasi lui pour moi… .

The Honeymoon

Living together while not married is a way of getting to know how compatible couples are. Better still is to travel together when more of life's surprises are involved.

Queen Victoria took Prince Albert to India for a honeymoon. That marriage worked out very well, but many modern-day trips can "trip up." For example, a travel agent will for profit send newly-weds to St. Lucia — a long, exhausting flight. In

June the West Indies is stiflingly hot and not worth the expenses involved, compared to a honeymoon in Europe — the same distance away, and cooler.

Where do the Japanese go for their honeymoon? They go to Atami, called the Niagara Falls of Japan. The British go to the Isle of Wight or to Brighton. Filipinos go to Baquiro, above Manila — Italians to Capri, but do Americans still take the Honeymoon Express from Grand Central Terminal? Many now prefer cruise voyages, and can even be married by the captain or take the families along with them if they can escape to be alone. This type of escape is even more romantic, since a challenge is involved, leaving the family members outside the stateroom with a "Do Not Disturb" notice on the door…for the entire trip, if desired.

The trouble with the perfect honeymoon is the fantasy world it creates, making the marriage a commonplace letdown. It is supposed to provide a lifetime together with a wonderful memory forever. The same with the second honeymoon, and even a third. But does it succeed?

When a second honeymoon is intended to save a shaky marriage, it is time to think now of separate vacations. They have a better proven track record, especially since you may well miss each other, based on the old "absence makes the heart grow fonder." If that fails, try your luck and marry your old sweetheart, if possible, or start from scratch. But find someone with a sense of humor, and money. Zsa Zsa Gabor married eight times, so don't be afraid of marriage. Just try to pick a good honeymoon and a good traveler, rich or poor.

Ignacio Arsenio Travieso Scull: René and Estella at the Park Plaza

On my first visit to Havana in 1940, I arrived in the midst of a Carnival. The photographer, Walker Evans, said he arrived there "in the midst of a revolution." Once the dictator Machado was overthrown, drumming was permitted during *Congos* (Carnival parade). The word conga means "rope," as one can deduce showing a chain of dancers. The 1940 Carnival was a particularly explosive affair since participants could break free of whatever slavery memories they still shouldered. It took awhile for their new sense of freedom set in after the 1937 permission was granted them by Colonel Batista during his first ascension to power. The Carnival's *tumbadores* demonstrated an angry ferocity comparable to Haiti's even greater rabid-sounding protest. They seemed to be blood-thirsty calls for revenge for the cruel injustice of its enduring suffering, while other black nations progressed. Haitians for this reason are considered to be the Olympian drummers.

Haiti's greatest exponent of its powerful drumming, Tiro Ro, asked me to spread the message out to the world that his drums were sending…He was despairing toward the end of his life, seeing the intense violence at his fingertips merely beating the air, falling on deaf ears.

As I joined in with the Carnivali along the Prado in 1940, from what appeared to be a celebration for Lent, I gradually became alerted to the fact that the celebrants were using Lent as a cover for rebellious activity, or at least the manifestation of newfound power, not as much in terms of gratitude as for revenge.

Chano Pozo, wearing a white hat and tails, was there with Miguelito Valdez, taking part with Los Dandy de Belén, since they were among the original organizers. Being a great deal smaller than Rio's present-day Carnival, it was easier to become personally involved. This feeling of a populus in arms expressing a love of liberty hit home for me, since I had just escaped to Havana from the clutch of the Great Depression in the United States.

The Illegal Alien

On December 8, 1951 I was arrested as an illegal alien in El Salvador. "Who would want to migrate to El Salvador," I argued. This did not go over well with the Immigration officials. My crime was "illegal presence" in the country. I was searched for stolen pre-Colombian artifacts and for drugs. There were no ATM's or credit cards for bribery in 1951 and I had little cash left at the end of my trip. Placed in the not-too-welcome custody of a Pan Am representative, I escaped jail and hand-cuffing, and was put up at a hotel, where I paid for my room, the soap, towel and toilet paper, the visa, the fine, and breakfast by selling my Bell & Howell camera to the desk clerk. You see, I had no visa!

The hotel was wooden and in a bad part of town. Graffiti said, "Yankee, go home." I will, if you let me, I thought to myself. The Pan Am rep had told me that citizens carried concealed weapons, and that I was a rich Americano. Tourists were strangers, and besides, a revolution was brewing. The hotel ceiling had a peephole that permitted a view of my bed, and sure enough, my floor board allowed a view of the floor below. I slept in the well-worn bed with the Roman poet Ovid's words in mind: "The conscious couch holds the enamored pair." There was no mosquito netting, since no one actually "slept" in this bordello, nor was there a bar, unfortunately.

This situation began in Miami when I convinced Bob Sheldon, President of TAN Airlines, *Transportes Aéreos Nacionales de Tegucigalpa* that, instead of carrying chickens, shoes, etc., as cargo to Central America, he should carry tourists to the recently-headlined *M*ayan ruins. "Take advantage of the newly-awakened travel business that was spreading from Nassau to the West Indies and beyond," I proposed.

So it was that I found myself sitting on cargo crates with no seat belt, flying on an itinerary survey of the project. Besides it being a dangerous adventure, I had time to watch natives on their way to Sunday mass, carrying smoking incense that filled the plaza with holiness. Mothers carried children like backpacks, clothed in locally-woven, colorful shawls. I saw many parrots, flamboyant flora, hamacas, heard flutes, and walked in a jungle.

The reason I arrived in El Salvador without a visa was due to my missing my Pan Am connecting flight to Miami. The TAN flight from Honduras to Guatemala had gone well, but the Pan Am flight from El Salvador to Miami that I was scheduled to connect with left before I landed. Whose fault was it? Mine, Pan Am's, TAN's, an incompetent travel agent, a time-zone error, the weather factor, or just a bad day to travel?

I never go to see the ruins of *Tikal* or *Copan* (as had been my primary motive, actually). Mr. Sheldon lacked financing and the pioneering spirit. I arrived home safe and sound (sano y seguro), stamped, sealed, and delivered.

Escudo, Peseta

On a metro city bus we may have to ask "Has anyone four quarters?" so that we can pay our fare with coins. I caused a fifteen-minute delay on the train from Compostela in Spain back to Lisbon. Because of the *escudo* and the *peseta* not compatible and not being accepted except in their country of origin. I could not pay my fare to the conductor. This would have meant being put off the train at the next stop and could have made me miss my connection back in Lisbon to Madrid.

I arose from my seat and addressed my fellow passengers in Spanish and Portuguese, explaining my plight, and asking for someone to accept my *escudos* for an exchange in *pesetas* so that I could pay my fare in the proper currency. Out of a carful of laborers, no one came to my rescue. In fact, someone phoned the next station, being suspicious of my request. It being a time of much unrest, with bombs and black markets and Basque tension in that area, I was met by an authority figure who called ahead to have me checked out by Interpol! This held up the train for a reply, making the laborers late for their jobs. After my passport was returned and my currency matter straightened out, we all took off—in fact, I found myself to be the only passenger in the coach all the way back to Lisbon, since all the passengers were workers, leaving me sitting all by myself, enjoying the most luxurious train ride I ever took, with the whole coach to myself!

Perhaps the recent (7.25.13) wreck near Compostela was caused by an overload of overhead baggage. Trial runs for training and testing at that curve perhaps did not take into account that the off-balance strain on the gravity involved added overhead weight, causing the train to tilt over on its side. It reminded me of a similar off-center balance that occurred approaching Aneel Falls in Venezuela. I announced that the best view of the falls was on the left, and everyone arose to film on the left, causing the plane to tilt over.

Introduction

Unlike prose, lists save reading time. They also allow quicker selection of material of special interest. Like statistics, they summarize the author's message. The longer the list, the stronger the impression made on the reader. I hope such will be the case here, since out of all the memoirs I have read, none resembled mine. Lucky in health, love, and money is made more puzzling since it resembled winning the lottery of life without ever having bought a ticket. Although this is about managing a lifelong handicap, it is not a how-to book. If it were, I would give it away free, in gratitude for all the bounties I received in addition to the gift of life itself.

The Dance of Life: Keep On Truckin'

"Music is the best art form to express the inexpressible," said Henry Miller. But the dance is an even greater influence. Without the movements that music inspires, there would be no life to express the inexpressible. Beyond the musical mating call, the lavish plumage, the seductive scent, the awkward or graceful wrestling, it is movement that resembles a dance that has the sperm wriggling to the egg to bring us life. We first imagine copulation as a dance our parents perform. From the fetus positioning itself in the womb, to the fluttering heart that cries love, to the spluttering voice that speaks good-bye forever, life is a dance that we jiggle with.

Music begets dancing but there is more dancing without music in life. There is a mobile connection that is essential to put events into actuality between motive and accomplishment. Life dies without movement, and each move we make is unique. It is this quality that allows an amateur to outperform a professional. By displaying the amateur facet of ourselves we are closer to life, since life makes us all contestants and unequal competitors. Were it not so, there would be no repeated errors. Besides, we all, including, eventually, clones, may be at the mercy of our daily astrological configurations and lunar influences. Astrophysicists embrace the string theory to explain the cosmos, but where would strings be without vibrations…without the dance that is a response to the music of the spheres?

Accidental Laughter

Rarely does one laugh at the scene of an accident, the victim least of all.

During the long voyage to Buenos Aires from New York, we organized prize fights out on deck for crewmembers. They were successful as entertainment and relaxation as well as a way of settling some minor disputes. Among the 300 crewmembers, we often had semi-professional boxers that taught lessons and gave exhibitions.

Why not have a prize fight in the main lounge, I thought, as part of our activities? We had been running musical chairs, horse races, costume parties, and were looking for something different. The captain outlawed crew fights in public rooms, of course, but passenger fights that were for amusement and harmless comical displays could be considered as part of workouts in the gym or as self-defense training. He OK'd the idea.

To carry this project further, it was decided that a boxing ring was to be set up in the main lounge, with two contenders chosen from the passenger list.

Prize fights during the forties and fifties were very popular, more so than today. The many scandals and ring injuries put the damper on them, but everyone knew of Luis Firpo, the Argentine heavy-weight world champion who had fought Dempsey. We decided to ask an Argentine passenger to enter the contest against an American opponent. Where the unexpected would enter the picture was in the selection of the fighters. We appealed to two elderly grandmothers to play the role of pugilists for the fun of it. Being fight fans and good sports, they agreed. We then supported them with backup managers and trainers and out-men, in keeping with actual ringside teams with towels, stools, etc.

Acting as announcer, I introduced the referee, followed by the fighters: "In this corner, fighting out of Jersey City, New Jersey, wearing the blue and weighing in at 120 lbs… . " In addition to the robes and shorts and boxing gloves, the two ladies were wearing sneakers, since ships in the forties were not stabilized. When the ship's drummer sounded the bell for the opening round, the audience began to encourage their fighter according to their selection, based on nationality.

(Early prize fighters concealed brass knuckles inside their gloves). Unknown to the audience was the fact that each lady held hidden from everyone's view some hair that had been cut prior to the bout, along with a pair of false plastic teeth. The first round featured the teeth falling to the floor after some "blows," followed by clumps of hair for all to see. For the second round, the fighters were seen with black eyes that were applied with shoe polish during the break. After some wrestling and wild swings at each other, the bout was stopped on a T.K.O. when one of the fighters sat on the dance floor pretending to need assistance from the referee to regain her feet. As she struggled upright, a large puddle was evident on the polished floor of the ring, that was quickly mopped up by the lounge steward.

Rather than being embarrassed by this unrehearsed display, the elderly woman arose with a gesture of victory by raising her arms over her head to loud cheering. "It was an accident," she cried out above the sound of much laughter.

Laughter in the Jungle

Have you ever jumped back in fright from something that suddenly showed up right in front of you? It could be a close call from a speeding New York taxi, but in the Amazon it's most likely to be a part of Mother Nature.

As we sailed, pieces broken off the mainland formed islands that floated past your porthole, with tall trees alive with chattering monkey sounds. Barely visible at night around the bend in the river, the captain of the "Ariadne" of the Hamburg-Amerika Line proceeded with great caution. It could be as deep as twenty-five feet or dry in areas after the rainy season.

We arrived in Manaus while the many unpaved streets were still muddy and unfit for sightseeing around town. The pungent smell of fish reminded me of Bergen, Norway, only in a hotter climate. Furthermore, it was the jungle that I had come to visit, where there were rumors of pygmy monkeys. Aside from some butterflies and birds, we had encountered no piranha, boa constrictors, anacondas, or alligators.

A short walk out of town brought me to a narrow river that discouraged crossing to where the rainforest was waiting. While resting on a log, I saw that the tall tree in front of me had its bark peeling off. Out of curiosity, I stood up, grabbed the loose bark and dislodged it. Hundreds of angry tarantulas slowly spread out like a carpet of red soldier ants. Jumping back in horror and surprise, I fell back against the log and onto the ground. They say it takes multiple bites from killer bees, but, like poisonous snakes, it takes but one bite from a tarantula to finish you off. Who knew that spiders lived in trees?

Suddenly, an outburst of laughter filled the air. Lined up along the opposite bank of the river was a cluster of Satera-tribe Indians. Naked they were, except for painted torsos, feathered arm- and headbands, shell ankle bracelets, and bows and arrows. Some wore loincloths but young women were bare-breasted, which, in 1959 I was unaccustomed to witnessing. They had all been hiding, silently spying on me behind the foliage. I got up and headed back to town, feeling like a fool, but wiser and frustrated, but lucky. It took me a while to laugh about it.

May the Best Music Win

If Rumba is a bolero in a state of sexual excitement, then Mambo is even wilder. When Rumba became Mambo during the beginning of a more liberalized national acceptance, testosterone found adrenaline. What was kept in the shadows of the Park Plaza came under the bright lights of Broadway at the Palladium. It took ten years to display sexiness on the dance floor. Even so, the Park Plaza dancers were better behaved because they were older; in spite of the few young hot examples, the Palladium crowd was younger and riper. The Park Plaza was more of a neighborhood-family environment, compared with the potpourri gang coming from five boroughs. The young of El Barrio during the Great Depression could not afford to go dance so much, so that dancing was more conservative, danced by their elders. The Plaza was never jammed, while the Palladium held more spectators than actual dancers, until people got up off the chairs to courageously confront the music. It never took prodding at the Plaza. Nor was there cheering, aside from Eléctrico's outstanding contributions. The adulation was kept for the band, especially loud when they took their breaks. Plaza needed no organized master of ceremonies, like Killer Joe at the Palladium. Many at the Palladium never got up to dance, but at the Plaza you didn't spend your money to sit. There was a definite feeling of separation at the Palladium between good dancers, beginners, mediocre, and between the audience seated and those dancing. Groupies existed even back in the Thirties when dancers followed the Happy Boys up to the Caborojeño Workers' Circle dance hall or to the Masonic temple. This practice continued when you would later see the same faces at the Embassy or La Conga or Versailles.

When we witnessed Machito, bigger than life on the Palladium stage, we knew we had been the advanced guard, the preceptors of what we were watching. We allowed ourselves to luxuriate like proud *abuelos*, like an old guard but not yet a retiree.

Amid the Broadway glitter, glamour, and glitz, "Macho" became louder in a larger room than at La Conga, but he never traveled far from his Afro roots, even when the band had sixteen plus a female vocalist who was not Graciela. Even so, one did not feel the Americanization influence as much as was evident in The Two Titos.

These three bands personified the character of Latinos in general that is more than charm or Respect, being, as it struck us, more genuine. This seems to arise from a tradition of authenticity similar to New Orleans jazz. By contrast, the R & R disco environment seems full—dancers as well as musicians—of poseurs needing outlandish accessories to appear important or talented. At the Plaza, everyone was satisfied with themselves, more "at home." Things were simpler at the time of the Plaza heyday. Having followed as a longtime witness to the phylogeny of Afro-Cuban music from the solares of Havana to the sell-out crowds at Madison Square Garden and Willie Colon's $850 p.p. admission to Posto Restaurant New Years' Eve, I can luxuriate like a proud grandfather, even though I "sit it out" now, involuntarily and reluctantly.

You can be inspired by a lecture or moved to tears by a movie, but with Afro-Cuban music and Latin music in general, you are dancing while you are sitting down.

My almost pathological loyalty to Afro after the Santero encounter in 1941 in Regla, may have been instilled in me by spirits unknown to me. It is unwise to permit unquestioned allegiance to a cause, culture, or choice. Thus, I enjoyed an original relationship with the music. Today I don't feel ostracized, since I was careful never to join in blindly, sheep-like. My devotion to Afro is that of a defender, so very passionately involved as to not reject argumentation if needed.... . Nor do I miss what I avoid in music. When one is not tempted, there is no need to resist. Should I find Rock 'n' Roll as irfresistible as Afro-Cuban, it is then that there could arise a conflict that would be welcomed with even more passion, but always con gran respecto for musicians. May the best music win.

Messed Up Music.

At the Park Plaza in 1939, Afro-Cuban jazz had a much different sound when Machito, under Mario Bauzá's influence, played timid jazz solo partitas on and off as though uncomfortable in that Latin stronghold. They tried it out on the road, so to speak, before introducing it at the La Conga Club downtown. Machito never dropped his proud identity as "Machito y sus Afro-Cubanos." Bauzá anglicized it. Tinkering with various descriptive names for his band, perhaps in desperation, Tito Puente announced before performing at the World Trade Center Marina, "I don't play Latin jazz, I play Latin!" He soon discovered that it was here to stay.

As a confused votary purist, I miss the symmetrical words-and-music format of unadulterated Latin music. I don't sense a proper commingling or easy synergism in Latin jazz. Like some canned output, it lacks soulfulness, which is very evident when heard separately in both jazz and Latin. As for the two Titos, a free spirit of artistic contention was evident in their rivalry. Like pugilists, they ended robust bouts in each others' arms. Latinos and jazzistas don't embrace enough. It's fair to say that Latinos do not have a streak of arrogance in them. They acknowledge the genius, spontaneity, rituals, universality, and sophistication that is found in both camps. But is a happy wedding possible when family roots are involved? The roots of both are in Africa, but Afro-Cuban *is* Africa. White musicians are less likely to have been taught to play by their grandfathers or family members than Latins or black musicians. Music teachers are less of an influence than family ancestors who are listening from the Great Beyond. Are the self-taught less acceptable?

The musicians of either choosing donate love as a sacred obligation. Their hearts are drums that pulsate with echoes in chambers, murmurs in cavities, fluctuations in their veins. They keep the world resounding within Nature's super bowl environment. They support a mystery that sings for humanity. They seem chosen.

As an orchestral organ, when silenced or expressed, the forte music of Life comes to us as grief or as gaiety from the heart. That internal metronome and ultimate timer is also a sounding board where the vibratos, crescendos, and tremolos of daily life are played by impulse, much of which is for our ears alone.

Imagine an integration of DaVinci and Vasily Kandinsky, of Franz Liszt and Hindemith, or Calder and Rodin — interesting, but one does not mess with the heart or with its music, especially since all musicians are brothers.

Mistaken Identities

As a global target for foreign visitors, New York was a sleeping giant badly lacking linguistics, guides, and know-how. During the early seventies, the birth of our travel industry was premature. "Go to JFK, meet 45 Spaniards and escort them to their hotel" was the order I received from the tour operator, which we did. However, this simple assignment almost created an international incident that threatened to turn friends into foes.

When the passengers were seated and the baggage loaded for departure, my bus driver turned on the public address system and handed me the mike. "Bien venidos a los Estados Unidos y a la Gran Manzana (the big apple), y viva España," was my friendly welcome. This was the customary greeting I extended to overseas visitors to New York. For the French, it was Vive la France. Suddenly, it was as though a bomb had exploded in the bus from the front to the rear. Hostile shouting resounded in a language I had never heard. These were all Basque nationalists jumping up from their seats, reacting in shock and awe as I also was, together with my driver. It was as though I were welcoming some Irish Protestants with a blessing from the Pope, or an Israeli/Arab confrontation.

Fortunately, my convincing sincerity and my repeated apologies simmered them down so that I was able to restore control; I mentioned my memorable visit to "la Perla del Cantabrico, San Sebastian, and beautiful Biarritz, as well as how warmly I had been welcomed by their countrymen.

Another meet-and-greet encounter involved fifty Argentine cadets on a good-will visit to the United States, coming to New York from Washington, where it seems they had been snubbed by our State Department. It was a moment in our history when we were obliged to condemn Argentina's treatment of its element and of *los desaparecidos*. The papers were loaded with photos of mothers carrying portraits of their missing children in streets of Buenos Aires. After Washington, it was understandable why they would identify me with the policies that were prevalent at the time.

Since I had had no advance briefing on any of the diplomatic intrigue involved in my assignment, and because I had always been received with *brazos abiertos* (open arms) when my ship laid over in B.A., I extended *un fuerto abrazo* (a warm embrace) as they boarded the bus.

On this occasion, a totally opposite reaction manifested itself, much different than the Basque fiasco. This was prompted by my mentioning at the mike that I was a soccer fan (untrue), and a friend of Luis Herrera, their international polo- and race-car champion (true). Having anticipated a cold-shoulder reception, the general and his cadets were in the palm of my hand. I solidified this newborn friendship by referring to tender beef, tango nights, and the floor shows at the Mar del Plata Casino. Since everyone had spent days eating Anglo food, I suggested a churrasco at El Rincón Criollo, the only Argentine restaurant in New York at that time. The cadets were traveling on their stomachs, so the offer was accepted by loud cheering. This was music to my ears since I would be receiving a commission for the business from the restaurant.

Furthermore, the officer-in-command had been forewarned concerning turning his wards loose on Times Square's 42nd Street, with its muggers, druggies, and prosties. The mean streets could not compete with home cooking, so the young men in their twenties who were hoping for a wild time in our town found an outlet of sorts in the liquor they were served at El Rincón. It was explained to all concerned that the fixed-menu dinner was prepaid but that all drinks were on the individual.

The food was a grand success but the beverages got out of control, of course, as I envisioned my growing commission. Unfortunately, my cut was used to cover the mishandled total bill, so that I ended up with a different compensation. The Argentines left America with a good impression after all, and the general handed me a medal from the *Círcolo Militar*, the one intended for the State Department.

Natural Disasters & Wild Parties

Chile is known for its wine, women, and festivals. The Viña del Mar Film Festival is the Latin American equivalent of Cannes. To get there from Santiago, a British-built railway runs along the coast, entering and exiting a long chain of unlit tunnels. Some tunnels run in and out of total darkness very quickly; others go on forever. The interiors of the carriages remain blacked out, except for emergency lighting.

Chile is a very friendly country, so that I began an introductory traveler's conversation with the young lady sitting beside me. She was ripe, plump, and sweet-smelling like the fruit Chile is known for. She was luscious, a delicious papaya called *la fruta bomba* in Spanish.

At first, we sat silent while passing through several tunnels, resuming talking only to refrain upon entering the next, and so forth. Since she knew her tunnels and I didn't, she began to talk just as we were exiting, stopping as we entered the darkness, until I found her hand searching for mine in silence. There was no need to talk, except to mention that I would be staying at the Hotel Miramar.

At the hotel as I was preparing for the beach, there came a gentle knocking at the door that coincided with sudden pounding at my window. A wave came crashing against it — we were having a Chilean earthquake! I opened the door. Rosita was calm, smiling, happy to see me. I was as rattled as the windows. She knew her earthquakes and I didn't. I embraced her with anxiety, urgency, intensity, and necessity. When the room began to swing, sway, rattle, and rock, I was shuddering, causing Rosita to laugh at me. When the bed hit the wall while we were acting like lunatics, I thought, Ride it out or run naked into the street. But this meant coitus interruptus. She silenced my fears with a prolonged kiss, as though it had all been fun and a wild party. As she prepared to leave me, still shaking, she laughingly said, "I hope you enjoy your visit to Chile."

Enrico Caruso said he would never return to San Francisco because of the earthquake, but I couldn't wait to someday return to Chile. Same thing in Japan, where a sudden landslide almost interrupted what we were doing. Atami, with its many bed-&-board hotels is known as the Niagara Falls of Japan. The many honeymooners, because of flooded streets, high tides, and mudslides, stay snug in bed, but not bored. A nasty hurricane caught us in bed in the middle of the Atlantic aboard the S.S. Oslofjord with no chance of escape. Looks like I'll die in bed somewhere, but not alone, and with a smile on my face, in spite of Mother Nature's idiosyncrasies.

The Old Park Plaza

I was not at the Park Plaza to meet women, as one does at some crowded bar. I was there to drink in the rhythms, lyrics, and excitement that were not part of my otherwise dreary world. Women entered the picture on the basis of their specific sizes, availability, ages, shapes, rather than their overall physical attractiveness, since I was more interested in selecting the right dance partner to better coincide with my absence of expertise. Actually, the older women suited me best, their having more patience with an eighteen-year-old beginner. The thermal quality of their very close seductive dancing contrasted with young girls who maintain a respectful distance. The more attractive women were the best dancers, having progressed further thanks to their popularity. They also had better knowledge of the latest moves, so that my advancement on the floor was now at a faster pace. To finally dance with the best was a trophy, a gold-medal accomplishment, especially since you had to bravely ask her or her partner's permission

When women are found to be less important in your formative years than dancing and musical influences, it is then that you assert your self-esteem, like a rite of passage. The woman in your life is in many ways superior to you. Dancing is a woman's sport. Dancing engenders a desire to excel, to be "good," to become perhaps one day a champion on the dance floor stage! Now you can lead the woman gracefully and capably, having shed your ungainly shyness.

Whatever inevitable competitive activity we encounter in our basic formation, dancing leads us to better-balanced decisions and sharp reflexes. We learn when to advance, when to retreat, etc. Sunday visits to the Park Plaza replaced Sunday mass. My manic dancing became a triangular routine: Saturday Rumba Matinee at La Conga Club, Sunday at the Park Plaza, and often evenings at the Havana Madrid Club. I arose in the morning after dancing in my sleep. My command of Spanish improved along with my footwork. Songs like "Oye, Mi Cachia," "Teng' Una Rumbita," "¡Pa' Que No La Bailes Como Baile Yo?"— translated: Sweetie, I have a nice rumba. Why don't you dance it as I do? I also learned to decipher the lyrics. The singer is telling her to forget the conservative *danzón*, in favor of the rhumba. Such exposure formed an autodidactic education, unequaled in any formal setting. It taught me to recognize stylistic variations of vocalists and of dancers like the Ballet Mambos of Mike Terrace

The beautiful composition called "Siloney," written by the sister of Maestro Ernesto Lecuona, speaks of the original native population of Cuba. It all formed an autodidactic education unequaled anywhere else. It also taught me about the vocal talents of personalities such as Pedro Flores, Pedro Ramirez, later Bobby Capo, and still later, Benny More and Celina and Graciela

Perez (Gracie), who sang at El Pasaje (the Passageway) Nightclub in front of the Cuban capitol with the Anacaona Castro sisters band, not to mention the truly very greatest female vocalist Celia Cruz. These names are as well known throughout the millions in Latin America as are Chaplin, Barrymore, Eddy Fisher or Sinatra. Unfortunately, most of our neighbors here at home have never known of them. On a more serious note, we attended the wakes of Tito Puente, Mario Rivera, Graciela, Max Salazar, Leo Fleming, Sr., Hector La Voe—names that represented Latin artistic excellence. Let us not forget Los Chaveles de España. All these performers and thousands of others come from the breast of Spain, a mother to them all!

In the case of many black and various mixed personages of extraordinary ability, we bow in particular reverence to musicians such as Bilingi, Carlos Vidal, Julio Andino, and perhaps the very greatest and most cherished—José Manheral, Sr. (Burú), whose greatness came from the breast of Mother Africa, and like Arsenio Rodriguez—who cried out "¡Africa, Soy Yo!" (I am Africa!). This reminds one of Geanni Versace "Io Sono Milano," (I am Milan).

The Park Plaza was the birthplace, the cradle, of many of these people. It grew nourishing a growing culture that today exceeds 34 million in America del Norte alone.

If the Palladium can very justifiably be known universally as the "Home of the Mambo," we can well refer to the Park Plaza as the manager of, the cradle of, dancing, singing, and exuberance (The Puerto Rican Day Parade, for example) that is growing strong and upright in our country today. There are no bronze plaques at the sites of the Palladium or the Park Plaza, few streets are named in honor of the many artists who built a reputation that is now... .

The Park Plaza

There was no mike, bandstand, spotlight, or amplifier, but two alarm bells were posted in opposite corners to alert the bouncers to where the trouble was. The printed exit sign was not lit and no fire safety equipment was to be seen. The emergency exit was surely locked to prevent illegal entry. It opened onto a narrow alley that was shared with the neighboring Teatro Hispanico, and ended out on Fifth Avenue. The entrance to the Park Plaza was through a narrow hallway, typical of Harlem buildings. On the left, a narrow stairway went up to the larger Park Palace Ballroom, which had better lighting, large windows, and twice the space, plus a bandstand with a mike. The lavatories were sanitary and brightly lit. We remember our preferring the Plaza.

Four iron columns supported the ceiling on the dance floor of the Park Plaza. The one in the darkest corners served as much to hold up the ceiling as to provide a bolster for the woman while her partner pressed his body against hers, grinding away in keeping with the music. Couples took turns. It took some skill to reach gratification before the song being played ended and the floor emptied. This unacceptable behavior was mostly conveniently ignored or politely overlooked as the exception rather than the rule. This, it must be remembered, was at a time when rooftops were obligatory venues for lovers.

"It's safer inside than outside," I told my friend Anatole Broyard, as we planned to bring some Villagers to the Park Plaza. We organized two taxi loads after briefing the party concerning proper behavior and safety measures regarding jewelry, etc. Like subway tracks in the thirties, taxi meters made loud clicking noises. We arrived in high spirits, tipping the drivers — ten cents each, the standard tip during the Great Depression, regardless of the distance traveled. A barricaded ticket window was unheard of downtown [Vincent, ticket window where? A taxi or at the Park Plaza?] making a bit of uneasiness among friends as we entered the hallway entrance to pay our admissions. Suddenly, a commotion arose inside, causing some screaming, followed by a minor stampede that plowed into our party. Half of our group ran back to the taxis and left, perhaps satisfied to do so.

With, I estimate, 200-300 Cuban and Puerto Ricans in the surrounding neighborhood, why was there never a long line waiting to enter? People desperate to dance were penniless. While some Greek and Roman stadiums and theaters charged admission, the old coliseum was free to all. Today we might consider this morale boosting as a project similar to City Meals-On-Wheels, part of a caring community that would also help unemployed musicians…and not a Lincoln Center scheme of some sort.

In the islands, dancing and swimming went together, as they do at Rio's Carnival when crowds swim along Copacabana to cool off, and return to continue festivities. Opposite the Park Plaza is Meer Lake. In 1939, there were three rowboats that we untied when the band took a break, allowing us to row out into the dark privacy of the middle of the lake under the stars, rowing back frantically when the sound of music came across the water to us.

In the Dominican Republic, behind the waterfront club Taino were shacks with mattresses for rent. In Montevideo dives, mattresses behind curtained areas on floor landings in the building served patrons. With no element of danger or stolen pleasure, unlike our rocking row boats, modern cruise ships are floating bedrooms with convenient cabins near your disco. Roman baths, Bangkok Brothers, Amsterdam walk in-walk out, Reno, Nevada ranches — none of these could give the romance of the open sky of Central Park's lake or the raw sex that took place against that iron column on the Park Plaza dance floor.

One of the more popular songs heard at the Plaza was "Camina Como Chencha." Chencha was a lame girl who was asked to dance every dance. This showed courage, spirit, determination, and a certain beautiful concern on the part of the males, who were determined to assure that she, in particular, enjoyed life, such as it was, in her condition. One night while saying good night to a friend living on West 114th Street, "the most dangerous street in the city," a woman ran screaming down the steps of the stoop we were on. She was being beaten by a man in front of us. Switchblades in '39 were today's box cutters. "We women carry razor blades," said my friend, showing me hers wrapped by a rubber band that she had hidden in her elastic stocking.

The enjoyment of having experienced an event like the Park Plaza compensated for having to go home by subway, or worse, for those who went to bed alone. It was when the trumpets fell silent and the bass began to pack, and the guitarists tip-toed off, that the show was over, honoring the piano that lastly tinkled good to the last note. Some New York Latin orchestras ended with "Good Night IRené." Once, while on the way out, I turned around to look at the dance floor. Nothing ever looked as vacant after that. It was a classic shock of recognition. So was the rest of the waiting world outside on West 110th Street, where it was Ford Madox Ford's "Parade's End." [Vincent, tell me more about this!]

The Park Plaza with the Afro-Cuban beat got a crippled country back on its feet, dancing! Twisa Moungu, Echale Salsita, Get Hot, Hot Shot, Hot Stuff, and that cool gal Hot Tomato, have become both hot and cool today, like those remarkable dancers at the old Park Plaza. We wonder whether our disco-club scene can do it, beginning with a cultural climate change. Viva *La Musica* — Afro-Cubana!

The Park Plaza

When one steps outside the circle of the family and by doing so, encounters the true world for the first time, whatever knowledge gained in that way has a tremendous impact on the future course of one's life. Americans taking *le grand tour* of Europe returned home with a cultural concept with high values. Thus, we became a society interested in learning. Students today whose parents send them off to Cancun, Jamaica, or Nassau, for instance, expose these young minds to inferior influences. The students quickly adopt as part of their formation unrefined behavior, mediocre interests, and less sophisticated lifestyles.

Next to visiting a foreign country is the familiarization gained through the literature that country produces. Visiting the West Indian Islands, where literary achievement is scarce, it is music that has the power to influence and formulate the direction of one's life.

What has this to do with the Park Plaza? Like a first-time encounter with a foreign country, the Park Plaza dance hall in '37-'38 helped to fashion a more salutary individual, thanks to the musical education found there. I traveled to the Park Plaza searching for music of a certain flavor — Afro-Cuban. I couldn't dance a step, I didn't know a soul, couldn't understand a word, couldn't play a note, nor could I spare during the Great Depression the carfare and the admission. At a time when there was little joy in the world, the music gave me the reason I needed to set off from Fort Hamilton, Brooklyn up to Harlem when it was dangerous to do so.

I found what I was searching for the moment I heard the Happy Boys Orchestra as I paid my $.25 admission. The ticket window was grilled like a Bronx bodega cashier's. The bandstand was a lighted area as I sought a chair near an exit sign. The ladies, young and old, were lined up facing the young and old men, all sitting on rows of chairs that lined the walls. For the first few numbers that the band played, I felt no need to do other than sit and listen, filled with the satisfaction of having found what I needed. I was not destined to remain a wallflower for long, for after my second visit I was approached by a girl who came and asked me to dance, something unheard of at the time. I wisely declined, feeling foolish. But better to feel foolish than look foolish on the dance floor. What I needed now was the ability to dance rumba.

On my third visit, a tall black fellow came up to m e. "I see you sitting. Why don't you dance?"

"I don't know how," I answered him.

"Show him how," he said to his partner.

So it was the René and Estella, the top Afro-Cuban dance team perhaps for all time, got me dancing. That brief encounter was the first step that led me around the world on cruise ships, hotels, night clubs, dance studios, and lectures, carrying Afro-Cuban rumba with me for others to learn. To popularize it was what now was needed, to its joyous content on to others.

When the management of the Park Plaza installed a very large upright fan, the admission went up to \$.35. It was set at the top of the stairway that led up from the basement, where the latrines were located. Currents of air carrying male and female pheromones floated over the dance area. In this way, ethereal substances, sex steroids, were added to the suggestive lyrics, the flirtations in progress, the orchestral vibrations, the sweet-smelling tobacco, the overlapping perfumes floating in the congested intimacy of a room one-third the size of the Palladium filled to the brim with sensuality. The large fan added spice to the feverish environment, increasing body temperatures to the maximum. The latrine windows were wide open to allow cold air to enter the building. A communal urinal, like a trough found on animal farms, served to allow a constant flow of water that kept the pipes from freezing in winter.

No one lingered long, for the glare of the white-tiled walls disturbed one's mood. You returned to the darkness of the dance floor, the music, and your partner at the sound of the first note of the rumba, buttoning up as you ran. If someone were to yell fire, dance might continue until flames were seen.

As one of the only sources of gaiety during thirty-percent unemployment in America, the Park Plaza's rumba world was vital. At a time when you would be asked to "please leave the dance floor" if your dancing was indiscreet, here the behavior was encouraged as an ingredient of joyful exuberance. The "Piropo," that titillating, sexy innuendo of everyday Cuba manifested itself in the physical activity on the floor, like intimate paintings that spring to life.

The Happy Boys Band with Doroteo Santiago did not take long breaks. The two-minute numbers allowed frequent change of partners. Particularly favorite pieces would be repeated. To tease dancers, the band employed a mock break, resulting in chairs being thrown into the middle of the floor, in jest, not in anger. (This display of bogus protest was inspired by cowboy-movie barroom fights popular in the Thirties.) The music resumed, with prostrate suppliants rising up off the floor to continue d dancing.

Eléctrico was a *live wire*, to use a post-Edison label. He was greased lightning, with his spasmodic *quelradas*, razor-sharp style, top speed, deadpan (*cara fea*) showmanship. His solos were the highlight of an evening of highlights. Every part of his body was in complete synchronization with the music. Perhaps it helps to imagine Killer Joe at the Palladium, except that Eléctrico was closer to a style of rumba called Columbia, which was closer to true Afro-Cuban ritual, with some break moves involving hitting the floor with the flat of your palms and your feet off the ground.

"Midnight," *negro como el telefono*, black as a 1930s telephone, was the only dancer who challenged Eléctrico, the dance master of the Park Plaza. He would hurry out onto the floor while applause for Eléctrico was still resounding, so as to cut into Eléctrico's performance appraisal. Midnight dressed entirely in black, including a rare vest, an encumbrance which gave him a fuller, more solid contrast to Eléctrico's string-bean frame. Midnight had a down-and-dirty, solid-man quality that contrasted with Eléctrico's height advantage (a four-inch difference). Where Eléctrico flew, Midnight was a glued deep into the music *heavy* man. Eléctrico was far out; he had the whole place stunned, shocked. Like two road-runners, their movements risked stress fractures. Amazingly, neither seemed to be out of breath off the floor. It was the audience that was left breathless.

The trumpets of the Happy Boys brought down the walls of the Great Depression. They were the pipers we followed to recovery. From a low-key romantic locale hidden away in El Barrio, they raised the level of intensity in their choice of more cheerful melodies, such as "Ahora Seremos Felices." Most Park Plaza patrons were from West 114th Street, "the most dangerous street in New York" at the time. Many of them did not own a radio. They went home singing along dark streets a music that disseminates happiness around the world.

Foreplay at the Park Plaza

Fancy footwork on the dance floor was a form of foreplay, complete with perspiration, panting, and pre-coital contortion. Friction caused internal combustion in such a pressure-cooker environment, this often leading to consensual mutual masturbation called dancing. Where else could such somatic satisfaction be bought for thirty-five cents admission price?...a price that could include outright orgasm? Cover and excuse for ecstatic behavior was provided by rhythmic overtones. Expert dancers abandoned concentration on agile footwork in order to create instead, intentional sexual excitement. They played the women like slide guitars. Males would find her center of gravity, located in the small of her back. By raising his supporting hand, or by lowering it up and down her spine, the couple achieved better focal contact. Raising his hand allowed him to brush her nipples as she rotated in front of him.

Like dancing itself, expert foreplay could be defined as grace under fire. It included a faster increase in movement called "montuno," first introduced by master Arsenio Rodriguez. Once securely interlocked, couples danced as one, increasing intimacy. Parting, they returned casually to their respective tables. Couples often chose to ignore faster rhythms in order to better experience foreplay in half-time.

Lowering his supporting right hand down her spine brought the lower part of his partner closer to him. For a much firmer pressure while dancing against his partner, the male gripped the pole behind his partner, placing her in a vice. It appears pole dancing has been around for a while. Whispering in her ear was intimate like modern phone sex, where the lyrics were substituted for her name in them. After what resembled an upright lap dance, couples parted, sharing the stolen forbidden fruit of risqué behavior and shared secrets.

Forward to 1999, Calle Ocho Fiesta, Miami. Two couples performing *El Baile del Gato*…doggie style on all fours. This dance never caught on—not in public, at any rate.

The Park Plaza crowd consisted of more women than men. I believe it was because during the Great Depression men had no paying jobs, whereas women were milliners (women all wore hats), seamstresses, and dressmakers with sewing machines. Women at the Park Plaza were either widows or mothers of young girls seeking husbands. You could see the difference in their dress: Widows had hats, many with feathers (we saw some with imitation paste cherries). The daughters were very well costumed in the latest patterns, since they as well as their mothers custom-made their dresses to show their shapes. What they all had was perfume, not cologne. Strangely, they all had the same scent, as thought the only acceptable perfume was Tabu. If it wasn't Tabu, it was a lesser kind that was cheaper and therefore not as fashionable. Tabu lasted in popularity for that reason well into the end of 1940. The mother and daughter duet was evident since girls were chaperoned and came looking for husbands among men who could afford the twenty-five cent price of admission. It was not fertile ground like long lines like the Palladium, since people had no money to spend for entertainment. You could not hear the band outside in the street as you could at the Palladium. To hear Latin music, you had to stand by a firehouse that put the radio outside (few people owned radios), or at West 116th Street you could hear *la musica* at the Rafael Hernandes music store or at the music store in Borough Hall, Brooklyn that sold Columbia, Casino de la Playa records for fifty cents in 1938. It also sold musical instruments.

The entrance to the Park Plaza was also known previously as the Golden Casino, perhaps hoping for a gambling casino-type establishment like the *Rhumba Casino*, a gambling locale that was never licensed but was intended to support gambling by the Mafia), in West End, Long Branch, New Jersey, like Asbury Park.

It was only after the dance hall was emptied out that the perspiration of the evening was very evident. Up to that point, because of the feeling of community engendered by the music, no one took offense or even notice of an odor—especially since it could have been described as more woman than man. Since I had never known the smell of grass, I innocently associated the distinctive sweet smell with the tropical West Indies as the cause of the smell—as a type of tobacco that was indigenous to that part of the world, just as pipe tobacco different from cigarette tobacco. In the men's room downstairs, in spite of all the open windows, the smoke hit me to where I really found the message in the drums, and especially in the loud trumpeting that opened up my deafness (My lead-poisoned brain), and brought the joy in the world closer to me at a time in our history when there was none. If you were stopped and frisked for grass, as I once was, they didn't arrest you. They just took it for themselves. In that way, the public, in most communities in New York, knew very little about grass. It was also not talked about in general, but cool. Even when Chano Pozo was killed, little was mentioned in the papers in general about the details or the reason.

The tall fan that was later installed and was located as to bring in fresh air for cooling up from the cooler basement windows, that fan also brought on to the dancers the sweet-smelling fumes that turned everyone on in a ------------. Also guaranteed, after five or six hours of such a setting of youth or old-age dancing, under Tabu, grass, or perhaps more, plus the need to find happiness in a strange land with the Happy Boys at their best, beating out even *descargas*, you can bet the Park Plaza would not remain unappreciated for very long. Where else in the whole wide universe could you go so delightfully out of your mind? It wasn't groovy, solid, or cool—it was all of it, and you were as much a part of it as the persons next to you that were jumping with you. If it were around today, or if the great Palladium had continued, perhaps the world that we know today would be better handled, better synchronized. It's not too late to continue hoping that people might one day find themselves "Strangers in Paradise," as I found myself that time back in 1938.

It was a very long train ride on the West End local from blond-haired, blue-eyed Fort Hamilton, Brooklyn to dark-skinned, flashing eyes in Harlem, but the music made the ride easy round-trip. If the Park Plaza was not the Pentecostal Church (Assembly) that it is today, I and so many others would be there sharing what could be called a carnival in paradise, or, better still even, a miracle on 110th Street. After all, the Park Plaza became bigger, if not better, when Machito and Noro showed up. The old Pan Art, Tico, Code, etc. records are still out there with the Happy Boys keeping *la musica* alive forever. Together with the mercurial mambo, we will always be ready to rumba.

Going north along Fifth during the Thirties made 110th Street the last stop, where buses, double-deckered, made Greenwich Village the last stop going south. Bus conductors came by to collect the five-cent fare. To take the bus was a joyful ride, made romantic and exciting by the sights passing by that included, for many blocks from 57 on, the refreshing scenery of Central Park, as well as the elegant mansions of the very wealthy. But when you got off at 110, you knew you were in another more unfamiliar world. To go to Harlem during the thirties, where the Great Depression was still raging, was a risky adventure, but strangely secure if you minded your own business. Today, with some people in the world behaving like animals, perhaps it was the music's influence in El Barrio that soothed savagery. Violence was, as it always has been, mainly love triangles more so than robberies—someone stealing your girlfriend, for example. Inside the Park Plaza, a certain decorum, like an understanding, prevailed. It was a heated, sex-prone environment. You parked your hostile jealousy outside. The bouncer was bored (he even found time to get in a dance mood), except for rare outbursts that as time went on became more prevalent, due to the increase in the number of men over women, the more-congested dance space, with the popularity of the Park Plaza becoming known, and the more prosperous participants emerging from the Great Depression now possessing money for hard liquor. Women also felt more liberated to behave less conservatively, just as society in general was.

Chano Pozo's death, followed by Malcolm X's at the Audubon Dance Hall, was condemned by the black and Latino communities. When Cugat and Miguelito Valdez were performing at the Waldorf Astoria in 1942, I was ordered to leave the dance floor because my flashy rumba was not "proper." Even though I obeyed the bouncers, who wore formal clothing, I could see that the ringside audience did not agree with him. They were curious to see more rumba, not Arthur Murray.

Returning Home

In 1959, I was about to leave sunny Florida for the Nord Cap, the North Cape Cruise aboard the Caronia. While packing my luggage, I discovered among some change from assorted countries I had visited, a coin from Iceland, a country I had never been to. Someone must have passed this tiny coin, small as a dime, off on me. Since we would be stopping at Reykjavik, of all places, I threw it in my bag.

Miami and Reykjavik are as different as night and day. Above the Arctic Circle, Iceland is the "Land of the Midnight Sun," and like jet-lag, your sleeping routine is upset when the sun never goes down behind the horizon, and midday is like midnight for most of the year. The Borg Hotel lobby bar was the brightest spot in the capital, where, like Nome, Alaska, the spunky citizens are proud of their stamina and ability to hold their liquor. The talk is mostly about fish, and the city smells much like Bergen, Norway. With no smart shops, cathedrals, or museums in 1958, Reykjavik was kind of "Why do people live here" place. Even so, I'm sure they miss it when they are away and are happy when they return home.

The language is impossible, the hard liquor hard to swallow, and aside from ice caves, there is not even skiing on its scrubby glaciers (Think *permafrost*). Like Easter Island, there were few trees to be found growing in the lava formations, few birds, and a sad beach with black sand, darker than Mt. Pelee's in Martinique. Being an inveterate tourist, I left the cheerful carousers at the Hotel Borg bar and took a taxi to see the sights. This was no Sun Valley or Snow Owl Inn in New Hampshire, more like Montauk. I closed my eyes and dozed off, helped by the "Welcome to Iceland" vodka toast I had, the uninteresting main street, and the scattered desolation of the outskirts. I would have welcomed a display of spectacular Hawaiian volcanic volatility. Sadly, Iceland went bankrupt in spite of being energy self-sufficient — thanks to its thermodynamic hot springs.

In the middle of nowhere, the taxi came to a halt. "Go see the hot water coming up from the ground," said the driver. I would have refused, except for the fact that I had to "go." Risking frostbite, I walked gingerly up to a small pool of steaming, bubbling, gaseous water. As I was about to rush back to the cab, the driver called out, "Make a wish. Throw a coin in the water. You will come back to Iceland." Now, I have thrown many pennies into fountains — even over my shoulder at Trevi, but a wishful thought of returning to Iceland — should I risk it? I searched in my pocket for a coin. Out came the one I had carried for thousands of miles from the sunshine state. As I was about to toss it into the gurgling, sulfurous pool of vaporous water, I stopped cold, then dropped it gently in. I returned to the taxi with a warm inner glow, mumbling, "I'm sure as hell never coming back here, but the little coin has."

The Revenge of the Whales'

Imaginary disasters make good fiction and sold-out films. But like a fire in a forest that rekindles itself once it has been conquered, let us put two catastrophes together.

The BP leak has been plugged but collateral damage has caused fissures, fractures, and ruptures that are vents, now widespread in the Gulf. Like an active volcano, the spill is alive, spreading into the hundreds of miles of subterranean cave systems that provide us with drinking water. These vast networks of invisible aquifers are now infiltrated by oil. Used for irrigation, this water kills crops.

Due to condensation, evaporation, and convection, the surface oil is drawn up into our rain clouds, assisted also by hurricanes or fog. Rain clouds carried across the U.S. eventually release poison down upon our lakes, reservoirs, and fields. This process is repeated when the rain falls back on the Gulf's surface, only to return to the sky. The rain, once a cleanser of the environment, now pollutes it further. Planes cannot enter these clouds and are forced to bypass them.

The reddish color of the contamination resembles the red tide, the "turned to blood" of the oceans mentioned by St. John the Divine. Oil is thrown on restless seas to calm them. The two don't mix, but detergents in the water can kill us in a no-win way. What is made by nature to float will never stay sunk. She balances our overflowing world population like water seeking its proper level, with disaster. The Deep Horizon leak is just one large-scale method of adjusting the world beyond our hopes, prayers, or "progress." Destiny is at work. "You want oil? We give it to you, and drown you in it." —Signed, Moby-Dick, 1851

Robert Farris Thompson

What's an old white man like me doing teaching Afro-Cuban music, art and history? I grew up in El Paso, Texas, an early training center for a globalized world. At El Paso's Dudley School, around 1944, I saw a good-looking Mexican-American girl lead the entire school in a mass conga line. She was clearly calling us to somewhere else.

I came closer to that "somewhere else" when my father gave me my first record, a 78 of "Canto Karabalí," by the great Cuban composer Ernesto Lecuona. I had no idea what "Song of Calabar" meant, but the melody got to me. It was an acoustical Tarot card that said, "This is your future."

Growing up in a Latino/Anglo city, I heard on the local radio station soul numbers like "Signed, Sealed, Delivered," and from a station broadcasting from Juárez, Mexican hits like "Amor Chiquito." There was a small black population armed with boogie-woogie and the blues that would shape my mind forever. I learned how to play boogie on piano from a young man named Lloyd Stevens and marveled at the train-whistle blues and sanctified beats performed by a black El Pasoan named Jesse Brown.

In the fall of 1948 I started to study Spanish. I studied for my first test to the beat of Afro-Cuban records. When I sat down to write my exam, verbs and vocabulary came tumbling down while music played in my mind.

From that moment on, Spanish language and Afro-Cuban music took over my soul.

But a most important inspiration struck me when I arrived, with my parents and sister, for a vacation in Mexico City in March 1950. While my family crashed in the Hotel del Prado I hit the streets. I wandered into the National Palace, where I saw Diego Rivera working on a heroic mural of the ancient Aztec city of Tenochtitlán. Returning to the Prado I was startled to find Anthony Quinn in the elevator with me, in town filming the "The Brave Bulls." I opened the windows to my room to discover what appeared to be the Duke and Duchess of Windsor having tea across the patio. Four celebrities in 45 minutes.

Something was going to happen. And it did. In the Prado dining room, I heard for the first time an exciting form of music that was to orient and anchor me forever: mambo.

Mambo is a blend: Afro-Cuban, jazz and classical. It took me from calm to excitement, like the jump from black and white into Technicolor. Mambo's hard-swinging minimalism gave me access to a style that challenged me to my very essence. Moving to the East Coast, I spent as much time as I could at the Palladium at Broadway and 53rd Street, epicenter of New York mambo.Mambo in New York made you realize that one of the luckiest things that happened to American popular culture was the Jones Act, which bestowed U.S. citizenship on all Puerto Ricans. Two of the major New York mambo kings, Tito Puente and Tito Rodriguez, were Puerto Rican. Songs like "La Familia" documented lives in transition from the island to New York. When Tito Rodriguez sang "En un sillón de bejuco solito me acomodé" ["In an armchair of rattan I made myself comfortable"] he brought back an aspect of Caribbean living, reassuringly cozy and Creole. The same impulse led Puerto Ricans in New York to build casitas, small, brightly painted island-style houses, in vacant lots in the Bronx or Spanish Harlem to offset the surrounding slablike tenement buildings.

I would go on to discover that mambo was dancing us all toward genuine being, becoming ourselves through caring about others. To proclaim this rich cross-cultural achievement became the goal of my teaching at Yale from the moment I started in 1964. In the '70s, mambo morphed into salsa. In 2008, it's called Latin jazz. I thank God for the Cubans, Puerto Ricans, African-Americans, Dominicans, Mexicans and other Latinos who keep it all going.

Mambo distills their cross-cultural insights, leading us, for example, to a Puerto Rican man who learned to live among the Anglos, Jews, Italians and Irish. In a wonderful book on his life, "Benjy Lopez: A Picaresque Tale of Emigration and Return," by Barry B. Levine, he shared this insight: "Imagine if you were twenty years old and didn't feel inferior to anybody or better than anybody. When you treat everybody the same, people open up to you." Those are words I have tried to live by.

Suitable Dancing at the Plaza: The Convergence of Bodies in Anatomically Correct Positions on the Dance Floor

Sexually transmitted euphoria required a comfortable adjustment, a proper "fit" that was natural in appearance, to conform to the rules of propriety. Only the dancers' self-control suppressed sudden raw, audacious contortions, even while performing with increasing vigor and inborn spontaneity.

When the evening began, the Happy Boys played short numbers to allow a process of selection, a change of partners. This was followed by longer numbers with better partnerships. The band would also mischievously pause, silent, stop entirely, teasing the dancers with spasmodic interruptions and pseudo-finales. This repeated trickery produced lingering waves of recurrent pleasure that mimicked an "after-glow." Endings were often repetitive, ejected at the very last note. When a satisfied male unfairly abandoned his malleable female partner during or at the end of this critical procedure, Mother Nature demanded ultimate fulfillment. She, the stimulated female, found even greater arousal in the arms of a second man that allowed her the pleasures of illicit promiscuity, like jumping from one bed to another, without stigma.

When daughters accompanied widowed mothers to the Park Plaza, both could be seeking mates. The Great Depression ruthlessly disrupted normalcy and tradition. Women often survived thanks to their God-given anatomy. All this was not a scenario of sex-hungry males and sex-famished females; even if performed horizontally, it would still be "wild party," slightly orgiastic but well within the perimeter of propriety, with discretion minus visible vulgarity (All the more admirable considering Latin impulsiveness). This was not 1990's bathhouse obscenity. The difference was also basically the control that the music demanded and its guidance, that both stimulated and facilitated proper, "befitting" dance-floor etiquette…no clutching the crotch or pelvic or "booty" expertise displays. These particular exhibitions would eventually appear at the Palladium, but with more or less humorous acceptance or embarrassed approval. At the Park Plaza, such boorish antics would have been rejected as robbing Latin dancing of its inherent dignity, of its La Raze

Mabuhay, Salamat

In Tacloban while at a terrific party in 1944, my vision suddenly became blurred. As pain in both eyes began, I called it an early night and left in panic. The next morning, I learned that two men were blinded by tupa, a homemade brew that is still feared today. Even so, my recollection of Tacloban and its fine people is a favorable one, and dear to my heart.

Watching the 2013 Miss Universe Contest, the Philippine entry came in fifth out of 82 contestants. Many travelers to Southeast Asia are taken by surprise at the unpopularized beauty of many of the women. My date at the party in 1944 was one of them. She was wearing a flowing silk gown made from a U.S. Army parachute that I had given her. But before she, in her fine attire, and I, in my uniform, could dance together, I left hurriedly, never to see her again.

In 1944, Tacloban's main street was unpaved and very muddy from the frequent rainstorms. Sixty-some years later, with a population of 22,200, and modern in many parts, I could still see it as it once was, plain as day.

When the Miss Universe Contest originating in Moscow ended, I tuned into Channel 539 where super-typhoon Haiyan was destroying Tacloban completely, my nostalgia traveled from the dramatic to the romantic, ending in the tragic (but gratefully not permanently) going blind, and for not being there now, thanks God.

All the South Pacific islands had rice paddies close by, as was the case in Bangkok, as late as the fifties, where, although paved, they were muddy. In 1940, the paved streets of Miami Beach were covered with sand. Minnesota's streets were covered with ice and snow in winter, and with leaves in autumn up in New England, whereas Venice has her flooded allies needing bridges to cross, not to mention our water main breaks.

Tagalog, the native language, borrows from the Spanish, Hindi and English, similar to Haiti's Kriol (Creole), borrowed from French. But there is one word in Tagalog that stands out today in any language—donayson. Spoken quickly, it reveals its message, one we all hear, if not with our ears, then with our hearts.

After graduating as a French military intelligence operative (along with Henry Kissinger, who was in the same class), I was assigned to Philippine Civil Affairs Unit. Our mission was to rebuild the societies and economies that were destroyed by the Japanese. This training later resulted in military government, the very successful policy used in assisting the Japanese mainland's recovery after the war.

My assignment took me from Guadalcanal to Samar Island, and to Leyte, Manila, Okinawa, and finally Tokyo. We did not win that war alone but with many thousands of Philippine casualties. Let us today show our brothers-in-arms the financial support and love that they badly need.

Travel Unpleasantries

Following all the drama of World War I, the world suddenly had an empty feeling to it. Compared to today, 2015, there simply was "no one around." Imagine standing today in front of Mona Lisa with no one else next to you, or lying on Copacabana Beach all alone. Walk Greenwich Village at 9 a.m. Sunday mornings and you feel back in time in a 19th-century neighborhood. Times Square at that time on most days is also "empty," not haunted but silenced, emptied. As we multiply we show more rude behaviors. The more space you have, the more life you own. People find peace far from people, say, on vacations, as a form of "vacating" a locale. On the go, only a mere handful of rather unexpected encounters called "unpleasantries" crossed my path. One here at home when an angry cab driver threw the tip I gave him back at me. It seems that when I went to sea the standard tip for taxi drivers, regardless of the distance traveled, was $.10. When I returned to life in New York, I still thought as I had prior to isolating myself on ships, so that I did not know the $.10 tip was an insult. This incident made me feel like a 1972 tourist visiting New York, quite uninformed regarding tipping. No visitor should receive such treatment, I believed. I decided to see the city from the perspective of a foreign visitor and, if possible, help change things by educating persons concerning the travel industry that was just beginning to see more foreigners.

In Spain, a Madrid shoeshine boy asked me to remove my shoes so that he could do a proper shine. This was back in 1952 when Spain was undergoing much poverty. When I complied, he ran off with my shoes, leaving me unable to run after him. In Cairo, even today, you never put anything in your handkerchief pocket. Kids run up and grab whatever they can before running off. In Morocco today, shopkeepers wrap inferior merchandise, which you don't discover until back home, believing that you received what you purchased. When the Egyptians wanted the British to leave Sudan (The English occupied Sudan at that time), a stone was thrown at my head while I was in Luxor. I must have been mistaken for an Englishman.

Some Middle Eastern people love us; others don't. A Tuareg spat at me in front of his son when I did not buy a trinket from him. In the Bekaa Valley, Lebanon, the natives turned the America flag upside down. In Iran, the Torah was on the floor at the entrance to an antique shop where customers entered, and, leaving, were obliged to step on pages of the Torah.

At Maxim's in Paris, the waiter was caught overcharging us by about $20 US. In Quebec, in a Chinese restaurant, my order contained leftovers from someone else's lunch. When I asked the waitress for an ashtray, she returned with one and said, "That will be one shilling, please." This happened in Nassau. In Rome, at an exclusive Bulgari jewelry shop, they did not give me the tourist tax exemption. I was unaware that I was entitled to receive it. When I returned to claim it I was told, "Sorry. The cash register is closed." In Damascus, the shopkeeper camouflaged the exit to keep me from leaving. In Tokyo shortly after the surrender, the shopkeeper's entire family rushed around the store erasing old prices when I came in. In Marseilles, porters on strike laughed at me breaking my back because I was carrying my luggage so I would not miss my train. In Yugoslavia, the captain left the dock, although he saw me running to the ship. I managed to jump onto the deck just in time.

In 1959, while exploring a jungle path, I tripped and fell, only to hear laughing coming from some Indians that, unaware by me, had been following behind me, hidden. In St. Martin, during the early Sixties, native people resented tourists, making visitors very uncomfortable, until the government put up a large billboard saying, Don't kill the goose that lays the golden egg!

Early tour buses had no onboard toilet facilities. We pulled up to a large restaurant on the highway, only to catch the owner putting up Restroom for customers only. A heavily sequined evening gown was missing when we left the Flora Hotel. By paying a reward, we retrieved our stolen passports in Rio. I didn't seek a path less traveled—the world itself was.

"I'd like a centrally located hotel in Prague," I advised the travel agent in London." "We have one just ten minutes from the main square," he said. When I arrived in Prague, I discovered that the agent meant by car, not within walking distance. Whoever heard of a hotel without an elevator? I had to carry luggage up three flights in three trips in France. While carrying and reading a conservative Italian newspaper in Livorno, I was insulted by the Communist dock workers. In Bombay, in 1952, I had to return to the ship and descend the gangplank, since my shirt had Muslim writing on it. In a Hindi city still recovering from massacres, an unscrupulous tour guide at a museum pocketed the entrance fee, saying, "It's closed."

After escorting sixteen very demanding Brazilian millionaires around the world for ninety days, I received no gratuity. Not only do Brazilians consider tipping belittling to a tour manager, but the travel agency told them it was not customary, I found out, adding that "the tip was already included in the package price!" In France, you can order a glass of Champagne. I did not know that if you ordered it in Argentina you must pay for the entire bottle. At La Conga in New York, I tipped the maitre-d' well for a ringside table, only to find more tables added to ringside as customers arrived all night.

At the Sert Room of the Waldorf in 1942, I was asked to "leave the dance floor" for dancing an authentic fast rumba, not Arthur Murray's rumba. Camel drivers on strike at the pyramids charged us the same for riding on a donkey. A cab driver in San Francisco charged us for a "return trip" after dropping us off at the airport for our flight. Same thing happened in South Korea. A carton of Marlboros to the chief purser allowed us to carry a puppy onboard from Barcelona to Naples. Otherwise, "No Dogs Allowed." Accepting a dinner invitation to dinner in Lisbon, I found myself starving until it was served after 10 p.m. In Buenos Aires, while in a dentist's chair, the electricity was suddenly shut off. The dentist continued using a foot pedal to operate the drill. In St. Bart's, a beach picnic party poisoned one hundred sixty of my passengers, due to potato salad left out overnight unrefrigerated. "You Jew, dirty Jew," a passing motorcyclist yelled out at me in Casablanca.

When talking of unpleasant subjects, one tends to exaggerate, but with pleasant happenings it would not be so to say that some are understated, especially if Lady Luck is involved. Perhaps we fear that we must pay back in some way, eventually. Without exaggeration, arriving in Havana in 1940 in the midst of Carnival, and not in the midst of a revolution—as photographer Walker Evans did—not only was it pleasing, it changed my approach to travel.

The Unknown Soldier

While dancing with a partner, Eléctrico was one of many, but as couples left the floor, including his partner, he went into a solo as the band continued playing, now for him alone. We soon saw that we were in the presence of greatness. Here was something stunning, like Mike Tyson's debut in the boxing world. He would arrive and leave alone. No one embraced or approached him, respecting his stature with distance, as we did on the dance floor proper. A low-key modesty characterized his social behavior. Only the musicians, the drummers in particular, were seen close to him. Respect was more appropriate than celebrity. In 1938, dancers dressed in a serious fashion, with jackets and ties and gray suits (except for Midnight's black suit and vest). The scene at the Park Plaza was incongruous with raw African moves dressed in Western garb. His partner was the seated drummer more than una Latina. They were working rather than performing, as we tried to catch their smallest gestures.

There were many Electricas in Cuba, but here in New York we were unaware of them. After his style became a name called Eléctrico, others became known as *dinamita, mecanico, el indio, Killer Joe, Cuban Pete*. He seemed embarrassed for having made us all look like unaccomplished beginners. It took years—almost ten—before the stars at the Palladium caught up to his style, but I never heard his name mentioned. In fact, no one ever knew his name. That is true celebrity, like the Unknown Soldier.

The Half Moon Club

The Half Moon Club was up a very steep flight of a narrow stairway. Although Julio handled his bass like a love object, it could be better described as an albatross. The place was dimly lit, more for economy than intimacy. A chilly silence hung over the scene that showed two couples at each of two tables, wearing their overcoats, huddling for warmth as well as closeness. The sweet smell of sugar cane rum brought back memories of the islands, adding to the mystique of the club. Irish pubs, smelling of oats, horses, and stables, have that same attraction for the average Irishman. Chinatown in New York smells like the Chinese city one has left behind, intentionally, perhaps.

There may have been others toward the rear of what could at one time have been a railroad flat with walls knocked down illegally. It was the first time I heard the name "Machito." He approached us like a maître d', embracing Julio like a "mano" and shaking my hand at the same time. At Machito's bidding, his men put out their cigarettes, and picked up their instruments. Soon, rum drinks were set on the long, hand-made bar. Julio sat in; so did the guitaristas.

Now one heard laughter, toasting. Couples arose to romance on the dance floor — the place became a nightclub. It rose from the dead!

As the Lucumí say: "Sangan Fimba Moropo' — the drink went to my head. I passed out when we reached the street. Heading home, Julio expertly walked me flopping like a puppet into the subway, to the West End local. It stopped at the end of the line in Fort Hamilton where I lived. As I went down to the train, I could hear the guys above me singing an aguinaldo: it was Christmas, 1938.

The next day, Julio phoned to inquire about my trip home and to tell me he had contacted a certain Mr. Chin Lee (Chinese restaurants in the '30's had live music, usually Hawaiians with hula dancers). He had arranged an audition there on 51st Street and Broadway for lunchtime. I admired his persistence. Like the exotic Hawaiians, we now blended in comfortably along the papier-mâché palm trees' tropical decor. We were confidently playing a precioso bolero for the noisy crowd of diners and hustling waiters when Mr. Lee politely asked us to "play Amelican.' So ended our sad, brief lullaby of Broadway.

But Julio did not allow the dream to vaporize. He went on to tear down that wall, chipping away at it so that in the early '50's, the Palladium opened across from the Ed Sullivan Theater, and in '64, Massucci and the Pacheco All-Stars played the Garden. Tito's "Mambo Diabolo" won in '85. Today, Latin bands play proudly.

When you hear that explosive opening rim shot that announces salsa, let us remember Julio, for it was he who first fired the shot now heard around the world.

When Kafka was the Rage

Whenever people thought of Greenwich Village before World War II, it was painters, speakeasies, and bohemians. But in the postwar error the bohemians and the speakeasies were gone while the painter image remained. Aside from poetry, little was left of literature's old guard. For culture in general, one thought of Europe. Henry James, Walt Whitman, O'Henry, O'Neill, and Melville were still around, but change was in the air.

It was into this setting that Anatole Broyard found himself in 1945. As one "Aroused by Books," the title of one of his works, Anatole's motto was vita sine litteris mors est (Life without literature is death.) Painters, poets, and musicians were more respected than the famished failure/writer stuck away in his cold flat. Painters held regular exhibits in Washington Square Park, where even the Ash Can School of art was on display, thanks to Beauford Delaney, a black artist supported by donations from writer Henry Miller and the Ascoli family. Jazz and bebop at the Village Vanguard and country music at the Village Barn or at George's at Seventh Avenue, corner of Bleecker brought the Village before a public seeking entertainment or wickedness.

For the literary minority it was off east of Fifth Avenue for the Fourth Avenue bookstalls or away over to University Place where business was slow.

The arts and crafts crowd had more place in the Village than bookshops, except for Pete Martin's excellent collection on West Fourth off Sixth Avenue. Cornelia Street with its former stables and difficult access from Bleecker was tucked away from people. It was as odd a location as were the books that Anatole hoped to sell when he opened his bookstore in 1945. No one had reason to enter Cornelia unless it was to visit Lenny's Fix-It shop that Lenny, a crippled black fellow married to an Irish girl, tried to pass off as an antique shop. Some of his leftover rusty artifacts adorn today's Cornelia Street Café's walls.

The bookstore failed when the winter arrived, not for lack of funds to keep it alive or because of location or the many other Village attractions. (Interest in it was beginning to appear.) It failed because there were actually few books for sale. Aside from three or four books displayed in the window, the shelves were ninety percent bare. Anatole's rare selection and taste in literature could have labeled the establishment "The Tomb of the Unknown Author." Nathaniel West, Henri Michaux, Celine, the Marquis de Sade, Huysman, Orwell, Zora Neale Hurston, Wallace Stevens, Blake, Saroyan, Gide, Verlaine — all are known today of course, but still insufficiently known.

The shop closed and is today Pearl's Oyster Bar, but it succeeded in two ways: besides making him a Village fixture, Anatole's influence contributed to an avant-guard milieu, a more wholesome atmosphere that erased the speakeasy, ash-can, hungry artist image. It turned from rebel bohemian to respectable intellectual, but not for long.

Perhaps pulp fiction, comic books or the science fiction categories could have saved things, but not in Anatole's eyes. Besides, there was now a growing demand for "good books" that turned people to Pete Martin, whose sales increased thanks to Anatole. Pete had been selling Anatole "rare" books at discount prices that angered Mrs. Martin. But Pete embraced Anatole as a fellow bibliophile. Reading all day and not circulating through the Village, the park or the bars, Pete was chained to his chair in his cubbyhole, disregarding business. To buy a book you had to pardon yourself for interrupting his absorption in Seneca's *The Pumpkinification of the Divine Claudius*. Classicism, rather than Romanticism favored by Anatole, was a hard sell. Readers are basically sedentary, lazy souls or prejudiced.

When Anatole became identifiable as what I call Village nobility, he became just a bit more sophisticated by dressing nattily or with smart sweaters and khakis that predated sport clothes. He wore his popularity well, underpinned by l'air sportif. He was not calculating, but spontaneous, with comments that were very much alive. More than something he'd mention was the nerve, the response he provoked in you as a verbal fencing master. He was one of the first to visit a psychoanalyst at that time. His "one drop" predicament encased him on four sides, he said, until he "climbed out of the box from the roof." He used Baudelaire's tragic example to caution us against Dr. Leary's "drop out," "if it feels good, do it" slogans. He was removed by his proper marriage from the poetry of the uncommon Village streets to a comfortable country family setting, where he felt boxed in once again.

This time it was by his own doing and not by a circumstance of Nature's coloration. He was apologetic, ashamed of his cubicle office on Madison Avenue and even Castro-phobic working in the Battery Park Whitehall Building, with its view of the Statue of Liberty, and among the tightly-knit desks at the New York Times. In his longing to be free, he established a new "freedom of expression" desire among Villagers. He was motivating attention to the Village at a time when it was still a "nice, quiet neighborhood," an orderly though tough working class in a majority Italian-American community. He brought Afro-Cuban and mambo music down from the Park Plaza Dance Hall in El Barrio, and was seen playing bongo while they were still unknown or called tom-toms. He jived in Spanish, using *hombre* before "hey, man." In his neat appearance he detained the appearance of ugliness in clothing that was to follow. Anatole, while helping out needy friends, including addicts, he cautioned against drugs by saying, "I want a clear head." Because of much attraction to and from the opposite sex, no woman gave him what I may have, namely, the freedom to feel himself as well as freedom from his dramatized literary world.

We melded in silent interaction. It was fellowship without the trappings of bonding or the horsing around of brotherly love. Astrologers call it the placement of our "nodes." He made free love more acceptable.

Although we lived apart from each other for ninety percent of our lives, we were forever bound by a secret we shared. We alone, by chance, witnessed the moment and place when the Village changed goals, ideals and vision. The world as well, we can say, lost its self-respect, due to the wrong friends (the Beats), but worst of all, the wrong reading material.

The World is My Oyster: Escape—Zora Neale Hurston
(Trying to understand me better)

As a retarded misfit of sorts with my hearing deficit, I've had to fashion a world unlike what is offered to us by God. Like a plant still alive but with dead flowers, mine is a world unlike yours. For impressions to reach me, I had to go travel to rare wonderments like Great Wall, Baalbek, Sarawak, Brunei, Ilban villages, the Sistine Chapel, or to find myself in the presence of *santeros*, or 90 celebrities, 88 countries, 64 ships, three colleges, three universities with five languages. Shock or amazement was needed to reach deep into me for the rightful *me*, for my patrimony. I was not to be excluded from a full life, except for what I wished to avoid. Being set apart gratuitously by controlling circumstances was comparable to poisoning. I didn't recognize my condition while still a formative "slow-to-learn" adult. That is why today I look back long years and rejoice now. The choices that I made or those that arose inexplicably empowered me to resist the forces that would have otherwise placed me in the bowels of the beset world of the twentieth and twenty-first centuries.

The thirty-billion-dollar cruise industry began with three second-hand slot machines that were pulled up from the Hudson River, where Mayor Fiorello LaGuardia had dumped them, in order to protect the public from organized crime. The three barnacled machines showed up in 1952 aboard the S.S. Nuevo Domenicano of the Eastern Shipping Company in Miami, placed on board by the Danio crime syndicate out of Chicago and Miami's Meyer Lansky mob. Lansky was just starting gambling in Havana as well. Since I was the Casino Manager as well as the Cruise Director, perhaps I can claim to be one of the guys who got gambling sailing on cruise ships out of Florida.

But whatever happened in 2014 with all those odd occurrences that crippled the cruise industry—the virus contamination, the engine room fires, steerage breakdowns needing tugboats? Remember how it all mysteriously normalized overnight? No doubt an agreement with the protection racket where a "piece of the action" was involved. Cruise billions attracted attention on this new turf afloat that made Al Capone look bad. It is Carnival Cruise Lines that dominates with controlling interests, and Holland-America, Caribbean Cruise Line, Costa, Crystal, and possibly Norwegian as well. They all stopped fighting each other with a "sit-down" à la *Cosa Nostra*. It wasn't only the stuffed toilets that stank up the industry, it was the cover-up. Now the casinos, the hotels, travel agencies, shops—everything from the price of your Coca-Cola to your cabin is "organized" to the average Joe's disadvantage.

Stabilized

Breathing exercise and balance form the basis of yoga. Without realizing it, I was engaged in yoga for many years, from 1948 until more or less 2004. How is it possible to perform the necessary yoga rules involved without consciously doing so? One day it dawned on me that the years spent at sea explained in a large way why my health, on a scale from 1 to 10—10 being the best—was, as my doctor said, "Twenty." It was only while watching a yoga instructor or showing the very basic slow-motion moves that involved the raising of the arms and extending them in front of you did I grasp the yoga concept. While slowly extending my arms, I began to realize that by doing so I was replicating the movement up and down of the ship as it plowed through the ocean, raising and lowering slowly and continuously, in the way that the ship carries on rising and falling continuously. In other words, it was doing my movements with me and for me; with me, since I was responding to the up and down effect that I was impelled to follow, due to the up and down carriage of the ship's motion. On land before the mirror, my arms would outstretch in front of me, but the ship obliged me to rise and fall, not just my arms but my whole body, rising and falling, day and night.

Of course, there were variations, depending on the state of the ocean, but these interruptions were also of benefit, pulling or pushing me, working me like a trainer or masseur would. I relaxed in the cradle of the sea. It was the gentle exercise that the ship did with me, plus the air that I inhaled continuously, the ocean air that is recommended as a wholesome therapeutic environment, free of contaminants and like nowhere on land anywhere except in the great wooded forests or high in the lofty mountains.

In the constantly active ocean, our bodies resist threats to our sense of balance. Our mental and physical reactions are continually involved with our muscular structure, being continuously exercised without a time out. On land, such odd activity would be impossible to endure consciously, due to normal fatigue. Land-based yoga in a gymnastic atmosphere or in a placid one, it is forever shackled by our limited endurance. On land, you are aware of and anticipate various pressures and challenges.

You are more unprepared on land; life is full of surprises, not always of the healthy kind. The ocean can be considered a psychotherapist whose manipulation massages our bodies as well as our psyches. It balances the yin and yang that makes us who and what we are. A sea voyage, like a tireless trainer, works on every part of our being. We arose from the ocean originally. It is the mother that rocks instinctively the new born. It is la mer. Present-day yoga—or we could say ancient yoga practice—has not been sufficient to the task of bettering mankind. On a ship, your organs are all experiencing harmonious effects absent on land. We are ninety percent water, and water seeks its own level.

Walking along corridors during rough seas, you rise and fall not of your own accord. A live, breathing, gigantic aquatic organism seems to control your every move. Man has forever sought to defy gravity with weight removed from his shoulders. With hydraulic buoyancy, like birds that skillfully sail across the sky, we discover the qi, the balance that is so beneficial and so essential in yoga's success. Like the mal-de-mer that tells us that we are off-balance, and that nature expurgates therewith, that which makes us ill in mind and body. Using hydraulic power, can we engineer a better mankind and a better world? While a ship is just a speck on a vast ocean—a slave to the wind and wobble of the weather that is, in this case, the rougher. The better like stepped up, intensified exercise with its odd behavior. Like riding atop an elephant, you are rocked about by its traction until relaxed into playfulness. You are in the saddle of the ocean that can never be harnessed, while asleep in this gigantic hammock that itself never sleeps.

Once back on land, we gradually readjust our equilibrium. We return to nature's requirement, that is, conscious thought of balance. This compels us to experience both mind and body in harmony. *Cogito ergo sum.* (I think, therefore I am). Without this combination, there would be no advancement to separate us from all other species. We alone walk upright and balance pro and con thoughts to reach suitable answers. Emerging from the ocean eons ago, we are at home on land while preparing ourselves for the weightlessness of traveling in space in the future.

With yoga afloat, the mind can enjoy a more carefree composure, while the body benefits from new exercises that include the total musculature, parts of which have been dormant or have never been activated.

Yoga afloat greatly calms the mind and invigorates the body. Yoga is a Sanskrit word meaning "union."

Resistance to the natural action of the ship's movement in any direction strengthens the muscular framework while helping breathe in pure ocean air. This was the normal before stabilizers, not today anymore. Since the ship is in constant motion beneath you, your muscles are contracting to compensate for otherwise improper balance. The compensation is 24/7 and at most times unnoticeable, except by the body-proper.

For many years, there was much swimming ashore and aboard in the pool. Ships are more crime- and germ-free, and I didn't ever need a doctor visit. My health was stabilized, even while ships were not. If you go to a spa, they give you a "body treatment" (expensive). On the ship, I enjoyed a free 24-hour "body treatment" as part of my job.

To obey the commands of the ever-restless ocean, every moment I spent sailing my body was unconsciously responding to the ship's reaction to the ocean's demands. By maintaining my balance, I was activating dormant muscles—even those unneeded on lands flat surface, but necessary on the ocean and in the practice of yoga.

The wide ocean is your gym. It offers the following benefits:

Balance needed—continuous exercise	No fatigue from repetitive workouts
Meditation - sunsets	No treadmill—danger to heart if excessive
Relaxation—deck chairs	No running—danger to knees
Breathing—fresh ocean air	Breaks—time out when on land only
Swimming—handy ship's pool	Discipline—your body is obliged to obey
Variety—calm or rough seas	Nourishment—good diet
Expense—none needed	Full-body treatment—no equipment needed
Safety—less crime aboard	Natural—no strained muscles
Activity—dancing daily	Fun when rough—walking like a drunk
Climbing—from deck to deck	Handy access—no commuting
Exposure—daily continuous movement	Spa aboard for additional care
Contemplation—night skies at sea	Socializing—dressing up for events
No boredom—spread-out activity	Upbeat environment in a health-promoting setting

Along with yoga afloat comes the concept of immortality. As humans, we are earthenware that turns us to dust eventually, but it is metal that keeps us alive with electrical currents for our beating hearts and synapses. Perhaps some day metals will materialize as robotic "people," capable of utilizing their vital properties to function just as we today are alive, supported by "we are what we eat." Thus, we will survive in a different form. We may use metals that in a proper formula benefit our advancement toward immortality, just like vitamins.

Dinosaurs perished due to an asteroid that shadowed the sun. It introduced metallic residue beyond a safe level compared to the amount already present due to the Big Bang. This amount continued to increase throughout eons and was accelerated by the industrial revolution. Bad metal attached to neurons is injurious to the functions in our brains that control our overall wellbeing. Overpopulation and climate change are secondary. Can good metals equal immortality? We arose from the oceans during the oceanic period. Salinity both preserves as well as corrodes, but there are compounds such as porcelain that resist corrosion, not to mention gold. Future robotic "people" will consume "healthy" metals just as we today, who are meat, consume meat. Until that day when we are one hundred percent imperishable gold robots, we will wear out as humans. Will the Supreme Being be El Dorado as Bolivian myth claims? Okinawans, with their food-based environment, are the longer champions. Dinosaurs had life spans unlike creatures today. The cars we drive generate XXXXXX of metallic subatomic particles. With yoga afloat (and the ten laps around the Promenade Deck, called a "constitutional," that equals one mile), are helpful, but we have many laps to go to immortality.

LISTS

What were the best
clubs in Cuba?
EL KURSSAL
EDEN CONCERT
JARDIN TROPICAIN
TROPICANÁ
MONTMARTRE
EL BOHIO
Sevilla Biltmore
Hotel.

did you travel outsi
of Havanah?
- CIENFUEGOS
VALLE DE VIÑALES

SALSALIVELLI.
BLOGSPOT
.COM

212 255 0508

Open House

Having lived for many years aboard ships, my cabins, large or small, were home to me. To enter someone else's private domain was always a fascinating, privileged experience.

In the late forties, a cruise director sold shore excursions whose itineraries often included permissible intrusions into many notable venues. Whether by invitation, by chance, or by virtue of occupation, my travels were the keys that opened the doors to a world of many mansions. Visited:

Ashford Castle, Ireland

Mohandas Gandhi's House, Bombay

Simon Bolívar's Home, Caracas

King Ludwig's Castle, Neueschwanstein

Betsy Ross's Cottage, Philadelphia

Hemingway's House, Key West

Ann Hathaway's Cottage, Stratford-on-Avon

Iban Long House, Borneo

The White House, Washington, D.C.

The Forbidden City, Peking

The Virgin Mary's Home, Turkey–Ephesus

King Farouk's Boathouse, Cairo

Vatican Apartments, Vatican City

Delmore Schwartz's Apartment, Charles St., NY

Washington Irving's Home, Phillipsburg, NY

Morgan Home/Library, NYC

Newport, Vanderbilt, Dupont Mansions, Casa Loma, Ontario, Canada

Goreme Cave Dwellings, Cappadocia, Turkey

Hitler's Wolf's Lair, Bergdesgaten

El Greco's Home, Toledo

Prado Family Dollhouse, Guaruja, Brazil

Pirelli Residence, Portofino

Governor's Mansion, Lexington, Kentucky

Peggy Guggenheim's Penthouse, Abingdon Square, NY

Christopher Columbus Home, Genoa

Hormel Ranch House, Austin, Minn.

Mayowood, Rochester, Minn.

D'Anjou Château, Orleans, France

Vaux-Le-Vîconte, Outside Paris

Versailles Palace, Versailles

F.D.R. Residence, Hyde Park, NY

Doges Palace, Venice

Grimaldi Palace, Monte Carlo

Shah of Iran's Palace, Teheran, Iran

Cardinal Minzenty Residence, Estergom, Hungary

The Kremlin, Moscow

Presidential Palace, Havana

Schönnbrunn Palace, Vienna

Josephine's Birthplace, Martinique

Crystal Pavilion, Brighton, England

El Escorial, Spain

The Alhambra, Granada

Sultan's Palace, Fez, Morocco

Topkapi Palace, Istanbul

Ben Franklin's Home, Philadelphia

Mt. Vernon Farm, Mt. Vernon

Native Indian "Chola," Canaíma, Venezuela

Santero Juan Besson, Regla, Cuba

Andrew Carnegie Mansion, 2 East 91st St., NY

Walter Annenberg Home, Ambler, Pa.

Red Fort Maharaja's Palace, Jaipur, India

Maharaja Palace, Jahor, India

Aaron Burr Carriage House, 17 Barrow St., NY

Alexander Hamilton Grange House, Sugar Hill, NYC

Marco Polo's Birthplace, Corchula, Yugoslavia

St. Anthony's Birthplace, Lisbon

Gracie Mansion, NYC

Thomas Edison's Home/Museum, Menlo Park, NJ

Deering Estate, Coral Gables, FL

Harvey Firestone Estate, Miami Beach

Alfred Lord Tennyson Retreat, Isle of Wight

Stafford (Family) Court, San Francisco

Braganza Palace, Sintra, Portugal

Emperor Dom Pedro II Palace, Petropolis, Brazil

Rambaugh Palace, Jaipur, India

Royal Family Palace, Bangkok

Museo Maritimo Palace, Venice

Tower of London, London

The Mansions of Newport, Newport, RI

Hadrian's Palace, Tivoli, Rome

Hadrian's Palace, Split, Yugoslavia

Maximilian's Palace, Jerash, Jordan

Shandala Temples, Kajuraho

The Bishop's Palace, Palace Hotel, NY

Queen Hatshepsut's Temple, Bier-Al-Hri, Egypt

Sir Harry Oake's Home, Niagara Falls, NY

The Morris Jumel Mansion, Washington Heights, NY

Villa D'Este, Lake Como

Isabella Stewart Gardner Museum, Boston, MA

Henry Clay Frick Museum, Fifth Ave., NY

George Eastman Museum, Rochester, NY

El Alcazar, Toledo, Spain

Duke & Duchess of Windsor	1952	Portofino
Prince Chulalonghorn of Siam	1955	Miami
Princess de Bourbon-Parme	1952	Rio
Princess Ilona Preston	1984	Glen Cove
Lady Meegan Lloyd George	1950	Barbadoes
Lady Jean Campbell	1950	Nassau
Baroness Rochas	1980	Paris
Marie-Terese d'Anjou	1981	Paris
Count & Countess J. de Launoit	1953	Miami
Duveen & Curzon families	1974	Cannes
Clemenceau Family	1978	Cannes
Maharani of Baroda	1950	Nassau
H.R.H. Queen of Roumania	1979	Monte Carlo
President Fulgencio Batista	1953	Havana
President Jimenez of Venezuela	1953	Miami
Count & Countess E. Martignone	1986	Milan
Lady Nancy Oakes	1950	Nassau
Charles Laughton	1938	NYC *NBC Rosen? Hall NYC*
Orson Welles Count Basie	1938	
Carmen Miranda Mary Martin	1938	NYC
Ethyl Merman Ella Fitzgerald	1938	NYC
Montgomery Clift Errol Flynn	1950	Nassau
Andrew Sisters John Barrymore	1938	NBC NY
Jack Dempsey	1939	NYC
Sugar Ray Robinson	1949	Roseland Ballroom
Claudia Cardinale	1982	NYC
Rudy Vallee	1950	Nassau
Jessica Dragonette	1950	Nassau
Rose Bampton Pelletier	1951	en route Rio
Baby Snooks Bob Crosby	1938	NBC NY
Linda Darnell	1938	by correspondence
Bea Wayne & Benay Venuta	1938	NY WOR
Loretta Young	1973	en route Genoa
Elsa Maxwell	1973	en route Genoa
James Roosevelt Señor Wences	1973	en route Genoa
Cornelius Vanderbilt	1972	en route Nassau
Leo Durocher	1941	Havana
Andre Watts Jan Peerce	1973	Aboard "Oceanic"
Tommy Manville	1940	El Morocco
Delmore Schwartz Sax Rohmer	1960	NY (Barbadoes)
Richard Tregaskis	1944	Okinawa
Michaux, Henri	1952	Paris
James Baldwin	1978	Cannes
Cardinal F.X. Spellman	1952	Rio
Robert Moses	1952	Maracas Bay Trinidad
Marc Chagall	1963	NYC
Dr & Mrs Charles Mayo	1949	Rochester, Minn.
Marjorie Merriweather Post	1951	Miami
Mrs Dodge Sloane The Olds Fam.	1951	en route Rio
Juan Trippe Anais Nin	1948	NYC
Ernesto Lecuona	1941	Havana
Santo Traficante	1951	Havana
Baron Otto de Bemberg	1949	en route Buenos Aires
Baron Carlo Banaz	1949	en route Buen os Aires
Prince P. de San Martino	1987	Rome
Tisch Family	1952	Rio

BABY SNOOKS (FANNY BRICE) 1938 NBC ....
BENAY VENUTA .1938 WOR NYC
CHARLES LAUGHTON 1938 NBC Studio NYC
COUNT BASIE " W.52nd ST. NYC
ANDREW SISTERS " NBC
JOHN BARRYMORE " "
ELLA FITZGERALD " ROSENKRANZ HALL
ORSON WELLES " "
CARMEN MIRANDA " PARAMOUNT THEATER
MARY MARTIN " "
ETHYL MERMAN " REHEARSAL STUDIO NYC
BOB CROSBY " NBC
JACK DEMPSEY 1939 DEMPSEY RESTAURANT NY
LEO DUROCHER 1941 NACIONAL HOTEL HAVANA
ERNESTO LECUONA 1941 TEATRO NACIONAL HAVANA
BEA WAYNE 1938 NBC STUDIO NY
TOMMY MANVILLE 1940 EL MOROCCO NY
MIGUELITO VALDEZ 1941 BEACHCOMBER MIAMI
RICHARD TREGASKIS 1944 OKINAWA
ANAIS NIN 194. NYC
JUAN TRIPPE 1948 PAN AM BLDG NY
BARON OTTO DE BEMBERG 1949 EN ROUTE BUENOS AIRES
BARON CARLO BANAZ 1949 "
BILLY ROSE 1949 COPACABANA HOTEL RIO
CLARE EDWARDS 1949 NYC
AMB. OSWALDO ARANHA 1948 UNO NYC
MARTHA RAYE 1939 IDLEWILD AIRPORT NY
MACHITO 1939 HALF MOON CLUB NY
JOSE TORRES 1948 JOES LUNCHEONETTE NY
LADY MEEGAN LLOYD GEORGE 1950 BARBADOS
LADY JEAN CAMBELL 1950 BRITISH COLONIAL HOTEL
MAHARANI OF BARODA " "
LADY NANCY OAKES ' NASSAU
DR & MRS CHARLES MAYO 1949 ROCHESTER, MINN.
RUDY VALLEE 1950 BRITISH COLONIAL HOTEL
JESSICA DRAGONETTE. " "
SUGAR RAY ROBINSON 1949 ROSELAND NYC
ROSE BAMPTON PELLETIER 1951 EN ROUTE RIO
ERROL FLYNN & ALEXIS NIHON 1950 NASSAU
MARJORIE MERRIWEATHER POST 1951 MIAMI
MONTGOMERY CLIFT 1950 BRITISH COLONIAL HOTEL
BESS MEYERSON 1950 "
SANTOS TRAFFICANTE 1951 SANS SOUCI HAVANA
VIRGINIA HILL 1941 BEACHCOMBER MIAMI
MRS. DODGE SLOAN 1951 EN ROUTE BUENOS AIRES
THE OLDS FAMILY 1951 "
THE TISCH FAMILY 1952 " RIO
ROBERT MOSES 1952 MARACAS BAY TRINIDAD
HENRI MICHAUX 1952 GALARIE RIVE GAUCHE PARIS
CARDINAL F.N. SPELLMAN 1952 RIO
PRINCESS de BOURBON-PARME 1952 RIO
DUKE & DUCHESS OF WINDSOR 1952 PORTOFINO
COUNT J. J. de LAUNOIT 1953 MIAMI
IGNACIO COCA 1953 "
PRES. JIMENEZ OF VENEZUELA 1953 MIAMI AIRPORT
PRES. FULGENCIO BATISTA " PRESIDENTIAL PALACE HAVANA

Travel Encounters

Baby Snooks (Fanny Brice): 1938, NBC, NYC. I was present in her dressingroom

Benay Venuta: 1936, WOR, NYC. I appeared on her program.

Charles Laughton: 1938, NBC Studio, NYC. Several encounters in the elevator

Count Basie: 1938, W. 52nd St., NYC. Photo with him on 52nd Street

Andrews Sisters; 1938, NYC. Autographs of all three

John Barrymore: 1938, NBC. Present in his dressing room

Ella Fitzgerald: 1938, NBC, Rosenkranz Hall. Present at her rehearsal

Orson Welles: 1938, Mercury Theater. Present at "Invasion from Mars"

Carmen Miranda: 1938, Paramount Theater. Kissed me in her dressing room

Mary Martin: 1938, Paramount Theater. Present in her dressing room

Ethel Merman: 1938, Rehearsal studio, NYC. Auditioned for her

Bob Crosby: 1938, NBC. Present in his dressing room

Jack Dempsey: 1939, Dempsey Restaurant, NYC. Greeted by him

Leo Durocher: 1941, Nacional Hotel, Havana. Asked me to come see training

Ernesto Lecuona: 1941, Teatro Payet, Havana. Flirted with me in his dressing room

Bea Wayne: 1938, NBC Studio, NYC. Lifted her onto the piano

Tommy Manville: 1940, El Morocco, NYC. Danced rumba with his date

Miguelito Valdez: 1941, Beachcomber, Miami. The great Miguelito Photo with me

Richard Tregaskis: 1944, Okinawa. Wrote me up in Saturday Evening Post

Anaïs Nin: 1946, NYC. We liaisoned at her place.

Juan Trippe: 1948, Pan Am Bldg., NYC. Handed me a fellowship

Baron Otto de Bemberg: 1949, en route to Buenos Aires. V.I.P. & his family NY to BA

Baron Carlo Banaz: 1949, en route to Buenos Aires. Liaisoned with countess

Billy Rose: 1949, Copa Cabana Hotel, Río. Got him on camera

Clare Edwards: 1949, NYC. Visited her in NY G.W.T. Wind

Amb. Oswaldo Aranha: 1948, Uno, NYC. Friend introduced us

Martha Raye: 1939, Idlewild Airport, NYC. She cursed at me.

Machito: 1939, Half Moon Club, NYC; 1938 introduced by Julio A.José Torres; 1948, Joe's Luncheonette, NYC. Ate together in the Village

Lady Meegan Lloyd George: 1950, Barbados. Nice conversationalist

Lady Jean Campbell: 1950, British Colonial Hotel. Met me before Norman Mailer

Maharani of Baroda: 1950, British Colonial Hotel. Asked me to buy "Detol."

Lady Nancy Oakes: 1950, Nassau. Friendly, she rode in a charity "Ladies' Race."

Dr. & Mrs. Charles Mayo: 1949, Rochester, Minn., Related, the British Colonial Hotel

Rudy Vallee: 1950, British Colonial Hotel. M.C.'d act-Nassau, Bahamas

Jessica Dragonette: 1950, British Colonial Hotel. M.C'd her act

Sugar Ray Robinson: 1949, Roseland, NYC. Rumba danced

Rose Bampton Pelletier: 1951, En route, Río. Sang for us

Errol Flynn & Alexis Nihon: 1950, Nassau. Met on the way to Miami

Marjorie Merriweather Post: 1951, Miami. Met & assisted her

Montgomery Clift: 1950, British Colonial Hotel. Conversed about the Village

Santo Trafficante, Sr.: 1951, Sans Souci, Havana. Santos invited me to join

Virginia Hill: 1941, Beachcomber, Miami. Bugsy Siegel's girl; we danced.

Mrs. Dodge Sloan: 1951, En route to Buenos Aires. She was going to buy horses.

The Olds Family: 1951, En route to Buenos Aires. The oldsmobile family

The Tisch family: 1952, En route to Buenos Aires. They put me up at the McAlpin.

Robert Moses: 1952, Maracas Bay, Trinidad. Robert & I went swimming.

Henri Michaux: 1952, Galerie Rive Gauche, Paris. Sold me an oil & watercolor

Cardinal F.J. Spellman: 1952, Río. Remembered me and my name

Princess de Bourbon-Parme: 1952, Río. One of two sister-princessesDuke & Duchess of Windsor: 1952, Portofino. Their dogs and mine met.

Count J.J. de Launoit: 1953, Miami. Invited me to transatlantic sail

Ignacio Coca: 1953, Miami. Invited me to help in Marbella

Pres. Jimenez of Venezuela: 1953, Miami Airport. Gave me a $25 tip.

Pres. Fulgencio Batista: 1953, Welcomed us at the American Municipal Association

Prince Chulalonghorn –Siam: 1955, En route Miami. Came to my house in South Miami

Delmore Schwartz: 1960, Charles Street, NYC. Threw me out of his house

Sax Rohmer: 1960, Barbados. Wrote Fu Manchu mysteries

Marc Chaga: 1963, Pier 80, NYC. Met and assisted on Pier 80

Duveen & Curzon families: 1974, Carlton, Cannes. Luncheon on the Carlton Terrace

Andre Watts: 1973, S.S. Oceanic. Played piano for us

Jan Peerce: 1973, S.S. Oceanic. Signed his program for me.

Clemenceau family: 1978, Cannes. Had us to the houseH.R.H. Queen of Romania 1979, Monte Carlo. Attended party in Monaco

Loretta Young & Frederick March: 1973, T.N. Raffaello. She refused my offer to dance.

Elsa Maxwell: 1973, T.N. Raffaello. Didn't invite me to her party

Señor Wences: 1973, T.N. Raffaello. Asked him to perform for free

James Roosevelt: 1973, Served as judge at my costume contest

Cornelius Vanderbilt: 1972, S.S. Oceanic. Was with us sailing south

James Baldwin: 1978, Carlton, Cannes. Was in Cannes with B. Delaney

Baroness Rochas: 1980, Racing Club, Paris. Tablemate at Bois de Boulogne

Countess Marie Terèse D'Anjou: 1981, S.S. Achille Lauro. Tablemate S.S. Angelina Lauro

Claudia Cardinale: 1982, NYC. Escorted her in New York

Cristina Fiorucci: 1982, NYC. Took her & staff around New York

Comm. Ettore Fil: 1982, NYC. Took him & family to Canada

Nino Benvenuto: 1970, M.V. Raffaello. Sailed from Italy to New York

Princess Ilona Preston: 1984, NYC. Almost married her

Beverly Paterno: 1984, NYC. Ran a high-scale escort club

Count & Countess E. Martignone 1986, Milan. Swam off their yacht

Prince Pepino de San Martino: 1987, Rome. Went to a fish dinner

M. Louis Vuitton: 1986, Paris. We argued. "You mistreated the luggage."

Skinny D'Amato: 1962, S.S. Oceanis. With Bodyguards. Mafia Boss

H.R.H. Zahir Kahn: 1973, Moana Clus, Monte Carlo. With his exiled family Afgan.

Ed Sulliva: 1973, Hotel Carlton, Cannes. Wore same outfits top & bottom

Brenda Frazier: 1949, Trinidad. Introduced him to tourist—Hindu

Ti Ror: 1968, Port-au-Prince. Haiti's greatest drummer

Sir & Lady Marc Potter: 2002

Joey Adams: 1949, 250 Charles St., NYC.

Bess Meyerson: 1952, Nassau. Miss America

William Gaddis: 1945, Greenwich Village. author

Petrillo: 1976, President, Musician's Union 108

James Brown: 2002, Edison Hotel, NYC

Paul Stewart: 1938, Mercury Theater

Celia Cruz: 1981, El Liborio Restaurant, NYC

Polito Vega: 1985, Beacon Theater & Madison Square Garden

Robert Farris Thompson: 2008, M.A.S. Restaurant, NYC. Professor of Religion, author

www.ingramcontent.com/pod-product-compliance
Lightning Source LLC
Chambersburg PA
CBHW041207100726

47911CB00017B/887